703 · 626 · 6685

GOD IN HELL'S KITCHEN

Neil Hare

ISBN: 1978178301
ISBN 13: 9781978178304

To my wife, Kate, and our children Sophie, Elizabeth, and Jack. When we see a child being born, especially our own, we cannot help but believe in God.

PART I

*"AND GOD SAW THE EARTH, AND BEHOLD, IT
WAS CORRUPT; FOR ALL FLESH HAD CORRUPTED
THEIR WAY UPON THE EARTH. AND GOD SAID
UNTO NOAH: 'THE END OF ALL FLESH IS COME
BEFORE ME; FOR THE EARTH IS FILLED WITH
VIOLENCE THROUGH THEM; AND BEHOLD, I
WILL DESTROY THEM WITH THE EARTH.'"*

GENESIS, 6:12-13.

1

At the sound of his name, Emanuel woke up from his dream. For a moment, he was disoriented because the dream had been so real and so frustrating. His heart was racing and he was breathing heavily. He hated the plane crash dream— it always made him feel like a failure.

"Mr. Adams. Mr. Adams. This is Judge Henry's clerk, are you there?"

Emanuel stroked the leather of his office couch to reassure himself of his location, and then reached down to his belt, unclipped his phone, and brought it up to his face.

"This is Adams," he said, looking into the minicamera on the phone so that the clerk could see him.

"Mr. Adams, the jury has reached a verdict. Could you please return to the courthouse?"

"Of course," Emanuel said. "I'll be there in ten minutes."
Emanuel jumped off the couch, rubbed his eyes, grabbed his suit jacket and headed off to D.C. Superior Court to hear the outcome of his latest trial.

Later that day, Emanuel strolled into the Old Ebbitt Grill. His favorite restaurant greeted him like a mistress at noontime, inviting but improper. Emanuel had picked up the habit of eating dinner alone at the bars of nice restaurants from his days living in Manhattan. New York is a lonely town, and people there would rather have strangers for company at dinner than sit alone in a shoebox apartment watching the television. He first latched onto the Old Ebbitt because it was right next to his office on 15th Street, but he stayed with it because of its warm, upscale saloon atmosphere. The food was hearty and affordable, and the bartenders were the best in town.

Emanuel's fingers clung gingerly to the jacket of his navy-blue, pinstriped suit, which was draped over his right shoulder as he sauntered across the Old Ebbitt's foyer to the bar. His red silk tie was loosened around his neck and his white shirt had lost its starch after the long day. A mischievous smile on his face suggested that he knew he was getting away with something.

Doc, the bartender, had Emanuel's Kettle One vodka martini ready as Emanuel sidled up to the bar. It only took a month of Emanuel's nightly visits before Doc started looking out for him and chilling the vodka as Emanuel twirled through the revolving front door. Doc would make sure the vodka was on the edge of freezing, rinse the glass with vermouth, and throw in three big olives, exactly the way Emanuel instructed him on the first night. It was a game between them now to see if Doc could have the martini ready at the precise moment Emanuel sat down. He was perfect this time.

"Counselor, how'd they treat ye today?" Doc asked with his thick Scottish brogue.

Emanuel shook Doc's hand and took a sip of his drink before answering. "Not too bad, Doc. Six months suspended, two years probation and another happy customer back on the streets where he belongs."

"Wonderful, mate. Another human being escaping a vacation in the clink, and all thanks to you."

"Cheers to that, Doc." Emanuel raised his glass and took another sip. "I love it when the judicial system works the way it should."

"And how's that, mate?"

"Fair and equitable treatment. You should've seen my client today, Doc. Eighteen years old and staring five years in the pen right in the face because he was busted with too much pot on him. The kid was pulled over randomly by the cops who asked if they could search his car. And he consented."

"They can do that?"

"Sure. The law allows them to make random stops and ask for consensual searches. If you say 'yes,' they go to it. This kid didn't know he had the right to say 'no.'"

"That's scary. We've turned into a police state."

"Almost. The kid was trembling next to me trying not to cry while we waited for the verdict. His grandmother, on the other hand, was standing right behind us howling like a sick cat. They were both sure he was getting the maximum sentence. I wasn't so sure myself. Luckily, I convinced the jury that the exact amount of marijuana they found on him was in question and they found him guilty of the lesser offense."

"Nice work, mate. You think the kid will stay clean?"

"Probably not. I sure hope so, though. He's a nice kid."

"Well, God knows I keep your card on me at all times, just in case."

"Doc, I would defend you with every last ounce of strength I have, because I like you and if you weren't here making my martinis that would really be a crime. One more, please," Emanuel said popping a vodka-soaked olive in his mouth.

"Ah, it's so nice to be appreciated. Ta."

Doc began the delicate process of making the martini while Emanuel looked up at the trophy heads hanging on the wall above the bar. He felt mixed emotions about how glorious the antelope and deer were, and feeling regret that they were stuffed on a wall. Then he felt a moment of self-pity since those figures seemed like the most familiar faces in his life. Emanuel shook off the sentiment and turned his attention to the large monitor behind the bar. Unlike bars outside the beltway where ball games entertained the patrons, the monitor at the Old Ebbitt was always tuned to C-SPAN. The sport of the Nation's Capitol was politics, and the Old Ebbitt was a main hangout for the players.

C-SPAN's billing for the night was the Reverend Jackson Emerson Winston addressing a large crowd at a political dinner at Washington's famous Hay-Adams Hotel as part of his campaign for the presidency. It was March 15, the November election was fast approaching, and Winston was pushing hard, gearing up for the stretch run. He was ahead in the polls of both the incumbent, Republican Stephen Taylor and Democrat August Fowler, and by most accounts he was going to become the first third-party president of the United States.

Emanuel took a sip of his new martini as he focused on Winston's talking head. As he felt the burn of the cold drink, he could not help noticing that Winston was an unbelievably striking man. His sandy blond hair, thick and wavy, was coifed in a conservative yet stylish manner that allowed a few strands to curl across his forehead. His eyes, translucent blue, forced you to look right into them whenever they focused on you. Winston had a chiseled face with a perfectly straight nose and a square, cleft chin. He exuded confidence and strength without saying a word. The fact that he was an eloquent speaker just added to his allure.

Emanuel looked down the bar and he noticed several people had stopped their conversations in order to listen to Winston speak.

"Friends," Winston began. His sonorous voice sang through the monitor into the dinner hour bustle at the Old Ebbitt. "When I started out my evangelical life, I honestly never envisioned standing before a group of people, asking for them to support me in a bid for the White House. I was a simple traveling preacher looking for a flock." Winston paused and smiled softly, humbly, remembering those early days.

"What I found in those days, my friends, were millions of Americans looking for hope. That's right, it was the 1980s and millions of Americans were still looking for light in their life. Believe it or not, with all due respect to President Ronald Reagan, the end of the Cold War did not fundamentally affect most Americans. The

Soviet Union was a distant enemy -- a faraway threat less imposing than so many things occurring right here at home."

"I found this out talking to people as I traveled throughout the country. Then I, like many others, benefited from technology; first, with my television shows, and then with the Internet, to find out first hand what America was thinking. And, you know what they were thinking, friends?" Winston paused again as a preacher addressing a congregation, not a stumping candidate.

"They were thinking: there is a moral divide in this country. No longer did race, or national origin, or even wealth divide America, but rather, faith. My brothers and sisters, there was a huge moral hole right through our society, that in my opinion still exists today, and it needs to be filled. It desperately needs to be filled." Winston was now stalking the stage with microphone in hand, eschewing the traditional staid manor of speaking to a formal dinner crowd.

"Who remembers the Columbine High School tragedy?" Almost every hand in the room shot up in the air in an obedient salute. "Who remembers fifteen-year-old Mary Stevens hiding under a desk in the school library when the two violent and lost souls approached her? They asked her 'Mary do you believe in God?' She, like the good Christian she was, responded 'Yes,' and then lost her life to a bullet. That gentle soul never fulfilled its earthly promise because our society was corrupt, filled with violent images in the media, movies, television, video games, and the Internet. Moral decay was pervasive, my friends, and people were tired of it."

At this point the camera panned throughout the Hay-Adams ballroom. Emanuel was amazed at the diversity in the room. It was not the traditional white, right wing, born-again Christians that might be expected to support a leader like Winston. Rather, there were faces of every shade of color, some with the smooth, glowing skin of youth and others with the wrinkles of old age. The eyes, hair, and noses likewise evidenced a crowd that stemmed from numerous races and cultures. And, Winston had them all enraptured.

"Need I even speak of the corruption in the White House in the late 1990s, my friends? Need I rehash the dishonor and ill-repute brought to that grand building right across Lafayette Square? I will not disrespect you with the salacious details of that era in presidential history, except to say that it was the ultimate indication that there was moral rot in America and the people were tired of it."

"And we all know when the chickens came home to roost, don't we? September 11, 2001. That attack on our society and our way of life was a wake-up call. A distant and foreign enemy shrouded in the guise of religious belief claimed moral superiority. They attacked our economy, our military, and more importantly, our values. That enemy started a war that we are currently fighting, and, unfortunately, losing. President Taylor's policies have led to the capture of some terrorist operatives, but we still live in fear. Why? Because every time we capture a terrorist, ten more sprout up, like weeds. Because, we've been afraid to admit that this is a cultural war – a war of two religions. It is time to cry from the mountaintop that fundamentalist Islam must be defeated!"

Winston was speaking at a fevered pitch at this point and paused to compose himself. Now, like all great performers he changed tempo.

"Remember, friends, God does choose sides. The Egyptians perished in the crashing waves of the Red Sea as the Israelites escaped bondage. God chose sides. When I'm elected President, we will fight and win this war, and God will be on our side. Remember though that the Israelites paid their price too. Their heathen and decadent behavior at the base of Mt. Sinai, worshipping golden idols led to forty years in the desert and cost Moses passage to the land of Canaan. Our lesson from scripture is that our eternal battle to become a more righteous society continues on. Not everyone was willing to look in the mirror after September 11 and ask, 'How can I become a better person from this? How can we become a better country?' I did."

"I am a humble servant of God, my friends," Winston whispered into the microphone. "All I have ever wanted to do was serve Him, in any way I could. There came a time, however, when I realized that to serve Him, was to serve America. This great country of ours, that gave me everything, had a moral hole, and I believe the Lord wanted me to fill it. That's why I started the Freedom party, my friends, and that is why I am running for President of the United States."

"We've made so many great strides to date. We've forced Hollywood to tone down its act, so to speak, and respect the fact that our children should not be exposed to gratuitous sex and violence. We've pushed for more religious activities in our schools to give our children a moral compass, and it's worked. We've worked hard to remove weapons from our streets, and to keep them out of the hands of children who might abuse them. We've made great strides, friends, but the largest steps are still yet to come." The crowd erupted in joyous praise of Winston's words.

Emanuel finished up his martini and ordered another.

"What do you think of Reverend Winston?"

"Excuse me?" Emanuel turned toward the voice of a woman who had come to stand next to him at the bar.

"I asked you what you thought of Reverend Winston, since you seemed so interested in what he had to say."

Before he answered Emanuel sized up the woman. She was in her mid-thirties with a wedding ring noticeably absent from her left hand as she nervously ran her fingers through her hair. Her suit and shoes looked expensive, as did the dye job on her shoulder-length auburn hair. While a few crows' feet around her yellowish eyes hinted at approaching middle age, her pale skin was still holding onto the luster and texture of youth. Emanuel had no doubt that she was a lawyer.

"I don't think Reverend Winston has the ability to change my life one way or another, even if he does get elected. I also care even less about politics than I do about religion, so that makes Winston a pretty unimportant figure in my life."

"Really? Then why were you listening to his speech so intently?"

"For a couple of reasons," Emanuel answered. "First, I am fascinated by the man. Even in the Twenty-First Century he's been able to instill the fear of God in people, probably enough to get elected

President of the United States. If that isn't the greatest scam I've ever heard, I don't know what is."

The woman laughed at Emanuel's cynical attitude.

"Second, up until a minute ago I didn't have anyone to talk to so I was forced to watch that damn monitor. My name is Emanuel Adams. How do you do?" Emanuel extended his hand.

"Faye Aldridge. Pleased to meet you."

The two shook hands in a long deliberate manner as if they would learn more about each other through the physical contact.

"Faye, I'm going to have to order you a martini since I have one, and Doc here makes the best in town. There's nothing you can do to stop me."

"I won't try then." Faye laughed; thrilled her pick-up attempt was successful.

"Doctor," Emanuel belted out across the bar while raising his glass. "Another one for the lady here."

Doc was almost finished making the martini before Emanuel asked for it. He delayed delivering the drink for a minute so as not to tip Faye off, and then placed it in front of her. Doc turned away and chuckled to himself. He had seen this move so many times before, yet it still worked. Emanuel would sit alone at the bar drinking martinis and inevitably a woman would approach him. He never approached them and hardly even looked around the bar in the typical searching gesture of the lonely drinker. Doc wasn't sure if Emanuel affected this pose to attract women, or if he really was that indifferent. Either way, Emanuel's self-assured and confident air always seemed to draw at least one woman over into his pensive world. Emanuel's tall, athletic build, thick salt and pepper hair, and swarthy features added to his allure. Doc always noticed, however, that Emanuel seemed much happier after he had some companionship.

"So, Faye, what do you do?" Emanuel had to ask the standard D.C. question even though he knew the answer.

"I'm an attorney for Powers & Boothe. Antitrust. How about you?" Faye took a sip of her martini.

"I'm also a lawyer, believe it or not. I do criminal defense for the prestigious firm of the Law Offices of Emanuel Adams. You must have heard of us?"

Faye laughed, appreciative of Emanuel's self-deprecating humor. She was delighted that she'd met a tall lawyer with a full head of hair who didn't take himself too seriously. Most men in Washington were so full of themselves they could hardly wait to tell you how important they were. And most often they never backed up this attitude with charm, wit, or looks. She was having a wonderful time already.

"Criminal defense, huh?" Faye said. "You don't meet many of those. How do you deal with defending people you know are guilty? I could never do that."

"I don't. I think we're all guilty of something. It's just a matter of degree. Society just decides to incarcerate some people for certain acts while letting other acts go unpunished. I also don't believe in prisons, and I don't think I'm in any position to make a moral determination about what acts are worse than others. For example, I could care less if someone uses drugs and I sure as hell don't think they should spend time in jail for doing so. I'm not saying they should be legal necessarily, but drug-related offenses should be decriminalized."

"What about dealing? Don't you think that dealing is worse than using?"

"No. It's a free market, isn't it? Nobody forces an individual to buy coke that first time and yank down a few lines. It's their choice."

"I'll agree with you on that one, and not a bad choice at that." Faye gave a coy little smile and Emanuel could tell the alcohol was taking quick effect.

"What about murder, though? That seems clear cut," Faye asked.

"Not to me. Sometimes we say killing is justified, like in war or self-defense, or when we execute people. Other times we just don't like the reasons people give us for killing. All I'm saying is I don't want to make the determination over what's legitimate and what's not. I'd rather just make an argument to keep people out of prison and let others decide the morality issue."

"So, you don't believe in right or wrong, good and evil?"

"Not really. The concept of right and wrong comes from religions that try to control human nature. I don't think you can really do that. People will do what their instincts tell them, just like animals."

"I thought those concepts came from God, like the Ten Commandments. God created us and told us not to do certain things, right?"

"I'm not sure I believe in God, so I can't believe that a higher power handed down laws for us. I think they were self-imposed by a certain segment of society like the right Reverend Winston."

"You don't believe in God? I thought everyone did these days."

"Nope, and I also don't believe in talking about religion when drinking martinis. It puts a bad taste in my mouth and changes the flavor of the vodka."

Faye laughed playfully and subconsciously inched closer to Emanuel. Her eyes were locked on his and he could tell he had captured her imagination.

"So, Faye, how about another round?"

"I'd love one."

2

A few blocks away from the Old Ebbitt Grill, Satya Grady was sitting in Lafayette Square smoking a Swisher Sweet cigar. He was staring at the White House, directly across Pennsylvania Avenue from the square. Such a beautiful building, Satya thought to himself. It was all lit up and so shiny white that it looked like it was scrubbed clean every day. It certainly was not a palace or a castle, but the White House did have a powerful and divine quality to it.

Satya's black eyes panned the White House and its surroundings in an effort to capture every detail in his memory. Pennsylvania Avenue was now a pedestrian promenade littered with enormous potted plants and barriers to prevent terrorist attacks and the wrought iron fence around the White House had been raised higher and electrified over the years. There were also more guards visible around the building heavily armed with automatic weapons. Instead of the old sports utility vehicles that used to carry Secret Service agents around, armored vehicles slowly patrolled Pennsylvania Avenue and the adjacent streets with powerful searchlights streaking across the sky.

These draconian measures were due to the increase in violent actions taken against United States government within its own borders. It started with the Oklahoma City bombing and then the attack in Congress where two Capitol policemen were killed. Then September

11, 2001, and the subsequent terrorist attacks changed everything. America became a place that expected both crime and terror. Satya Grady was keenly aware of this fact since it was part of his everyday life. As a New York City cop, his whole life was filled with violence and unfathomable acts.

Satya took a long pull of his cigar, inhaling a tad before exhaling into the night. He loved America. It had been good to his family ever since they stepped off the boat at the turn of the twentieth century. His family had moved all over the world for centuries, like nomads. They would stay someplace for a while until they felt they had worn out their welcome due to their religion and culture and then they would move on. Finally, they had arrived in the land of religious freedom. At that time, before immigration reform closed America's borders, America opened its arms to the poor refugees of the world, and they came in a flood of humanity.

Satya's grandparents were so grateful for the opportunity that they instilled in their children a great love for the United States. His parents instilled this same value into him and as he stared across at the White House he felt a lump in his throat and tears welling in his eyes. Satya knew one thing for certain: his love for his country had not wavered over the course of his life.

Religious freedom and economic prosperity were the ideals that brought most people to America as it did Satya's family. They certainly enjoyed this freedom, instilling in Satya as great an appreciation for his faith as they did for the United States. Satya thought back to his childhood when his grandfather used to sit him down on his lap and tell him stories with his thick accent. He would recount old fables that had been passed down for generations. Then Satya's grandfather would whisper in his ear, "In America, you can be who you are with pride, not like in the rest of the world. Here there are laws that say you can be any religion you want. Never forget that, and never forget who you are."

Satya never forgot his roots. He was a religious man. He had participated in all the rituals of his religion growing up and attended religious school three days a week in addition to regular school. At twenty-two he married Kim Morris, a girl from his neighborhood who had a similar background. Satya and Kim had three children, all of who received the same religious upbringing that Satya had.

Satya took another pull off his cigar and contemplated how all he really cared about was being an American and a man of God. He loved both ideas dearly.

The night air became a touch colder and Satya pulled the jacket of his uniform closer around him and turned the collar up. He took a last puff on his cigar, and then tossed it onto the red bricks of the square and stomped it out with his standard issue boot. Next, Satya knelt on the ground and clasped his hands in front of him. He began to pray, bowing down to God and asking Him to protect his family. As Satya prayed, the tears that had welled up in his eyes spilled over and streamed down his cheeks. He prayed on and on while the tears kept flowing.

When Satya was finished praying he stood up and brushed himself off. He looked up at the night sky for a few moments and then stared again at the White House. He pulled out his handkerchief, wiped his eyes and cheeks and blew his nose. Then he unholstered his nine-millimeter and checked it to see that it was clean, loaded with a full clip, and that the safety was off. Satisfied, Satya put the gun back in its holster and took one last look at the White House before setting off toward the Hay-Adams hotel.

"Ladies and gentleman, I want to sincerely thank you for coming out tonight in support of my bid to become the first third party President of the United States."

Reverend Winston paused to allow the crowd to give him the due applause. He looked out at the beautiful old ballroom of the Hay-Adams Hotel relishing in his position of power. Then he looked into the eyes of his supporters and knew that he had them mesmerized.

"While I am ahead in the polls, we all know it's a long road ahead and that road is filled with uncertainties. What is not uncertain, however, is my pledge to you and the rest of the American people that I will devote every ounce of my energy to this campaign. I think the time is right for a new order in this country of ours and it is my destiny and that of the Freedom party to fill this new order"

Reverend Winston shook his fist as he said this, and once again stepped back from the podium. The crowd, elegantly dressed in black tie and evening gowns, rose to its feet in raucous applause. They were in a trance, and acted in unison, like a fleet of automatons controlled by Winston. They all had the same smile on their faces and gleam in their eyes as they clapped rhythmically in sync.

Winston held up his hands in an attempt to quieten the crowd, and eventually they returned to their seats. He continued on:

"My fellow Americans, brothers and sisters, before I leave you tonight, I will make one more pledge. I pledge that if I am elected president of this great country you will see a change in government the likes of which Washington has never experienced. Politics will no longer be about infighting and partisan tactics that do no one any good. Rather, the American people will come first again. We are all in this together whether Republican, Democrat, or Freedom party. And each and every one of us, is a spiritual person who has faith and an inherent understanding of what is right and wrong. America has strayed from the path of righteousness and together, you and I will find that path again. Thank you and God bless you."

With his emphatic last words, Winston stepped away from the microphone and waved to the crowd. Winston's wife Judy joined him on the dais and they linked arm in arm. She gave him an innocent kiss on the cheek and together they waved to the crowd, now giddy with excitement. Judy was a perfect complement to Winston; tall, slender, blonde, blue eyed, and attractive. When she smiled her eyes lit up in a genuine fashion, and there was no doubt she had complete faith in her husband. Not since John and Jacqueline Kennedy had American politics seen such a beautiful couple.

After soaking in the adulation for a moment the couple walked off the stage and out a side door of the ballroom. As they exited the door, security agents surrounded them and led them through the hotel to the limousine waiting for them out front. Winston and his entourage crossed the foyer of the Hay-Adams and then burst through the front doors of the hotel. As they broke into the night, they were confronted by a mob of reporters and cameramen blinding them with bright lights and shoving microphones at them. Photographers took pictures in rapid fire with flash bulbs going off like fireworks.

Winston was forced into an impromptu press conference so he took the opportunity to answer a few questions.

"Reverend Winston," a reporter shouted, "is it true that you plan to expand military spending to increase our armed forces even more than President Taylor?"

"That is true indeed, but the enlarged military would be for humanitarian purposes, not for threatening other governments or waging war. Rather, it is my belief that we as the most powerful nation in the world should use our might to help the less fortunate in the world. We will nation-build."

"Reverend Winston, could you discuss the abortion issue for a moment please?" another reporter shouted.

"Unlike President Taylor, I'm one hundred percent against it. It's murder, plain and simple, and against everything that all religions stand for. Terminating a life just because the parents don't want to care for the life is disgusting. There are far too many people in our society who are willing to care for children if the biological parents don't want to."

"My first order of business as President will be inserting into the federal budget money for federal adoption centers to place unwanted children with people who want them, and second, to work towards a constitutional amendment criminalizing the act of performing and receiving abortions. Physicians take an oath to protect life and then they capitalize on women who want to destroy it. I quote you the story of Adam and Eve. When they violated God's law, they were punished and banished from the Garden of Eden. And, the serpent who facilitated the evil . . . well, we all know who he was."

"My policy will be, across the board, whether it be abortion or crime, you either turn to your government for help which will be abundantly provided, or you suffer the consequences. In the case of abortion, I'm telling women that if you have an unwanted pregnancy, don't make your child suffer. Endure and have the child, and then the state will take care of it for you. Nine months is a small price to pay for a human life."

As Winston was expounding his abortion policy, he noted something strange out of the corner of his eye. There was a man standing behind the reporters in a policeman's uniform. At first, Winston was not bothered, as it was perfectly normal to have policemen around during public appearances as a security measure. Slowly, however, Winston mentally registered the bothersome fact that the man was wearing a uniform that did not resemble that of a D.C. cop or Capitol policeman. It was a subtle point, but one that Winston could not ignore.

"I'm sorry ladies and gentleman, no more questions. I must be on my way. Thank you." Winston concluded the press conference and tried to proceed to his waiting limo. The crowd of reporters parted, making a path for him.

As Winston started to move, he was compelled by some invisible hand to turn toward the strangely dressed policeman. His eyes locked onto those of the cop who was staring directly at him. Winston saw a dreamy yet intense look in the man's eyes, and sensed danger. He slowed down, and gave the man the once-over. When he saw the "NYPD" badge on the front of the man's uniform he stopped moving.

Winston raised his eyes from the man's chest back to his eyes. He sensed that he could almost look into the man's soul his eyes were so wide. The two were locked together, unable to take their eyes of each other. Winston felt hypnotized and could not comprehend when he heard people yelling about a gun. Satya Grady's eyes were the last things Reverend Winston saw before he heard the gunshots.

3

The thin rays of the rising sun sneaking through the blinds were enough to wake Emanuel from his alcohol-induced slumber. When he first opened his eyes, he wasn't quite sure where he was, then he spotted the used condoms lying on the parquet floor. He rolled over and saw a mop of auburn hair cascading down onto toned, white shoulders, and he remembered he was at Faye's house.

The night could not have gone better. The martinis went down so fast the olives barely had time to marinate in the vodka. Faye wanted oysters so they devoured three-dozen Wellfleets. Emanuel thought back, reveling in the memory of Faye sucking oysters right out of the shell without cocktail sauce or horseradish masking the slimy, salty taste. Faye's eyes rolled back in her head in mini orgasm each time an oyster slid down her throat.

The conversation flowed as easily as the vodka and oysters. It was one of those evenings when every statement Emanuel made was exactly the right thing to say. He was like a basketball player in the zone, incapable of missing a shot. When Emanuel stated with conviction that he believed everything in life happened for a reason, including bad things, Faye shot him a look that said, "I've finally met a man who shares my outlook on life."

When Emanuel picked up the check and suggested they go back to his place for a nightcap, Faye insisted they go to hers. This was yet another bonus for Emanuel who preferred the comforts of a woman's home to his Spartan, bachelor apartment. Plus, he liked having the freedom to leave when he felt the urge instead of having to gently nudge a companion out the door before they wanted to leave.

In the cab to Faye's Georgetown townhouse, her hand went instantly into Emanuel's lap before they even kissed. She looked at him right in the eye as she brazenly fondled him through his suit pants. Emanuel just sat back ran his fingers through Faye's luxurious hair and enjoyed the feeling of blood rushing to his face as Faye stroked him.

Emanuel loved encounters like this one because there was no emotional work involved. As they drove down K Street, he knew he was guaranteed a delicious night of sex, complete with feigned intimacy. There was no protracted courting period or tortured dinners, just a few martinis, three-dozen oysters, and presto, the opportunity to play husband and wife for the night. The next day or even that very same night, he could walk away, retreat to his solitude, and not have to deal with another person's day-to-day emotional needs.

They had stumbled into Faye's Georgetown townhouse groping each other. Faye was giggling and repeating over and over again that she normally didn't invite men she had just met back to her home. Emanuel just smiled to himself having heard these excuses so many times before. For some reason, he had thought to himself, women still felt guilty about cavalier sexual encounters, and needed to pretend they didn't normally happen.

Faye dropped her bags in her foyer and asked Emanuel if he wanted a drink. Despite the fact that he was already quite drunk he thought it would be rude to refuse, and so he accepted a glass of white wine. He waited in her living room, running his hand over Faye's expensive couch, and trying to keep his head from spinning. All of a sudden, Frank Sinatra's "Fly Me to the Moon," began playing, and

Faye walked into the room with the wine. For the first time, Emanuel got a full view of her body, which was fit and in perfect proportion.

Faye had removed her suit jacket, and was now wearing a sleeveless, white silk blouse and blue skirt, which hung two inches above her knees. She had well-toned calves and slender ankles that Emanuel liked, and bright pink toenails that were visible since Faye had removed her shoes. The sight of her bare arms and upper thighs gave Emanuel a sexual charge that in his drunken state, he knew he would not be able to control for long.

Faye sat down next to Emanuel on the couch and they each took a sip of their wine. There was a brief moment of silence before Emanuel grabbed Faye and kissed her. The taste of the wine still lingered on her lips and tongue. He remembered thinking the fruity wine flavored with a hint of smoke must be a Chardonnay. Faye was a great kisser, knowing the right mix between soft and delicate kisses, and more aggressive ones. Emanuel became more aroused with Faye's kisses and he began running his hands over her body. He massaged her breasts through her silk blouse, pinching her nipples, which were poking through her delicate bra underneath. The initial shock was soon replaced by a look of pleasure on her face, which was now highlighted with rosy cheeks and lips red and moist with saliva.

In a moment of lucidity, Faye requested they go upstairs to her bedroom where they could be more comfortable. Once there, they made love twice in a delicious haze, and then fell asleep back to back, on different sides of the bed.

Just past Faye's head a clock read 6:09 a.m., and Emanuel knew the time had come to slip away. He sat up in bed and tried to clear his head and wake up. His head was throbbing and he was covered in dried sweat and bodily fluids. He was exhausted and was not looking forward to a day at the office.

Quietly, Emanuel put his suit back on, stuffing his tie in his jacket pocket. He turned to the large, oval mirror Faye had hanging on the wall and was not pleased with what he saw. His hair was standing up straight in a weird crown and the bags under his eyes were heavy. Emanuel rubbed his chin, rough with a day's growth, and noted he was too pale and thin.

He walked over to the bed and sat down next to Faye. He gave her a kiss on the forehead and she opened her eyes begrudgingly.

"I need to go," Emanuel said while stroking Faye's back.

"Have a good day," Faye croaked back.

"I'll talk to you soon."

With a final kiss Emanuel was out. These parting exchanges were always stilted and awful, yet necessary. Emanuel was certainly not going to creep away like a thief without saying good-bye. It was a small gesture, but one that he fastidiously adhered to, as if to attach one modicum of civility to this type of encounter, which he viewed as seedy despite the fact that it represented his own lifestyle choice.

Emanuel walked through Faye's house admiring its decor. It was one of Georgetown's coveted row houses, which are old, beautiful, and expensive to buy and maintain. He had not really noticed how nice it was the night before, but he certainly appreciated the original art and antique furniture as he made his way down the stairs and out the door. Faye was obviously doing well at Powers & Boothe.

Emanuel hit the sidewalk and took a look around to find his bearings. The street signs told him he was at 30th and P, and suddenly, he was aware of the weather. It was mid March, but the morning had a stark, wintry feel. He looked at the sky, which was cloudy with only a few holes. He could see that the gray clouds were moving fast to cover up the last remaining blue patches.

Emanuel flipped his collar up and hugged himself as he set off by foot. He lived in West Dupont, which was only a fifteen-minute walk from Faye's straight up P Street. He made a note of that for future reference, as he liked having women near-by. He also liked Faye and contemplated calling her again.

As Emanuel neared his apartment building he popped into the market across the street for a cup of coffee and a bagel. He almost never had food in his apartment and amused himself by thinking that he single-handedly kept this market in business. Emanuel picked up a *Washington Post* to go with his breakfast and together they cost him twenty dollars. Convenience came with a price in West Dupont.

When Emanuel stepped back out onto 21st Street the sky was totally overcast and the clouds had turned from a light gray to a more ominous charcoal. He lowered his eyes from the sky to the front page of the newspaper, and in an instant his hunger pains were replaced by a sickening fear. The cup of coffee, which had been hot in his hand, suddenly felt cold and the blowing wind cut through his suit as if it were paper. Emanuel read the headline over and over again in order to make sure it was real:

"Reverend Winston Assassinated by New York City Cop"

For some inexplicable reason, Emanuel had a feeling that came from the pit of his stomach that he would be drawn into this event that was sure to rock the nation.

4

Satya's night had not been nearly as pleasant as Emanuel's. Moments after he had unloaded his clip into Reverend Winston, he had been tackled by numerous security people and members of the media. It was fortunate that the media had been involved, since police officers and armed security were not able to shoot back at Satya for fear of hitting an innocent bystander.

When Satya was physically brought down he did not put up a fight. He had accomplished his mission, and there was nothing left for him to do but surrender. He never planned to try and escape, but merely to accept responsibility for the act. This fact was unknown to Satya's capturers who proceeded to dish out a fine thrashing.

As the blows sunk into his face and body, Satya felt no pain. He was at peace because he believed in what he had done. However, he also had the vision of Reverend Winston's eyes staring him down. Just before his life came to an end, Winston's eyes told a story of understanding. He knew what was coming and accepted it. There was no fear in his eyes or despair, simply recognition of events that were beyond his control. Satya would never forget those eyes as long as he lived.

After he was subdued, Satya was cuffed and thrown into the back of a police car. All the while, camera flashes were going off around him. The media wanted shots of Winston's bloodied body and of his assailant. Cameramen were frantic, uncertain of what to film next, while the reporters began giving a play-by-play. This was the kind of event that drove ratings through the roof.

The last thing Satya saw before the police car sped away was Winston lying on the ground in a pool of blood. His handsome face had holes in it and the charisma and vigor had left his body in an instant. Satya had seen many dead bodies in his life, but this one was starkly different and infinitely more disturbing.

Satya sat back in the car, starting to feel the welts and cuts on his face and body. He wanted to touch his face but couldn't, his hands cuffed firmly behind his back. He looked down at the front of his uniform and noticed that his badge had been ripped off and that two buttons were missing from his coat.

The cop car raced through the streets of D.C. down to central lockup. When they arrived a horde of policemen and reporters were waiting for them. Satya was practically carried from the car to the police station. Microphones were thrust in front of his face and the bright lights from the television cameras blinded his eyes.

Satya was in shock. His brain had shut off, and his body was limp. He had the vision of Winston's corpse etched in his mind and nothing else was registering. The whole scene was surreal, and he watched it unfold as if he had become part of some television cop drama.

Reality came back to Satya when he was thrown into a chair in the interrogation room. He had been in these rooms hundreds of times himself, but on the other side of the table. He knew well what was coming. The officers left the room, leaving Satya by himself. This was standard procedure. The cops want the suspect to feel alone and scared so when they burst into the room they are halfway to a confession.

Satya felt neither scared nor alone. He was actually relieved to have the silence and the solitude. He felt relaxed, as though he had just enjoyed an intense and enduring orgasm. His limbs felt like rubber hoses and his face wore and expression of inner peace.

"Would you take at look at that guy," Detective Phil Horahan said to his colleagues as they looked through the two-way mirror at Satya. "He looks like he's lying on the beach catchin' rays."

"Maybe he's on somethin'," Horahan's partner Detective Mike Baxter answered.

"We'll find out in a minute, I guess."

A uniformed officer opened the door to the anteroom where Horahan and Baxter were standing.

"Detectives, here's the report. He is NYPD."

"No shit? A cop assassin. Now I've seen it all. Thanks," Baxter said still looking at the report in disbelief.

"Come on, Mike. Let's work him over."

The two detectives entered the room with heavy steps. They were not happy about interrogating one of their own. Satya watched the door open and the two walked in, and their presence snapped him out of his reverie.

"Officer Grady, I'm Detective Phil Horahan, and this is my partner Detective Mike Baxter."

Satya sized the two up. Horahan was mid-forties and, by the sound of his voice, a very heavy smoker. He was thin except for a belly that could only come from too much booze, and his face was heavily lined. What little hair Horahan had left was cropped short, and his red, bulbous nose was too big for his face. Satya figured Horahan would be the good cop and do most of the talking.

Baxter was black and much younger. He had shaved his head bald and looked like a middle linebacker. His trapezius muscles were visible through his cheap shirt and his enormous biceps restricted him from straightening his arms. His enormous hands were placed on his hips in a defiant gesture as if he was waiting for a reason to dish out some punishment. Clearly, Baxter was bad cop.

"Officer Grady, you want to tell us why a police officer would kill a presidential candidate on live TV?"

"Not really," Satya replied. He noted the muscles in Baxter's forearms flex.

"Okay. Were you acting alone on this?"

"I really think I'd like to talk to my lawyer, if it's all the same to you two."

"Do you have a lawyer?" Horahan asked incredulously.

"Not officially, but I know one here in D.C. that I'd like to represent me."

"Who's that?"

"His name is Emanuel Adams. He used to be a DA in Manhattan. Do you know him?"

"Yeah, I know him. He's slimy. He'll do anything to get guys off the hook. Good choice."

5

Emanuel walked into his office and instinctively looked at his telephone. The red message light seemed to be blinking faster than usual, and seemed more like an alarm than anything else. Emanuel lamented his hangover and picked up the phone.

"Mr. Adams, this is Detective Horahan of the Metropolitan Police Department. We have a Satya Grady in custody at Third District for the murder of Reverend Winston. He requested you as his attorney. Could you please call down to the station, or just come on down if you are able to take the case? Thanks."

Emanuel hit the number one on the phone to repeat the message. He could not believe that it was real, but it sounded official. He had been expecting something to happen, but was still amazed that his premonition had materialized. After hearing the message for a second time, Emanuel slumped into his chair and let the phone fall off his ear onto his shoulder.

"Who the hell is Satya Grady, and why does he want me as his lawyer?" Emanuel asked himself.

Emanuel thought back to his days at the DAs office in Manhattan figuring he had run into Grady at some point. He was NYPD after all. His mind was a blank. He had dealt with so many cops that they all ran together in his memory. He hated most of them anyway and tried to forget them as soon as he no longer needed them for a case. Most cops were just thugs who liked having the authority and ability to bash skulls. They couldn't care less about justice.

There would be only one way to find out who Grady was, and that was to go meet the man. Emanuel slowly peeled himself out of his chair and went to the window of his office. He had a view from 15th Street over to the East Wing of the White House. There were news vans parked along the street, and Emanuel could see reporters and cameramen standing around drinking coffee and smoking cigarettes. The wind was blowing hard and the flags on top of all the buildings were whipping around furiously.

Emanuel took a deep breath and walked out of his office, grabbing his briefcase on the way. He locked the door and took the elevator down to the street. He hailed a cab and headed downtown to central lockup.

As was his habit during cab rides to meet new clients, Emanuel started working up possible defenses even before hearing their side of the story. Emanuel had learned two things in his years practicing criminal law as a prosecutor and then as a defense attorney: people under arrest are always guilty, and they always lie about what happened. As far as Emanuel was concerned, defending people was not about proving their innocence, but rather, simply finding a way to manipulate the facts to keep them out of jail or keep them in for as short a time as possible.

In this instance, Emanuel was drawing a blank. Why would a New York City cop blow away a presidential candidate and religious leader in cold blood in front of so many witnesses? The cop made no attempt to get away with the crime, disguise himself, or flee the scene. Just as Emanuel was formulating a defense, the cab pulled up to the Third District police department.

Emanuel was brutally awakened from his thoughts by a mob of television crews and protestors surrounding the station. Television vans were double-parked along the street in front of the building with their satellite dishes buzzing atop their roofs. Reporters were already in front of cameras making reports on what was surely paper-thin information.

The really frightening scene, however, was the mourners and protestors making a stand for the deceased Reverend Winston. People were weeping and shaking their fists, calling for the assassin's head. Images of Christ in every possible incarnation were everywhere. One person had strapped himself to a cross in only a loincloth to bring the image to life.

Preachers were standing on crates yelling out scripture over bullhorns while dozens were kneeling in silent prayer. Winston had become a martyr to these people and the passion on their faces was evident to Emanuel as he stepped out of the cab. As he did, the reporters rushed at him from all sides, asking who he was and what he was doing there. They sensed the first piece of the story and were desperate for information. Emanuel just put his head down like a running back breaking through the line, and he kept his mouth shut. As he made his way up to the front door of the station, he was grabbed and prodded by the reporters until finally he had to wave his arms violently to keep them at bay.

Emanuel burst into the police precinct thrilled to be free of the media hounds. He smiled to himself, amused at the irony of feeling free while entering a police station. Usually, he felt claustrophobic when he came to interview clients even though he knew he could leave at the end. Despite his years of experience, he still had the fear of being thrown in jail through mistaken identity or some mishap. The thought of imprisonment was too much for him to bear.

Almost immediately upon entering the building, Emanuel was approached by Horahan, who was smoking a cigarette in the lobby.

"Jesus, Adams it's about time you got here. This place is jumping. Plus, we haven't presented the guy because he insisted on waiting for you. You know we only have twenty-four hours."

"Morning Detective. It's always a pleasure to see you, too."

"Whatever, Adams. I have a job to do."

"Horahan, you're not still bitter about the Robinson case are you?" Emanuel said, responding to Horahan's antagonistic tone. Emanuel had won an illegal search and seizure motion in a case where Horahan had been the investigating officer. Fred Robinson walked on a murder rap because Horahan searched Robinson's apartment without a warrant. Horahan claimed he was in hot pursuit of Robinson after the shooting while Emanuel argued that Horahan arrived an hour after Robinson and broke the door off the hinges to enter the apartment -- end of case.

"I got over it. It just surprised me since you are about the only lawyer I know who cares enough about criminals to argue that thin-ass shit."

"Are you referring to the Constitution of this great country of ours as 'thin-ass shit'?"

"I'm referring to scumbag murderers who need to go to jail, not back on the street," Horahan said, standing closer to Emanuel.

"Let's argue that one over a beer sometime," Emanuel said, trying to calm Horahan down. "What's the story with my new scumbag?"

"You don't watch CNN? They must have shown the footage a thousand times of this cop, Grady, blowing away Reverend Winston outside the Hay-Adams last night."

"Actually, I missed it." Emanuel felt like vomiting at that moment. Video footage the whole world had already seen did not help the defense. It meant brain dead jurors who don't read newspapers or watch the news.

"Listen, Horahan, what does a guy have to do for a cup of coffee around here, beg for it?"

"Coming right up counselor. I think you're gonna need more than that after you meet with this guy. He's NYPD for Christ's sake. Whacko."

Horahan poured Emanuel some awful-smelling coffee into a Styrofoam cup and put a spoonful of sugar into it without asking how Emanuel took it. He handed the coffee over and then led

Emanuel through a few secured doors to the interrogation rooms. A group of people stood outside one room and Emanuel figured that had to be the jackpot. He noted the uniforms, a large black man and a woman in her mid-thirties wearing a tan suit, with a French blue shirt underneath the jacket. They turned toward him as he approached.

"Adams, this is my partner Mike Baxter and U.S. Attorney Sophie Mitchell. Everyone, Emanuel Adams."

Handshakes were exchanged all around followed by an awkward silence. Emanuel wanted to size up his opposite number for several different reasons, but backed off for fear of starting off on the wrong foot.

"Any confessions?" Emanuel asked, breaking the silence.

"Not yet. He wouldn't talk without a lawyer." Baxter replied.

"Good. Then I'd better go see our boy and we'll talk more after."

"Enjoy," Horahan said, opening the door for Emanuel. "Remember, though, you only have a couple of hours before we have to head over to the courthouse. We've already given this one special treatment, so please don't fuck with it any more."

"I'm not even sure I'm taking the case," Emanuel responded with a slight smile.

"Yeah, right," Horahan said.

As Emanuel entered the interrogation room he had a feeling of dread the likes of which he had never experienced. The moment he met his clients was usually when he was at his most confident and brash in an effort to give them comfort. This time he felt as if he needed the comfort.

Satya was sitting serenely in his chair, seemingly in a semi-conscious state. His eyes were half shut and his hands were folded neatly together on the table in front of him. He had a slight smile indicating an inner peace that was an odd contrast to the state of his face. Somehow his gray hair was brushed back and neatly parted, and Emanuel wondered how he had maintained such a kempt appearance in an interrogation room.

"Emanuel Adams." Emanuel introduced himself and extended his hand.

Satya got up slowly from his seat and extended his handcuffed hands. "Satya Grady. Thanks for coming so soon."

"Not a problem. So, did you get beat up here in the station last night or some time before."

Satya smiled. "Sorry Emanuel. They played it by the book with me last night. I took the beating right after the shooting."

"We can't have all the breaks now can we."

The two sat back down at the table. Emanuel broke out a legal pad and took a pen out of his inside jacket pocket. After he was settled, he turned his attention to Satya. There was a long silence as Emanuel sized him up. Emanuel was used to seeing people after they had killed someone and there was always the same aura about them. They were always fidgety and nervous as the repercussions of the act sank into their heads. They were like children who realized they had done something really wrong and had to face mommy and daddy. Satya, however, did not exhibit those qualities, but rather sat intently watching Emanuel.

"First, Officer Grady, I'm interested in why you requested me as your lawyer," Emanuel began. "Have we met before?"

"Yes, we have. I met you once when you were a DA in Manhattan. It was only briefly since you decided not to prosecute the collar my partner and I made."

"Oh yeah? What collar was that?"

"You remember Jesus Cruz?"

Emanuel took a nervous sip of his coffee and felt a trickle of sweat begin descending down his temple. He had not heard that name in years and had no desire to. It was the Cruz case that effectively ended his tenure as a district attorney and changed his outlook on life.

In his third year as an assistant district attorney, Emanuel was fortunate enough to have a felony case come across his desk. It was a drug case that his superiors felt he could handle after two and half years of misdemeanors. For third years, felonies were like badges of honor since they were so hard to come by. When you got one, it was like a reward from the top.

Up until that point, Emanuel had been the perfect young prosecutor. He gave very little ground on plea bargains, and played everything straight by the book. His bosses loved him because they could tell Emanuel relished his job. Emanuel did love the intrigue of the criminal courts and the characters that came through the door everyday. At that time, it mattered little to him that he was putting people in jail because he just wanted to be part of the action.

The Cruz matter was a straightforward case meant to help Emanuel's career, but it didn't play out that way. Emanuel remembered the day he walked into his office and picked up the memo waiting for him in his in box:

MEMORANDUM

Jesus Cruz: Twenty-five year old Hispanic male. Married with one child: 6 months old. Occupation: Electrician, currently unemployed. Crack cocaine addict arrested for the third time on possession with intent to distribute charges. Under New York Penal Code Section 24.138, if convicted must serve a mandatory fifteen-year sentence.

Just as Emanuel finished reading the memo, the arresting officers walked into his office.

"Mr. Adams?"

"Yes."

"I'm Officer Grady, and this is Officer Chow. We arrested Cruz last night for possession with intent. We were told you'd be expecting us."

"Right, I definitely was. You guys want some coffee?"

Grady told Emanuel the brief story of the arrest and he took notes while sipping the watery coffee.

"Martinez, our undercover guy, had been lurking in Cruz's neighborhood for a few weeks and had seen him buying on street corners. Then he heard that Cruz was making a big score last night. We missed the actual buy, but picked up Cruz moments after with ten grams of crack on him."

Everything looked legitimate on the arrest report. The cops were following a lead that checked out, so they had probable cause to stop and search Cruz. He was read his Miranda rights, brought down to the station and booked. Emanuel knew there would be no Fourth Amendment illegal search and seizure issues so off the top of his head he could only imagine that defense counsel would argue that there was no intent.

Moments after Grady and Chow left, Toni Fuentes stormed into his office. Fuentes was from the Public Defender's office and militant. She started blasting Emanuel without the slightest salutation.

"Adams, how can you work with these fascists? These fucking cops make me sick!" Toni yelled, pointing an accusatory finger at Emanuel.

"Now, now, Toni, that's no way to begin a plea bargain."

"Who said anything about a plea bargain? There was absolutely no intent."

"Toni, ten grams is one hell of a party for one guy and it's above the statutory limit for simple possession. It's Cruz's third strike, so you better start haggling," Emanuel said confidently.

"Forget it. This guy's an addict. He can't control his habit or how much he buys. If he has the money, he buys what he can. He's no dealer. He definitely gets high on his own supply."

Emanuel had to laugh because Toni's accent sounded just like Al Pacino's in "Scarface."

"Is something funny, Adams?" She was pissed.

"No, no, I'm sorry. Listen, I don't think the jury is going to buy the addiction defense. I sure don't."

"Oh yeah, why don't you try stopping chain smoking Camels and then we'll talk."

"Touché. Unfortunately, though, Camels are still legal, thank God. Look, are you really going to risk fifteen years on this when we can work something out?"

"Cruz has a wife and a baby to support and any time served will be a disaster. He told me that he can't afford to do time. He needs to work. He also admitted he's addicted and wants treatment. I'm tired of the government locking people up when what they really need is positive help."

"I'm not going to debate the merits of the war on drugs with you, Toni. The man committed a crime with specific penalties and there's nothing I can do about that."

"Bury the case, Emanuel."

"What! The first felony of my career and you want me to bury it." As soon as Emanuel said that he knew he had made a mistake. Toni cared about a human life and a family and with that statement it seemed Emanuel only cared about his career.

"That's great Emanuel. I thought you were a compassionate DA. You're all the same. Let me tell you something, either you throw this case out or I am going to debate the war on drugs with you . . . in court."

Fuentes stormed out of Emanuel's office and he was left with a lump in his throat and a queasy feeling in his stomach. Fuentes was going to put the system on trial and Emanuel was going to ruin a family to further his career. All of a sudden, the thought of trying a felony wasn't so exciting, because Emanuel agreed with Fuentes. Putting Cruz in jail would ruin his life and place his family in an even worse position than having a drug-addicted man heading it.

That was a pivotal moment in Emanuel's life. For the first time in his career he sat in judgment of a defendant, and he could not justify sending Jesus Cruz to jail for fifteen years. He thought of Cruz's family, and concluded that removing him for drug addiction was unbelievably wrong. Emanuel couldn't care less about addiction since he figured everyone had one. Some were just legal, and others weren't.

He decided to bury the case and quit the DAs office as soon as his three-year commitment was up. It was a rash decision, but one he was happy with. He also quit smoking Camels.

Emanuel was in a trance, thinking about his past when Satya spoke, bringing him back to the present.

"I know you buried that Cruz case. That file somehow slipped away, and he never even came in front of a judge."

"I didn't think it was a strong case."

"Come now," Satya said sympathetically. "It was a softball, and you know it. It was your first felony and it was a gift. You let it go because Cruz had a family. It was the right thing to do."

"A cop in favor of letting criminals walk? Are you kidding me?"

"I've walked the beat for twenty-five years. I've seen the worst of everything this life has to offer. It's not always simple. Sending Cruz up would not have served any purpose."

"It would've kept a drug dealer off the streets. Prison stopped being about rehabilitation a long time ago, Officer."

"If you thought he was a drug dealer why'd you bury the case?"

"I told you, I didn't think it was a strong case, unlike yours. Would you like to talk about that now?" Emanuel asked, trying to change the subject away from the painful memory.

"What would you like to know?"

"For starters . . ." Emanuel paused because he had a feeling he was not going to like the answer to his question. "For starters, why'd you do it? You're an experienced police officer and last night you murdered a presidential candidate on live television." The veins in Emanuel's temples were bulging and he was sweating out the vodka from the night before.

"Emanuel, when I tell you why I killed Jack Winston I want you to take me seriously?"

"Of course."

Satya paused and composed himself before continuing.

"I killed Winston because God told me to do it."

Despite his best efforts to control himself, Emanuel allowed a tiny smile to appear on his face and sat back in his chair. Experienced police officer or not, Satya Grady was obviously delusional or temporarily insane. It was still weak and a probable loser, but at least he would have something to work with.

"Is something funny?" Satya asked.

"No, not at all. I just want to make sure I understand. You're saying that the only reason you killed Winston was that God told you to do it?"

"That's right."

"Officer Grady, when you killed Winston, did you think that what you were doing was wrong?"

"If you mean did I know that killing another human being is against the law, then the answer is yes," Satya replied with conviction.

"Were you aware of the consequences of your actions?"

"Absolutely. I'm a police officer after all." Satya was looking directly into Emanuel's eyes and the tone of his voice was firm and assured.

Emanuel began to sweat again. Satya had just convincingly failed the McNaghten Test for establishing insanity as a defense to criminal conduct.

"I'm not insane Emanuel"

"With all due respect, when you say that God told you to kill Reverend Winston, I made the assumption that perhaps you are not quite compis mentis. Every other guy hauled up on murder charges claims 'God told him to do it.'"

"You don't believe in God?"

"My beliefs have nothing to do with your case," Emanuel said, irritated. He could feel the sweat soaking through his undershirt.

"Of course they do. If you believe in God, isn't it reasonable to believe that God told me to kill Winston?"

Emanuel started to feel better again. Satya might have thought he was sane, but this kind of talk said something different. Emanuel decided to engage him to determine his competency.

"Okay, let's say for the sake of argument that I do believe in God. Tell me why that makes it reasonable to believe that God told you to kill Winston."

"Just look at the Bible. The Old and New Testaments are filled with stories of God talking to people. Moses receiving the Ten Commandments directly from God, and God asking Abraham to sacrifice Isaac in an act of faith and then stopping him at the last minute. There are whole books on prophets who talked to God."

"Jesus Christ walked the Earth for 33 years, so everyone who came into contact with Him came into contact with God. So, why is it so far-fetched that I had an encounter with God?" Satya said, exasperated that he had to defend himself to his lawyer.

Emanuel sensed Satya's anxiety and tried to calm him. "Officer Grady, let's say for a minute that I believe you talked to God. Why don't you describe to me when and how this miracle took place?"

"Fine." Satya took a deep breath and began telling his story.

One of the proudest achievements in Emanuel's life was quitting smoking. The physical and mental addictions were intense, and it had taken a long time to overcome them. Despite this personal triumph, the minute he walked out of the interrogation room he bummed a cigarette off Detective Horahan, who was still standing with Baxter and Sophie Mitchell.

The thing that Emanuel had liked best about smoking was its self-destructive element and that was what he needed after talking to Satya. He had lost control to a client for the first time in his career. From the minute he walked into the room, Emanuel knew he was the reactor not the actor in the situation. Satya was the one at peace and calm while Emanuel was completely on edge, and he was the lawyer.

"I didn't know you smoked Adams," Horahan commented with a smile as he fished for a cigarette out of his soft-pack of generic cigarettes. He was thrilled to find another member of the socially unacceptable smoking club.

"Yeah, well, I quit. But today seems like a good day to start again."

Horahan lit Emanuel's cigarette with a yellow Bic lighter, ignoring the fact that the police station was a non-smoking building.

"Was it that rough in there that you have to start smoking again?" Mitchell inquired.

"Let's just say it was a bit unnerving. I'm not sure what this guy is all about." Emanuel took a long drag off the cigarette and relished in the pain the smoke caused in his clear lungs. "Horahan, do you think I could take a look at the footage of the shooting? You guys have the tape already, don't you?"

"We sure do. You can see it, but I'll bet you'll need a drink after that one," Horahan said, enjoying Emanuel's predicament. "Let's go to the video room."

The group walked down the long institutional corridor, through a pair of swinging double doors, and then turned into a large room filled with high-tech equipment. In one corner of the room a large-screen monitor was set up with elaborate video and web browsing attachments. There were ten movie theater style seats in front of the screen.

Horahan offered everyone a seat and then called over a technician to roll the tape.

"You're in luck, Adams. We've already compiled a master tape that shows the shooting from practically every possible angle. There were so many television crews on hand we had the luxury."

The tape started to roll and the group went silent. The first angle was simply focused on Winston as he was walking out of the Hay-Adams. It showed him striding confidently with a broad smile as he talked to reporters on the way to his limousine. Then the camera picked up how the expression on his face changed as he spotted Satya in the crowd.

Emanuel noted how Winston's face at first emoted bewilderment, and then a kind of placidity. At no point did Winston show fear or surprise, but rather an eerie calm. Finally, the cameras showed Winston's face contort as bullets sunk into his body, and then as bullets hit his head, his face disappeared.

The next segment was a close-up of Satya. With so many cameras around, Satya had been picked up in the background and the tape was edited and enhanced to make him the focus. Satya had a look of determination on his face. He never blinked and showed no signs of nervousness. Satya picked his moment, drew his gun, took careful aim, and unloaded.

Emanuel watched the footage of Satya carefully. He was perplexed at Satya's demeanor. It seemed as if he was on the firing range aiming at a paper target. His hand was steady and he hit Winston with every bullet. For the brief second between Satya's last shot and the time he was tackled, he had a look of relief on his face – not happiness, but satisfaction.

The next shot included both Winston and Satya. You could see Satya standing in the background with his eyes trained on Winston. Then Winston turned toward Satya sensing his presence. As Satya raised his gun you could see the two locking eyes and staring at each other. Emanuel had never seen anything like it. In that instant, there seemed to be complete understanding between the hunter and the prey. Winston made no effort to move or shout out, but rather stood there, as if accepting what was about to happen.

Horahan hit the pause button on the remote control and the group sat in silence. Everyone was unnerved by the last scene, which was now frozen on the large screen. Emanuel looked at the faces around him and he could tell everyone was trying to determine what had happened between Satya and Winston. To Emanuel, it looked like the two were in some conspiracy where Winston had hired Satya to kill him.

Perhaps God had appeared to Winston to tell him that the end was near, Emanuel thought. Perhaps we all know when death is staring us in the face and at the last second accept it gracefully as Winston had. Emanuel shook his head as if he was shaking off a punch. These were crazy thoughts, and he could not believe he was having them. He tried to tell himself that this was just a straight murder by someone who was probably legally insane.

"What do you think, Adams?" Mitchell asked. "Looks like you have your work cut out for you." Emanuel did not appreciate her editorial comments.

"Ms. Mitchell, I am not ready to talk to your office just yet. At the appropriate time, you'll know exactly what I think."

"Take it easy, Adams. I was just making the observation that with this video footage you have a tough case."

Emanuel's tone had been too sharp, but all of a sudden, he was not happy about sitting in the presence of the government attorney and the investigating police officers. They were the enemy now and it was time to draw a line in the sand.

"Sorry for my tone Ms. Mitchell. I'd like to go back and talk to Grady now if you don't mind." Emanuel barked.

"Sure, Adams, anything you want." Horahan said.

Emanuel stormed back into the interrogation room where Satya was sitting quietly as before. He had the same serene smile on his face and his hands were neatly folded in front of him.

"What the hell happened last night, Grady? I just saw the video, and you and Winston looked like you were in on it together."

"Mr. Adams, I've told you everything. Reverend Winston and I had never met before. It was simply God's will that I took his life and I think Winston understood that somehow."

"I'm really tired of this God bullshit. The deal is I'll plead you not guilty by reason of insanity, and believe me when I tell Mitchell out there your story, I should get you a pretty sweet deal."

"I'm sorry Mr. Adams, but I can't do that. I want you to defend me on the basis that I was following the word of God, and therefore, cannot be guilty for killing Reverend Winston."

"Justifiable homicide because God told you to do it! If I do that, I'll be disbarred. That'll never fly even if we're blessed with a jury of born again Christians. If it did, every goddamned criminal in America would be saying God told them to rob liquor stores and steal cars!"

"I can't speak for other people Mr. Adams, but I know that God came to me and told me to do this. If you explain that to the jury, I'm sure they'll believe you."

"Grady, I think you're insane."

"How can I convince you that my story is true?"

"You can't."

"Well, how about we make a deal?"

"What kinda deal?"

"My arraignment won't be for several weeks. In that time, you go up to New York and try to confirm my story. If you can, then you defend me my way. If not, I'll plead insanity."

"How the hell am I going to confirm your story?"

"I don't know. I just have faith that God will somehow show you that I'm telling you the truth. It was meant to be."

"Why would I waste my time searching for some sign from God? Then I'd be crazy, too."

Satya stared at Emanuel with his black piercing eyes. "Emanuel, I think somewhere deep inside you believe my story. I also know that you are a man in need of faith and if you don't do this, you'll spend the rest of your life wondering. It's only a few weeks. What's the worst that could happen --you find nothing and you defend me your way."

Emanuel studied Satya carefully. Satya was not pleading with Emanuel to accept his offer. He merely stated his argument clearly and calmly. He was so self-assured, it was if there was no doubt in his mind that Emanuel would actually agree to his proposal. Emanuel was unsure of what to say. This was the case of a lifetime and could catapult him into the ranks of America's most high-profile lawyers, but he had a client who was trying to dictate terms. Finally, Emanuel realized there was no harm in agreeing to Satya's plan. He would have to go to New York anyway to investigate the case, and if he somehow found God along the way, so be it.

"Fine, we'll do it your way. I'll go in search of the Holy Grail and if I find it, I'll defend you your way. If not, we go insanity and I try and save your ass. Deal?"

"Deal. I know it'll work out."

"I'm sure it will too. Now, I'm going out there and I'm telling those people that we're ready to go to the presentment. Okay?"

The two men shook hands. "Thank you, Emanuel. I knew you wouldn't let me down. That's why I chose you."

"Right," Emanuel said as he got up to leave.

Outside the room, he confronted Horahan and Mitchell, who were anxiously waiting to head over to D.C. Superior Court for the presentment. In the District of Columbia people arrested must be brought before a judge within 24 hours of their arrest, except on Sundays.

"Alright, we're ready to go," Emanuel announced to the group, who remained standing outside like the interrogation room was in fact a delivery room.

"I knew you'd take the case," Horahan said with a sneer.

"Everyone needs a lawyer at some point in their life; even you Horohan. I'll meet you over at D.C. Superior."

"Beautiful," Horahan said blowing smoke out of his thick nose.

"We now go to Jude Michaels outside the Third District precinct of the District of Columbia police department. Jude . . ."

"Thanks Ron. As you can see behind me, the scene here is emotionally charged. More and more people are showing up here to mourn Reverend Winston, and to protest his death. The crowd has taken on a mob-like quality calling for instant retribution against Winston's assailant, Officer Satya Grady of the New York City Police Department. The cry has been 'an eye for an eye and a tooth for a tooth.'"

"We have learned more about Officer Grady," Jude said, brushing a strand of sandy blond hair out of her face. "He has been a member of the police force for twenty-five years, and has a distinguished record. He has received two commendations for outstanding service and has no blemishes on his record for any misconduct or poor performance."

Jude was in her element now. One of CNN's rising stars, she was thrilled to have such an exciting story. Jude covered the Washington beat, but there'd been nothing of true significance since she had started the job two years before. She had the kind of looks the television demanded— attractive but plain. Her small, upturned nose was almost hidden in her wide face, which was scattered with freckles. The feature her producers most liked was the smile that didn't disappear when she talked. When she was reporting on breaking news, like at the moment, the smile seemed to grow with each new morsel of information.

"My source inside the police department, tells me that the investigating officers assigned to this case, Detectives Phil Horahan and Mike Baxter, have no idea yet as to why Grady took the life of Reverend Winston."

"We've also been told that Grady has met with a lawyer, and that the lawyer will most likely address the media shortly. In fact, there are some officials stepping outside of the building right now."

Jude stopped reporting and the camera panned across the sea of protestors who were cordoned off at a safe distance from the building, and faced with a line of riot police. It then focused on Emanuel stepping out of the building to face the press corps. Jude ran over to where Emanuel was standing as he began to speak.

"Ladies and gentleman, my name is Emanuel Adams. I was summoned here today by Officer Satya Grady of the New York City Police Department, the man accused of murdering Reverend Winston. I met with Officer Grady for approximately an hour and discussed his case with him. Obviously, those discussions are protected by the attorney/client privilege and therefore I cannot disclose the specifics of that conversation with you. Following my consultation with Officer Grady, I decided that I would represent him, and we're now going to Superior Court, for his presentment. Thank you. That's all I have to say."

Reporters began blasting Emanuel with questions that he did not entertain. He was ushered toward a police car and driven off. The camera focused again on Jude.

"Officer Grady now has a lawyer, criminal defense attorney Emanuel Adams. We don't know much about Mr. Adams, but we will certainly look into who he is, since he is definitely not, a nationally recognized legal figure. That being said, he is now in charge of the biggest case of the twenty-first Century. Back to you, Ron."

As soon as Jude finished her report, she grabbed her cell phone and dialed into her office.

"Hi, it's Jude. I'm following the Emanuel Adams lead, okay?" This was the story that Jude had been waiting for her entire career.

Emanuel arrived at D.C. Superior Court on 5th and D Streets in Northwest D.C. The building was an imposing, modern structure that served as more of a community center than a courthouse. There were always people hanging around outside of D.C. Superior, smoking cigarettes, eating hotdogs from the nearby vendors, and having private discussions with their lawyers or looking to hire one. Inside the courthouse, there was a constant bustle of activity as people rushed to courtrooms, filed complaints and motions, registered wills, and filed divorce agreements. And many, like Satya Grady, faced criminal charges.

Emanuel walked in, passed through the metal detectors and took the escalator down to the basement where the hearing commissioners sat to decide the fate of the people arrested the previous day.

Emanuel first walked into the clerk's office to fill out the necessary paperwork. He found Satya's name on a list of prisoners and copied his arrest number onto another form that indicated he was representing Satya. He then looked at the charges against Satya, and felt a chill when he read: "First degree murder."

The District of Columbia reinstated the death penalty in 2000, after years of going without it. The crime levels in the city had risen steadily every year and finally the decision was made to reinstate it as a means of deterring violent crime. The levels of violent crime had not decreased since the District adopted the death penalty, but several people had been executed, adding to the killing occurring on the streets.

The death penalty statute allowed the prosecution to seek the death penalty in cases of premeditated murder committed with malice aforethought, or felony murders -- killings that occurred while committing rape, robbery, arson, and similar crimes. Emanuel knew that assassinating a political candidate was usually considered premeditated since it usually required some planning to get close to such figures.

After filling out the paperwork, Emanuel walked around the corner to the courtroom. He pushed his way through the two sets of doors, sat down on one of the pew-like benches reserved for the gallery, and waited. Whenever Emanuel entered this room, he was always struck by how unimpressive it was. There was no grandeur like the courtrooms in the movies. It was basically a poorly lit, small basement room, with cheap furniture. There was always a disinterested clerk, a court reporter, the hearing commissioner, and the bailiff running the show. That was the whole operation to determine whether people could walk away and go home or remain in custody to await trial. It was an awfully meager room for such a decision.

The prisoners were kept in an adjoining room in two small cells called the "bull pen." Lawyers usually had a few minutes to go back there and talk to their clients before they were presented before the commissioner. The lawyer then had to make a quick determination if an argument existed to secure release of the prisoner. Emanuel was lucky that he met with Grady for an hour before his presentment.

Since most people arrested can't afford a lawyer, a motley crew of Criminal Justice Act lawyers hung around the courthouse all day hoping to pick up clients. The Criminal Justice Act paid lawyers $50 per hour to represent indigent clients. It wasn't a great living, but for many of the lawyers it was the only work they could find. They would just sign up with the courthouse and the judges would call them in if necessary. The really desperate could hang around in the lawyer's room drinking horrible coffee and waiting to jump right in. Most of the lawyers who lurked in the courthouse had some kind of deficiency that made them unsuitable for any other kind of work. There was a blind one, one in a wheelchair, and several alcoholics. Poor people accused of crimes don't have much choice in who represents them.

Finally, Mitchell walked in and stood before the prosecution's desk. She looked over at Emanuel and gave him a quick smile and a greeting.

One minute later, the commissioner came in and sat behind her desk. She brought some weightiness to the room with her black robe, short gray hair, and reading glasses resting on the tip of her nose. The bailiff called the People versus Grady, and Satya was brought in by a police officer. Emanuel immediately jumped to his feet and approached the bench, as did Mitchell. When they were before the commissioner, Mitchell handed Emanuel a copy of the "Gerstein", or police report, and a copy of the felony complaint. The "Gerstein" must establish a prima facie case of the allegations, such as the defendant was witnessed shooting the victim. In addition to the first-degree murder charge, they also charged Satya with carrying a pistol without a license. In the District, there were no permits for handguns.

"The government requests the defendant be held without bond," Mitchell said after Emanuel had reviewed the documents for two minutes.

"Counselor?" the commissioner said awaiting a response.

"Your honor, Officer Grady is a police officer of high distinction, who poses no threat to any person or property. Also, he is from New York, he is still employed by the New York City police department, and he has strong community ties. He is not a flight risk and, therefore,

I request that he be released on his own recognizance to await trial." Emanuel did not waste too much energy on an argument that he knew would be denied.

"Your request is denied," the commissioner said. "The defendant will be held without bond and the preliminary hearing will be set within 20 days."

That was all there was to it. The police officer came back over to take Satya back into custody.

"I hope to hear from you soon," Satya said as he was led away.

"Good luck," Emanuel responded instinctively. He was not sure if Satya heard him as the door to the bullpen was snapped shut abruptly behind him.

6

After returning to his office under police escort, Emanuel took a nap on the couch. The combination of his long drunken night with Faye, and the highly emotional day dealing with Satya had taken its toll. He told Paula, his secretary, to hold all calls, loosened his tie, kicked off his shoes, and passed out.

Emanuel woke up two hours later without having moved, without dreaming a thing, and feeling like a crash test dummy after a full day's work. Emanuel rubbed his eyes and ran his fingers through his hair. He just lay on his couch looking up at the ceiling and contemplated what Satya had told him that morning.

Could there be any truth to that story? His first instinct was that Satya was crazy. He had heard that kind of story plenty of times before in his career. Just blame it on God and you'll be forgiven. It was always bullshit.

This time, however, Emanuel had a different feeling. He could not get the videotape out of his mind. The look in the eyes of both Satya and Winston had an eerie quality about it. Emanuel could not say what that quality was, but it made him give some credence to Satya's otherwise doubtful story.

Then, of course, there was Satya himself. A New York City cop with an unblemished record and no history of mental illness, comes down to Washington and calmly unloads his gun into a presidential candidate and nationally recognized religious leader. It made no sense. Emanuel understood crime and the criminal mind. There was always some fact in a case that made everything clear. Either the motivation of the defendant or the actions of the victim always explained the incident. The patterns were similar in violent crime— but not in this one. Emanuel was left only with Satya's explanation, and he was not happy about it.

Finally, and perhaps most disturbing, was the way Satya described his actions. He wasn't ranting like a schizophrenic, or shaking his fist foretelling of the end of the world. He didn't glance around the room furtively or stroke his head relentlessly as he told his tale. Rather, Satya calmly and convincingly explained what happened to Emanuel, as if he was describing a trip to the grocery store or an outing with his family. Satya was sure of himself and what he had done that it was disconcerting. He was either a sociopath or a prophet, Emanuel mused.

Emanuel walked outside to the balcony of his office to get some much-needed fresh air. The sun was starting to lose some of its brightness in the waning afternoon, and a brisk wind was swirling. He directed his gaze across 15th Street toward the White House. People had already gathered in Lafayette Square to protest and burn candles. Emanuel wondered why they were holding a vigil outside the White House, and then he heard someone speaking through a megaphone.

"Impeach Taylor for killing an angel of the Lord!" the man was yelling.

Emanuel actually smiled to himself for the first time in what seemed like days. People were actually blaming President Taylor for Winston's death, as if he had gone to New York and hired Satya to kill off his political rival. It was a ludicrous proposition, but then again, Taylor did have the most to gain by Winston's death. Emanuel imagined Taylor was probably celebrating inside the White House with a bottle of champagne and a Cohiba. With Winston out of the picture,

Taylor's reelection hopes took a dramatic turn in a positive direction and, barring a major slip-up, almost guaranteed four more years.

Stephen Taylor was a moderate Republican who had parlayed his military heroics in Vietnam into a successful political career. Taylor served as a Navy SEAL and was captured behind enemy lines on an assassination mission in 1968. After two years as a POW, Taylor returned home and immediately entered politics, first serving in the Navy's government liaison office, and then running for the House of Representatives in Florida. He later ran for the Senate and gained prominence in Washington during the Reagan era. During the Clinton administration, Taylor became the leading Republican opponent to Clinton's policies, and decided to run for President. Taylor's formula for victory was taking the traditional Republican policies of small government and lower taxes even farther towards the libertarian stance that the government should stay out of people's lives as much as possible.

In so doing, however, he had to take moderate views on social and moral issues. He advocated an increase in educational spending, especially in the inner cities, and tolerated the right to choose an abortion in certain defined circumstances and across the board in the first trimester. Most importantly, perhaps, Taylor tried to distance himself from religious influences. He hid from the prayer in school issue, and when cornered simply referred to the Constitution, which he said spoke for itself. Taylor was careful with the family values rhetoric as well, since he acknowledged that the face of the American family had changed over the last twenty years. The days of mom and dad and the picket fence had given way to dad alone or mom and mom with the picket fence and, even as a Republican, Taylor accepted this.

Taylor's libertarian stance was severely challenged when he began waging the war on terrorism. First of all, he was very careful not to make it a war against Islam because he didn't want to bring religion into the equation. He also had to protect civil liberties at home because he didn't believe the government should impose itself in people's personal lives. Therefore, racial profiling and stepped up law enforcement efforts were slow in coming. He was aggressive in the foreign arena by pursuing terrorists, but he was still having trouble on the home front. The terrorists had eschewed large scale attacks and weapons of mass destruction for small scale operations blowing up buses and nightclubs, Palestinian style, and he was slow in clamping down.

Now Taylor was having trouble with Winston as a result of Winston's focus on the issues of morality, personal behavior, accountability, and the government's role in pointing the people in the right direction. Winston was not afraid to call the war on terrorism a religious war in which the enemy was clear. Not all Muslims were terrorists but all terrorists were Muslim, Winston argued, so he advocated cracking down on Muslims both at home and abroad in the name of protecting Christian America. Winston successfully turned Taylor's libertarian stance against him and was gaining momentum up until his death.

Standing on his balcony, Emanuel smiled at the little twists and ironies of politics in Washington. Power ebbed and flowed in Washington often for no apparent reason. Sometimes candidates lost elections because people didn't like their personalities, and other times people just changed their mind on certain issues or put their priorities in a different place. The Democrats and Republicans had been tossing the same issues back and forth for years, trying to distinguish themselves from one another. Domestically, health care, education, Social Security, tax cuts, the deficit, and regulating the Internet, were the hot button issues for both parties. And both parties had become so centrist they were afraid of extreme views, like overturning *Roe v. Wade*. Then, as if out of nowhere, Winston appeared and surprised them all. Apparently, there were a whole lot of people in America who did care about morality and religion and figured that schools and care for older Americans would improve if we were a more righteous nation -- if we treated our neighbors how we would like to be treated. The two major parties were completely unprepared.

Thinking about Winston's role in American politics made the smile fade from Emanuel's face as he realized he was now involved in that same drama. No matter on what grounds he defended Satya, God or no God, the issue was larger than just murder. "Last night I'm drinking martinis, eating oysters, and making love to a beautiful woman, and now I'm defending a crazy killer," Emanuel said to himself. "How the hell did I get into this mess?"

The next morning, Emanuel arrived at the office at 8 a.m. ready to make some preliminary investigations into his new client. He felt refreshed from a good night's sleep and a day without alcohol. When he really had to be sharp Emanuel eschewed the delights of the Old Ebbitt and one of Doc's martinis for some Chinese food and a movie in the solitude of his apartment. The MSG put him to bed early.

Emanuel's plan for the day was to make some calls up to New York and find out a little more about Satya, and set up some appointments for his trip up. Who was this man? What kind of police officer was he? What kind of husband and father was he? The issue was really character since Emanuel would either have to show him as a loose cannon who was heading for a mental breakdown, or the most righteous man alive who was destined to talk to God. Emanuel hoped he would find the former to be true.

He also needed to find out more about Winston. Emanuel followed politics as much as anyone who lived in Washington did. It was impossible not to if you wanted to talk to people at a cocktail party. He had started reading about Winston and watching him on the Sunday morning talk shows. At first, like most people inside the Beltway, Emanuel did not take Winston's presidential bid seriously. There was no way a religious zealot was going to challenge for the White House. If Ross Perot and Ralph Nader could barely capture a few percentage points of the national electorate, how could a televangelist do it? However, when Winston began making a serious impact, Emanuel began to take notice.

Winston's past and his present motivation still remained a mystery to him. Several points struck Emanuel as he thought about Winston and his new client's intense desire to kill him. If Satya was insane, as Emanuel suspected, something about Winston had to have triggered Satya's violent response. Satya could have picked any high-profile person for an irrational murder, but why Winston? Even John Hinkley had a reason for shooting Ronald Reagan – the desire to impress his unrequited love, Jody Foster. Apparently, Satya was trying to impress God by killing Winston. But, if Winston was as religious as he claimed to be, then it was completely irrational for God to order his assassination. This was a point in favor of an insanity plea, requiring Emanuel to show how righteous Winston was if it came down to it. Only an insane person would kill one of God's most vigorous workers, and then claim that God ordered the hit. It was a good start, Emanuel thought.

However, what if Winston turned out to be a fraud? Perhaps Winston was just a con man taking money from little old ladies in God's name, and running for President was just a way to take his sting operation to the highest level possible. With both God and the American people on his side, Winston would make a killing. Now, *there* was a man that God would want to be stopped. That would certainly help the "God told me to do it," defense. Emanuel shook his head and ran his fingers through his hair in disbelief that he was even contemplating that line of reasoning.

After making a list of people to call, Emanuel summoned Paula into his office. Paula was in her early fifties and diminutive with nondescript short hair dyed a deep red. She was British but had moved to America thirty years earlier as an au pair and never left. She had a sarcastic sense of humor and loved to tease Emanuel for anything she could think of. Paula constantly complained about her job, but, in reality, she loved it and was excellent at it. She was the only help Emanuel needed since she could do legal research, track people down like a private investigator, and do any administrative work in a flash. Paula also knew the procedure of D.C. Superior Court inside and out, and often helped Emanuel with the little details of law practice that he despised. She had been with him ever since he had started his own practice and was Emanuel's confidante and friend.

"You're certainly looking a bit more chipper this morning, Emanuel. You looked like hell yesterday afternoon," Paula said, staring Emanuel down over her glasses and a steaming cup of coffee.

"Thanks, Paula, you always know just the right thing to say."

"So, how are we going to defend this lunatic? My God, killing someone on the bloody nightly news."

"Luckily, we have a great defense: God told him to do it."

"Fantastic. God told me not to come to work today and I should've listened. An insanity case— we haven't had one of those in a while."

"I don't think it's that simple. He's a New York City cop, after all. And, he was so convincing."

"Oh, dear God. I think you're losing your mind," Paula said, exasperated.

"I told you it was complicated. Anyway, what's the docket looking like? I might need to go to New York for a few weeks and when this thing heats up I'm not sure how much time I'll have for anything else. I'm assuming they're going to fast track it."

"Not too bad. We have several new potential cases that I suppose we can turn down and the only other biggie is the Henderson trial in May. There's some other small matters, but we can manage."

"Great. I'm gonna start investigating this thing, so I'll trust you to handle the rest. I don't want any calls today."

"Very good."

After Paula left, Emanuel picked up the phone and started calling.

About four o'clock that afternoon Emanuel was exhausted and decided to head down to the Old Ebbitt. Much to his chagrin, after all his calls and some research into press Satya had received over the years and some of his arrests records that were available online,

Emanuel concluded that Satya was far from a powder keg who was heading toward some antisocial behavior. The insanity defense, at least from this initial inquiry seemed a long shot. Unless he could find a psychiatrist to evaluate Satya and certify that temporary insanity was possible, simply testifying that God told him to kill Winston would not meet the elements of the insanity test.

As far as Winston went, Emanuel didn't turn up anything interesting. All the news reports basically described him as a straight shooter. Being a televangelist with a rich collection plate didn't make you an evil person, and there were no reports of any marital infidelity or true fraud. He was no different that any multi millionaire with presidential aspirations, except for his right wing religious leanings. Again, by no means unusual in the political arena.

Emanuel was now back to square one and felt like contemplating his options down at the Old Ebbitt over a martini instead of brooding in his office. On his way down 15th Street, Emanuel bought a pack of Camel Lights from a hot dog vendor, and presto, he was back where he loved to be.

The Old Ebbitt was relatively quiet at four o'clock since the happy hour crowd had at least an hour of work left. Only the tourists and the hard-core drinkers were at the bar. Doc was not expecting Emanuel this early, so the martini was nowhere near ready when he slumped over the bar. Doc started making it in a hurry after sensing that one of his best customers was not in the best of moods.

"I saw you on the telly today, counselor. You're a mighty handsome man," Doc said, trying to lighten Emanuel's mood.

"Thanks Doc, but I don't think you have to flatter me anymore. As long as my martini is cold I'll tip you."

"No, I mean it. You looked great. This case is really gonna make you, Emanuel. I knew it was just a matter of time before you landed a big one. You'll have your own TV show at the end of this."

"What if I lose the case and Grady gets executed? I'll be like the plague, nobody would want to come near me, and I'm telling you Doc, this case is a loser if I've ever seen one."

"That attitude's not like you. You always find some angle to work with. Why're you so down on this one?"

"I just don't like it. It's not straightforward and it's making me nervous. There's no doubt my client did it; the question is why? And, the answer stinks."

"They always do, pal. You still looked good on the telly."

"Thanks Doc. Why don't you make me another?"

"Sure." Doc walked away, realizing Emanuel wanted to be alone.

Emanuel thought back over the conversations he had had that day. First, there was Satya's captain on the force, Joe Doolan. The man had practically burst into tears when Emanuel identified himself as Satya's lawyer. Doolan stated unequivocally that Satya was the best police officer he had ever worked with in his tenure at the New York City Police Department.

"You know the old motto of 'to protect and serve?'" Doolan had said. "Grady was probably the only officer who really tried to live up to those words."

Doolan described Satya as a cop who looked at his job as more public service that law enforcement. He was interested in making a better society one neighborhood at a time, and that meant looking after the potential criminals just as much as the potential victims. Satya never got pleasure out of making arrests, especially if was a teenager or people with families. He tried to look after the people who lived on his beat.

"If Satya heard of a kid heading for trouble," Doolan explained, "he'd pull that kid aside and tell him he was watching over him. Not in a threatening way, but in the sense that he would help the kid if he needed it, just as long as he didn't break the law. It was the best deterrence I've ever seen."

Doolan went on to say that walking with Satya through the neighborhoods he patrolled was like walking down the street with the Mayor. Everyone knew him, and he knew everyone by their first names. He would know little facts about people's lives like what jobs they had and how their kids were doing in school. The people viewed him as someone to turn to in a crisis, not a cop trying to beat them down.

"This attitude came from all races and backgrounds, too," Doolan had made very clear.

Satya was also a leader on the force, Doolan explained. Strangely, despite Satya's great record he had rejected promotions that would have taken him off the streets. He wanted to be with the people to help them and work with them. Despite his rank, all the officers and detectives in the department looked up to him. He was always discussing potential ways officers could be more effective, using communication skills instead of force in the bid to fight crime. People would gather around him to listen to him talk about keeping the peace in New York, a state of being that few had ever thought possible.

"Satya made them believe," Doolan proclaimed.

This did not sound like a man ready to blow holes in a presidential candidate, Emanuel thought, lighting up a Camel. All Sophie Mitchell would have to do is put Doolan on the stand and an insanity plea would immediately be stopped dead in its tracks.

Next, Emanuel had talked with Kim Grady, Satya's wife. Unlike Doolan, she could not contain her tears, and had cried for the first fifteen minutes of the conversation. The only words she could get out were "Thank you," as she sobbed over the phone.

Finally, she composed herself and started talking about Satya and the life they both shared. She said that Satya and their children were the most important things she had in her life, and the thought of losing Satya was almost too much for her to bear. She said that when she met Satya she fell in love with him immediately. There was never a doubt in her mind that she wanted to spend the rest of her life with him.

"He was so powerful," Kim reminisced. "I was at a party and he walked into the room and it was like sticking my finger in a light socket. He wasn't the best looking boy in the room, but there was something about his smile, and his face, and the way he walked that struck me. Satya walked through the whole room shaking everyone's hand and sharing a few words with everyone. It was effortless. Then he came right over to me as if I was his destination. He said he'd been thinking about me and wanted to know if I would take a walk with him sometime. I blurted out, 'how about now?' He took my arm and led me out of the party. I never wanted him to let go of me ever again."

Emanuel had asked Kim the painful question of explaining why she thought Satya would kill another human being, especially someone like Winston. She explained that Satya's whole life was spent caring for other people. Kim recounted how often people Satya had arrested appeared at the house to talk to him. Or, other officers would stop by to have a quiet conversation with him.

"People always turned to Satya in times of need and he was always there for them. For Satya to do something like this there must have been some positive reason for it," Kim had said. "I believe that in my heart."

A positive reason for killing Winston, Emanuel thought, sipping his martini. Why couldn't Satya have just rallied the vote against the man? Why did he need to take such drastic measures if he didn't like him? What good ever came from violence? Emanuel pondered. Even the act of killing a person deemed "bad" by society serves to uphold the viewpoint that taking another life is acceptable under certain circumstances. Always a dangerous message, Emanuel thought.

Emanuel took a break from his reflections and looked up at the television behind the bar. It was broadcasting a special report on the Winston assassination, chronicling Winston's life and making him out to be one of the greatest public figures the United States had ever known. Emanuel chuckled at the irony and lit another cigarette.

"Reverend Winston started his evangelical career in a beat-up Ford pick-up. He had a few boxes of bibles in the back of the truck that he would sell to supplement his income. Otherwise, he traveled from Southern town to Southern town, looking for a pulpit that needed a preacher."

"Winston had no formal religious training, but was a self-taught Bible scholar. His parents took him to Church every Sunday and were impressed at their son's interest in the Lord and the teachings of Jesus Christ. Soon, he was spending more and more time poring over any religious works he could get his hands on."

"When he graduated from high school, Winston decided to attend college at Liberty, a Christian college in Virginia. Strangely, he majored in history, leaving his religious study to his spare time. His classmates told me that Winston did not trust others to explain the teachings of God to him. He felt that a person had to uncover the mysteries of the spiritual self on his own, through study and prayer."

"Winston graduated at the top of his class, and then hit the road to spread the Word. He wanted to expose others to the form of religion that he had decided was the best: living one's life as dictated by the Bible."

"It was tough going for Winston at first. Winston's confidants told me that in the mid-eighties, when life in America was all about money and greed, people were not that interested in living a straight and narrow existence. He did find a certain following, however, and word traveled about the charismatic young preacher."

"In Montgomery, Alabama, in 1987, Winston met one follower who struck him powerfully: Judy Billows, a preacher's daughter. The two fell in love instantly, were married in her daddy's church, and then set off to continue Winston's mission."

Emanuel found himself moved by the pictures of the newly married Jack and Judy Winston. They looked the all-American couple right out of the movies. They were both beautiful and made a stunning pair. More than that, though, was the look on their faces that screamed that they were certain they were meant to be together, as if their meeting was preordained by a higher power. It was everyone's dream to find the chosen person, but how many people really do? Satya and Kim seemed to fit into that category, too, Emanuel thought.

"Winston's big break came in Houston, Texas, in 1987," the reporter continued. "Stuart Simpson, an oil billionaire, saw Winston preach and decided to make a large donation. It was never disclosed how much that donation was, but it was rumored to be well into the seven figures."

"Winston took that money and produced his own television show in order to more easily reach the masses. The move was hugely successful and soon Winston was a household name -- at least in the houses of evangelical Christians. Along with his popularity came enormous wealth as his army of followers showered Winston with donations for his new church, the Divine Light. When we come back from a short break, we'll look at Reverend Winston's jump from the pulpit to the campaign stump."

Just then Doc came over with another martini.

"It must be your lucky day because that beautiful blonde at the end of the bar just bought you this drink. Some bastards have all the luck."

Emanuel turned to look down the bar and sure enough a woman with perfectly styled and highlighted sandy blond hair was staring at him with a broad smile on her face – her teeth were almost too big for her face but they were perfect. Emanuel raised his glass in appreciation, but did not call her over. He was not in the mood for any companionship after his day. Unfortunately for Emanuel, the woman got up off her barstool and walked over to him uninvited. He watched her out of the corner of his eye, appreciating her tall stature and posture. The head mistress at her finishing school would be extremely proud, Emanuel thought.

"You looked so lonely over here, I thought you might want some company," the woman said on arrival. She was immaculately put together from her make-up, to her designer suit, to her expensive shoes. She had a confident air about her, and the broad smile seemed uncontainable.

"Actually, I'm not lonely, I'm just alone with my thoughts. There's a difference." Emanuel replied with a hint of annoyance in his voice that was slightly forced.

"I don't think there is a difference. It's always better to be with another person than to sit alone at a bar, drinking a martini, and examining your navel." The woman's tone was mimicking Emanuel's annoyance, yet she still maintained a pleasant demeanor. Plus, she had a valid point so Emanuel began to soften his stance.

"I'm sorry. I suppose I should be more grateful when someone offers me a drink. In my line of work, you never know where your next drink may come from sometimes."

"You're a lawyer, right?"

"I sure am. What gave me away?"

"Any stiff who'd rather be alone than have a drink with a beautiful woman must be a lawyer," she said.

"Touché," Emanuel answered raising his glass.

"Actually, I saw you on TV yesterday. You're representing that cop who killed Reverend Winston."

"I'm afraid that was me."

"That's pretty impressive. How'd you even get involved?"

"I knew Satya when I was a district attorney in Manhattan. I was the only lawyer he knew in town, so I got the call."

"Were you two friends?"

"No, we just crossed paths once, that's all." Emanuel took a sip of his drink and thought back to that pivotal day when the Cruz case came across his desk. He had no idea how big it would actually be in his life.

"What's his defense?" The question broke Emanuel away from his memories.

"Do you smoke?" he asked.

"Sometimes?"

"Would you like one? I just started smoking again and it feels wonderful."

Emanuel lit the woman's cigarette and one for himself. When she leaned over for the light her blouse fell forward and he got a nice eyeful of her cleavage. She was wearing a black lace bra that pushed her breasts up and together. Along with the eyeful, Emanuel got a large dose of her perfume, which was flowery but subtle. It smelled expensive.

The two smoked in silence for a minute and then Emanuel spoke.

"Do you believe in God?" he asked.

"Isn't that a little serious for happy hour conversation?"

"Just answer the question, please," Emanuel said a bit too harshly.

"Sorry, Mr. Lawyer. Of course I believe in God. I went to Catholic school when I was a kid. I had no choice. Actually though, despite the Catholic guilt, I genuinely do believe in God."

"Why?"

"Just think about all the things in life we can't explain. There just has to be a higher power."

"What can't you explain?"

"Lot's of things. Take babies for example."

"You don't know where babies come from?"

"Of course I know how to make a baby in practice, and I know the scientific explanation. But, look at it on a more esoteric level. You take one sperm and one egg, and the next thing you know you have another creature growing inside of you. Nine months later you squeeze out another human being with a brain and thoughts and feelings. There is so much to giving birth that is beyond my comprehension that I have to believe that God has to have a part in the process."

"I never thought about reproduction like that."

"Well, you should. I'll tell you something else I can't explain."

"What's that?"

"How you plan on defending a man who killed a presidential candidate on live television? You got an answer for that one?"

"Well, Ms. Michaels, I suppose you'll have to ask God after you find out about the babies."

Jude took a long drag off her cigarette, exhaled and then smiled.

"When did you make me?"

"Let's see, I spend more time with you in the mornings than any other woman. So, I guess, as soon as you got close enough for me to see your face clearly, I knew you were my favorite reporter."

"I'm sorry that you wake up next to CNN, but at least it's good to know someone's watching. So, do you have an answer for me?"

"Now, Ms. Michaels, you've been around long enough to know I can't reveal what was said in my interview with Officer Grady."

"Of course, but you can still give me something, can't you? I know the guy's a cop so it makes no sense. He must have told you something."

"You know, Ms. Michaels, I'm really disappointed."

"Why's that?"

"For a minute there, I thought that the most beautiful and insightful TV reporter I'd ever fantasized about was interested in me. Now I just feel like a news story, and I don't like that. Even worse than that, you've ruined the sanctity of my favorite watering hole. I guess I'll have to find a new joint."

Emanuel dropped some cash on the bar, stood up and left.

Emanuel now felt ill at ease. Finding out that Satya was an upstanding citizen and family man, and having Jude Michaels interrogate him, brought home the seriousness of the situation. He didn't want to return to his office or go home, so he just started walking. He walked down 15th Street in the direction of the Washington Monument. The bright white obelisk, the common symbol of virility dedicated to the father of American independence, was glowing in the night sky, and served as a beacon for Emanuel who had no idea where he was going.

Things were happening so fast around him, and he was starting to feel as if he had no control over the situation. There seemed to be an invisible force pulling him into this case. It was the same feeling he had the morning before when he first read the news about the killing. He had experienced the same feeling again when he walked into his office and saw the red light blinking on his phone. Emanuel had dreamed of a high-profile case like this where all the odds were stacked against his client, but now that he had it, he was scared. It was one thing to defend an eighteen-year-old for drug charges when no one really cared about the result, but a political assassination was something totally different.

Emanuel walked past Pennsylvania Avenue with the White House on his right-hand side, and the sweeping avenue leading up the Capitol on his left. It was a dramatic part of D.C. where you could see all the images of power from one vantage point. Those two buildings and the people working inside them, sitting one mile apart, controlled the fate of the greatest country in the world. Satya's actions had potentially changed this fate in an instant.

Emanuel turned right on Constitution Avenue, another sweeping Parisian-style boulevard, and then headed for the part of the National Mall where the monuments lay. Since it was dark, there was an eerie feeling to this wooded area that guarded the monuments to America's greatness like an enchanted forest. Emanuel walked along the reflecting pool in front of the Lincoln Memorial and watched the image of the marble monument shimmering in the water.

There were definite parallels between Lincoln's assassination and Winston's, Emanuel thought. Lincoln freed the slaves and went to war with his own country to support that move— one of the boldest in American history. He was killed for his actions, although by that point it was too late to stop the societal change he had started.

Winston, while not yet a president, was also talking about a radical social change in America. He wanted to impose Christian values on the entire country and, in so doing, force his brand of morality on the nation. Instead of ending the racial divide like Lincoln,

Winston was seeking to end the moral divide in the country. By killing Winston, Satya stopped this movement before it really began, unlike Lincoln's death. Emanuel wondered if this was a good thing or a bad one. If Winston had become president and succeeded in his plan to make America a Christian country united in one sense of morality, would that have made the country better?

Definitely not, Emanuel surmised. America's greatness came from a sense of individual freedom of thought and action. Lincoln freed the slaves so that blacks could live the lives they wanted to, not so they could be shackled to a new order imposed by the government in place of the plantation owners. America is the most heterogeneous society in the world, and to try and unify it under one belief system could not be good, Emanuel thought. In fact, the freedom to be immoral, as long as it didn't affect someone else's freedom, was what America was all about.

Emanuel veered off from the Lincoln and strolled down by the Vietnam Memorial. This memorial was unique on the Mall in that it was a reminder of one of America's greatest military failures. Sure, it was meant to honor the men and women who sacrificed their lives for their country, but at the same time it left open the question of "why?" Why did those people die? It wasn't like fighting against the tyrannical regimes of the great wars, or the wars of American expansion in the nineteenth century. Vietnam was a political and diplomatic war. America needed to make a stand against the perceived Communist threat, so Vietnam was the proving ground and the dead soldiers were the players.

We trusted our leaders in Vietnam, Emanuel thought, as he walked along the marble wall chiseled with the names of the 57,000 dead. There were so many names, and all of them trusted their leaders. "That's what Americans do, and that's what makes us great," Emanuel uttered out loud. What would a man like Reverend Winston have wanted us to do? Emanuel wondered. Winston was filled with religious fervor and strong convictions based on the Bible. He advocated a war against Islam that could be World War III and send American soldiers all over the world. Would Americans give up their lives for such a religious crusade? Could we win?

Next, Emanuel meandered past the Lincoln Memorial again, and headed in the direction of the Memorial to President Franklin Roosevelt. This relatively new and sprawling memorial was across the tidal basin from the Jefferson Memorial. It was a stark contrast to the Jefferson, which like the Lincoln and the Washington, was a beautiful white marble structure that glowed in bright lights at night. These were happy and bright memorials that made a person's chest swell with pride.

The Roosevelt Memorial, however, depicted something different. Its walls showed the struggle of American workers during the Depression, standing in soup lines, gaunt and bitter. There was no fulfillment of the American dream at that time -- just wanting. Then there was the leader that pulled America out of that dark time, FDR. Emanuel went up to his image, which after a great debate showed him in his wheelchair, a disabled leader that had the strength to reinvigorate and inspire a nation.

It was amazing, Emanuel thought, since at that time, nobody even knew that Roosevelt was crippled by polio. The press never described him that way and there were no television cameras to hound him wherever he went. In the modern era, a president couldn't smoke a cigar in the White House without the press decrying the act as a kowtow to Big Tobacco.

Roosevelt's physical limitations were irrelevant, since his strength of character and creative vision led America out of an economic abyss and through the most violent war in the history of the planet. His leadership was so strong that Congress amended the Constitution to impose term limits on the president so that he could only serve two four-year terms. So, despite Roosevelt's accomplishments, the American people feared that one man could become too powerful if allowed to sit in office too long— even if constantly reelected. This decision hurt America at times, when a third term might have been beneficial for Ronald Reagan or Bill Clinton, but it seemed to be a trade-off people were willing to make.

"Could a President become too powerful?" Emanuel wondered. Could the Constitution, with all its checks and balances, and the American people, allow a president to assume the role of dictator or despot? Perhaps if a president was aligned with God it could happen, Emanuel concluded. Like the kings of old who claimed they were descendants of God, maybe an American president who claimed he had the ear of the Almighty, could claim that kind of power. It was a strange thought, but it made sense to Emanuel. A man like Winston could be very dangerous in a democracy that always fought to separate the Church and the State. Maybe Satya Grady, whether God talked to him or not, just decided that Winston was a threat to the American way of life, and that he needed to be stopped.

It was logical to Emanuel who didn't believe in God, anyway. Perhaps Satya, who had devoted his life to public service, was willing to make the ultimate sacrifice for the public good. Maybe Satya was the martyr in this case and not Winston, the purported man of God. As a criminal defense attorney, Emanuel knew that the truth was a relative term. Often rape victims were turned into women with loose morals who "had it coming," and sometimes cops who used the term "nigger," were instant racists framing an apparently guilty man. And, maybe sometimes a good deed is doing the world a favor by killing a man unfit to be President of the United States.

Emanuel turned away from the statue of Roosevelt and started walking back home. The assassination of Reverend Winston was a major event in American history, and Emanuel was going to play his role in it. While he still didn't believe Satya's story, he appreciated the historical importance of the case. This was indeed the kind of case Emanuel had envisioned fighting when he dreamt of becoming a lawyer. The fact that Satya's life was at stake was obvious, but the fact that the country would have a strong reaction to these events finally hit him with full force.

PART II

*"FOR IT IS A REBELLIOUS PEOPLE, FAITHLESS
CHILDREN, CHILDREN WHO REFUSED TO HEED
THE INSTRUCTIONS OF THE LORD; WHO SAID TO
THE SEERS, 'DO NOT SEE,' TO THE PROPHETS,
'DO NOT PROPHESY TRUTH TO US; SPEAK TO
US FALSEHOODS, PROPHESY DELUSIONS, LEAVE
THE WAY! GET OFF THE PATH! LET US HEAR
NO MORE ABOUT THE HOLY ONE OF ISRAEL!'"*

ISAIAH 30:9-11.

7

When Emanuel emerged from Penn Station onto 34th Street, the noise hit him like a violent attack. With a garment bag slung over his right shoulder and a duffle in his left hand, the ordinance came in the form of honking horns, carbon monoxide fumes, blaring music and voices. The most overwhelming force was the sheer number of people milling about on the streets. The volume of humanity made Emanuel feel like a solitary soldier in a war against a vast army that he couldn't possibly win. Nevertheless, Emanuel grabbed his bags tightly, steadied himself and started walking.

Emanuel had booked a room at the Sheraton mid-town, which was only a short walk from Penn Station. The hotel was three blocks east of Hell's Kitchen, the site of Satya's alleged encounter with God. It was also only ten blocks from Central Park, which was Emanuel's favorite part of New York. Often during his DA days, Emanuel would jog or simply meander through the park when he had a case on his mind. The teaming humanity playing together was very soothing for him. While people roller-bladed, shot baskets, or just sun-tanned in Sheep's Meadow, all the turmoil that was Manhattan dissipated.

Every block he passed on his walk had a little grocery store and coffee shop, and, of course, every corner had its bar. Just like Central Park, New York could not survive without its booze. The people needed a sedative or else they'd all start killing each other. Emanuel always laughed at people who claimed that alcohol caused much of the crime in the city. He believed there would be much more without it, and he wouldn't want to be witness to that little experiment.

He reached his hotel, a modern glass skyscraper with thousands of lights framing its entrance. He checked in and settled into his room on the 43rd floor. He was happy to be off the streets, high above everything where it was quiet. Emanuel scanned down 8th Avenue as he unpacked. He hung up his clothes in the closet and then inspected the mini bar. He found a bottle of Chivas, poured it over ice, and lit a cigarette.

Later that evening, Emanuel gave into his egotistical impulses and turned on the television. He couldn't resist turning to CNN to see what was happening with the case. President Taylor was about to give the world his views on the assassination. Emanuel poured himself another drink and lay down on his bed to watch.

"Good evening ladies and gentleman, this is Ron Fitzhugh in Washington. In just a few minutes, President Taylor will address the nation from the Oval Office concerning the assassination of Reverend Jackson Winston. Our sources inside the White House informed us that President Taylor was deeply disturbed by Reverend Winston's untimely death, despite the fact that they were engaged in a heated battle for the presidency. President Taylor is also obviously aware that millions of Americans were loyal followers of Winston, and are grieving his death. Furthermore, the President wants to condemn this type of lawless behavior. Here is the President now.

President Taylor was sitting behind his imposing oak desk staring directly into the camera. He had the furrowed brow look of concern on his face that all president's affect when addressing the nation in times of crisis. His dark eyebrows contrasted with his thinning hair that had turned completely white during his prisoner of war years in Vietnam. Taylor's face still revealed some of the suffering with his eyes droopy and uneven wrinkles visible despite the make-up he was wearing. He sat in front of the camera with his shoulders straight and broad, as always, and perfectly framed in a navy-blue suit.

"Good evening, my fellow Americans. This is truly a sad time in American history. Reverend Jackson Winston was a real American and a man of God. He was a man of great convictions and beliefs, and he wanted to bring those values to this office."

"While I am seeking reelection to the presidency, I looked forward to engaging Reverend Winston in the political process that has served our country for well over two hundred years. I was looking forward to allowing the American people to decide at the voting booth who was to lead our great country for the next four years."

Emanuel scoffed at Taylor's claim, knowing full well that no politician would choose a long and bitter fight over an easy and decisive victory on Election Day.

"It saddens me beyond words that the violent act of one person who refused to allow our political process to proceed has ended the life of a man who, while I might have opposed politically, I nevertheless greatly admired," Taylor continued.

Emanuel took a long sip of his drink. That "one person" was his client. The significance of the words sought him out in his New York City hotel room and smacked him across the face. He became keenly aware that the full weight of the United States government would be against him. Emanuel could sense from Taylor's words that he was happy to have an easy scapegoat to target for the removal of his political adversary.

"Today, I grieve with all Americans for the death of a great asset to our country. Reverend Winston's words have touched the lives of millions, and brought hope to those who needed to get closer to their God. He devoted his life to God and to spreading his word. He was hoping to serve his country as best as he knew how, and I respected that."

"I am further saddened that there are still those in our country who would rather turn to violence to settle differences, rather than to engage in a healthy debate. I had envisioned a twenty-first century in which we would not have to suffer through tragedies that have befallen great Americans in the past— Presidents Lincoln and Kennedy, and the Reverend Martin Luther King to remember a few."

"It is my hope that we can learn from this tragedy, and realize that violence should never be the way we settle our national differences. We are all Americans despite our political party, despite our religious affiliations, despite our different races and cultural backgrounds. We are all Americans and, ultimately, we are all in this together. By 'this', I mean the long struggle to uphold the values that have made this country the greatest nation on earth, and our society the freest the world has ever known. This is the society I personally fought for in Vietnam along with so many other Americans. It is incumbent upon all of us to remember that we must all do our part to ensure that America's greatness and prosperity will continue on for our children and generations to come."

"Finally, I would like to assure you that our judicial system will work swiftly and fairly to resolve this terrible act. I am sure many of you would like retribution for Reverend Winston. Keep in mind, however, that part of our great heritage is to give everyone a fair trial, and the right to defend themselves in a court of law. Reverend Winston believed in those ideals, and it would only tarnish his legacy if we would seek less for the man charged with his murder. I can assure you all that justice will be served."

"Tonight, I will pray for Reverend Winston's family and remember him as a great American, and I ask all of you to do the same. May God Bless the United States of America. Good night."

"That was President Taylor from the Oval Office addressing the nation concerning the assassination of Reverend Jackson Winston," Fitzhugh resumed his report.

"The President expressed his sorrow for Winston and asked all Americans to pray for his family. He further assured the nation that justice would be meted out in a fair and swift manner. All in all, I must say, a very moving speech by the President."

"We're now going to go to Jude Michaels outside of the White House for more on the President's speech. Jude."

Jude was standing in the White House Rose Garden along with the rest of the press corps. Her neatly fixed hair was barely blowing in the evening breeze, and her blue eyes were sparkling from the excitement.

"Thanks Ron. It was a moving speech indeed. There is no doubt that the President was disturbed by Reverend Winston's death, as any political leader would be. However, President Taylor is also going to use this tragedy for his own political gain. It is uncertain at this point if the Freedom Party will continue to seek the presidency in the wake of Winston's death. If it decides to do so, it is unlikely that it will produce a candidate at this point who possesses the mass appeal or following of Reverend Winston. If the Party decides not to seek the presidency, then it is likely that most would-be Freedom voters will return to the Republican Party and President Taylor. So, Ron, from a political standpoint, the President has gained tremendously from Winston's assassination. I believe, and sources confirm, that the President used the speech tonight to rally the country around him in what is clearly becoming a national crisis."

"Jude, are you saying that the President is using Winston's death as a political tool?" Fitzhugh asked.

"Ron, it's no secret in Washington that President Taylor was not very fond of Reverend Winston or his religious ties. The President is a staunch believer in a literal reading of the Constitution and he is on the record as saying that if Winston was elected, the separation of the Church and State would be in jeopardy."

As he watched, Emanuel thought back to meeting Jude at the Old Ebbitt. His first thought was that she was much better looking in person, and then he found it amusing that he was watching her report on the case. He liked what she was saying. Jude was showing the same aggressiveness she showed by stalking Emanuel at his favorite bar. This was inside Washington politics and she was reporting the facts.

Of course, Taylor hated Winston. He hated him for acting holier and more honorable than Taylor, who had risked his life for his country.

"Jude, do you therefore believe that the President was disingenuous in his remarks about Winston?"

Almost on cue, Jude picked up Emanuel's thoughts.

"Ron, the President is on the record as disliking the way Winston claimed the moral high ground on social issues. The President always used his own morality and belief system as the backbone of his political career, and resented the way Winston punted morality around like a political football. Therefore, while I think calling the President's speech tonight disingenuous might be a tad strong, I will say that the President is saying he believes Winston was a 'great American' might have been more for the voters than straight from his heart."

"Thanks, Jude, for that report."

While Emanuel was gulping down his drink in his hotel room, back inside the White House, President Taylor was sipping a Johnnie Walker Black and meeting with his Chief of Staff Paul Tobias alone in the president's private study, upstairs in the White House residence. It had been a long day and Taylor had been dreading his speech about Winston. He was glad it was over.

"What'd you think Paul?" Taylor asked, taking a sip of his drink.

"It was perfect, Mr. President."

"Was I sincere enough?"

"I think so. I mean, he was your opponent so you could only go so far, but I think it was believable." Tobias was a former Marine with direct combat experience in Vietnam, and he gained favor with Taylor by giving him straight answers even when they might hurt. "We'll have to wait for the polls tomorrow to know for sure, but I think you should improve your position."

"Between you and me, Paul, I'm not sorry the son of a bitch is dead. He may have fooled a lot of people, but that religious crap would have ruined the county."

"Are you saying you think you would have lost to Winston, Mr. President?"

"I'm saying it would have been close. He took a lot of Republicans over to his side, not to mention some Democrats. I'll tell you something else, I'm still not sure I'm going to win."

"How can you say that with Winston out of the picture?"

"His supporters think he's a fucking martyr, and they may stick with the Freedom party despite his death. I can't afford to take that chance." Taylor made this last statement in a tone that Tobias had heard many times before. It was a tone that demanded action.

"What do you suggest, Mr. President?" Tobias responded, stepping up to the challenge.

Taylor took a long drink before answering his Chief of Staff. "Paul, I always had a feeling deep inside that Winston was not as clean as he appeared to be. To put it another way, I think he was a big hypocrite with some major skeletons in his closet. I wasn't going to take that approach because I felt it was a no-win situation. Even if I had found something on him, it would have made me look spiteful and his followers would have rallied around him."

"But now that he's dead . . ."

"That's right. Now that he's dead I can expose him without looking mean and put a stop to the Freedom party before it really begins."

"I understand completely. I'll go through the usual channels and see what we can find."

"Excellent Paul. Pour yourself a drink. I hate drinking alone."

8

Emanuel woke up with a throbbing head and a dry mouth. It took him a minute to remember that he was in a hotel room in New York and not in his apartment in D.C. He rubbed his eyes and then started slowly massaging his temples in an attempt to clear his head. Emanuel had stayed up half the night watching television and drinking almost every bottle of liquor in the mini-bar. The pressure of the case had got under his skin after watching Taylor's speech and drinking seemed to be the only way to feel better.

Like an old man, Emanuel gingerly sat up in bed. He looked over at the circular glass table in the room and saw the empty bottles beside an ashtray full of cigarette butts. The image brought him back to his younger days as a Manhattan DA when the coffee table in his East Village apartment always looked like that. The thought made him smile and, by chance, gave him a plan for the day.

Emanuel got out of bed and walked to the window. He was completely naked and gave himself a small thrill by pulling open the curtains of his room and exposing himself to mid-town Manhattan. He looked out onto the surging city and felt a rush of energy. "There is no fucking place like this," Emanuel said to himself, pressing his nose against the window. He yearned to hear the inaudible, stifled New York street noises through the triple-panned glass. Inspired, Emanuel jumped in the shower and got ready for the day.

Emanuel needed to investigate Satya to figure out who he really was, because he was still uncertain. Part of him still hoped that Satya was, at minimum, temporarily insane when he killed Winston— or otherwise completely crazy. However, in order to keep his promise to his client, he intended to give him the benefit of the doubt and try to discover how righteous a man he really was.

In order to help with this investigation, Emanuel decided his first stop would be the DAs office and his old partner Turc Tophet. DAs did not really work with partners, but Emanuel and Turc started the same year, shared an office, and commiserated on many cases. They did try several cases together over the years, but the partner moniker in Emanuel's mind really came from the hundreds of nights they had out together.

Emanuel and Turc were drawn together from the first day of orientation at the DAs office. Emanuel spotted Turc sitting a few rows behind him in the small amphitheater where the District Attorney welcomed the new recruits. As Emanuel boarded the Nine train heading downtown, he thought back to that day. He was struck, first of all, by Turc's appearance. Turc looked like a model, with blond hair perfectly coifed; sharp, defined facial features; and florescent blue eyes. All of Turc's features were perfect from his thin, slightly sloped nose to his white teeth. To this day, Emanuel had never seen a more beautiful man.

Emanuel remembered back to when Turc first walked into the office that they were to share for the next three years. He was wearing a custom tailored, charcoal gray suit with a metallic blue tie. Turc had the kind of physique that fashion designers envisage when they create their clothes—tall, with broad shoulders and a slim waist.

When Turc greeted him, and shook Emanuel's hand it was an awkward moment. Turc was smiling, trying to be friendly, while Emanuel gazed at him in wonderment. Emanuel's idea of a district attorney was a straight-laced, do-gooder with a crew cut and a lean, hungry face, not a pretty boy. Turc seemed out of place at the DA's office and Emanuel was intrigued. He was delighted to have Turc as an officemate and looked forward to learning more about him.

What Emanuel quickly discovered was that despite Turc's pretty exterior, on the inside he was probably the "dirtiest" man in New York. Turc liked living on the edge and everything he did, including working as a DA, was designed to push boundaries. The idea of arguing to put criminals away in front of a judge, jury and gallery excited Turc so much he had decided to be a Manhattan DA from the first day of law school.

Turc was also concerned about appearances and wanted to be the very best at everything he did. He knew Manhattan had the best DAs office in the country, so he just had to work there. Emanuel remembered the first day they met, when Turc told him he planned to be the best DA New York had ever seen. Turc wanted the high-profile murder cases that would get his picture on the front page of the *New York Times*. The DAs office would be his ticket to celebrity.

The reason Turc wanted fame so badly, most of all because he loved to party. Turc loved to booze hard, and would do any drug put in front of him that did not require a needle. But, more than anything else, he liked sex. Emanuel came to see that for Turc the feeling of adoration that women bestowed on him before, during, and after sex was the most addictive drug— and one he could not live without.

Luckily for Turc, he was incredibly proficient at sexual conquest, and so feeding his addiction was easy. Emanuel had seen handsome men initially attract women, only to turn them off when they opened their mouths, but Turc had both looks and charm, and he used them masterfully. The ultimate in satisfaction for Turc was to go out to a bar with some friends for some heavy drinking and then, during the course of the night, have a beautiful woman approach him. He would seduce her or manipulate her into his way of thinking and, ultimately, they would end up in bed together.

Emanuel had shared and benefited from this scenario countless times before. More often than not, the woman who approached Turc had a friend who needed companionship, and Emanuel had no difficulty playing Turc's second. After only a few nights out together, Emanuel and Turc had their partnership down, and it was a formidable team.

Emanuel's flashbacks to his running days with Turc were interrupted by the subway train's arrival into the 14th Street station. He jumped out of the train and headed outside.

The day was unusually hot for springtime New York. The humidity caused Emanuel to sweat right through his light cotton dress shirt the minute he stepped out of the subway station. He ran his fingers through his hair and they emerged damp with sweat. Emanuel's hangover got suddenly worse and he put on his sunglasses to shield his eyes from the hazy sunlight.

Emanuel walked down to Hogan Place to the home of the Manhattan's DAs office. He could not help feeling nostalgic as he opened the front door and stepped into the mayhem that is the criminal justice system in New York City.

Like Turc, Emanuel had also dreamed about being a Manhattan DA from the time he thought about practicing law. Unlike Turc, Emanuel did not want it for the fame, but rather he thought of it as the toughest proving ground for any future criminal lawyer. Emanuel always knew he wanted to work on the defense side of the battle, but he figured he should first figure out how the other side worked. It is far easier to conquer an opponent when you know how they think and operate.

The lawyers in the Manhattan DAs office were the brightest in the country. All of them had the qualifications to land big law firm jobs that paid the top salaries, but they were people of a different breed. As Emanuel came to find out in his years working as a DA, every prosecutor had a different reason for choosing the low-paying public service lifestyle over the riches that Wall Street law firms offered. Some were hardcore and actually loved the idea of putting people behind bars, some believed in public service, and others, like Turc, sought glory. There was a common thread, however, among them— they all loved the drama. All of them craved that feeling in the pit of their stomach right before they stepped in front of a judge to prosecute a case. It was a few moments of pain and then the rush of adrenaline as instinct took over and a trial began. These moments did not exist for young associates at big law firms, who typically sat in conference rooms all day churning through documents, but at the DAs office they were thrust upon you daily.

It was an exciting time in Emanuel's life and he felt a similar excitement as he walked into the office again. He passed through the metal detectors and joined the throng of people hurrying through the foyer. He made his way to the elevator and headed up to the twentieth floor to where his office used to be.

The elevator opened up onto a busy office that only seemed quiet in contrast to the chaos in the lobby. Emanuel went over to the reception desk to make sure Turc was still on the floor. There was a young woman working the phones who had not been there in Emanuel's day.

"Is Turc Tophet's office still on this floor?" Emanuel asked politely. The woman was talking on the phone and ignored Emanuel completely. He had forgotten that in New York you have to demand something if you really want it.

"Excuse me Miss, but is Turc Tophet still on this floor?" Emanuel said in a loud, stern voice that startled the woman.

"Take it easy barrato, or we'll have to arrest you for disturbing the peace." It was Turc standing in an adjacent doorway with an amused look on his face. His arms were crossed and he had the same bravado as Emanuel remembered. He was still wearing a custom-made suit and a designer tie, and while his face showed signs of wear and tear, he was as good looking as ever.

"So, Johnny Law, still grinding it out on the beat?" Emanuel said, needling his friend.

"Of course. Somebody's got to put the bad guys away and stop slimy defense lawyers like you." Turc approached Emanuel and gave him a big hug, as was the tradition between the two men.

"It's good to see you, barrato. It's been too long. I was beginning to think you were afraid of the big, bad City," Turc said.

"Come on Turc, you don't need me around to get it done."

"I know, but it's still a lot more fun when you a have a good buddy to party with. The women are always going to be there at the end of the night." Turc had the devilish grin on his face that always appeared when he talked about late nights and women.

Emanuel followed Turc back to his office, which was considerably bigger than the one the two had shared years before. Turc's office was in immaculate order without so much as a paper clip lying around haphazardly. Files were neatly arranged, pens and pencils packed into a coffee mug, and stacks of paper perfectly aligned.

"I'll order us some coffee, since I know my boy loves his java."

"Thanks, Turc."

A few minutes later, a pretty young woman entered the room with two steaming cups of coffee. She placed them on the desk and gave Turc a quick smile that told Emanuel she'd fallen victim to Turc's charm in the past. He didn't even need to ask.

"So, you finally pulled in the big one. I can't believe you did it first," Turc said, taking a sip of coffee.

"I guess you could say that. It doesn't seem like the big one though. To me, it seems like a big loser."

"They're all losers on your side of the table my friend. The question is can you do a good enough job so that the whole world thinks you're a great lawyer."

"That's why I'm here. I need to investigate Grady to have any chance."

"How is he?" Turc asked.

"You know him?"

"Of course. Everybody knows him. He's the cleanest cop on the beat. I've never heard anyone say he was takin', or usin', or runnin' roughshod over guys on the street. Everybody on the force loves him and he was certainly a model witness to have on the stand." Turc paused and smiled, "So, what made him do it?"

It was precisely this type of story that Turc really enjoyed— human failure. Emanuel never quite understood why it was so important to Turc that other people showed weakness. He was like the characters in the movie *The Highlander,* who gathered strength every time they decapitated a rival. Emanuel had never liked that aspect in Turc, and thought it showed weakness in him.

"What the hell happened?"

"You'll never believe it."

"Try me. I've heard it all."

Emanuel paused, uncomfortable that he had to repeat Satya's story.

"He told me God came to him and told him Winston was an evil man who had to be stopped."

"Holy shit," Turc said, sitting back in his chair. "He's claiming the God defense? I never pegged Satya as the postal type. He always seemed so calm and together. I guess something must've set him off and he went nuts."

"That's the thing Turc, I'm not so sure about that."

"What?"

Emanuel shifted nervously in his chair. Turc sensed Emanuel's discomfort and opened his desk drawer and pulled out a pack of cigarettes.

"Here you go buddy, it looks like you could use one."

"Thanks," Emanuel said as Turc lit the cigarette with a silver Zipp-O. "You know I quit, and this case has me smoking again."

"Sure," Turc said, again with a smirk.

Emanuel inhaled deeply and blew the smoke out of his nose before answering. "Here's the thing, Turc. I'm pretty sure Satya's crazy and pleading him insane is his only chance. But . . ."

"But what?"

"But, something about it still bothers me. It just seems odd that this great cop would snap one day, then come all the way down to D.C. to shoot a presidential candidate in cold blood."

"All of a sudden, assassinations are unheard of?"

"No. But what if Satya isn't crazy and is the dutiful cop everyone says he is, and what if Winston isn't the righteous man of God he appears to be?"

Turc smiled at Emanuel and took a drag off his cigarette. It was a smile that slightly mocked Emanuel for his naivety. "So, you think that maybe he did talk to God?"

"Who knows what talking to God means? Maybe he had a dream or a vision. Or maybe the idea just popped into his head and it seemed like God put it there. All I'm saying is maybe Satya felt he was doing a public service by wasting this guy. Maybe Satya knew something the rest of us didn't and wanted to stop the guy from being President. I just want to check it out."

"It is a strange one. I'll give you that. But, we've both around a long time, Emanuel, and you know sometimes people just do bad things. Sometimes, there is no explanation for why people break the law. Half the criminals I deal with say they just didn't think they'd get caught."

"You feel like helping the investigation then?" Emanuel pleaded.

"Help the defense? Are you kidding me?"

"Come on, Turc. It'll be just like old times."

"Well, if you put it that way. You have to promise me one thing, though," Turc said pointing his cigarette at Emanuel.

"What's that?"

"We go out like old times before you go home."

"Deal," Emanuel said, knowing exactly what that meant.

"Great. Let's go talk to some cops."

The two friends took the back elevator, which led from the DA's offices down to the First Police Precinct. The offices were connected to allow easy consultations for the police officers and the DAs who worked so closely together.

The New York police station made the D.C. Superior Court building seem like a petting zoo. Hundreds of uniformed officers were swarming around, escorting handcuffed criminals or interrogating witnesses. There was an electricity in the air that came from a tense environment where so much was at stake.

Emanuel tried to envision Satya in this place. His client had such a calm demeanor it was hard to picture him with a wrinkled brow and sweaty temples striding around the room like the others were doing now. These cops looked haggard and overworked, trying to keep their fingers in a dyke that was destined to give way.

Turc led Emanuel through the main room where the intake was handled to a quieter back room where officers could do administrative work. They approached a desk where an Asian-American officer was filling out forms on his computer screen. He was small and looked fit. His black hair was slicked back neatly. When he stopped to take a sip of coffee, he noticed the two lawyers.

"Turc, what's going on?" the Officer said.

"Not much Derrick. I'd like to introduce you to Emanuel Adams, a former D.A. here, and Satya's attorney. Emanuel, this is Officer Derrick Chow."

"Of course. We met before with the Cruz case," Chow said, standing up to shake Emanuel's hand.

"So, you remember."

"Sure I do. I don't forget when my collars end up back on the street without ever seeing a judge."

"What?" Turc said.

"That's how I met Satya and Chow here. They were the arresting officers on a case that came across my desk— a drug bust. After talking to the PD, I decided it was better to let the case go."

"Interesting call, Emanuel. I guess we can talk about that one later," Turc remarked sardonically.

"Anyway, that's why Satya called me after his arrest."

"How is he?" Chow asked.

"He's okay, under the circumstances. I'm sure he's not enjoying the D.C. Jail, but otherwise I suppose he's fine."

"Everyone around here is thinking about him. Nobody could believe what happened. It was so unexpected."

"You saw no indication that Satya was agitated or acting strangely in the days leading up to the shooting?"

"Absolutely not. Satya was my partner. I saw him almost every day and nothing seemed unusual. He was a little shaky after a run-in he had with a burglar a few weeks ago, but that was it."

"What happened there?" Turc asked.

"He was shot tracking a B&E. It was no more than a flesh wound to his shoulder. I was off that night. Satya was riding alone so I'm not sure exactly what happened."

"I don't remember hearing about that," Turc said. "Where was it?"

Emanuel tugged at his collar. He suddenly felt warm and dizzy. He thought back to the story Satya had told him in the interrogation room of the 3rd District. Emanuel thought it was best not to mention it at the present time.

"Apparently, he was riding in Hell's Kitchen when he caught a flat. 9th Avenue, I think."

"A cruiser getting a flat tire?" Turc said incredulously. "You never hear of that."

"I know, but it does happen occasionally. Satya got out to check it out when he heard a noise down an alley. He went to investigate it and came across someone trying to break into one of the buildings off the alley. When Satya surprised him, the guy pulled a piece and shot him, hitting him in the shoulder, like I said."

"Did he shoot back? What happened to the perp?" Turc asked.

"No, he didn't. The shot knocked Satya down, and, the guy got away. Satya called for help and he was taken to the hospital. He was back to work the next day with just a few stitches and a little bit of shock."

"I'm sure he was rattled. After the incident did you notice Satya starting to act strangely?" Emanuel asked.

"Not really. He was a little quieter. He seemed a little more introspective than usual. But, we all have our down times in this job."

"Did he ever mention Reverend Winston to you during the time up to his going to Washington, or before for that matter?" Emanuel continued his examination.

"We don't talk politics around here much, so I don't think so. It never came up."

"Officer Chow, Satya's files don't report much violent activity in his arrest records. He never killed anyone in the line of duty, the records say. To be honest, I'm having a little trouble imaging how a police officer can go twenty-five years without killing anyone in the line of duty and then decide to assassinate a politician. You see what I'm getting at?"

"No, I don't, Mr. Adams. His file is his file."

"Come on, Derrick," Turc broke in. "You guys can bust as many heads as you want out there and we all know it, and most cops have. Did Grady ever have any incidents that weren't reported? We need to know."

Chow looked over both men and ran his fingers through his thick, black hair. He wasn't quite sure if these men were friends or the enemy. "Look, Satya was my partner and a friend. I want to see him get out of this. If he killed Winston, the mother fucker probably deserved it. I'm not sure I should be telling you stuff."

"I understand your concern Officer," Emanuel said, "but here's the situation. I need to find a defense to get Satya out from under this mess, and it's a big one. If I don't learn as much about him as possible, I won't be able to do that."

Chow thought it over briefly and then began to speak. "Okay. There was one incident where somebody got hurt. "

"Go on," Turc said, eager for another story of human weakness.

"A couple of years ago, we responded to a call up in Harlem. It was an old friend of ours, so to speak, a mid-level drug dealer named

Pete Hawkins. We got a tip that Pete was working on a deal to buy a fairly large amount of heroin. It was a step up for him, and Satya was hoping we could stop Pete's expansion which was certain to get him killed or arrested."

"So, we showed up at his apartment for a pow-wow. He was alone and looked anxious. He was just wearing shorts and a tank top and he was sweating. I thought he was high but I wasn't sure. We talked for a few minutes and told Pete what we knew. Satya tried to reason with him, and begged him not to make the buy. Pete didn't want to hear it and became increasingly agitated. Finally, he got up and walked over to a dresser. He reached into the top drawer and pulled out a weapon. He asked us to leave, that he'd heard enough."

"I was definitely for leaving, but Satya calmly approached Pete still talking to him. I don't remember what he was saying since I was scared, and things were happening fast for me. I'm not sure what happened next except that Satya and Pete started struggling for the gun. Then a shot rang out and Pete lay dead on the floor."

"Satya was stunned. It was definitely an accident, but he could have prevented it. He was trying to help Pete and the next thing he knew, he'd shot him. At this point, I started to think more clearly. I told Satya that it'd be better not to report the incident as it happened, but rather to say we found Pete dead. He agreed, and so it never went on his record."

"Well, Derrick, that's an interesting story," Turc said a bit exasperated. "First, Emanuel buries a case and then Satya shoots someone and doesn't report it. What the hell is going on here?"

"Come on Turc, don't play that game," Chow snapped back. "You know how this business works. Sometimes you just keep quiet. It's easier."

"Listen, we're here about Satya. Let's stay focused," Emanuel said, trying to remain calm despite the story. While the shooting might have been an accident, it was a black mark on Satya's seemingly squeaky-clean record. The man had killed before, which made the assassination less of an anomaly. There may have also been other stories Chow was unaware of that might show more violent tendencies. This was a major blow to the insanity defense.

"Thanks, Officer Chow. You've been very helpful. Let's go, Turc." Emanuel didn't want to learn anything more.

"Tell Satya I'm thinking of him and to hang in there," Chow said as Emanuel and Turc walked away.

"Maybe Satya isn't such a great cop after all," Turc said with a smirk.

"Thanks, buddy. You always know the right things to say."

Emanuel and Turc spent the next few hours talking to cops in the First Precinct to get their impressions of Satya. Fortunately, no one else had any surprise stories indicating Satya might possess violent tendencies. They all stayed true to Satya's image as the cleanest cop on the force, continually trying to help the community in any way he could. They stood up for him as a leader on the force, a highly skilled police officer, and a solid family man. The comments served to soften the blow of the Pete Hawkins story and left Emanuel feeling slightly better.

When Turc had to return to work, Emanuel went to the records room for the rest of the afternoon. Again, he found nothing but normal arrest reports showing no unusual use of force in Satya's career record.

Emanuel walked out of the First Precinct at ten o'clock that night. He was immediately struck by the heat and smell of the night, after spending all day in a climate controlled environment. The temperature had remained constant since mid-day, as had the humidity. He decided to walk for a while to clear his head after the long day. The mixed results of the day had brought Emanuel no closer to plotting a defense except to poke holes in a possible insanity plea. That left Satya's explanation, and Emanuel had certainly not discovered evidence of God in his conversations with the men and women of the New York City Police Department or the mountains of arrest records.

If Satya was not insane, then why the hell was he saying God told him to kill Winston? The entire concept didn't mean much to

Emanuel who was not a religious or spiritual man. He never prayed and asked God for anything, and he had certainly never felt that God had spoken to him. Perhaps Satya was speaking in metaphorical terms. He had told Emanuel his story of talking to God but it could mean so many different things. Satya was clearly just instilled with the notion that Winston must be killed, and he did it. This was still not really a defense unless Emanuel could get God on the stand or find a way to justify Satya's actions in another way for the jury and hope they nullify an otherwise open and shut case.

Emanuel walked slowly for about an hour mostly looking at his feet and mulling over his impossible case. Every few moments he would look up and see where he was and what was around him. Sometimes he would catch a glimpse of someone walking by him. It was never a full picture, a pair of eyes maybe, or the color of someone's hair, or maybe their mouth engaged in a conversation or frowning. It was just bits and pieces of humanity.

Back in his hotel room, Emanuel lay awake in bed. The events of the last few days had happened so quickly that he'd hardly had time to realize that he was working on "the big one." He had the case every lawyer dreamed of, and it was an incredible feeling. He felt powerful like the famous lawyers he had read about as a child: Clarence Darrow and Sam Leibowitz. Satya's life was in his hands and the whole world was watching. The difference was he had no idea how it would turn out. If the Scottsboro Boys had all been hanged maybe no one would have written a book about Leibowitz. Perhaps, if Emanuel failed to keep Satya from executioner's needle, he would just be a loser in a country that hated them— far from a superhero. Emanuel was scared and exhilarated at the same time, and struggled to sleep.

In a moment of desperation, he pulled open the drawer of the bedside table and looked inside. Sure enough, there was a copy of the Bible. Emanuel took it out and began to read it for the first time in his entire life.

9

Paul Tobias marched into the Oval office at 6:45 in the morning holding a manila folder stuffed with papers. President Taylor was sitting at his desk drinking a cup of coffee and reading the morning papers.

"Good morning, Mr. President, how are you today?" Tobias asked in a cheerful voice.

"Well, the Heat lost again last night, Paul, but other than that I'm fine. And you?"

"I'm very well, sir." Tobias paused. "I wonder if we might have coffee in your private study sir."

"Certainly, Paul," Taylor said, raising his eyebrows and throwing down the sports page.

When Tobias requested a meeting in the private study, it meant the matter at hand was extremely confidential. The Oval Office was monitored by both video and audio devices for a confidential presidential record. The public was not privy to this information but, due to several White House scandals, it became policy to monitor events to protect the President from himself. The private study, made famous by President Clinton and Monica Lewinsky, was for the most discrete conversations.

The two men walked into the study and sat in the two oversized leather chairs. Taylor took a sip of his coffee and asked Tobias to proceed.

"Mr. President, late last night I received this dossier from the men I deployed to investigate Winston, and you'll be happy to know that there are some interesting results."

"Please Paul, go on."

"The first revelation is definitely substantial. In a nutshell sir, Winston had been siphoning money out of his Church for years. He set up several off-shore bank accounts, with hundreds of millions of dollars in them."

"What was Winston doing with the money? Personal use?"

"Our people have sources who will attest that Winston was planning on establishing an army of his own mercenaries to accomplish objectives here at home and world-wide."

"What kind of objectives?"

"Basically, to fight his own crusade. He wanted to convert the world to his brand of Christianity, especially the Muslim world. Apparently, he found them just as unholy as they found us and was willing to play it their way. If bin Laden could do it then so could Winston. Further, he was planning on using the resources of the United States to accomplish it if he became president."

"You can't be serious?"

"Mr. President, I am very serious. I have the documentation in my hands and we will produce live witnesses as needed."

"Paul, I want this leaked to the press today."

"Of course, sir." All of a sudden, Tobias took on a more somber air.

"What is it, Paul? There's something else?"

"Yes, Mr. President, there is, and its of a much more personal nature . . ."

Jude was sitting at her desk reviewing her notes on the Winston story. She was completely frustrated because the story was not going any-where. CNN gave her the lead on coverage and she fully expected to parlay this story into a major advancement of her career. Stories like this could make a career, lead to multi-million-dollar book deals, television shows; in other words, everything Jude wanted.

Unfortunately, after the first few days of hard news she found she was doing retrospectives on Winston that, so far, were mere biographical sketches. The Freedom Party still had not decided whom if anyone was going to step into Winston's shoes. He had not picked a vice presidential candidate prior to his death and there really was not anyone else as powerful as Winston to turn to.

The Satya Grady angle was a dead end. He was so squeaky clean that it made reporting on him absurd. She could not find one person who questioned his integrity, his honesty, or his sanity. Jude had covered enough dirty cops in her career to know the signs. She knew, however, that dirty cops are interested in money, not murder. They usually turn dirty because working a tough job for little pay frustrates them. Murder might only happen to protect illegal activity but not as an end in itself. Unless someone paid Grady to kill Winston, there appeared no signs of corruption. Anyway, if he did it for money, Jude thought, he would have tried to get away with it, and that was not the case here. What was his motive?

President Taylor did not even bring an angle with his sweet speech made in honor of Winston. Jude knew full well that Taylor despised Winston. However, Taylor was too smart a politician to slip up now. His reelection was almost a lock due to Winston's death. The polls were already starting to reflect Taylor's advantage; end of that story.

Jude was reading and re-reading her notes, because she knew there had to be something more, on everyone involved. Jude was a great reporter. She definitely had a beautiful exterior that made her shine on television, but she started out as a print reporter without a camera in sight. Now she had the opportunity to take her career to the next level once again, and yet she was stumped. Where was the story? She looked over her notes again, scratching her forehead with red manicured nails. There was definitely something odd about Grady's choice of lawyers, she thought. While she assumed Grady couldn't afford a million-dollar defense, he didn't even pursue the big names to see if they would take it. Johnnie Cochoran, Roy Black, and Alan Dershowitz weren't even brought in for a consultation on this matter.

Adams was a decent criminal defense attorney. Jude had looked into his record and he had done fairly well arguing cases in D.C. Superior Court with a full roster of guilty clients. He'd had a few cases tossed out on illegal search and seizure grounds, which was remarkable since the Supreme Court had all but eroded that Constitutional protection. Adams had represented more drug offenders than anything else and seemed to be a proponent of legalization based on the arguments he made. With small time hustlers, he always made out as if dealing drugs was the best opportunity for kids in economically depressed neighborhoods and it was the American way to fulfill a demand. The fact the government decided to outlaw certain drugs and not others, like tobacco, was not the concern of these ambitious entrepreneurs. It was an argument that only worked with the right jury, but Adams had received some press on it.

As for violent criminals, Adams lacked a certain amount of experience. He'd represented a few, but nothing close to a high-profile murder charge. Jude had nosed around the courthouse and nobody claimed that Adams was the lawyer you needed to beat a murder rap. That being said, why did Grady reach out to Emanuel when he undoubtedly needed the best. Adams had been a Manhattan D.A., and maybe the two had met before, but that was certainly no basis to choose a lawyer, Jude thought. There must be more to it.

Then there was Winston. Jude had peripherally covered his rise to national prominence as a politician. At first, no one in Washington took Winston seriously. There had always been men of the cloth in Washington, but usually as political consultants or spiritual advisers. Never before had a member of the clergy as big and powerful as Winston tried to make the transition to national politics.

Jude's experience told her, though, that anyone with the ego to want to run for office, especially President of the United States, probably had something to hide. The desire for power is like an addiction, and Jude knew that where there is one addiction, there are often others. What were Winston's?

Jude's intuition was burning, but she needed a break. The next moment, the phone rang.

"Jude Michaels."

"Hi Jude, it's David."

Jude groaned. David Bauer worked at the White House for Paul Tobias. Jude met David at a black-tie function where she was seated next to him and was forced to listen to his White House stories all night. She made the mistake of drinking too much white wine and ended up letting David drive her home. Then, she made the mistake of inviting him up to her apartment for a nightcap, and finally, she completed the evening of blunders by sleeping with him.

She didn't really regret it. David was nice enough and not bad looking by Washington standards. The problem was that David didn't realize it when the night was over and reality set back in. He called Jude incessantly and was not concerned when Jude turned him down time and time again. In his defense, every once in a while, Jude said yes to David, usually when she was really lonely or when she wanted to see what was happening behind the scenes in the White House.

"Hi David. What a surprise to hear from you."

"Don't be sarcastic Jude, it's very unbecoming."

"Sorry, David. I didn't mean to be. I'm just bogged down with this Winston story."

"Well, that's part of the reason I'm calling Jude. I thought we could have a drink tonight and I'll give you a little info you might find interesting."

"David, are you bribing me to go on a date with you?"

"Yes."

"Ok. What time are you picking me up?"

"I'll see you at 7:30."

Strangely, Jude did not have to sleep with David again in order to get his information, although she was so happy about what she heard that she thought about propositioning him. After two martinis at the Lounge, one of D.C.'s extremely dark Euro bars, David told Jude about Winston's secret bank accounts and plans for a modern-day crusade. At first, she did not believe David because, for a reporter, the story was too good to be true. Once David gave her names, numbers, and places so she could investigate the story on her own she believed him. Then she got scared.

The one truly interesting angle Jude had covered since Winston's assassination was America's reaction to it. In towns all across America, prayer vigils were held, crosses were erected, photos of Winston appeared everywhere, and preachers found any pulpit they could to teach the Gospel. Winston's death had brought religion in America to the forefront in a drastic way. The religious right had waited for years to have a candidate like Winston who did not waiver on moral issues, and his death had spurred the movement on.

America had always been a country that tried to live by Christian ideals. The Founding Fathers decided to separate the church from the state and to ensure the free expression of religion in order to protect religious minorities, but there was always a large segment of American society that tried to circumvent this notion. The school prayer issue never disappeared, and school districts across the country continually tried to raise the bar concerning what was constitutionally permissible. Prayer at football games, graduations, before school, after school, or in Bible clubs were all attempted, sometimes with judicial acquiescence.

These cases were all about Christian prayer, not about whether an Islamic or Jewish prayer could be uttered in school. In 1925 the state of Tennessee passed the anti-evolution law which forbade the teaching of evolution and required teachers to explain the creation of human life from the story of Genesis. The law led to the arrest of high school biology teacher John Scopes who was teaching that man was just another mammal and had evolved from primitive life forms. Scopes' arrest brought America the famous legal battle between Clarence Darrow and Williams Jennings Bryan known as the "Scopes Monkey Trial." While the anti-evolution law was ultimately upheld, Darrow for the defense effectively proved that the Bible could not be read literally. Darrow did this by putting Bryan on the stand and questioning him about the words of the Bible. Did Eve really come from Adam's rib? Who was Cain's wife? Did a whale really swallow Jonah? Was the world really flooded and all civilizations destroyed? What about the ancient Egyptians and Chinese? Bryan and his fundamentalist movement were discredited, and evolution was once again taught in schools.

Winston's rise to power showed that America did not evolve very far from 1925. The same people who supported the anti-evolution law and fought for prayers before high school football games backed Winston all the way. He was finally their voice, and like Ronald Reagan's relentless pursuit of the Soviet "Evil Empire," Winston never wavered from the idea that everything we needed to govern our society was found in the pages of the King James Bible.

Winston's supporters were now beside themselves and were expressing their grief very publicly. During some of the prayer meetings, preachers likened Winston to Jesus Christ. They said he walked the Earth for a number of years teaching people of a better way of life and then was executed. They still did not know why Grady had killed Winston, and so the preachers could not explain Winston's death other than to say he died to save America the way Jesus died to save the world.

Jude covered these rallies and was amazed to hear people spout their explanations for why Winston was killed. Many suspected a government conspiracy led by President Taylor who feared losing the White House. Many blamed foreign terrorist groups who did not want to see a true man of God assume the leadership of the most powerful country in the world. Still others blamed forces within the

United States that sought to preserve their decadent and Godless way of life.

When David revealed to Jude that Winston was far from a clean character and had a questionable motive for seeking the White House, Jude wondered how Winston's supporters would take it. And, like in Roman days, she did not want to become the messenger executed for bearing bad news.

Emanuel spent several days in a dreary pattern of research that rarely makes it into legal television shows. He sat in the records room of the First Precinct pouring over Satya's arrest records looking for clues into his character, and photo copying any page that looked remotely interesting. If anything jumped off the page at him, like a person's name, or a difficult arrest, then Emanuel would lumber to the copier and add it to his growing file. He knew that later when he was building his case, one of those bits of information might come in handy. Sometimes the smallest detail could lead to a great idea.

Certainly, nothing in any of the reports hinted at mental illness. Satya never portrayed erratic or unexplained behavior. By all accounts, he usually followed procedure by the book and if anything, seemed more lenient on criminals than he might have been. While he always met his quota of arrests, Satya never exceeded it tremendously as other police officers did, who looked at their job as a challenge to arrest as many people as possible. Was this an indication of insanity or vice versa, Emanuel wondered.

The one case that really jumped up at Emanuel was that of Jesus Cruz. That was the connection after all, and maybe it had some meaning. The file was straightforward with just the intake form and nothing else. It reflected the two prior drug arrests. In the margin, there was a note that said "Looking at strike three." In the box for comments, it simply said that Jesus was a drug addict and not a major dealer. "He needs rehabilitation not retribution," Satya had written. "So, Satya agreed with Toni Fuentes on this one," Emanuel said to himself.

He needed to track down Jesus Cruz. Even if Cruz didn't have anything helpful to offer for Grady's defense, Emanuel had a strong desire to see Cruz and find out how his life turned out. Was letting Cruz go free a worthwhile gesture or a gratuitous breach of the public's trust?

Emanuel immediately called Toni Fuentes. He figured hard-ass public defenders like Toni never give up and move on to other careers. They love the long hours and low pay because they feel like they are making a difference. Sure enough, Emanuel was correct.

"Fuentes here," Toni answered the phone when Emanuel called.

"Toni, this is Emanuel Adams."

"Oh my God, Emanuel! How are you?" Toni asked with a sympathetic tone to her voice.

"I'm fine, Toni. I'm in New York investigating Satya Grady."

"Of course, I should've figured as much. Grady was one of the good guys on the force, Emanuel. We've all been in a state of shock. I was glad to see that you took the case, though."

"You were? Why?"

"Because you're a good lawyer, and you have compassion. I'm sure he needs both right now."

"Thanks, Toni. Satya has an interesting story, I can assure you."

"What is his story?"

"I'd rather not talk about it over the phone. Can I come down to your office?"

"Absolutely. Why not come down about six tonight. That's when things slow down a bit."

"Great. One more thing Toni . . ."

"Sure, Emanuel."

"Could you dig up Jesus Cruz's address for me. I need to go talk to him."

"Jesus Cruz? Still on your mind after all these years, huh?"

"I guess so. Can you do it?"

"I can probably handle it. I'll see you at six."

Emanuel walked over to the Public Defender's office, which was only a few blocks away from the court house at Hogan Place. The waiting room of the PD's office was filled with mostly young men of color. Some had a nervous, scared look in their eyes— the first offenders— and some had an annoyed, irritated look like they definitely had something better to do than meet with some lawyer— the veterans of the judicial system. Emanuel noted that like all waiting rooms where people's lives were on the line there was a funny smell that was earthy and animal, and no amount of cologne could ever cover it up.

The waiting room was sparsely decorated with art prints and a few plants. The table in the middle of the room was littered with well-thumbed magazines, all several months old. In one corner, there was a vending machine selling sodas, imitation coffee, and snacks.

He walked up to the receptionist, introduced himself, and told her he had an appointment with Toni Fuentes. Luckily, Toni had told the receptionist to bring Emanuel right back, saving him from the menacing stares of the people in the waiting room who would somehow know he was a lawyer and not a lawbreaker.

When Emanuel got outside Toni's office he saw she was just finishing up with a client so he gestured awkwardly to her and then stepped back and leaned against the wall to wait. He rested his head against the cool cinder blocks and took a deep breath. He then looked to his left and right and took note of the lawyers and staff of the PD's office walking about tensely. Much like the First Precinct, at the Public Defender's office there was always too much work and far too little time.

Finally, Toni appeared at her door. She shook hands with her client who walked away, leaving the two old adversaries alone facing each other.

"Together again after all these years, Emanuel. Quite a surprise I must say."

"It sure is Toni. I bet you thought you'd never see me again."

"I guess I probably didn't, but we both know how strange this life can be. Come on in."

Emanuel followed Toni into her office, noticing as she walked that she was wearing the same black, pin striped suit she wore the day she stormed into his office over Jesus Cruz. The suit was faded, showing its age, and Toni filled it out a little more than the last time, making it tighter than desirable. Toni was still attractive, however, and despite her stressful job, the olive skin on her face still had a youthful freshness to it. She was wearing her hair in a bun that revealed a few streaks of gray, but the bags under her eyes were nothing compared to those Emanuel was sporting.

Emanuel sat down and looked into Toni's brown eyes that were asking him a million questions. He knew she wanted to know everything but didn't want to start cross-examining him. It was like the first appointment with a therapist.

"So, how's Satya?" Toni finally asked trying to keep a casual tone.

"The last time I saw him he was being held at the police station, so he was doing okay. They were treating him somewhat deferentially since he's a cop, but it was still custody. The detectives assigned to the case are also straight shooters, so I'm not worried about any funny business. Right now, though, he's sweating it out in D.C. jail."

"Have you talked to him?"

"Not since I've been up in New York."

"How's it looking?"

"Not good. He shot Winston in front of about fifty witnesses, including several law enforcement officers. The incident was also caught on film as you've probably seen. So, he has no alibi, and admits to committing the act. He does have a defense, however, and it's a winner," Emanuel said sarcastically.

"And that is . . ."

"He told me that he had a vision of God who told him he had to kill Winston for the greater good of mankind."

Toni sat back and looked at Emanuel without blinking. Slowly, a smile appeared on her face.

"The old 'God told me to do it defense,' huh? You know how many times I've heard that bullshit over the years? You can't be serious. What the hell is he trying to pull?"

"I don't know for sure. You hear that, you're thinking insanity all the way— a lifetime at St. Elizabeth's, no problem. But, he told me an incredible story about what happened, and that he definitely did not want to plead insanity. He assured me it really happened."

"Talking to God?"

"That's right."

"How'd you leave it?"

"I told him I'd investigate the case and if I find God or any other reason to believe him, we go with justifiable homicide. If not, we go insanity."

Toni burst out laughing. "That is the most ridiculous thing I've ever heard. You agreed to that. Man, you've gotten soft down in D.C. I think it's time you came back to the show."

Emanuel let Toni have a good laugh before continuing. "The thing is, Toni, I don't think he's crazy and I've seen nothing so far to make me believe he is."

"Other than the fact he shot Winston in cold blood and told you God told him to do it."

"Right."

"Let's assume for a minute that you do confirm his story." Toni made quotation marks with her fingers when she said "confirm," and was still laughing. "I'm not sure the court will allow that as a defense."

"Why not?" Emanuel asked, taking a more serious tone. "You have to swear to tell the truth with one hand over the Bible, so why not this defense?"

"Because there's no way to prove it, and when Satya gets convicted, you'll be disbarred for agreeing to defend him on that basis. I hope the judge will try to protect your career."

"If I test Grady and he comes up sane, and he wants to get on the stand and try and convince a jury that he talked to God, how can I stop him? It's his right."

"Maybe, but there's no precedent for it, and I'm just warning you, you'll have to convince the judge to allow it."

"Thanks for the tip," Emanuel snapped.

"Don't get angry at me, Emanuel. I'm simply telling you from years of experience hearing every possible defense under the sun, 'God told me to do it' doesn't take you very far."

"Why not? What does 'talking to God' mean, anyway? I'm not saying that I believe Satya actually talked to God like Moses did. I'm just saying why do any of us do the things we do. Arguably, all our ideas come from God because He created us body and soul. Winston was running for president, and winning, I might add, on the idea that everything this country needs is represented in the Bible— the word of God. Maybe when I let Jesus Cruz off the hook years ago, I was really following God's orders, even though I didn't know it at time."

Emanuel had become agitated as he spoke. He was listening to his words in disbelief. He had never believed in God and now he was arguing that perhaps God had influenced his own decisions. It was a philosophical question he'd never contemplated before. He wiped his sweaty forehead with the sleeve of his suit jacket. His face was red and he was breathing heavily. Toni got up from her desk and walked around to him. She didn't say a word, but simply knelt beside him and gave him a hug. When she did, Emanuel broke down and started to cry. It was a whimper at first and then he let go completely and started to weep. He couldn't understand why. The pressure of the case, his client's life, and the whole issue of God suddenly become overwhelming.

Toni just rubbed his back to try and soothe him. She put her forehead against his temple and held him tightly. She didn't say a word and didn't try to stop his tears. Toni had seen people break down many times in her career and knew it was best to let them go.

Finally, Emanuel stopped crying but wouldn't break Toni's embrace.

"I don't know what's happening here Toni," he said. "This whole thing is just affecting me in the strangest way. I've never had a case like this."

"This is a big one, Emanuel. And a tough one."

"When I talked to Satya right after the shooting, it was so surreal. I wanted to disbelieve him. I wanted so badly to think he was another homicidal lunatic, or public servant who just snapped. But, everything about him and what he said made me believe him. He was so calm and composed. I've never seen anyone in custody look like that, as if he knew beyond a shadow of a doubt that everything would be okay. That he would get out and go home to his family. It was incredible, Toni, and it won me over."

"Okay, Emanuel. Okay. I trust you and I know you're a good lawyer. I also know Satya Grady, and I know he's a good cop. So, it's possible. But, I think you're holding on too tightly with this one. Maybe, it's because you've never believed in God that you want Satya to be telling the truth. I don't know."

"Why don't you go see him and talk to him, Toni? You can judge for yourself."

"You know I can't leave here, Emanuel. I have a caseload you wouldn't believe. Like I said, I trust you. I'm just telling you that raising this defense probably won't get past the judge, and if it does, I have no idea how you prove it to a jury. Satya's life is in your hands, Emanuel. You have to remember that."

"I know. I know. That's why I'm trying to sort it out. Maybe I'm the crazy one."

"Well, they probably thought Jesus was crazy when he was going around telling everyone he was the Son of God," Toni said with a smile.

Emanuel burst out in a cathartic laugh that made him cry again. He finally stopped and wiped his face with the sleeve of his jacket. "Speaking of Jesus, do you have Cruz's information for me?" he asked.

"Yes, I do." Toni said as she stood up and walked back around her desk. She pulled out a piece of paper from a file and handed it to Emanuel. "He's living over in Queens. Let me know how he's doing. I'd be interested to know myself. And listen, keep me up to date on this case. If there's anything I can do to help, I'll do it. Or, if you just want to talk."

"Thanks Toni," Emanuel said standing up. "Thanks for everything." The two hugged and Emanuel left.

Emanuel spent another sleepless night reading the Bible, and periodically raiding his minibar for another scotch. Just before dawn he passed out in a mixture of drunkenness and fatigue.

When he woke up it was one o'clock in the afternoon. He took a long, scalding hot shower, put on a suit and headed out to find Jesus Cruz. It was another unseasonably hot and humid day that caused him to start sweating the minute he hit the sidewalk. He entered the subway which offered no relief to the oppressive heat and took the Q train from midtown out to Queens. Jesus lived in Astoria, which was only a fifteen minute train ride from Manhattan.

When he got out at Astoria, he walked down from the elevated platform and hailed a cab. The cab rumbled through the side streets of Astoria past the foreign-language signs of the Greek section, into a quiet neighborhood of respectable row houses. Emanuel paid the fare and got out. The address was 777 Broad Street, the home of Jesus Cruz.

Emanuel walked up the stairs and knocked on the door. He heard a baby crying inside and people running around. Eventually, a woman came to the door with a baby in her arms.

"Can I help you?" she asked.

"Yes, Ma'am. My name is Emanuel Adams. I'm an attorney from Washington, D.C., and I'm looking for Jesus Cruz."

"Why?"

"I kind of knew him many years ago when I was an Assistant District Attorney in Manhattan, and I was hoping to speak with him. Is he here?"

"He's not in any trouble, is he?" she asked with a worried look on her face.

"No, not at all. This is a social visit, really. Is he here?"

"He's still at work, but he should be home soon. Do you want to come in and wait?"

"Thank you. I would."

The woman opened the door and let Emanuel in. The first thing Emanuel noticed when he walked in was a large painting of Jesus on the cross hanging over the fireplace. The living room was very clean except for a few toys scattered on the floor. A little boy was watching television while a little girl played with some Barbie dolls.

"My name is Marie, I'm Jesus' wife. These are our kids, Jesus, Jr., Christiana, and this little one is Carlos."

"Hello, everyone," Emanuel said awkwardly. He wasn't around children very often and was not sure how to act.

"Why don't you sit down. You two go upstairs," Marie said to Jesus and Christiana. "Would you like some coffee, Mr. Adams?"

"Yes, thank you," Emanuel responded even though he didn't really want any. Marie put Carlos into a baby seat, and walked back through the dining room to the kitchen. Emanuel sat down and tried to keep himself at ease. He noticed additional icons like a statue of the Virgin Mary and a fairly large crucifix nailed to the wall. There was also another painting of the wall of a bowl of fruit.

Before Marie came back with the coffee, the front door opened and Jesus Cruz walked in, sweating and out of breath. He carried the jacket of his tan poplin suit over his arm and his red striped tie was loosened around his neck. When he saw Emanuel sitting on his couch, he took out a handkerchief from his trousers and wiped his forehead and the back of his neck. He took a deep breath before asking calmly, "Who are you?"

"I'm Emanuel Adams," Emanuel said, getting up and walking over to Jesus with his arm extended to shake hands. Jesus shook Emanuel's hand and looked him over contemplatively. The name had struck a cord with Jesus, and he was trying to place it.

"Aren't you the man representing Officer Grady?" Jesus asked, finally placing Emanuel.

"I am. I guess you saw me on TV?"

"Yeah, I did. I couldn't believe it when it happened. I know Officer Grady."

"I know." Emanuel said.

Just then Marie walked back into the room carrying a tray with the coffee and a plate of cookies. When she saw Jesus, a smile came over her face. She put the tray down and went to give him a kiss. It was longer than the typical hello peck, and it came with a hug. In Emanuel's emotional state, it made him choke up.

"How was your day?" Marie asked taking Jesus' jacket.

"It was fine angel. How was yours?"

"Good. The kids were well behaved today. Would you like something to drink?"

"Please bring me a glass of water. Sit down, Mr. Adams," Jesus said. Marie went to fetch the glass of water. Emanuel sat down and put some milk and sugar into his coffee. Jesus didn't say anything until Marie came back with the water. She left the two men, taking the baby upstairs with her.

"So, Mr. Adams, why are you here and how do you know that I know Satya Grady?"

"Mr. Cruz, I know that once Officer Grady arrested you for possession of narcotics with the intent to distribute. I also know that you were never prosecuted for the crime and walked away a free man. I know this because I was the prosecutor assigned to your case, and I buried the file."

Jesus took a sip of his water and sat back in his chair, taken aback by the news.

"Why'd you do it?" he asked with a hint of defiance.

"Part of the reason was your lawyer Toni Fuentes who convinced me that jail time was not the answer for you, and part of it was your family. And I guess something just snapped inside me. I figured you were just an addict and that prison wasn't going to cure you of that. I hoped that maybe if I let you off, you would find a way to turn your life around. That's part of the reason why I'm here. I wanted to see if I made the right decision, because basically it ended my career as a DA. I couldn't do it anymore with a clean conscience."

"So, you want to know if I'm still using and dealing. You've come into my house to ask me that?"

"No, Mr. Cruz, I'm not here to ask you personal questions. I just want to know what you've done between now and then. If you don't want to talk to me I'll understand. But, it's your case that linked me with Satya. It's why he called me to defend him in his case. I'm in New York investigating the case, and for some reason, I felt I should see you."

"In that case, I'll talk to you. I'm not using or dealing drugs anymore, Mr. Adams. I have a good job working as a software consultant. I also do community service work, counseling young Latinos with drug problems. And as you see, I have a beautiful wife and beautiful children."

"I do see that, Mr. Cruz."

"I'll tell you something else. None of this would have been possible without Satya, and I suppose you too, Mr. Adams."

"Satya helped you out."

"Helped me out? Mr. Adams, Officer Grady saved my life."

As Jesus began to talk, Emanuel sat back in his chair, realizing he had finally found some answers.

After leaving Jesus, Emanuel took the train back to the city. The last thing Jesus said to Emanuel as he walked out the door was, "tell Satya I'm praying for him." It was a simple request and one that Emanuel would have ordinarily thought ridiculous. Prayer had never figured into his defense plans before. To him that was like hoping a lucky break would win your case, which only happened in the movies and never in real life. A great lawyer who had command of the facts and the ability to sway a jury was what a criminal defendant needed, not people praying for him. But, when Jesus uttered those words, Emanuel felt, for the first time in his life, that prayer might help Satya in this case. The facts and the law were totally against Satya, so maybe faith was the answer.

Emanuel took the train to Penn Station, exited, and started walking towards Hell's Kitchen. He was thinking about Jesus' amazing story, and how in many ways it validated Satya. The idea of inherent righteousness was new to Emanuel, who never thought of right or wrong before. Everything was gray to his legal mind, but his views were changing. Maybe a person could be so pure of heart and spirit that if they did something like kill another human being, it could only be a righteous act. Maybe it was this kind of moral dilemma that the idea of God was designed to handle for human beings, and maybe that was gravely missing from Emanuel's life. God answered the unanswerable questions and Emanuel realized that up until this point in his life he had never even asked these questions. Perhaps it was easier to live without pondering the intricacies of life and obsessing over how to live a better one, but it was also one-dimensional. As Emanuel strolled the streets of Hell's Kitchen, he thought how tired he was of that life.

10

The next day was Friday and the shrill ringing of the hotel phone snapped Emanuel from his sleep. He'd had another late night thinking about the case and periodically flipping through the Bible. When he saw that it was seven in the morning, Emanuel realized he'd only been asleep for a few hours. He also wondered who was calling him so early.

"This is your wake-up call, barrato."

"Turc, is that you? Why the hell are you calling me so early?"

"It's the weekend bro, and you promised me a night out."

"I changed my mind," Emanuel growled.

"Nice try. I'll be in court all day, so meet me at Dante's at 5:30." Turc hung up.

A feeling of dread swept through Emanuel's body and he fell back into his pillow. After regretting agreeing to an outing with Turc, he fell back asleep, knowing he would need it later.

Dante's Steak House was on 44th Street between Park and Lexington. Emanuel had never been there, but he knew they served the best sirloin in town and that there was a major Mafia slaughter that occurred at Dante's in the 90s. The Scalino family gunned down one of their own made men, Tony "the Ox" Romano and his two capos.

Just after the Ox had taken the first bite of his tartuffo, he opened his eyes and saw the two hitmen striding toward him. His mouth was full so he couldn't cry out and his capos were too busy eating to notice. The three were shot twice each, a bullet between the eyes and one in the heart— extremely professional. Emanuel thought it was decent of the Scalino's to let the Ox finish his steak before they killed him, however when John Scalino brought that point up at his murder trial as a mitigating circumstance, neither the judge nor the jury gave it much weight. Around the DAs office at the time, Scalino's argument became known as the "Last Supper defense." Scalino got life.

The defense was a propos to the one Emanuel was plotting for Satya, and he wondered if Turc had picked the place for that reason. Emanuel was feeling much better about the defense. His talk with Jesus and a call he had made that day to the doctor who saw Satya after he was shot gave him some nice facts to work with. He also had Satya's nearly impeccable arrest record and fellow officers as character witnesses. Emanuel also inherently believed that Satya was not insane now or at the time of the shooting. And anyway, since Satya was not interested in that defense, Emanuel would not set out to prove his client was insane at trial. Now Emanuel just had to prove justifiable homicide.

While Emanuel knew that he would have to tell both the judge and jury that Satya believed he had talked to God and was following His orders, he would couch it in the rubric of justifiable homicide. For example, the law allows deadly force if a violent intruder enters your house and threatens your family. The analogy here was that Satya was a public servant who believed Winston was a threat to the nation and deadly force was necessary. It was still a far-fetched defense, but it was logical and made Emanuel more comfortable than simply arguing Divine Intervention. If he could somehow present facts showing Winston was a bad actor, he would be better off still.

Emanuel walked into Dante's at five o'clock and took a long look around. It had just opened for dinner and was empty, giving it a deserted and eerie feel. The restaurant was decorated with heaviness in mind, with wood throughout, paintings with thick frames and massive chairs at the tables. Everything was the finest quality, but big and obvious. Emanuel had no doubt that the steaks, if nothing else, would be huge.

The bar was definitely open and a lone bartender was standing behind it cutting limes. He was wearing a sparkling clean and pressed white shirt with a black silk tie tucked into a starched white apron. He had shoulder-length, thick black hair, and the biggest nose Emanuel had ever seen. It was long and fat and made his eyes look beady because they seemed so far away. Strangely though, despite his nose, the man was handsome in a swarthy way.

"How are you tonight, sir?" the man asked in a thick Italian accent.

"Fine thank you," Emanuel answered, sitting down on a bar stool and laying his cigarettes on the bar.

"Let me see now," the bartender said leaning over the bar and rubbing his cleft chin. "You want a martini, vodka, with olives. Am I right?" he asked with a sly smile.

"You are indeed," Emanuel said amused. "Can you guess which vodka?"

"No, I don't do that, I'm not commercial. I'm a, how you say, equal opportunity barman." The man laughed a cartoon character laugh as if he knew he was being cute.

"Kettle One," Emanuel said bluntly.

Two martinis and Andreas the bartender's life story later, Turc sauntered into the bar. He always had an air about him that was cool and breezy, as if he was completely confident that nothing but good would come his way. As was his custom, he came up to Emanuel and gave him a big hug to greet him.

"I see you've started early, brother, as I should have guessed," Turc said, immediately lighting a cigarette.

"I had a little down time so I figured why not. By the way, this bartender makes an incredible martini."

"Oh, I know it," Turc said with a smile.

Just at that moment, Andreas arrived with a martini for Turc. He had a wide grin on his face and extended his hand to shake Turc's.

"Turc, my friend, it's so good to see you. How are you?"

"I'm fine Andreas, and yourself?"

"You know me, Turc, I'm just struggling to survive. Hey, let me have one of your cigarettes?"

"Sure, Andreas, anything for you," Turc said taking out his pack from his jacket pocket and handing it to Andreas.

"Thanks Turc. I'll be back in a second." Andreas walked off to make a drink for another customer.

"You guys must be pretty friendly if he bums cigarettes off you," Emanuel said.

"I've been coming here for a long time, so we've gotten to know each other fairly well."

"While I was waiting for you he told me the most amazing story about his life . . ." Emanuel began.

"The one about him being wounded in the Balkans war, becoming a model in New York, and losing his wife in a drunk driving accident?" Turc added nonchalantly while sipping his drink.

"I suppose you've heard it since you're a regular."

"Are your kidding me? He tells that story to everyone he meets."

"You make it sound like the story's not true."

"It's not. It's all total bullshit."

"That can't be. The way he told it. He was so impassioned. I could see the joy and pain in his face when he got to certain parts. There's no way that story's bullshit."

"I'm telling you, it's just one big cover-up. Andreas is one of the biggest coke dealers on the East Side."

Emanuel was stunned. He put his drink down before taking a sip and stared at Turc in disbelief.

"What about his daughter? That has to be true."

"His quote daughter is the best excuse he has for leaving the bar to make a deal. Who would question a guy who needs to go home to his sick child? It's actually brilliant."

Andreas reappeared and handed the cigarettes back to Turc.

"Thanks Turc. So, I see you two are friends. Small world."

"It sure is, Andreas. We have to run. How much for all the drinks?"

"I'll give you a deal, $30."

"Great," Turc said peeling off two twenty-dollar bills from his money roll. "Come on, Emanuel let's get out of here."

Emanuel finished the last bit of his martini and shook Andreas's hand in parting.

"I hope to see you again soon," Andreas said with the same impish smile on his face.

When Emanuel and Turc got outside the restaurant, Emanuel had to ask more about Andreas: "You're telling me that Andreas is a coke dealer and none of that story is true. I just can't believe it."

"Believe this buddy," Turc said, removing a tiny plastic bag of cocaine from his pack of cigarettes. "You didn't even notice did you? The perfect little transaction."

"You just bought coke in there?"

"You put the money in the pack of smokes, Andreas takes it out and puts in the white. He's in there selling like that all night."

Emanuel was definitely disappointed. Andreas seemed so real and believable. His story was an epic struggle to find happiness in life. It reminded Emanuel of the stories he'd been reading in the Bible every night. Andreas had lost and gained everything multiple times in his young life. Emanuel wanted to believe that a petty criminal from the streets of Rome could become a successful model in New York, marry a supermodel from Connecticut and have babies. Not to mention his comeback from a nearly fatal wound in battle. Perhaps it was farfetched, but then so were some of the biblical stories, like Joseph and his brothers. Andreas had found total joy and then lost it all with the death of his wife— an example of the fleeting nature of happiness in life.

The thought that Andreas was just another coke-dealing bartender was disturbing. It shook Emanuel's confidence in Satya and his story.

Was Satya acting for some higher purpose or was he just a bull-shitter trying to cover up wrongdoing? Andreas created an entire alter ego to cover up his drug dealing, so maybe Satya invented a tale about God to rationalize his murder. This was not the thought that Emanuel wanted at a time when he was starting to feel better about his upcoming defense.

"Get that puppy dog look off your face, Emanuel. I'm sorry your new friend is a lying drug dealer. Get over it. It's party time," Turc said, not making the same connection Emanuel had between Andreas and Satya.

Instead, Turc took out the bag of coke, dipped the corner of his credit card in, and took a big snort. As he did, he threw his head back and let out a little groan.

"Goddamn that's nice. Nothing like a little of the kind after a day working for the Man."

"Do you think you should be doing that right on the street where everyone can see you?" Emanuel asked.

"Relax man, you forget, I'm Johnny fucking law," Turc said with a wink. "Who's gonna fuck with me? You want some?"

"No thanks, I'm okay for right now." Emanuel responded meekly. "Where're we heading?"

"We're going to a thing on the Upper East, but it doesn't start until later. So, I figured we'd go to American Trash and shoot some pool first and get drunky. Sound good?"

"Great," Emanuel said, trying to sound enthusiastic.

The two hailed a cab and set off into the bustling Friday night traffic. Emanuel was already somewhat buzzed from the martinis and introspective. Emanuel had always been fascinated by the human condition. It was another reason he went into criminal law. There are very few times you see people at the truly animal level; after they've been arrested is one of them. From an early age Emanuel wondered why people did the things they did, from the innocuous to the blatantly reckless. There always seemed to be a driving force behind the actions and inactions of people.

In criminal law, every perpetrator had an alibi or an excuse. Emanuel had known guys who were caught on videotape committing their crime and who would say, "That looks like me, and walks like me, but man, it ain't me."

At first Emanuel tried to explain away why people committed crimes. He rationalized that people who grew up in poverty naturally turned to crime for economic reasons, or people who had terrible family lives became antisocial. Quickly, however, he realized that people from all walks of life and financial backgrounds committed crimes— well-educated stockbrokers trying to swindle old ladies out of their pensions, or lawyers plotting to kill their wives. Emanuel had seen it all and after awhile he stopped trying to explain it. Instead, he just took note of it all and wrote it off to the human condition. He figured that sometimes people just could not deal with life in acceptable ways and turned to the unacceptable, and when they were caught there was no explanation.

Emanuel looked over at Turc who was simply gazing out the window enjoying the effects of his first bump of coke. Turc had the look of a man about to begin a daunting task that he felt confident he would accomplish. Emanuel was confident Turc would, too. He always did.

The cab pulled up next to American Trash at 81st and 1st Avenue. Trash was a biker bar set among the Upper East Side high-rise apartment buildings that were filled with New York's most conservative people. The Harley's were parked in a neat row outside and the Skynyrd was blaring from inside. An odd scene for a Manhattan street, but a classic example of the City's menu of diversions that leaves no one unsatisfied.

Turc and Emanuel sauntered into the bar, both in their suits and both with cigarettes dangling from their lips. They stopped in the front and let their eyes adjust to the dark, smoky room. It was fairly crowded for early evening with a mixture of tough-looking bikers and people like Turc and Emanuel who just wanted to hang around them.

Men and women dressed in mounds of denim, leather and cotton tee shirts with sayings like "Kill 'em all and let God sort 'em out," lined the bar. Everyone had a cigarette in their hands and seemingly, a minimum of two drinks in front of them. There were a couple of mangy dogs lying on the floor with their tongues hanging out, trying to breath in the putrid air.

The bar was a small rectangle like most Upper East Side joints. It had a pool table, a pinball machine called "Tits and Ass," a driving game with 3-D graphics, two large monitors and a juke box— enough side dishes to go with the main course of booze.

Turc immediately took off his jacket, loosened his tie and went to the bar. He shook hands with Pig the bartender, and ordered two Budweisers and two shots of Cuervo. He also got ten dollars in quarters from Pig before bringing the drinks over to Emanuel.

"Cheers, barrato. It's great to see you. Things have never been as good as when you and I stormed around this town together night after night."

The two slugged down the shots without salt or lime and then headed directly for the pool table.

"Best three out of five for twenty bucks, and the loser of each game has to buy a round of shots. Got it?" Turc said, violently slamming the quarters into the table.

"Got it," Emanuel said, taking off his jacket. He was beginning to accept the fact that he was going to get insanely drunk and the thought actually started loosening him up.

Turc racked the balls and Emanuel broke without sinking a shot.

"So, Magnum, how's the investigation going?" Turc asked, brusquely grabbing the cue out of Emanuel's hands.

"It's going pretty well. I've definitely got a much clearer picture of Satya in my head," Emanuel said, watching Turc sink the ten.

"And, does that picture help his case?"

"I'm not sure anything can help his case, but it's certainly not making it worse. I've found no evidence that he's now insane or was on the verge of a breakdown before the incident. And, I've found no evidence that he was anything but a great cop."

"What about evidence of God?" Turc said with a hint of sarcasm as he lined up a shot.

"That's where things get a little thin. I really have to show that Satya was justified, in some tangible way, in killing Winston. I need to shift his story about talking to God to a debate about morality, right and wrong. That way it'll seem less weird."

"How are you going to do that when your client is a killer? It doesn't get more wrong than that," Turc said, sinking another ball.

"Well, Jesus Cruz had some interesting things to say on the subject."

Turc stopped playing and stood upright. "You talked to Cruz? How'd you find him?"

"Toni Fuentes gave me his address. She was his lawyer back when, you know . . ."

"No, I don't know," Turc said. "I meant to ask you about that little case."

"What do you want to know? I used my prosecutorial discretion."

"You call burying a clear-cut drug distribution case, 'prosecutorial discretion?'"

"Give me a break, Turc. It was a long time ago. You want to bust me for it now? Don't you want to hear what Cruz said?"

"I do, but I want you to know that I was a little stunned to hear what you did with Cruz. I'm no angel but I think, if you commit the crime, you should do the time."

"What! You just committed a crime half an hour ago. Should you go to jail?" Emanuel asked, annoyed.

"I didn't get caught, did I?"

"That's your standard? The old cliché, 'it's only a crime if you get caught?'"

"That's right, barrato. You talk about morality in your defense, but what is morality? It's what society says is wrong if they see something they don't like or don't understand. If Satya kills Winston while he's committing a crime, people understand that and he's not even arrested. If he blows Winston away for no apparent reason, he's a murderer. If I get caught buying drugs, I've committed a crime. But, if no one sees me I've done nothing wrong because there's no one watching in order to judge me. You were in a position to bring Cruz to justice for his crime and you made some lofty decision to let him go, and since I know about it, I have every reason to tell you I think it was bullshit."

"Satya knew I let Cruz walk, and he never said anything about it. What do you think that means?"

"It means neither one of you knows how to draw lines. You both live in some middle ground where you think you can make decisions that transcend the social order. You did it with Cruz, and Satya just did it with Winston. I guess you two are a good match."

Emanuel took a sip of his beer and tried to digest what Turc had said. Turc could compartmentalize his life and how he looked at criminal conduct. He had no problem violating the law by buying drugs because he supposedly accepted the consequences of his actions. If he got caught, he would take his punishment. He did not believe, however, that buying and using drugs was inherently wrong, it was simply against the law of the land. Emanuel realized that most Americans probably felt that way, which would be his major hurdle in defending Satya. He needed to raise the level of right and wrong from the laws of the United States to a higher level— the level of God.

"So, by that analysis, Satya's had it?" Emanuel asked.

"I'm saying, bro, that you better come up with a concrete, real justification for why he killed Winston, or yeah, he's done for. And, as far as you're concerned, I forgive you for the Cruz deal," Turc said looking Emanuel right in the eye as he sunk the eight ball. "Looks like it's your round, buddy. Make it Grand Marnier. That'll bring us both closer to God."

Four games of pool and four shots later, Emanuel found himself staggering around the thirty-ninth floor of Byron McGregor's Upper East Side apartment. Somewhere along the way to taking Emanuel's fifty dollars, three games to two, Turc explained that he had a friend named Byron known for throwing elaborate parties.

Byron was a pure capitalist. He was a product of the bull market that stampeded through the mid to late 90s. Once the Internet gave people direct access to financial markets, investing changed and people like Byron were the real beneficiaries. Trading stocks, options, bonds, and futures became as American as baseball. It was a national obsession that encompassed the great American ideals of gambling, winning, and, most importantly, making money.

Byron started out as a broker in the late 1980s making cold calls selling dog companies to anyone stupid enough to buy them. He was good, though, and built a reputation as an aggressive and intelligent salesman. Byron made decent money even during the recession of the early 90s, but when the technology boom hit, he thrived. All of a sudden, he was selling tech companies that would rise in value two hundred percent in an afternoon. After managing huge portfolios, he realized he could make even more money on his own, trading his own account and funding start-up companies. Byron saw the game before anyone else. The perception of value in a dot.com company was much more important than actual profitability. He was an excellent judge of business plans and managers, and funded as many companies as he could. Most were successful, and when the companies went public Byron walked away with hundreds of millions of dollars.

The difference between Byron and some of the other venture capitalists and entrepreneurs of the late 90s, was that Byron knew when to get out—he always saw the end coming. By the beginning of the twenty-first century, Byron stopped funding these companies after realizing that everyone else was catching on to the scam. By this point, he had so much wealth he just diversified into real estate, commodities, traditional companies, and smaller businesses. One thing was clear: he would never be able to spend all the money he had.

This fact did not stop Byron from trying, however. He loved making money because he loved spending it on a decadent and depraved lifestyle. Byron never saw a point in marriage and instead surrounded himself with the world's most beautiful and unattainable women. He avoided high-profile women like big name actresses or models because he loathed the public eye. Byron's unique deviance was tracking the young talent on the verge of discovery. Like picking the right companies to fund, Byron had an uncanny ability to pick the young actress, model, or dancer, who would one day grace magazine covers and command audiences worldwide. By that time, they'd already entered and left Byron's twisted world, almost like a right of passage for stardom.

Byron had residences in Paris, Los Angeles, Milan, Hong Kong, Rio, Greece, and, of course, Switzerland. He owned his own Boeing 757 and a yacht that sailed interchangeably around the Mediterranean and the Caribbean. Byron was an international party unto himself because he never forgot that the money he earned was only worthwhile if he spent it the right way.

Emanuel was numb from drinking when he walked into Byron's apartment, but was nevertheless amazed at what he saw. The apartment was almost entirely white except for splashes of black and red that popped out from time to time. The floor was white tile, which gave the place an antiseptic feel and created an unnerving soundtrack as the heels clipped along. The apartment took up the entire floor of the building, which allowed for open spaces and a spectacular view of New York from every angle. It was by design that the apartment was all white; because the Manhattan views were so over-stimulating Byron opted for the minimalist approach inside. Emanuel couldn't help staring out the bay windows in a daze, marveling at the absurd creation that is New York.

While the skyscrapers stacked one on top of another outside was a jarring sight, the bizarre characters walking around Byron's apartment were equally as startling to the eye. Emanuel was amused because he had always wondered who wore those outlandish clothes he saw modeled in fashion shows. He had finally found all of them at Byron's.

The guests at Byron's party matched the décor of the apartment. No one was wearing anything that had any color to it, with the majority in black and white. The only thing that gave any depth to the fashion statements was the texture of the blacks and whites; some leather, some spandex, some polyester, and more rubber clothing than Emanuel had every seen. The faces were equally stark. Everyone ascribed to the model look of startling, protruding cheek bones, full lips, and thick hair cut into all manner of jagged angels. It was all achieved through the New York diet of vodka, cigarettes, cocaine, and the very occasional low-fat snack. They would all photograph well, but in real life they looked like wax figures.

Emanuel had lost Turc amongst the throng, and now set out to find him. The jungle bass mix emanating from speakers embedded in the walls was loud and never-ending, and made Emanuel feel like he was on some trippy urban safari. People huddled in small groups drinking multicolored martinis and passing around mirrors with thick lines of coke. One group seated on Byron's white leather couches was passing around a hookah, smoking some foul-smelling weed. Women and men would casually touch Emanuel as he walked by as if to inspect him for a future sexual interlude or stare at him because the skin on his face wasn't stretched taut or because he was wearing khakis and a blue, patterned oxford.

Emanuel grabbed a martini off a waiter's tray and continued his search for Turc. The smoky atmosphere and the alcohol from American Trash caught up with Emanuel. He was feeling closed in and trapped in this hedonistic world where everyone was inhaling some kind of mind-altering drug and seemed to be plotting some invasion of personal space.

Emanuel weaved his way over to a window in order to look outside and tune out the inside. He put his hands to the glass, gently resting his forehead there at the same time. The cool glass soothed Emanuel's feverish skin. His head was spinning and all he could focus on was the tops of his oxblood loafers.

"Are you alright?"

Emanuel turned to see a very beautiful woman standing in front of him with a glass of clear liquid. The woman was elegantly dressed in a low-cut, black velvet cat suit that highlighted her breasts, which seemed slightly too big for her frame. She had long, straight brown hair that was pulled back off of her face and cascaded down to the small of her back. She was wearing very little make-up and her face had a fullness to it that made her seem like a Botticelli in a room full of Picassos.

"I brought you some water," the woman said, holding out the glass. She had a strange formal accent that hinted at the influence of various foreign languages. Emanuel took it gratefully and drank the water down all at once, staring at the woman the entire time.

"I've lost my friend," Emanuel said, wiping his chin with his sleeve. "Do you think you could help me find him?"

"Don't sound so helpless," the woman said gently. "Of course I will help you. What is his name, your friend?"

"Turc. Turc Tophet. Do you know him?"

"Sure, I know him. Turc is the lawyer everyone calls when they get in trouble. Somehow, he always finds a way to fix those pesky little legal problems. He is best friends with Byron so he's probably back in the inner sanctum."

"The what?"

"Byron's private room where only a select few can go. He likes having all these people out here drinking and using his drugs, but he considers them the proletariat. The elite are in the inner sanctum."

"Can you get me back there?" Emanuel asked.

"Yes, I'm considered one of the privileged few. Byron appreciates my occupation and my terrific pedigree."

"I'm sure he'd appreciate neither of mine," Emanuel mused.

"If you're a friend of Turc's, I'm sure he'll accept you. I'm Clea d'Orleans, by the way."

"Emanuel Adams. Pleased to meet you," Emanuel said, shaking Clea's hand, while she leaned in to kiss him on both cheeks. He caught on after a second, but it was a less than graceful introduction.

"So, what do you do?" Emanuel asked, trying to recover from his oafishness with the standard D.C. question.

"I'm an archeologist," Clea responded with pride. "And yourself?"

"I'm a criminal defense attorney. I used to be a DA with Turc." Emanuel paused before asking his next question, pondering whether he should bring up Satya, but he could not help himself.

"Have you ever come across anything in your work that you thought might prove the existence of God?"

"That depends on which God you're referring to; there are quite a few of them out there," Clea said with a clever smile of slightly crooked teeth. She liked the question though and inched closer to Emanuel, her big brown eyes lighting up.

"That's a good point," Emanuel conceded. "How about Jesus? Ever find any evidence about Him or who He was?"

"My goodness, two minutes ago I thought you were going to jump out that window in a drunken stupor and now you want to know if I have seen evidence that Jesus was the Messiah. I will tell you this Emanuel, I've seen and read about proof that Jesus existed, walked the earth so to speak. But, as far as I know there is no way to prove he was the Son of God. I'm not sure how you would test for that anyway."

Emanuel had a deep frown on his face that concerned Clea. She wondered if he was going to pass out as his face took on a grayish pallor and beads of sweat appeared on his forehead. Emanuel was suddenly distraught that he was losing his mind for even undertaking a search for God on Satya's request. Of course, there was no proof that a God walked the earth, so why would one be doing so now? All that exist are stories passed down for generations about Gods that last appeared to man thousands of years ago.

Why would God have appeared to people during biblical times and then disappear? Why would Jesus appear during Roman times, allow himself to be killed, and then ascend to heaven without ever returning? Why start something and then walk away, leaving human beings to figure out the meanings and applications of a set of ideologies?

Emanuel needed another drink. Lucidity was becoming too painful for him, and so he grabbed another martini off a passing tray.

"Do you really think you need another one of those?" Clea asked.

"Yes, I really do."

"If it helps, I believe that God does exist," Clea stated, sensing Emanuel's discomfort. "Despite the fact that I've spent years digging in Middle Eastern deserts and never uncovered hard evidence that God exists doesn't bother me. The fact that I can even find any evidence that human beings lived so long ago reinforces my belief that there is a God. The thread of humanity through time has a God-like quality to it."

"I can also tell you that that things have not changed that much. We're still as violent as people of old. Wars have not become obsolete as I thought they might be. People still hate each other for petty reasons. Humans are wonderfully creative. We build magnificent cities with fabulous architecture and art, and then we find ways to destroy it all like on September 11. It took a few extremists to bring down those tall beautiful buildings that it took thousands to build. I suppose human nature will never really change and reach an ideal. We just have to accept that."

"That's not very optimistic."

"I know, but it's fact. Maybe humans need to both create and destroy in order to appreciate the positives in life."

Emanuel leaned down and gave Clea a kiss on her red lips. They were full and soft and comforting. She kissed him back, not at all surprised that he kissed her only minutes after meeting her.

"Let's go find Turc, okay?" Clea said. Emanuel just nodded in agreement.

Clea took Emanuel's hand and led him through a maze of rooms to an intricately carved steel door that was a copy of Rodin's "Gates of Hell." An enormous man with a body builder's physique guarded the door. He was wearing a tank top that exposed two pierced nipples. The man was quietly smoking a cigarette, seemingly unbothered by the scene if front of him.

"Good evening, Mark. How's it feeling?" Clea asked.

"Tight, baby. It's feeling real tight. What can I do for you?" Mark said exhaling smoke through his thick nose.

"I'd like to take my friend Emanuel here back to the inner sanctum. He's with Turc who I imagine is already back there."

"Yeah, he's there, but he didn't mention a friend."

"Would you mind calling through and asking?"

"Anything for you princess," Mark said unsnapping a miniature phone from his belt. He said a few words and then, after a moment, snapped the phone shut.

"Go ahead, but be careful," Mark said with a smirk on his face directed at Emanuel. With that he grabbed the handle of the heavy door and swung it open, the muscles of his arms bulging under the strain.

Clea and Emanuel walked into a fairly bright and cold room that smelled clean despite the fact that everyone in the room was smoking something. Unlike the rest of Byron's apartment, this room had no windows and seemed to have no white anywhere. The walls were dark red velvet, and the floor was stone with Persian rugs strewn about. Huge, black marble statues of mythological characters like the Phoenix and the Griffin were haphazardly placed around the room.

People were lounging on plush couches and huge armchairs big enough for three people. There was a fully stocked bar at the back of the room with a topless woman in a dog collar making drinks and delivering them throughout the room. In the background, low ambient music was playing, giving the room a peaceful, other-worldly quality.

Turc was sitting with a group of people around a glass coffee table. When he saw Emanuel, Turc gave him a lazy smile, before getting up and coming to greet him. Emanuel noticed that Turc had changed out of his suit and into black leather pants and a black silk shirt, which he'd left completely unbuttoned. He had a long necklace hanging to his belly button with a bizarre metal amulet in the shape of a sun.

"What's up, barrato? I knew you'd make your way back here eventually. Let me introduce you."

Turc pulled Emanuel over to the group where one man was holding court. It was Byron wearing a white tuxedo jacket with a shawl collar, a white shirt unbuttoned to mid-chest, and black tuxedo pants. Two women were leaning against him, stroking him casually while he intermittently pulled on his Dunhill, took a sip of his drink, or continued talking. His black hair was slicked back with a razor thin part on the left side of his forehead.

"Byron, this is my friend Emanuel. The one I was telling you about," Turc said.

"Nice to meet you." Emanuel said extending his arm to shake Byron's hand. It was the kind of half handshake that politicians use when working the rope line.

"And you," Byron said, reaching again for his martini glass. "But, I'll tell you something right now: you won't find God in this place. Here we do the Devil's work." Byron said, laughing smugly. Emanuel felt his face go flush in embarrassment and anger at Turc for having told Byron of his mission.

"Don't be mad at Turc, Emanuel. He tried not to tell me but as you'll soon find out, it's very difficult to lie to me. Anyway, I saw you on television and I knew you were representing that cop. By the way, hello Clea— come give me a kiss."

"Hello Byron," Clea said as she walked over and gave Byron a long kiss on the lips.

"Have a seat you two," Byron said after disengaging from Clea. "I want to talk more about your case."

"Why are you so interested?" Emanuel asked, slightly annoyed. He couldn't figure out Byron's angle and thought he was taking a mocking tone.

"I'm so interested, my friend, because I knew Jack Winston rather well. He made me buckets of money over the years and I'm extremely sad he's dead."

"You did business with Winston?" Emanuel asked. The hairs on the back of his neck were standing up and he suddenly felt very sober.

"I did, and I'll tell you all about it, but, before I do, you should try some of this coke. It's fantastic and you look a little weary." Emanuel was taken aback by this request, which seemed like a childish initiation ritual. However, there was no time to protest as Byron snapped his fingers and one of the women stroking him leaned over to a mirror on the coffee table and cut the lines.

Emanuel had done his share of coke during his days of "youthful indiscretions," but had put it behind him when he started to pursue more mature goals. As Emanuel looked around the dark room and stared into the vacant eyes of those sitting around the coffee table, he did not have the will to reject the drug. Emanuel leaned over the mirror on the coffee table, took the gold tube, and inhaled a long line, pausing in the middle to switch nostrils.

The burn in his nostrils felt good as did the feeling of the coke dripping down the back of his throat after he tilted his head back. Emanuel got a warm feeling in his face and a tingling sensation in his fingers and toes as the drug took instant effect. The coke cut through his alcohol buzz and made everything in the room seem a little bit clearer. He closed his eyes for a minute, relishing in the feeling and remembering briefly how much he used to enjoy "partying" like this. He had either forgotten how good cocaine could be or else the quality had improved over the years, because the lines brought him a happy lucidity.

"It feels good, doesn't it?" Turc said, slapping Emanuel on the back. He had a huge grin on his face, clearly pleased that his friend was joining in on the decadence.

"Yeah, Turc. It feels good," Emanuel said before turning his attention back to Byron. "So, tell me about Jack," Emanuel said.

"Jack was a dirty son of a bitch, and smart as hell— the dirty ones usually are. He was a real man of God, too, but that was all on a personal level. He had found a relationship with the Almighty that worked for him, but he kept quiet about that, except to the extent it drove him to succeed in business."

"For Jack, religion was just business— totally different from spirituality or closeness to God. He was the biggest capitalist I've ever met, other than myself. Jack realized early on that he could use his charisma, intelligence and religion to make obscene amounts of money."

"When did you meet him?" Emanuel asked.

"I first heard of Jack in about 1986. I was an investment banker with some rich clients including Stuart Simpson, Jack's first benefactor. Simpson was a bible thumper who needed some tax breaks so he gave Jack a huge donation. This deal was even sweeter because it was really an investment in Jack's television show and he was prepared to treat it as such, off the books of course. Simpson would get the deduction, a huge return on the money, and an initial kick back in cash. I just had to help paper the deal so Scott brought Jack to New York to meet me. I was expecting some hillbilly with the sophistication of Gomer Pyle. I figured Scott had found a sucker to use as strawman for this deal. Well, I had Jack all wrong."

"He showed up in Manhattan like a Roman emperor returning from a conquest. The way he looked, the way he dressed, the way he walked and talked—all screamed confidence. He was no redneck. He was slick and all business."

"The first night I met him, we went out with Simpson and the lawyers and Jack ran the whole show. He ordered the wine and a seafood bouquet for the table with lobster, crab legs, and the biggest oysters you could imagine. More importantly, he ran the discussion. It became clear to me that he put the deal together, not Simpson. Jack thought the plan up and then found the richest person he could to finance the deal. It was brilliant. He had everyone in the palm of his hand when he was talking about God, the American way of life, and about money. The only thing he didn't talk about was sex, but the tension was there. One of the lawyers was a pretty, young associate at one of the Wall Street firms. She couldn't take her eyes off him. Every once in a while, Jack would glance directly at her with a special smile all for her. I'm sure no one else noticed, but I did. He was a master. I never asked but I bet Jack had a private consultation with that lawyer after dinner that she never billed him for." Byron's monologue had everyone enraptured.

"Winston cheated on his wife?" Turc blurted out. Again, this type of information thrilled him. That a famous cleric was also a philanderer revealed his weakness and Turc loved that.

"Are you kidding me?" Byron responded. "Jack was the biggest deviant I've ever met— even bigger than you, Turc. As you can imagine, that deal went through beautifully. Jack's career took off, Simpson quietly made over $10 million, and I walked away with a decent payday myself. Then, much to my pleasure, Jack started contacting me directly to do more work for him. He knew a kindred spirit when he saw one."

"He started coming to New York regularly for meetings, and we started doing some horrible things. Jack needed to be discreet, and that's always been my game. No public antics like so many of these assholes pull; everything in one of my places with only my closest associates. Anything we did in public was the height of civility. We'd hardly even drink when we went out and there were never trashy women hanging around. Behind closed doors, however, it was a different story."

"What'd you do?" Turc asked, still enthralled.

"Jack felt so close to God that sometimes he felt like a prophet or the second coming. Not all the time, but sometimes. This was an incredible feeling of power and he had to find a release for it sometimes. I think running for President was just another outlet for this power surge. Running the most powerful country on earth was intoxicating for Jack."

"Here with me, he would just play sick games. Setting up exorcisms and healings of very young girls. Jack loved them young, barely old enough most of the time. We'd bring in the teenage models and Jack would try and purify them in his own special way. Much of the time he didn't want me around but I could hear the screams— theirs and his. I'm not sure what he had them do but it was painful, and he loved it. The look in their eyes after they came out of a room with him said it all. Something horrible had happened that they'd never forget it."

Everyone paused for an instant trying to imagine what Winston would have young girls do to him. It was a tantalizing thought to think of a preacher with demons of his own that needed to come out in some sadomasochistic ritual. One night he'd be on television preaching the word of God and healing the sick, and the next night he'd be tied up and beat or cut by a pretend vestal virgin.

"What were your business dealings like?" Emanuel asked.

"As I said, Jack was a savvy business man. He started making money in droves and he needed to protect it and make more. He was never satisfied with what he had. I helped finance his other ventures like the theme parks and the website. Jack got into retail as well, coming up with Jesus dinner sets and clothing lines. These were conventional moneymakers, but Jack also had some private dealings that I was not privy to. He asked me to set up several offshore accounts and foreign subsidiaries for him in order to take his business global, but I never knew what types of businesses exactly. Jack wanted a worldwide empire more powerful than the Catholic Church. He truly believed that his Church and form of Christianity would be the new order, and that he would be the first Pope."

"What did you think of that idea?" Emanuel asked.

"I thought it was good racket. Jack made people happy with his brand of morality and his belief system, and those people rewarded him with money. It's a very similar notion to the Catholic Church. So, if Jack could pull it off, great. He was making me a fortune as well, so I couldn't complain. I'll admit that every now and again, he became too messianic for my tastes. I mean, sometimes he really sounded convinced he was a prophet. I'm not very religious so it didn't bother me. But, it just sounded crazy. I think it was having all those followers that did it too him."

"What about his Presidential bid?" Emanuel kept up his examination.

"That part I thought was strange since it could've jeopardized what he'd established. Unfortunately, it cost him his life, but I didn't foresee that. I advised him not to do it when he asked me because I thought he'd give up too much of the personal freedom he loved and needed. How would he come up to New York for his usual binges when he was President?"

"So, you thought he'd win?" Emanuel pressed.

"I thought he had a good chance. He had unlimited funding to run a campaign and a built-in base that spanned almost every sector of the economy. Plus, Jack had the personality and looks that Americans want in a President. Americans want someone they enjoy looking at everyday, and Jack had it."

"He didn't listen to you though," Emanuel said.

"No, he didn't. It came back to his connection with God. Jack felt America needed a religious leader in power to combat the religious movements governing so many other parts of the world. America needed to show a different front to the world, Jack believed, in order to change its image; a new morality at home and a tougher brand of foreign policy abroad. Jack thought he could spread American Christianity around the world with F-16s and Marine units. That was the way to ensure American dominance for centuries to come, he believed. Maybe he was right. He was winning after all until your client stepped in and stopped him."

"That's right, Satya changed it all," Emanuel said almost to himself.

"Funny how Jack thought he was a prophet and apparently so does your client. They can't both be, can they?" Byron said laughing loudly and taking a drag off his cigarette.

"I suppose not," Emanuel said.

"Enough of this talk now," Byron said abruptly before Emanuel could contemplate that last thought. "Let's party."

After several more hours of gratuitous drinking and drugging, Clea asked Emanuel to see her home, and he obliged her. They took a cab to her mid-town apartment building, a block away from Carnegie Hall. All the way there, Clea snuggled up against Emanuel, nuzzling him like a cat.

When they got out of the cab, Emanuel looked up and could barely see the top of her building. The doorman opened the door and tipped his cap. They walked into the elevator and Clea hit the button for the penthouse.

When they got out, Clea took Emanuel's hand and led him past the only door on the hall to the stairwell. He followed her up the stairs to the roof of the building. The sun was just beginning to rise, creeping slowly above the horizon. Clea backed up against the railing and gave Emanuel a gentle kiss on his lips. She kept her eyes open and looked at him with an intense stare. Then, she crouched down and unzipped his fly, while Emanuel looked out over New York, sprawling in the dawn. The morning light slowly began illuminating the metropolis, inch by inch, block by block. Then, in a flash of light and pleasure, the sun exploded over the horizon with bursting rays.

11

After sleeping most of the day away in a dreamless haze, Emanuel left Clea's apartment with the usual gossamer promise to call. The experience lacked reality for Emanuel as they often did when he met a woman after a few cocktails and parted company with her before his hangover had really begun. As he walked back to his hotel Emanuel felt the pangs of guilt from another sexual encounter devoid of any emotion or attachment. "I have to stop doing that," he muttered to his shoes as he watched them march along.

The whole night at Byron's came into question in Emanuel's pickled brain. The revelations about Winston were certainly powerful and fit into Emanuel's emerging analysis of the case. If Winston was an evil man, then killing him could be viewed as a positive act. However, Emanuel knew that to argue justifiable homicide, Winston would have had to pose a threat to Satya directly. Simply acting on God's behalf for the greater good of mankind would not pass muster. Then again, how reliable were Byron's statements? Stories told in dark, smoky back rooms did not hold up in court and Byron assured Emanuel as he led him out the door that his story would change dramatically if he was called to testify. Emanuel was free to try and corroborate the stories but Byron would certainly not jeopardize his private world for Satya Grady's defense.

So many questions remained unanswered, but Emanuel didn't have much to contemplate them. He had promised Turc another night out and he didn't have much time or the energy for legal reasoning.

Back in his hotel room, Emanuel again looked onto Manhattan as the sun was slowly descending over the skyline. He couldn't help thinking that just being in New York made him believe in God. The fact that human beings had the vision, the creativity, and the gall, to build such a place lent credence to the idea that there was a higher power behind everything.

Emanuel decided to walk over to Turc's Upper West Side apartment in order to enter the street side fray. There were so many people walking up Broadway he didn't seem to move, but felt swept along in the current of humanity.

As Emanuel walked he could not help marveling at how "The Great White Way" was still thriving. Despite the merging of cable television and Internet that brought interactive entertainment to people's homes twenty-four hours a day, people still liked to go to the theater. Broadway had even expanded over the years to accommodate the new productions and the old favorites. Emanuel mused that despite electronic access to myriad forms of entertainment, witnessing a live performance still captivated people's imagination. Seeing people act on stage made it seem more real and less manufactured, Emanuel thought, knowing full well he was in for some theater that night with Turc.

Turc still lived in the same one bedroom apartment on 60th and Columbus. Ten years earlier when he first moved in, the 32nd floor apartment had a breathtaking view straight down 9th Avenue, and over the Hudson River. Now, however, because of the incredible amount of development that is a constant in New York, you could only see a thin slice of 9th Avenue peeking through the forest of high-rise apartments.

Bob, the doorman, let Emanuel in, still recognizing him and remembering his name after all those years. Emanuel took the elevator up, and sighed to himself. He was still exhausted from the night before and was not really looking forward to another night of debauchery.

As he left the elevator and walked down the hall he could hear the music from Turc's getting louder and louder. It was some angry rap with guitars and drums playing like automatic weapons.

When Turc opened the door, he had a mischievous grin on his face like he had been up to no good, which Emanuel could only assume was the case. Turc was not wearing a shirt and his hair was sticking straight up in jagged edges instead of his usual prosecutorial part on the side.

"Hey big boy," Turc said, giving Emanuel a hug. The two were the same height at six foot two, making the embrace one of equals. As they let go, two pair of blue eyes locked on a pair of brown. There was a lonely quality to Turc, Emanuel thought, although he looked so happy to have his old friend back in town.

Emanuel walked into the main room to find a porn flick playing on the huge plasma screen monitor hanging on Turc's wall and a pyramid of cocaine sitting in the middle of Turc's glass coffee table. Emanuel sighed, pulled out a cigarette from his jacket pocket and sat down. He lit up and stared at the graphic images passing in front of his tired eyes.

"I was just making the first martini of the night," Turc said, grabbing two glasses off the kitchen counter and carrying them out to the living room.

"Thanks, pal," Emanuel said, taking the glass and bringing it to his lips immediately.

"What a night. I ended up in a threesome with two of Byron's concubines," Turc said nonchalantly as if that sort of thing happened every night. "And, how was Clea?"

"She was great," Emanuel responded, trying to muster enthusiasm. He still had a touch of the "guilties." Emanuel recounted the rooftop scene knowing that Turc would enjoy the story. He then changed the subject back to Winston. "What did you think of Byron's comments about Winston?"

"I think they're probably accurate, but big deal," Turc said, desecrating the coke pyramid with a razor. "So, Winston was a capitalist. Is that really a surprise to anyone? A televangelist was in it for the money and not just for saving souls. Those suckers out in middle-America might have hurt feelings, but the rest of us cynics have seen this act before."

"What about the infidelity?"

Turc stopped mid-line and looked up at Emanuel with one eye. He then finished the line before answering.

"First of all, infidelity is no longer immoral in America even if it's rough sex with young girls, especially when it comes to politicians. It's not like he was a Catholic priest molesting pre-pubescent boys. Second of all, unless Satya caught Winston in bed with his wife, it still doesn't add up to justifiable homicide."

"But it does give Satya some credibility, I think. He starts to make sense when you look at Winston as a man with a dark side. And, who knows maybe there's more lurking beneath his bed."

"Sure, Emanuel, it shows that Winston might not have been the cleanest president we've ever had, although, if I knew this stuff about him he would have had my vote. I think it gives you something to build on and ask Satya about. If he had some insight into Winston's character, whether from God or a earthlier source perhaps you can legitimize the killing for the jury. Let me add that thank God we all have a dark side. Life would be incredibly boring without it," Turc said handing Emanuel the gold tube for a line.

There was a brief moment of silence while Emanuel did a line. When he was finished he asked angrily, "So, what are we doing tonight?"

"We're going hunting," Turc answered.

The two men ended up walking down 9th Avenue to start the night at a dark and smoky lounge in Hell's Kitchen. The Red Lantern had an urban décor of low couches and metal café tables with uncomfortable post-modern chairs. Hundreds of white candles in crystal glasses shed the only light on the diverse crowd that turned up in Hell's Kitchen. The neighborhood was famous for it's seedy under-world of gangs, drug dealers, prostitutes, and working-class ethnic families. Housing was cheap and for some reason it never evolved as other New York neighborhoods had. Several years earlier some eager entrepreneurs tried to gentrify Hell's Kitchen with some hip bars and restaurants. They had performed fairly well but the neighborhood stayed the same. That's why at a place like the Red Lantern you had a funny mix of cool struggling artists, gays, Latinos, and some older locals just wanting a quiet drink at the bar.

Turc liked the Red Lantern because early in the night he just wanted to talk and drink with his friends and not worry about women. But, then again, every once and a while the Red Lantern delivered some edgy young ladies that could take the night in an interesting di-rection. Plus, it was only a few blocks from his apartment so his buzz wouldn't get dampened by a long cab ride downtown.

They ordered more martinis from the waitress who flashed a smile of imperfect teeth that failed to detract from her bare midriff and gold belly button ring that sparkled in the candlelight. Turc gave her a long careful look as if filing her away for a later conquest.

"So, that President Taylor is one lucky son of a bitch, isn't he Emanuel?" Turc asked.

"I don't know. I don't think the election was a foregone conclu-sion. Taylor might still have beaten Winston in a fair fight."

"Come on. The guy hasn't won the war on terrorism and it's been years since September 11. The economy is still lagging and people aren't buying what he's selling anymore. On the other hand, Winston was really playing hardball with his cultural war rhetoric. He was gin-ning us up to take on the entire Muslim world."

"You really think that's what people liked about Winston?" Emanuel asked.

"I do," Turc responded. "And, maybe that's the way to go. Aren't you tired of those flag burnings in the streets of Cairo and Beirut? How are we going to change that? With force, that's how."

"That's great, Turc. We'll just take the whole place over, kill millions of them, and then terrorism will go away. I thought the terrorists hated us for that kind of culturally dominant, imperialistic behavior," Emanuel said.

"No, they hate us because we have New York, good drugs, and hot women that walk around exposing their bellies. They're just jealous, those extremist mother fuckers. Remember where the terrorists went the night before 9-11," Turc stated. "A nudie bar to drink and smoke and look at some tail before they flew into Paradise. Now if they had that growing up in Saudi maybe they wouldn't have become American hating terrorists," Turc argued tongue in cheek. "So, let's make the world safe for nudie bars."

"Brilliant argument, counselor," Emanuel said laughing. Just as Emanuel said that he looked to the front door of the Red Lantern. A young man with olive skin, thick black hair and an unkempt beard came striding in through the open French doors. His hands were around his belly like a pregnant woman feeling for the first kick and his face had a deranged look to it. The Red Lantern attracted an unusual clientele but this man was over the top. Before Emanuel could point him out to Turc the explosion came in a deafening roar and a bright flash of light. The two men were sitting in the rear of the crowded place and were blown over by the force of the explosion.

Emanuel felt himself flying backwards effortlessly like a feather caught in the wind. Then he hit something hard and everything went quiet. Emanuel felt very peaceful and could feel the smile on his face. He had no worries or concerns. He felt euphoric and happy for the first time in weeks. Then his eyes opened and Satya was standing right in front of him.

"Satya, what are you doing here?" Emanuel asked in a sleepy voice that didn't sound like his own.

"I came to save you, Emanuel."

"Did they let you out of jail?"

"In a way. I just knew you would need me so I'm here. How are you?"

"I don't know. I can't tell what happened. I feel so light and peaceful."

"That's good, Emanuel. And how is the case going?"

"I think it's going fine. I've learned some things about you and about Jack Winston. It should make for a hell of a story although I'm not sure it'll be a great defense."

"Don't worry about that, Emanuel. I just want you to make the case for me. Whether we win or lose doesn't matter."

"Who are you?" Emanuel asked.

"I'm Satya Grady, Emanuel. I'm here to protect you. I'm whomever you want me to be—an angel of mercy . . . or death."

"Am I dead, Satya?"

"No, Emanuel. You're lucky. That terrorist blew this place apart but you made it. You're alive. You are very much alive."

"That's good Satya, that's good."

When Emanuel woke up he was lying on the sidewalk on 9th Avenue being attended to by a paramedic. He heard sirens and saw the reds, blues, and whites of flashing lights everywhere. He looked around him and saw others lying on the pavement, some missing limbs and others badly burned. Still others were being zipped into body bags. It was a surreal moment, after seeing so many scenes like this on television and in pictures, to be living one.

Emanuel looked up at the paramedic and asked him how he was.

"You have a bad bump on the back of your head and a few scratches on your face. You are one lucky guy," he said.

"How about my friend?" Emanuel asked.

"Don't know about that. There were others who made it out in one piece, but not many."

"I need to find him," Emanuel said starting get up."

"I'd take it easy, buddy."

"I'm fine, really," Emanuel said getting up on wobbly knees. He started walking around the carnage looking for Turc. He couldn't believe what he saw. What had been the Red Lantern was a torn and twisted gaping hole of wood and steel. Broken glass was scattered on the pavement like jigsaw puzzle pieces, and blood and chunks of flesh gave the picture color and texture. Smoke and the wind carried the sweet smell of burning flesh through the air. Rescue workers were running to and fro attending to the wounded and shuttling victims into waiting ambulances. Emanuel staggered around looking for Turc. He had an awful feeling in his stomach, fearing the worst. How could anyone survive such a blast? How did he? Then he remembered Satya Grady. Had he been there or was that some kind of dream?

Emanuel didn't have to look much further because there was Turc lying on 9th Avenue. He had that same mischievous smile on his face and his blue eyes were open and gazing skyward. "Turc!" Emanuel yelled, but his friend did not move. At first, Emanuel was perplexed that Turc didn't answer. Then he looked down to Turc's chest and discovered that his deviant compatriot did indeed have a heart. Unfortunately, though, it was no longer beating.

12

Emanuel spent the next few days tending to his head injury and making sure Turc's body was shipped home to his family in California. Although the cat scans of his head showed no damage, Emanuel's brain certainly felt bruised. He was still in shock from the attack and wavered back and forth between grieving for his friend and contemplating his own survival. Shrapnel from the blast had ripped open Turc's torso, yet Emanuel had escaped with a bump on the head, and the two were sitting right next to each other. Despite the element of randomness associated with acts of violence, Emanuel still felt there was a greater force at work. And, of course, he had the image of Satya to reinforce that feeling.

The bombing, in and of itself, was not unusual. Al Qaeda and other terrorist groups had resorted to smaller scale, conventional attacks post 9-11. Taking a page out of the Palestinian's terrorist playbook, they had opted to scare American civilians and disrupt the economy rather than delivering a knockout blow. The result was minimal. After a while the public began to accept such attacks as they had previously accepted violent activity in the rest of society. It was one more thing to worry about after being hit by a car or caught in a gun battle between drug warlords. Despite the occasional attacks, in mostly larger urban settings life went on as usual.

Emanuel's life was far from usual anymore and he decided to re-turn to Hell's Kitchen to look for some answers. The lawyer in him hoped that some of the perpetrators of his drama might return to the scene of the crime. As he walked, he realized that any doubts he had about Satya's sanity were now assuaged since he himself had had a similar encounter with a "vision." His client, who had claimed contact with God, had appeared to Emanuel as an angel of mercy. Was the vision real or simply the delusion of a person knocked un-conscious in a bomb blast? Emanuel didn't know the answer except in the proof of his own vitality.

Emanuel had come to New York in an effort to save his client from a likely death sentence and perhaps, his client had saved him from the same. The irony for Emanuel personally was apparent, but how did this now fit into Satya's defense and his killing Jack Winston? Satya's violent action was still a violation of the law and no different than the work of the man who blew up the Red Lantern. Can we take lives just because we believe it's what God would want? The suicide bomber probably thought he was acting on God's orders, so why was Satya any different? Emanuel didn't really believe Muslim terrorists had the mandate of God on their side, but if he believed Satya, then his killing was acceptable. Killing Winston, while an act of violence, was still permissible if Satya truly talked to God. If Satya is a prophet or angel, Emanuel rationalized, then Winston's death was justified; if not, then he was nothing more than a murderer.

Emanuel's walk had brought him back in front of the Red Lantern. The area was cordoned off with yellow tape and FBI inves-tigators were sifting through the rubble looking for clues that might track where the bomber came from and built his weapon. No group had taken responsibility for the bombing, and the man was simply identified as Khalid Mohammed, a twenty-year-old who had been liv-ing in Jersey City. He had overstayed his visa and had worked as a day laborer and busboy to support himself. No one claimed to know him very well and no one had reason to suspect he was a member of a ter-rorist cell. In theory, it was an act no different than the disgruntled postal worker who mows down weekend diners at a McDonald's or the man who opens fire in the day trading office where he lost money in the market. Mohammed was angry and he blew up a café in Hell's Kitchen.

As Emanuel surveyed the wreckage, still in disbelief that he had survived, he noticed that the Red Lantern was on the block between 53rd and 52nd Streets where Satya claimed he was shot pursuing a criminal. Emanuel stopped and looked across the street to see if the alley was there that Satya mentioned and sure enough, it was there stuck between a bodega and a dive bar. He looked quickly up 9th Avenue and seeing a break in the traffic, sprinted across the street.

While the hairs on the back of his neck stood on end, Emanuel stood before the small break in the buildings and thought "Did God come into this alley?" Slowly, Emanuel walked into the alley, which was littered with newspapers, old lottery tickets, and cigarette butts. After twenty paces, the alley came to an end. There was a large door flush against the right side of the alley and the back wall, made out of metal corroded with age. The color had changed a strange hue of green, and the hinges and bolts on the door were so rusty that there seemed no possible way it could open. The cracks between the door and its metal frame where also fused together.

Emanuel turned to walk out and then his eye caught a brown colored spot on the opposite wall. He jumped to it and crouched down for a closer look. He couldn't be sure, but Emanuel had been to enough crime scenes to know what dried blood looked like. He ran his fingers over the spot and gave himself a chill. Emanuel turned and fell back against the wall, sitting in the filth on the ground.

He lit a cigarette and sat back and waited. He expected Satya to appear again and explain the unexplainable. Or he expected God to appear and tell him what the master plan was; what was happening in the world and how Emanuel fit into it. As he sat there, Emanuel realized he needed some changes in his life. Somehow his solitary lifestyle no longer seemed appealing in the face of imminent death.

He had survived a bomb blast, but death is inevitable. Was this the way he wanted to spend the rest of his days? He thought back on the countless lonely meals at the Old Ebbitt and the occasional superficial sexual encounters—Faye back in Washington and Clea here in New York. Not only were these moments self-destructive but they were also incredibly selfish. He was sure these women and others were not as detached as he was, simply hoping to feign intimacy for a night as a crack addict just needs a fix to get through another day. Did he want to go through life using other people to satisfy his occasional needs for an emotional high?

Emanuel sat in the alley a while longer just thinking and waiting. No images of God came to him, but rather the smell of trash and the occasional gust of wind that snuck into the alley. Finally, he pulled himself up and headed back to his hotel.

Emanuel had been walking with his head down, watching his feet stomp along the pavement. Suddenly, he lifted his head up and saw that he was standing right in front of a little church called St. Stephen's. Emanuel had never gone into a church before except to attend a wedding or a funeral, but as he stood before the small but ornate Catholic church he decided to go inside.

As he walked in, he was filled with embarrassment and awkwardness for participating even marginally in Catholicism. There was the image of Christ, hanging on the Cross in the front of the church, and stained-glass windows showing Jesus healing the lepers, turning the loaves into fishes, and water into wine. The church had a quiet feeling to it due to the absence of people inside, and it had a musty smell. Emanuel started walking up the aisle, running his hands over the wooden pews as he strolled forward.

As he stared up at the image of Christ, he mulled over the idea that Christ supposedly died for the sins of humanity. To what end? Emanuel wondered, since to sin was, in fact, to be human. Perhaps, it was just about forgiveness and the thought of eternal peace in the afterlife. Maybe that's why people like the idea of Jesus so much.

"Can I help you?"

A priest who had come out of nowhere startled Emanuel.

"I'm sorry Father," Emanuel said. "I hope you don't mind me being here . . . I don't know why I'm here."

"Don't apologize, my son, this church is here for you. Do you need to pray or would you like to take confession?"

"Actually, Father, I'm not really Catholic. I mean, my mother was, but I never practiced it. I've never really prayed or taken confession, so I don't know."

"Don't worry about those things. If today is the day you need God, then start today."

"Could we, maybe chat for a minute?"

"Of course, sit down here." The priest motioned to the front pew and Emanuel sat down.

"I'm Father Frank O'Brien," the priest said extending his hand.

"Emanuel Adams." They shook hands and Emanuel noted how soft and delicate Father O'Brien's hand was.

"You're the lawyer defending Satya Grady. A troubling case, no doubt."

"It is Father. Every case comes down to one fact that needs resolution. In this case, it's when, if ever, does God sanction killing another person?"

"The Catholic Church sanctifies life. 'Thou shalt not kill,' Emanuel."

"That's right Father, but, with all due respect, religion has led to more death and destruction than any other force in history. Killing in the name of God dates back to the first religions and continues today."

"Is that what your client said, that he killed Winston in the name of the Lord?"

"More or less. And I can tell you he isn't insane. So, can I try and justify such a claim?"

"Do you want to? Do you want to prove that Satya talked to God and out of all the possible things God could have said he chose to order an assassination?"

"Not particularly, Father. I was raised without organized religion and haven't given God much thought until recently. I suppose I'd hope that God would stop mankind from violence and not the opposite. But that doesn't seem to be the case, does it?"

"You assume God plays an active role in how we humans treat each other. I think God has given us all the opportunity to live a righteous life full of peace and love, but the decisions to follow that path are ultimately our own. Remember, God sacrificed his only son to a violent death to show us sin and cruelty. We were supposed to learn a lesson there."

"But again, Father, what lesson? The Kings of the Middle Ages set out conquer the world in the name of Christianity at the point of a sword. They went into the Middle East and killed millions who didn't believe. Then later, the Muslims set out to do the same in the name of Allah and accomplished the same bloodshed. Now today it looks like we're about to go at it again. So, what was the lesson?"

"The lesson is there are principals by which we should all live our lives. For Christians, those principals come from the teachings of Christ— doing unto others as you would have them to unto you. Just because some in history have distorted this and other messages of peace, doesn't mean that God sanctioned their actions. You need to decide, Emanuel, what God means to you, and then act accordingly."

"Why are you personalizing this Father, we're talking about my defense."

"Are we? If Satya Grady's actions make sense to you in your understanding of God and perhaps religion, then you can make the argument. And, you might even convince a jury that God had reasons for this act. If not, you'll simply be trying to prove something that is unprovable and that you, yourself, don't believe. I can't see you winning over a jury under those circumstances."

"How do I come to that conclusion, Father?"

"Why not try praying. Talking to God is a two-way street, Emanuel. If you start first, He may answer."

"Thank you, Father. I'll give it a try."

13

After having drinks with David, Jude rushed over to her office clutching the file to her chest and looking over her shoulder. Suddenly she had the feeling that everyone knew what she had and wanted to stop her from reporting it. Since it was a Saturday evening there was only a skeleton crew working the bureau. Jude entered her office, closed the door, and immediately called her producer, Paul Avanti. Paul was an old-school newsman who would know exactly how to handle the story, and Jude needed his help.

"Avanti," Paul said answering his phone brusquely.

"Paul, I've got a big one here," Jude said.

"Jude, is that you? What have you got?"

"You know my source inside the White House?"

"Sure, the lovesick puppy."

"Right. I guess I must be wonderful in bed, because he just gave me a file on Reverend Winston that has evidence that Winston was embezzling Church funds, and stashing the money in offshore bank accounts. The kicker is that the money was allegedly for a paramilitary unit that Winston was going to use to spread his gospel by force worldwide, like a modern-day crusade."

"Jesus Christ, Jude, that *is* big. You better have some hard facts before I'll let you go on the air with it."

"Well Paul, I've got a man's name here in front of me who is one of Winston's financial advisers. According to my boy, the guy is willing to tell all. I also have numbers and locations of bank accounts."

"That's a damn good start. I want you to get a hold of the guy and try and book him for tomorrow morning. We'll let him spill the beans to the world. I assume the White House wants nothing to do with this story."

"That's right, Paul. I can't so much as mention Pennsylvania Avenue in this story, and David was dead serious."

"Those dirty bastards. Let's meet tomorrow morning at five and see where you are. Hopefully, we can get you and this guy together before the 11 a.m. show."

"You got it, Paul."

At 11 o'clock the next morning, Jude was sitting in CNN's Washington studio with Matthew Johannsen. As Peter predicted, Johannsen was responsive when Jude called him the night before. He claimed that Winston's death was a relief to him because of the planned Crusade. Johannsen stated that, at first, he willingly participated in Winston's scheme, but ultimately, he realized how dangerous it was. When he wanted to extricate himself from the situation, Winston threatened him with bodily harm and he stayed on the job out of fear. Johannsen was now perfectly willing to tell Jude everything he knew on camera. He agreed to fly up to D.C. in the morning and appear on CNN's Sunday morning talk show.

Jude was exhausted, but wired at the same time. She had been up all night, talking to Johannsen, pouring over the records in her possession, and reading everything she could on Winston's Church. Jude was well aware that this was the biggest story of her career. There was no indication that any other journalist was close to this story, and the evidence seemed to be clear. She wanted the interview to go perfectly.

The format was going to be a special report that would preempt CNN's normal Sunday morning political talk show. Jude would be in total control.

"Good morning, this is Jude Michaels with a special report on the life and death of the Reverend Jack Winston. Through our comprehensive coverage of this story, CNN has learned that Winston was involved in some allegedly illicit activities that may shed some light on his assassination."

"According to our source, Winston was embezzling funds out of his Church's coffers in order to finance a modern-day Crusade to spread his word around the globe. In addition, Winston was planning on using the power of the U.S government and military to aid him in this mission if he achieved his goal of winning this year's presidential election."

"With me here in the studio this morning is one of Winston's top financial advisors, Matthew Johannsen. Good morning, Mr. Johannsen."

"Good morning, Jude."

"Mr. Johannsen, when did you first start working at Winston's Church of the Divine Light?"

"In 1994, I started as a mid-level financial planner in the chief financial officer's office. I helped map out the Church's financial strategy, what our investments would be in the long and short term."

"Were you dealing with a lot of money at the time?"

"Back in '94 the Church was probably grossing $50 million a year. Then, of course, with advances in technology we really started raking it in. We were everywhere."

"What is your position now?"

"At present, I'm second in command after the CFO."

"So, you are intimately involved with the day-to-day operations of the Church?"

"That's correct."

"Can you tell me, then, about Winston's secret financial activities and this paramilitary organization?"

Johannsen took a deep breath and a sip of his coffee before beginning. "Winston first mentioned his desire to become President during the Clinton impeachment hearings in 1998. He was disgusted by the whole mess and felt that it brought dishonor to the United States, which Winston believed is a country founded upon the Bible. He didn't tell anybody except his closest advisors about his aspirations. I was one of those few. Winston mapped out a strategy and a timetable for making a run at the White House, and the first thing he decided to do was set up a political slush fund. We began cooking the books, skimming off money, and funneling it offshore to the Caymans and Channel Islands. The Church was taking in a tremendous amount of cash so it wasn't difficult. We spent so much money on charitable activities that no one, including the Internal Revenue Service, saw any red flags. Certainly, our members were happy with how their donations were spent."

"Several years later, Winston brought up the notion of forming an 'Army of the Lord,' as he called it. He suggested that due to globalization, focusing only on America might be shortsighted. He felt that if we were going to fight battles on many fronts just like in the original Crusades, foot soldiers would be necessary. Winston figured that if he became President, he could secretly control the mercenary forces without anyone realizing, sort of like Reagan and the Contras. If he didn't become President he argued that the force would help us bring more sheep into the flock. Really though, he never doubted that one day he would become President of the United States."

"So, what steps did you take to organize this paramilitary group?" Jude asked.

"We set up shell corporations in several small countries without the regulatory structure we're used to here at home. Then we used the companies to hire personnel and purchase weapons. Winston was close with several ex-military figures who believed in his vision. They agreed to serve as military advisers and to help in recruitment. We started with Americans and then moved over to foreign mercenaries. The force was small at first, but then it grew consistently over the years. Today, we have base camps set up in fifteen locations worldwide with men who train either on a full time or part time basis. They're there just waiting for the call."

"A call that now will never come."

"Let's hope not."

"Mr. Johannsen, why are you telling us this today?"

"Jude, it's quite simple. Reverend Winston was not the man that America thought he was. I admit that, at first, he was a deeply religious man, but then something happened. He changed. He began thinking that he was a messenger of God— like Moses or even Jesus Christ. He felt so strongly about his vision of religion that he wanted to attain as much power as he could to spread that vision. It became dangerous. He was a power-hungry dictator who would stop at nothing, even a holy war, to achieve his ends. I know it's wrong to say, Jude, but America is better off without Winston in the picture."

"And what are your plans now?"

"Honestly, Jude, I'm afraid for my life. By exposing Winston for what he really was, I'm sure I've signed my own death warrant. Winston still has many supporters who believe in him and will try and continue his dream. The word 'martyr' is being used pretty widely in reference to Winston, and that kind of adoration can drive people to do anything."

"Mr. Johannsen, thank you for bravely coming on the air today to shed light on Reverend Winston. Good luck to you."

"Thanks Jude."

Up in New York, Emanuel turned off his television set. Emanuel was stunned over what he had just heard. In an instant, he flashed back to his first interview with Satya and what he had said about his encounter with God. Immediately, Emanuel started frantically searching through his papers. Satya had spoken of similar qualities possessed by Winston. God had told him it would be so. Emanuel was manic, ripping through the mounds of notes and yellow stickies. Finally, he found the legal pad he had used during his first interview with Satya. There were the words he had written down: "Dark, depraved, leader of an army, power over people and nations." Maybe it was true, Emanuel thought. Maybe Satya had talked to God.

Emanuel knew it was time to go home.

PART III

"AND THE LORD PASSED BEFORE HIM, AND PROCLAIMED: 'THE LORD, THE LORD GOD, MERCIFUL AND GRACIOUS, LONG SUFFERING, AND ABUNDANT IN GOODNESS AND TRUTH; KEEPING MERCY UNTO THE THOUSANDTH GENERATION, FORGIVING INIQUITY AND TRANSGRESSION AND SIN; AND THAT WILL BY NO MEANS CLEAR THE GUILTY; VISITING INIQUITY OF THE FATHERS UPON THE CHILDREN, AND UPON THE CHILDREN'S CHILDREN, UNTO THE THIRD AND UNTO THE FOURTH GENERATION."

EXODUS XXXIV, 6-7.

14

As the cab sped out to Queens and LaGuardia on a fairly slow Sunday afternoon by New York standards, Emanuel felt good about things. First of all, he always found it liberating to leave Manhattan. Whether it was through a tunnel or over a bridge there was always a feeling of survival and escape that came with seeing the New York skyline in his rear-view mirror. The sky seemed bigger, the sun shined brighter, and the air was cleaner off of that island. Freedom.

Mainly, however, he felt euphoric that he had a defense for Satya. He knew it was tenuous and, if he was honest to himself, probably a loser, but most of his cases started out that way. The fact was he believed Satya was sane despite his pronouncements about divine communication. Emanuel's vision of Satya after the suicide bombing helped him to gradually accept that there is another layer of spirituality in life, one that gives direction and even protects you from harm. Satya's claim, while impossible to prove, was supported by two provable facts: Satya lived a righteous life as a police officer, serving his community above and beyond the call of duty, and Jack Winston was an evil man intent on world domination. If Emanuel could convince the jury of those facts then perhaps they would believe Satya's act was justified and acquit him.

The cab pulled up to the departure gate at LaGuardia and Emanuel jumped out hoping to catch the four o'clock shuttle. He was ready to fly home and get to work.

As soon as Johannsen finished his public confession, President Taylor went into action. He started with a call to the Justice Department to dispatch the FBI to arrest Johannsen. He also instructed them to obtain subpoenas to search the Church of the Divine Light's headquarters and seize all financial records and any other potential incriminating evidence. He told Justice to bring as many criminal indictments against as many people as possible associated with the alleged conspiracy.

Then Taylor called the Internal Revenue Service and the Securities and Exchange Commission and ordered them to assemble auditing teams to review Church records. He ordered them to use all legal means possible to bring civil suits against the Church and all members remotely responsible for raising funds and then misappropriating these funds for the alleged subversive activities.

Finally, Taylor placed a call to the Pentagon and convened a meeting of the Joint Chiefs of Staff. He also called the Central Intelligence Agency, his National Security Adviser, and the State Department. Taylor told all of them that he planned on using the full might of the United States military to seek out the paramilitary groups assembled by Winston.

Taylor prepared to go on television that evening to tell the American people that he took the allegations against Winston very seriously and that he was planning on using his executive powers to investigate the matter to the fullest extent possible.

As he did the day after Winston was killed, Taylor sat at his desk in the Oval Office in front of a camera. He had been preparing his speech since he knew the story was going to break. The whole world would be watching.

"My fellow Americans, it saddens me to appear before you tonight under these circumstances," Taylor began his address. "As many of you may know by now, allegations were made today to both the media and government officials, that Reverend Jackson Winston was building a subversive force to spread a new religion throughout the United States and the world. That religion was not the word of Jesus Christ as we Americans know it, but rather the vision of Reverend Winston."

"While all the facts are not clear at the present time, I feel it is my duty to investigate this matter fully and completely. Two of the cornerstones of our democracy as set out in the First Amendment to our Constitution are the separation of church and state and the free exercise of religion. If the allegations are true, Winston was set on violating both of those cherished ideals."

"I want you to know that I too believed Reverend Winston was simply running on a conservative platform based on a general sense of morality, a morality that Winston believed was needed in our country. I think we all agree that more moral and spiritual influences in our society are positive goals. I did not think or know, however, that Winston, as a purported man of the cloth, had a grander and more sinister agenda."

Emanuel was sitting on the couch in his apartment watching the speech. He was certain he detected a gleam in Taylor's eyes as he talked about Winston's "grander and more sinister agenda." Taylor could not have scripted this outcome better, Emanuel thought. For the first time, the extreme candidate was not just stealing votes from the mainstream candidates, but he was out-polling him, too. No Republican or Democrat had ever dealt with that before, and up until Winston's death, Taylor was not doing a very good job of dealing with it. Then Satya solved his problem. Even if these allegations against Winston were never proved, Emanuel thought, Taylors' chances of winning the election were improved in a way no campaign tactics would accomplish.

"The use of religion as a means to suppress and coerce other people," Taylor continued, "was one of the main reasons our Founding Fathers saw fit to expressly forbid in our Constitution the commingling of government and Church. Our forefathers left their homelands because they were not allowed freely to practice their own religions in nations where kings claimed to be descendants of God. That environment led the creation of the most free, open, and democratic society the world has ever known."

"If these allegations are true, Winston wanted to return to the days when the ruler of the land was once again a self-proclaimed proxy for the Lord. As your President, I vow that this will not occur on my watch. Since Winston's dead and no longer a candidate for President, he can no longer pursue this course of action. However, I fear that the infrastructure he created while he was still alive may still exist and may pose a threat to our national security. Therefore, today I mobilized our armed forces and our civil defense units in the FBI and other agencies to seek the truth in this matter, and, if it is true, deal with it quickly and efficiently."

Emanuel felt a chill as he heard those words. He knew Taylor was not afraid to use military force if he deemed it necessary. As a military man, he viewed loss of life as a necessary contingency if other peaceful means of handling a crisis were unsuccessful. Emanuel had a dawning sense that force would definitely be used in this case.

"I will not stop until I feel confident that Winston's alleged army either does not exist or is stopped whether here at home or abroad. I say this to ensure the safety of our democracy. Rest assured that the freedoms we have fought for countless of times throughout our history will be protected."

"Thank you and good night."

Brilliant, Emanuel thought. Taylor will now save America from the forces of evil and protect our democracy.

After his speech, Taylor once again convened in his private study with Paul Tobias. He poured himself a much-needed single malt scotch and sat down in his leather chair.

"How'd it go, Paul?"

"Excellent, Mr. President. Everything is going as planned."

"Paul, I want a poll conducted tomorrow to see where the people stand on this issue. I have a feeling it's not going to be all smooth sailing."

"Yes, sir."

"Also, I want all the teams from the IRS, SEC, and Justice to be small, crack units, headed by our people. We can't afford to have some do-gooder, Bible-thumper trying to exonerate Winston."

"Yes, sir."

"Paul, have we located any paramilitary groups that we can claim are associated with Winston, yet?"

"Yes, Mr. President. There are about six such groups in Latin America that we know about. They're all fringe groups not really associated with any major liberation movements. A couple might even just be bandits in the drug trade. None are very well armed so it won't be difficult to terminate them. We will have to deal with the governments of the countries where they're holed up. They probably won't be thrilled by a U.S. military operation on their soil, but I'm sure we'll find away to sweeten the pill. I have men on the ground already negotiating such contingencies."

"Good."

"We also have a few groups targeted here at home. They're right wing extremist groups with strong religious ties. It may be a little trickier since they could disavow affiliation with Winston. We can set up some moles within the organizations to tell the press what we want, or alternatively, just create assets who can claim they once were part of the groups. We do have to be careful to avoid a Waco scenario, however."

"That won't be a problem, Paul. I'm not going to negotiate. I'm just going to send in the troops with express instructions to destroy."

"And if there are survivors who claim no knowledge of Winston's plan?"

"Well, of course they will. The guilty always deny any wrongdoing. Don't they Paul?"

"Yes, sir."

15

Taylor's remarks to the American people that Sunday night caused an instant rift throughout the country. There were those who stood by Winston and his Church. They disbelieved Johannsen and automatically suspected a government conspiracy at work. Winston's supporters were suspicious of the revelations and began to mobilize. Messages were posted on the Internet rallying the faithful for marches and letter writing campaigns. They wanted to reveal the truth that they believed had to be on Winston and God's side. They mistrusted Taylor and feared that he was using the government to suppress the Word of God.

On the other side of the equation, the people who had always doubted and feared Winston's message felt vindicated. A large segment of the population did not feel comfortable with a religious leader entering politics, especially at the presidential level. Like Winston's supporters, they too rallied, calling for a renewed stand for religious freedom. The accusations against Winston and Taylor's words proved to this group that the imposition of religion into politics smacked of the oppression of religious minorities. Winston's near rise to power became a motivating tool for civil libertarians throughout the country.

All the groups decided to descend on Washington to have their voice heard. It was a trend that had developed over the last few decades in American life. Protest, non-violent and sometimes violent, was stronger than it had been since the civil rights movement in the 1960s. Americans seemed angry with their government and they weren't sure what to do about it. In 1999, there had been violent protests in Seattle and Washington over world trade and non-governmental organizations like the World Bank. The Seattle riots were extremely destructive as protestors broke store windows and clashed with police. The D.C. and Capitol police handled the Washington protest more adroitly, but the feeling of anger was still there.

People who didn't feel strongly about these issues sat back and argued that if these people were so angry they should just use the democratic process and the power of votes to bring change in the government. Then came the presidential election of 2000 when the muddled voting process in Florida decided the election, giving the White House to the candidate with less overall popular votes. Now, all of a sudden, the whole political process was brought into question. People questioned how America could be a true democracy if the candidate with a majority of the popular vote didn't win. "We tried to bring change," people yelled, "and it didn't work."

The word "disenfranchisement" was used constantly from all corners of the country and all walks of life from African-Americans to elderly Jewish Americans. "If the Supreme Court needs to step in and decide an election, is our democracy really working?" people asked. Some people felt that five justices decided a presidential election, and that made many Americans angry.

The first outlet for this anger came on inauguration day 2001 when thousands gathered in Washington to protest the election. The throng convened early in Dupont Circle to mobilize for their march to the Capitol. They were wearing the army fatigues and black ski hats that had become the trademark garb of the protest movement. They held placards stating, "Hail to the Thief," and chanted "hey, hey, ho, ho, he must go!" The protestors clashed with police clad in riot gear. It wasn't the most violent meeting of protestors and police, but it still provided the desired contrast with the marching bands and pom-pom girls of the inauguration parade. The entire day was dark and rainy, as was the mood of the country. The first election of the new millennium was a tainted, tawdry affair.

From that point on, it was easy for the protest movement to find a rallying cry to descend on Washington. It didn't really matter what the issue was because the protest was what was important. If the voting process was marred, and corporations were buying politicians and access to Capitol Hill, then the people would simply unite, hold hands, and scream. The right to free speech, many Americans now believed, was the last true vestige of democracy.

The protest over Winston and his death, was a big one, however, since it covered all possible areas. The political process was in doubt because death had taken someone out of the race, and people were ready to believe that perhaps Taylor had something to do with it. "Forget about manipulating vote counts," people screamed, "now they're just taking out candidates prior to the election!" And now, even after Winston's death, Taylor was using his executive powers to ensure Winston's memory was sullied and there was nothing the people could do.

On the policy side, people were angry about either Winston's desire to push the country in a moral direction or Taylor's perceived desire to stop it. It was time, Winston supporters yelled, for America to become less concerned about profitability and more concerned about humanitarian concerns. "The pursuit of wealth has gone too far and we've lost sight of our soul," more screamed. Wasn't it time for religion, the clergy, and community service to take charge of American life? "Winston was taking the country in the right direction, and Taylor stopped him!"

America's national identity now seemed up for debate. What kind of country did we want to be? How did we want to act? Did we still need to be assassinating our leaders in the twenty-first century? Should we pursue Winston's agenda without him or be glad we veered off that path? The people were seething and needed to vent. And the man who really brought on this national debate was now sitting alone in a D.C. jail cell.

The day after his return from New York and Taylor's speech, Emanuel went to the D.C. jail to meet with Satya. As if the nature of the visit was not depressing enough, the weather added to Emanuel's unpleasant task. Black clouds had been coming in all morning like angry soldiers ready to lay siege to the Nation's Capitol. Ultimately, they opened up in a torrential downpour of cold spring rain as Emanuel drove over to the jail.

D.C. jail is located in Northeast Washington, next to Robert F. Kennedy stadium and D.C. General Hospital. All three sit along the Anacostia River, a murky body of water. Northeast is a far cry from clean and beautiful Northwest, which is filled with monuments to democracy and art-stocked museums. Rather, Northeast resembles many American inner-cities where economic opportunities are scarce and violent crime is a way of life. Most of Emanuel's clients came from Northeast or Southeast, so he spent much of his time investigating in the areas. There were nice parts lined with brownstones and old, small houses, but other parts were made up of tenements, housing projects, and burnt-out and boarded-up buildings. Somehow, economic prosperity never makes it to inner-city America. Sure, lots of people got out and find prosperity elsewhere, but still, far too many end up victims of crime, or in places like the D.C. jail.

Emanuel parked his car and started the long walk up to the building. He couldn't find his umbrella and had only an overcoat and an old Redskin's cap. His head was bent down and he watched his feet splash through puddles on the pavement as he traced the familiar route up a small hill, through a wrought iron gate to the entrance of the jail.

As he walked, he noted the television crews parked out front with their satellite trucks. There was nothing for them to see or do, but they were staked out nonetheless. Emanuel was relieved no one recognized him as he made his way in.

The guard buzzed him in and right away Emanuel was hit by the sour smell of the institution. It was even more putrid than the smell of the New York Public Defender's waiting room, a combination of sweat, horrible food, human excrement, and fear. It was the tangible smell of fear that set the jail apart. It was a similar smell to a hospital, except in the jail, there was no attempt made to preserve the human dignity of the inmates.

Emanuel presented his D.C. Bar card to the guard and then filled out the requisite paperwork. He had a short wait before another guard came to escort him upstairs. He was buzzed through another door that slammed shut behind him, and then taken to an elevator. The elevator ride up always gave Emanuel the creeps because it seemed like he was entering the innards of a horrible monster from which there may be no escape. Outside the elevator Emanuel walked down to the visiting rooms where another guard sat in a bulletproof booth. Emanuel handed him a slip of paper and the guard called through for the prisoner.

Emanuel sat in one of the little visiting rooms overcome by the smell and the heat of the place. There was no ventilation and the institutional smell just sat in the air permeating his clothes, hair, and skin. The longer Emanuel waited the more anxious he became. He yearned for a cigarette, and contemplated lighting one up despite the consequences.

Finally, a buzzer from the door leading to the cells sounded and Satya Grady was escorted into the visiting room. He was wearing the prison issue orange jumpsuit, and both his hands and feet were in shackles. Satya's face was ashen and gaunt from the lack of sunlight, sleep, and food. No new prisoner can stomach a meal or sleep at night. It is hard to sleep when countless prisoners are yelling obscenities at you all night.

Satya's eyes had already taken on that thousand-mile stare that soldiers get after months in the field. He made sure not to look anyone in the eye because that can get you killed in jail, and he pretended not to see what was happening around him. The guard led him to Emanuel's room and left, locking the door behind him.

When Satya sat down across the table from Emanuel his face eased up a bit and the wrinkles on his furrowed brow slowly disappeared.

"How are you, Satya?" Emanuel asked.

"It's not the Plaza, but it's better than some of our jails in New York," Satya replied.

"They gave me my own cell, and they keep me away from the other prisoners most of the time which is good. It doesn't stop them from screaming at me all night, but at least I feel a little safer."

"How are the guards treating you?"

"They've been fairly civil for the most part. I think some of them respect the fact that I'm a cop, even if they think I'm a murderer . . . I suppose there's no chance of getting out of here?"

"No, I'm sorry."

"So, what's my defense going to be?"

"I think you know the answer to that question."

"What made you change your mind?"

"Many reasons. Your stellar record as a police officer and family man, my conversation with Jesus Cruz, Winston's nefarious activities, but mostly a vision I had."

"Really. What kind of vision?"

"It was a vision of you, Satya. Did you happen to hear news of a suicide bombing in New York a about a week ago?"

"I did. It was in a bar in Hell's Kitchen."

"That's right. I was there, Satya, with a friend of mine. When the bomb exploded I was knocked unconscious in the blast and that's when I had a vision of you." Emanuel looked for some recognition from Satya, but he just sat there with an unimpassioned look on his face.

"What did I say?"

"You said you were whom I needed you to be— an angel of mercy or an angel of death."

"And, what do you think about that?"

"I'm not sure. I can't tell if it was just a dream, a hallucination, or something more real. What I do know is that I survived the blast. My friend and many others did not."

"I'm sorry to hear that, Emanuel."

"Thank you. I also know that the experience gave me faith in you, and made me think about the way I'm living my life."

"That's good, Emanuel. A man should always take stock of his life and determine how far he's strayed from the path of righteousness. It's the only way to come back to it."

"How far have you strayed, Satya?"

"I've never been closer, Emanuel. I've never felt more whole or justified in my entire life."

"I'm glad, but you have to know something right now." Emanuel paused and looked Satya over. "Our chances of winning aren't very good. I have to convince a jury not only that God exists, but also that he told you to kill Winston, and that that's reason enough to set you free. I hope you understand how difficult that is going to be."

"I do realize, Emanuel, but faith is difficult. Nobody alive today actually saw or spoke to Jesus, but most of us believe in him and what he stood for. I think the jury, whoever they will be, will have faith in me and my story."

"I hope so, Satya. I really do."

Emanuel pulled out a retainer agreement from his briefcase, which in D.C. all lawyers must sign with their clients. Satya signed the agreement.

"You left out the space for your fee," Satya said.

"I didn't think you'd want to talk about that now. We can work it out later."

"I'd rather do it now. How much is this going to cost me?"

"How much you got?" Emanuel asked with a smile. "I mean if I bill you by the hour it's going to be a hefty fee. I want to be fair to you."

"I've already spoken to my wife. She's going to send you a check for $20,000 for starters. We can take it from there."

"That's fine, Satya."

The two men shook hands and looked at each other for a moment.

"There's one more thing you should know, before we go forward," Emanuel said finally. "I'm almost certain, the government will seek the death penalty on this one."

What little color remained in Satya's face drained away.

When Emanuel walked outside the D.C. jail, a mob of reporters encircled him like the dirty birds circling above the Anacostia River. Somebody had recognized Emanuel on the way in and the call went out. It didn't take long for more satellite trucks packed with hungry journalists to arrive on the scene. The hungriest of them all, Jude Michaels, was in the throng with her microphone cocked like a pistol.

Since Emanuel was carrying a signed copy of a retainer agreement in his briefcase, he figured it was appropriate to talk to the media. He was not that thrilled that it would be an impromptu press conference on a Monday morning, but he had no choice. He gathered his strength and tried to calm the surging press corps.

"Ladies and gentleman," Emanuel yelled above the cacophony of questions the reporters were hurling at him. "If you'd settle down for one minute I promise I will make a statement and take a few questions." The reporters responded to Emanuel's plea and stopped asking questions. They were packed with nervous energy however, and it was painful for them to stay quiet for too long.

"As you obviously already know," Emanuel began, "my name is Emanuel Adams and I'm a criminal defense attorney here in Washington. A few minutes ago, I met with Officer Satya Grady who retained me as his counsel. Effective immediately, I will begin preparing his defense."

"Does that mean he's pleading innocent?" Jude asked. She was not going to let some other reporter get in the first question. Emanuel paused and stared at Jude for a moment before answering. He forgot how what a nice smile she had.

"That's correct. At the present time Officer Grady plans to plead not guilty to all of the alleged charges," he finally answered.

"On what basis, counselor?" Jude asked.

"At this time, I'd rather not discuss the basis for our defense. It's still too early in the game."

"How's Officer Grady holding up?" another reporter asked.

"He's obviously finding his stay in D.C. jail draining, but his spirits are high, and he believes he will be exonerated in this matter."

"What did you and Officer Grady just discuss?" another reporter asked.

"I briefed him on my investigations into the case and some strategy, which I won't discuss at the moment. That's all I have to say at this time," Emanuel concluded and stormed towards his car. The mob of reporters did not give up and followed him all the way into his car peppering him with question after question. It was dizzying for Emanuel and he suddenly felt trapped. He couldn't get away fast enough and almost had to run over a few reporters in order to leave. Once he drove away, some rushed back to their vans in order to follow him as if he might lead them to more answers. Suddenly the reality of how big and taxing the trial would be hit Emanuel and he was not sure he was up to the task.

Emanuel drove back to his office looking in his rear-view mirror the entire way. He had gone directly to the jail that morning and it was now time to get down to his legal research and get into the proper mindset for the case.

The elevator opened up into the foyer of his office and Emanuel shook off the rain like a wet puppy. Paula jumped up from her desk and ran over to give him a hug. Emanuel did not call her the whole time he was in New York, nor did he tell her he was coming into the office that morning.

"Emanuel, I'm so glad you're back," Paula said, inspecting him in a motherly way. "I was so worried about you. You could have called." Paula's tone instantly changed to one of annoyance.

"I'm sorry, Paula. I was just so busy and preoccupied up in New York I didn't have a chance." He omitted the bombing incident so as not to worry Paula.

"So, what's happening with this bloody case? The phone's been ringing off the hook with reporters looking for some answers."

"I'm sure. I was just over at the jail, talking to Satya and then I held a mini press conference. Hopefully they'll leave us alone for a while."

"Please tell me we're going insanity on this."

"Sorry, Paula. God told him to do it." Paula let out a groan. "Do you have the numbers of those religious scholars? We need them now."

"I have them," Paula replied, defeated.

Emanuel walked into his office feeling grateful for the familiar surroundings. It was like his home, since he spent more time there than anywhere else. For that reason, he had invested time and money in making the office a sanctuary. For starters, he bought a massive, antique desk made of sturdy mahogany. He had always thought a lawyer should have an imposing desk so clients feel safe and adversaries intimidated.

The desk was usually cluttered with papers, court documents, and files. Emanuel was organized in his disorganization. He knew where everything was even if it took him awhile to find a specific paper. He liked to have things at his fingertips so he usually didn't put active files back in the cabinet where they belonged.

Next to his desk, Emanuel set up a more modern computer table and ergonomically designed chair. Emanuel preferred to draft all his documents by himself on the computer and then have Paula make any edits. This meant hours in front of the monitor typing or dictating using voice activated software. He also did all his legal research himself, which meant more time in front of the monitor. Every legal decision since the beginning of United States jurisprudence and every statute was available to him online by simply telling the computer what he wanted. It made legal research far easier than the days of libraries and databases that were difficult to search.

Across the room, Emanuel had a long, chocolate brown leather couch that he used for multiple purposes. He took afternoon naps fairly regularly on the couch, when he worked late and would just sleep in the office, and occasionally he would share a quiet moment there with a woman. There was a coffee table in front of the couch and two leather chairs across from the table. Next to the couch, he had an entertainment center with a large monitor, and DVD system for music and movies. The monitor was on a wheeled unit that Emanuel would simply rotate around in front of the couch when he wanted to watch something.

On the walls Emanuel had a combination of art, personal effects, and his diplomas. He had a photograph of his parents when they were young. Emanuel loved the photo because it made him think of the promise of life, before you know how everything is going to turn out. His parents were cheek to cheek and he could tell they were in love when he looked into their eyes. It was taken soon after they were married and before the long years of true responsibility had weighed heavily upon them as it does with everybody.

Emanuel also had a photograph of himself walking out of court after his first big win as a criminal defense attorney in Washington. It was a murder case like Satya's, but far more clear-cut. The defendant was named Ronnie Templeton and he was accused of killing a woman in Southeast during a robbery attempt at her house. No one witnessed the crime, but the cops had magically produced one witness who said he saw Ronnie coming out of the house about the time the murders occurred. There was also some suspect forensic evidence, including carpet fibers from the woman's apartment found at Ronnie's. The woman was shot with a 9-millimeter Glock, the kind every gangster in town used. The cops found one in an alley three blocks away from Ronnie's apartment and tests found it had been fired within a similar time period to the murder.

Despite the sketchy evidence, the prosecutors took the case all the way to trial. Ronnie told Emanuel he did not commit the murder even though he had no real alibi. Nevertheless, Emanuel believed him. At trial Emanuel first got the forensics expert to admit it was possible that the police who were at both scenes tracked in the carpet fibers. In the coup de grace, under cross-examination a young officer admitted he was directed by a superior to plant the gun in the alley. It was a rare moment for a defense attorney and Ronnie was acquitted. When Emanuel exited the courthouse, there was some press waiting and a photographer took his picture. It reminded Emanuel that anything was possible when you had justice on your side.

Emanuel also had some original art on his walls. He loved landscapes with bodies of water in them. The water conveyed motion to Emanuel and he liked to look at the paintings with the idea that there is always somewhere else to be and a way to get there. The paintings helped him scare off the feeling of being trapped that occasionally overcame him during bouts of insecurity and depression.

Emanuel worked all day skipping lunch and at about seven he decided to head down to the Old Ebbitt for some dinner. He was looking forward to one of Doc's martinis and a hearty meal before he went home for some much-needed rest.

Emanuel strolled down 15th Street and twirled through the revolving door of the Old Ebbitt. This time, however, he felt a new sense of purpose. Despite being alone he wasn't lonely. Emanuel was inspired by both the case and his new outlook on life. As usual, the place was bustling with activity. It never mattered what time of day it was or which day of the week it was, the Old Ebbitt was always humming. Even though it was Monday, the bar was fairly packed with people enjoying a drink.

Despite his several weeks of absence, Doc had Emanuel's martini ready as he jumped on a bar stool and sat down.

"Counselor, it's good to see ya again. I was beginning to think you were angry with me."

"Come on, Doc," Emanuel said taking a big sip. "How could I be angry with a man who makes martinis like this? I'm an intelligent man."

"Thanks counselor, and a true gentleman, too." Doc paused awkwardly. "Listen, Emanuel. I saw you on the TV today talkin' about the case. I know it's gonna be hard on you so if there's anything I can do . . ."

"I appreciate that, Doc. You're a pal. I think if you just try and keep things normal for me around here that'll be enough. I'm going to need several of your best martinis over the next few months," Emanuel said pointing to his glass. "Speaking of which, how about another."

"Coming right up."

As Emanuel popped the last olive of his martini into his mouth, he caught a whiff of a familiar perfume. He turned quickly, and was once again face-to-face with Jude Michaels. Before he could say a word, she began defending herself.

"I know you don't want to see me here, but I just wanted to talk to you alone. I broke this story, and I want to keep on top of it. That being said, you're going to need a reliable channel to make statements regarding the trial. I think we can have a mutually beneficial relationship here."

Just then Doc arrived with Emanuel's new drink.

"Doc," Emanuel said. "Put that martini on Ms. Michael's tab, and bring her one too."

"Sure thing."

"Does that mean you'll talk to me?"

"That means, I feel like some company right now. I'm tired of eating here alone."

"Wow. I'm honored."

"And, I guess it means that I agree with you. I do want to have a means to get our point of view out when I want it out. If you can do that for me, then maybe we can help each other."

"What is your side? I mean, what possible defense can Grady have? Was he aware of Winston's covert activities somehow?"

"I don't want to talk about it now, but you'll be the first to know, okay. Now, will you join me for dinner?"

"Sure," Jude said, feeling very pleased.

"I hope you don't mind eating at the bar. Doc here would kill me if I sat at a table."

"No problem," Jude answered.

Emanuel and Jude spent three hours eating and talking at the Old Ebbitt bar. She told him how she knew she wanted to be a television journalist from her college days at George Washington University. Jude had worked as an intern on Capitol Hill and in the White House and knew she liked the intrigue of politics and law. She wanted to be a journalist, however, so she could write about the political process and play the watchdog role over the government.

She recounted how after graduating from the Columbia School of Journalism, she went to work for the *Hartford Chronicle*. The *Chronicle* was a well-regarded newspaper in a less-than-prominent market. Hartford was a mid-sized city with a prominent financial sector, but it was definitely a second-tier town. Jude covered local politics and Connecticut's representatives in Washington and received wide acclaim for her work.

"I always got the story first," Jude said with pride.

"I guess you haven't changed much," Emanuel replied.

"That's right. All that work paid off too, getting me onto local television up there. I became the expert on Connecticut politics weighing in on the talk shows. It's not easy for a woman in television journalism. Most of the time producers are after looks rather than journalistic talent and integrity. It's a constant battle."

Jude was high energy and filled with excitement. Emanuel always admired people who loved what they did for a living.

"Anyway, I kind of knew that my future was with television not print. Soon enough I was hosting my own Saturday evening talk show, "Hartford This Week." I'm sure you've seen it," Jude mocked herself. "And, after a couple of years of that gig, I got the call from CNN. They were looking for another reporter in Washington and asked me if I was interested. I couldn't move down here fast enough."

Emanuel and Jude had moved onto dinner and a bottle of red wine. Jude's pale complexion was now rosy with the warm atmosphere and she was talking non-stop. Emanuel was happy to eat his beef stew and listen to her.

"My goal is to be the most respected journalist in America. I'll be honest, I think this case can do it for me."

"I hope so," Emanuel replied. He was definitely enamored by her. Jude had an idealistic quality to her that Emanuel found refreshing. He had been idealistic once, but the years of criminal law and failed personal relationships had taken their toll.

In turn, Emanuel told Jude about his past, including his stint at the DAs office. He regaled her with stories of his biggest cases and she seemed genuinely interested in them. She asked several pointed questions as reporters are prone to do, but Emanuel liked that. He enjoyed having someone interested in his work.

Emanuel wanted to tell her about his recent experiences in New York but he held back. He knew it would make her story ultimately much better to know how he came to believe in Satya, but now was not the time. He did not feel comfortable discussing a search for God on behalf of his client, or adding to the sensationalism he knew was sure to come when he unveiled Satya's defense.

The two also talked about more mundane things like where they liked to go out in D.C. Jude liked to hit the town when she had time, which wasn't very often. She always had to look and feel her best, so staying out late drinking was rarely part of her agenda. When she did go out, though, she went to the political hangouts near the Capitol and in Georgetown. If she could pick up some gossip while socializing, all the better. She told Emanuel that despite actively dating, she had yet to meet a man in D.C. who intrigued and excited her. "Most guys in town are either gay, boring, stuffy lawyers, or all three" Jude said, adding, "No offense intended."

Emanuel laughed at Jude's assessment of Washington's male population. He agreed for the most part even though he was not gay and did not consider himself boring or stuffy. He confessed to Jude that he didn't get out much. He had to work too hard to make a decent living and after a day fighting in court, all he wanted was a quiet drink. "Standing around a crowded bar with a bunch of posers, isn't my idea of fun anymore," Emanuel said.

"No offense taken," Jude replied.

"I don't think you're a poser, Jude. You know what I mean."

Finally, and disappointingly to Emanuel, there was nothing left to eat or drink. They had shared an apple cobbler a la mode for dessert, and each had two cups of decaf coffee. It was time to go home and think about the mountains of work they both had ahead of them. Emanuel picked up the tab and they walked out of the Old Ebbitt together onto 15th Street.

"I really enjoyed myself tonight," Emanuel said. "You've no longer ruined my favorite restaurant. You've made it better."

"Thanks, Emanuel. I had a great time," Jude replied. "I'm looking forward to this." Jude shook Emanuel's hand and jumped into a cab. As Emanuel stood alone on the street corner watching her drive away, he wondered what she meant.

16

Three days later, Emanuel returned to D.C. Superior Court for Satya's preliminary hearing where the prosecution must convince the judge that there is probable cause to send the case to a grand jury. Probable cause is the thinnest legal standard to prove, sitting on the complete opposite end of the spectrum from the hardest, "beyond a reasonable doubt." To prove probable cause the prosecution need only show there is a "possibility" that the defendant committed the crime with "possibility" being between 50 and 51 percent. The judge does not weigh the evidence at a preliminary hearing, but rather, just receives enough information from the prosecution to reach the conclusion that it is likely that a crime was committed and the defendant is the person who committed it.

In order to prove probable cause, the prosecution usually puts on the stand the homicide detective or FBI agent investigating the case who adopts all the investigation reports as his own. Hearsay is also admissible.

The preliminary hearing is a formality in most cases, so much so that the prosecution often starts grand jury testimony in advance. The prosecution has the right to do this in a secretive manner although seasoned defense attorneys usually find out through back channels that it has happened. Emanuel had talked to his sources that told him the grand jury had already heard testimony on Satya's case. Emanuel was not surprised. Grand juries will always do what the prosecution says anyway, and in this case, with several witnesses and video, there was not doubt the grand jury would indict. Emanuel knew the case was going to trial and there was nothing he could do procedurally to stop it.

Emanuel arrived at D.C. Superior and was immediately confronted by a circus atmosphere that made the usual mayhem at the courthouse seem tepid. The media was waiting with a full battalion of reporters, cameramen, and light and sound technicians, backed up with a division of satellite trucks. All the players in the media game were there with numerous foreign networks also represented.

More daunting than the media hordes were the mobs of protestors from both sides of the religious and political issues surrounding Winston's assassination. Police barricades cordoned off the protestors on either side of the entrance to the courthouse along D Street. On the right-hand side were Winston's supporters screaming for Satya's head on a spike, and holding placards denouncing the alleged government conspiracy currently slandering the holy name of Reverend Winston.

On the other side were Satya Grady supporters clamoring for his release as an instrument of justice. Their signs accused Winston of plotting to bring down the American democracy. They also held signs supporting President Taylor in his efforts to find the truth about Winston and to bring any of his legions to justice.

The groups were yelling across the plaza at each other as Emanuel exited his cab. That noise combined with the hundreds of questions hurled at him by the media was a physical knock against his senses that almost bowled him over. Emanuel steadied himself and ran the gauntlet of people into the courthouse, which seemed eerily quiet in comparison.

Emanuel passed through the metal detector and took the escalators up this time to the fifth floor. He wasn't sure who the judge would be and was anxious to find out. The judge always makes a big difference in a criminal trial primarily on evidentiary matters, jury instructions, and determining penalties. Some judges were more sympathetic to defendants and tried to give them the benefit of the doubt while others figured that if they've come this far into the system, they were most likely guilty.

On the fifth floor there were more people milling about crowding the hallway. There were more media personnel there including Jude, who immediately rushed up to Emanuel and thrust a microphone in his face.

"How are you feeling this morning, counselor?" Jude asked.

Emanuel inhaled a large dose of her perfume before grumbling, "No comment," and storming toward his assigned courtroom. Jude's smile quickly faded, as she expected a nice sound bite from Emanuel.

When Emanuel reached courtroom 519, he saw the name Judge Bernie Wallace on the door and he knew he'd received a tough draw. Wallace was an African American judge who had no sympathy for the predominately African American criminal defendants who appeared before him. He was a product of Benning Road, Southeast, one of D.C.'s worst neighborhoods. Wallace had survived the drug wars and gunfights to make it to the bench. His attitude was "if I did it, you can too." Being poor was no excuse for crime in Wallace's mind.

Defendants were always encouraged to plea out their cases in Wallace's courtroom because he usually imposed the maximum allowable sentence under the law. If a crime had a range of 10 to 20 years, Wallace would hand down the 20. Likewise, Wallace would only allow pleas to lesser charges if the defendant agreed to the maximum sentence for that offense.

Emanuel was disappointed because he knew Wallace was not going to react well to the "God told me to do it defense," and that when the prosecution asked for the death penalty, Wallace would have no problem granting it. On the positive side, Satya did not want to cop a plea anyway and Wallace was a fair jurist. His decisions were tough but at the end of the day, justice was served.

So, with mixed emotions, Emanuel entered the courtroom, which was packed with more observers, and sat down at the defense table. The main courtrooms at D.C. Superior were slightly larger and more impressive than the room for the presentment in the basement, but were nevertheless lacking in any marble grandeur.

After a few minutes, Sophie Mitchell walked in wheeling a box of documents on a small hand truck. Another U.S. Attorney joined her who Emanuel had never seen before. Mitchell stopped at the defense table to greet Emanuel and introduce her co-counsel Carl Hoffman. Emanuel did not feel like making small talk so he just said hello and put his head back down into reading his notes.

Emanuel was so engrossed in his review that he did not hear the side door open or see the bailiffs bringing Satya into the courtroom. He was wearing a navy-blue suit and a solid blue tie in order to give the appearance of wearing his police uniform. Satya was pale and thin, but was happy to be out of the jail even if it was for a court hearing. At least he could act like a human being and not live in fear for a few minutes.

"Here's the prisoner, counselor," one of the bailiffs said to Emanuel.

"Oh," Emanuel responded, somehow surprised that his client would be there too. "Satya, how are you? Just sit down next to me here."

"I'm fine Emanuel, and how are you?" Satya said, sitting down next to Emanuel.

"Good, good," Emanuel responded, answering both of Satya's statements.

Satya looked around the courtroom and immediately spotted his wife Kim sitting in the gallery. Kim was an attractive woman with straight black hair streaked with gray and olive skin that did not show too many wrinkles. Her brown eyes began to fill with tears at the sight of her husband. Unable to contain herself, Kim jumped out of her seat and rushed over to Satya. Her quick movement startled Emanuel who was still reviewing his notes, and he flinched as Kim threw her arms around Satya smothering him with kisses. It was a tender and painful moment cut short by the bailiff who came over and gently ushered Kim back to her seat. Satya's eyes were now also filled with tears.

The next minute the loud knock on the judge's door sounded and Judge Bernie Wallace entered the courtroom to the familiar "All rise."

Wallace sat down and growled "good morning" to the courtroom. Everyone present responded in kind like an orderly congregation. Wallace then fell silent as he looked over some paperwork seemingly at leisure. He wanted to quickly establish that this was his courtroom, and things would be done at his pace and for his convenience. Finally, he was ready. He looked up and gave his clerk a subtle nod. The clerk then made clear for the record that the first case of the day was the United States versus Satya Grady.

The hearing went exactly as Emanuel expected. Detective Horahan took the stand and described the events of the night when Satya killed Winston and then supported his testimony with the same video he had shown Emanuel in the police station. Mitchell then put a few witnesses on who actually saw Satya shoot Winston, including one of Winston's bodyguards, an ex-Marine named David Pritchard. His testimony was so precise and detailed it could have convicted Satya all by itself, Emanuel thought to himself.

Emanuel did not waste the court's time with any kind of procedural arguments or claims of innocence. There was no point irritating Wallace at this early point in the proceedings. Emanuel knew he would have to fight Wallace just to defend Satya on the grounds of justifiable homicide, and wanted to save up goodwill for that day. At the end, Wallace found probable cause and sent the case to the grand jury. The only question left in Emanuel's mind after the preliminary hearing was how long it would take Mitchell to get the indictment. He figured it would not be long.

After Wallace adjourned, the hearing the bailiffs came to take Satya back to prison. Emanuel tried to reassure him and told him not to take the finding of probable cause as a defeat. "You know we have to fight this thing at trial," Emanuel said. Satya just gave a thin smile and then looked longingly at his wife before being led away.

When Emanuel left the courtroom, he decided he needed to give the press something. With Jude front and center and her microphone most prominently sticking in his face, Emanuel recounted the fairly brief hearing. "My client intends on fighting this thing all the way," Emanuel said before walking away.

Two weeks after the preliminary hearing, the grand jury indicted Satya for first degree murder. Mitchell at least had the decency to call Emanuel personally to tell him, in addition to serving him with the written indictment. She also told him that the government, without question, would be seeking the death penalty.

Emanuel began working on his defense with the Bible as Exhibit A. He had to convince the jury that if they were religious and believed in God, then they could believe in Satya. People pray everyday and ask God for guidance and often make important life decisions only after prayer or religious contemplation. In this case, Satya felt he received guidance from God to act and proceeded accordingly. Emanuel figured that he'd have to know the Bible inside and out to cite examples similar to Satya's.

He started with the Old Testament and just moved forward. There were, of course, many instances in the Old Testament when God communicated with human beings starting with Adam and Eve. There the message was clear and relevant: If you disobey God's orders you will be punished as Adam and Eve were banished from the Garden of Eden and lost their innocence by eating from the Tree of Knowledge.

In the story of the great flood, on the other hand, Noah obeyed God's command and survived the deluge as the rest of humankind perished. God saved the righteous Noah while He took vengeance on humanity that had become too evil to live. It showed a God willing to take lives in the greater interests of mankind.

Much like Satya's case, God ordered Abraham to sacrifice Isaac, despite having waited a lifetime to have him. It was a test of devotion and faith and Abraham lived up to his end of bargain. At the last minute, God intervened and stopped him and made the covenant with Abraham to circumcise all Jewish males eight days after they are born. That order is still being carried out thousands of years later, Emanuel noted.

The greatest prophet in the Old Testament was Moses since he received the Ten Commandments directly from God. Ten direct orders for Moses and all the Israelites to follow. Those ten laws formed the foundation of modern, civilized society, yet are rarely followed, Emanuel thought, including in Satya's case. God always creates and ends life but can he do it through another human being in violation of His own commandments? That would be a tricky hurdle to leap at trial.

Jesus Christ, the human face of God on earth, walked throughout the ancient world, talking and preaching to hundreds of people. He gave new rules and lessons that everyone who came into contact with Him heard. Jesus performed miracles, filling fishermen's nets, turning water into wine, and healing the sick. Those who witnessed these acts ultimately wrote them down to be believed by millions of people.

After Jesus died, He appeared to Mary Magdalene, the Apostles, and Paul on the road to Damascus. That meeting led Paul to become the greatest Christian prophet, spreading the Word of Jesus and founding the Church.

The whole New Testament is the recitation of those who had, in fact, witnessed the acts of Jesus Christ, and heard His Word. The whole story shows that man communicated with God. If not, the whole religion would be invalidated. So, under that theory, Emanuel had every reason to believe Satya Grady. If Mary Magdalene, Peter, and Paul, could talk to God then so could a good cop from New York.

All the reading made Emanuel feel euphoric. The Old Testament was the foundation of a religion that had lasted over five thousand years, and the New Testament was the foundation of a religion that had lasted over two thousand years. Both required the faith that God was intertwined with human beings; so much so, that He told them what to do, what was right and what was wrong. God had supposedly told Satya what was right and wrong, and gave him a specific act to follow, which he did. It was no crazier than believing Jesus walked on water, or that God told Abraham to sacrifice his only son as an act of faith. Why did God talk to people thousands of years ago and then stop? Emanuel wondered. That wouldn't make sense, especially since both books were testaments, testimonials, affidavits, legal documents in the court of human imagination and belief. Maybe, Emanuel thought, no one had the courage to report interactions with God over the last several thousand years. Maybe, he thought, the time was right to do so again. Maybe it was time for a new testimonial with Satya Grady's experience killing Jack Winston as the foundation.

17

Emanuel lost track of the days and nights. He barely slept because the ideas and the stories he was reading were so heavy that they made his mind work at an incredible speed. He would just collapse from exhaustion and then wake up and begin again. When he would come across a passage that he found interesting in some way, Emanuel would jot it down on a yellow sticky note with an annotation about why he found it interesting.

Emanuel was obsessed and overcome at the same time. It was invigorating. Never before had he engaged in an activity of self-discovery. All his life he had diligently studied other subjects. Emanuel was a good student, finishing at the top of his high school, college, and law school classes. He loved learning, and while his classmates would bemoan having to spend long hours in the library, Emanuel always saw it as a great luxury. Being a student meant reading great works of fiction and nonfiction written by some of the greatest minds the world had ever produced. This was a challenging, mind-expanding process and Emanuel relished it.

Even in law school when he had to read case after case, he enjoyed learning about the laws of the United States, without which the country would fall into disarray. He wanted to understand the way judges think and their rationales for deciding cases certain ways. After all, he reasoned, this is a country of laws and if you don't know what those laws are you are at a distinct disadvantage. Emanuel wanted to know those laws better than anyone. He read every case assigned to him outlining the facts, the holding, and the analysis behind the holding. During lectures, when the professors would employ the Socratic method, Emanuel was always prepared and actually looked forward to sparring with the professor to test his understanding. He often came close to winning some debates, bringing up new theories and analytical directions that his professors often had not considered. For Emanuel, education and understanding were the most important things in life.

What he was doing now was very different, however. Instead of looking externally to understanding the legal system, or studying politics or international affairs or reading novels about far away lands and different time periods, he was looking only at himself. As he read the Bible, it was with a skeptical eye, always asking, "Do I really believe this?" or "What does this really mean?" Due to the fact that the Bible had been read for thousands of years, Emanuel figured that whether God existed or not, it was a weighty document. People had based their decisions and lived their lives by what was taught in the Bible, and this fact made Emanuel think about his own life.

After reading certain passages, he could not help but think about how he did things and whether perhaps there could be a better way. He started thinking that perhaps things in his life should be more intertwined. The Bible stories were so universal. Human beings had the same fears and faults and made the same mistakes over and over again throughout the ages. That's why they need each other, Emanuel thought, to know they're not alone in their inadequacy. That's why people like the Bible and religion, because it unites them in a common cause to survive life. It was a new concept for Emanuel who never before had felt the need to be part of a group. That was beginning to change.

While the judicial system was dealing with Satya, the political system continued the process of determining the next President of the United States. Despite the fact that the reliability of the electoral process was questioned after 2000, it still marched on. No matter what else happened, a presidential election occurred every four years. And, the campaign stormed forward through the summer towards the national conventions.

After Winston's death, and the revelations about his organization, the presidential race became a two-party affair once again. Taylor was pitted against the Democratic Party nominee, August Fowler, a Senator from Georgia. The campaigns were traditional with massive advertising efforts and regular whistle stop appearances.

Fowler was a left-wing Democrat who was running against Taylor's center-right policies. He was a pacifist and didn't want the United States to be engaged in police actions or preemptive wars around the world. Further, he believed in civil liberty protection and wanted strict controls on the new Department of Homeland Security. He acknowledged that we needed to protect ourselves against terrorism but not at the expense of losing the freedoms we enjoy. Fowler was vocally opposed racial profiling at airports and national identification cards. On domestic policy, Fowler advocated universal, government sponsored health care, an increase in the minimum wage, and harsher environmental standards. Taylor had not done much with those issues during his first term. Rather, he kept his campaign promises and cut taxes, and true to his background, he spent money on building up the military. He had argued that the prospect of regionalized conflicts around the world required a diverse and specially trained military with the right type of equipment to meet the challenges of terrorism and guerilla warfare. Luckily for Taylor, the world played along and he had several opportunities to use his new and improved military. Now he could once again employ is troops in his "war against Winston."

Fowler had a tough challenge battling Taylor, and one that really did not become easier with Winston's death. Fowler was never a proponent of family values or a moral leader. He supported a woman's right to choose an abortion, a position that immediately alienated him from everyone in the Freedom Party. Winston had been so persuasive on the campaign stump that he had convinced many moderate voters that abortion needed to be outlawed for the benefit of the country. Winston called it a matter of national security, saying that we kill more Americans every day than any foreign power ever has. People were ready for his message. Fowler was still not in a position to win those voters back. Even though Freedom Party voters no longer had a candidate, they were not going to backtrack on their ideals so quickly.

Taylor was also having trouble wooing the Freedom Party voters because most of them believed he was manufacturing the case against Winston. He refused to even engage in debate over this issue, feeling it was beneath him to answer questions about whether he was possibly "wagging the dog." He did hold views on social issues closer to Winston's ideology, and hoped to convince at least the ex-Republicans in the Freedom Party to come back. There were rumors, however, that some Freedom Party members were planning on backing a write-in candidate just to erode some of Taylor's support or voting for Fowler in protest.

Before Winston's death, Taylor was trailing him by seven points in the polls, and Fowler was another ten points behind Taylor. Now, Taylor maintained a mere six point lead over Fowler and was concerned about his chances. If he could not win back some Freedom voters he could be in trouble, and if the rumored backlash occurred all would certainly be lost.

The missions against Winston's operation were coming off perfectly. Taylor had ordered three military strikes against Freedom militia groups, one in the United States, and two in Central America.

The strikes were all successful with complete annihilation captured on video for the entire world to see. No American soldiers were killed in action, and all but four Freedom soldiers were killed in the attacks. The surrendering soldiers were considered prisoners of the United States military, and were kept incommunicado and tried by military tribunals in secret. They would not receive the due process in the civilian judicial system.

The governmental investigations into Winston's affairs were also bearing fruit. Money laundering violations were pervasive, and numbered bank accounts were uncovered in the Cayman Islands and Switzerland. The church's books had been doctored to divert charitable gifts to the private accounts and away from intended projects. In fact, millions of dollars from Winston's considerable holdings had been pouring into off-shore accounts for years. The case against senior church members was so tight, all of them agreed to plead guilty and accept whatever mercy the government chose to show. The accused were immediately whisked away to their own Federal minimum security penitentiary to serve twenty year sentences for fraud, conspiracy, and violations of RICO--the Racketeer Influenced and Corrupt Organizations Act, the organized crime law.

Still, much of the public did not fall in behind Taylor. People had become cynical about what the government told them. None of the militia members or convicted church officials had a day in court to defend themselves. All were either dead, or agreed to government terms and only issued statements apologizing for their behavior and asking for forgiveness. People viewed what they were seeing with a skeptical eye, and the hard-core Freedoms did not care if what they saw was the truth anyway. Many believed that if the allegations were true, Winston was doing the right thing. They saw no problem with Winston using donations to his church for pursuing what he believed was God's work. If Winston felt a religious army was necessary to spread the word of God, then it had to be done. These people pointed to the Crusades as an example of governments raising troops to spread the word of God at the point of a sword. If it happened then, why should it not happen in the modern era? No one ever criticized the old Crusades, the hard-core argued. According to the allegations of Taylor's government, Winston was planning on using the might of the United States to spread his religious ideology, and the hard-core were all in favor of that.

This reaction surprised Taylor. He had thought that patriotism would exceed religious fervor, but he was wrong. The Freedom extremists, and there were many, cared more about the Gospel than the Constitution; they cared more about the Ten Commandments than the Bill of Rights. Taylor was an American to his core and thought that most people believed like him, that God created the United States to be the most powerful country in the world and the most wonderful human experiment that ever existed. For Taylor, the stories in the Bible represented a good ideology metaphorically, but more of a Utopian dream than a reality. For him, the democratic process of the United States, where every émigré from the far reaches of the earth, of every color, ethnicity, and religion could live in relative harmony, was the true embodiment of God's presence on earth. The Freedom extremists thought differently.

They vocalized these views on the National Mall all summer long. Freedom party loyalists set up camp on the Mall, complete with prayer tee-pees where they would pray daily for Winston and the morality of America. Occasionally, they would clash with police who now stood ready twenty-four hours a day. Fairly regularly, the protestors would become angry and engage the police. Batons were brandished, and arrests were made, only for encounters to occur again a few days later. Their leader was gone but they wanted his voice heard through their vigil and recordings of his sermons that blared from loudspeakers.

Taylor witnessed it all from the White House, which was only a few blocks away. He knew he needed something more against Winston to stop the backlash. It would have to be something personal to Winston that would undermine his credibility as a moral and holy figure. It needed to be something to actually stop the whole Freedom movement in its tracks. If he could make Winston look like a hypocrite, then people might realize following a zealot was not the way to go. Once again, Taylor's faithful National Security Advisor would come to the rescue.

18

On September 1, fifteen days prior to the trial date, Emanuel received the *Jenck's* material from the prosecutors. The *Jenck's* material— named for the Supreme Court decision that authorized it— was part of the discovery process and consisted of any prior statements made or adapted by a witness who had testified on direct testimony to the grand jury. It basically gave the defense insight into the minds of the prosecution's witnesses in order to try and find some hole in their stories.

In this case, however, the *Jenck's* material was solid. The actual witnesses to the shooting gave lucid and vivid recollections, the forensics experts matched the bullets found in Winston to Satya's gun, and there was no problem with the chain of custody of the evidence to suggest any tampering or contamination. Finally, Horahan's statements and those of the other police officers involved in the case were, as expected, beyond question.

After reviewing the *Jenck's* material and finding no problems, it was time for Emanuel to notify the court and the prosecution that he wanted a competency hearing for Satya. It was time for Emanuel to drop the bomb that he was going to defend Satya on the "God told me to do it defense."

As Emanuel expected, Judge Wallace was not pleased with Emanuel's announcement in court.

"Mr. Adams, are you trying to make a mockery of this court? You know that's not going to fly and you can forget about an ineffective assistance of counsel defense on appeal. Not coming out of my trial court."

"Judge, you know I have a great respect for this court, but the simple fact is my client firmly believes he was following God's orders and I believe him."

"You believe him!" Judge Wallace yelled. "Mr. Adams, I must say this is original. You're trying to go one step further than ineffective assistance of counsel to the "my lawyer was insane" defense. Your client may be going out of his way to prove his insanity to me before we impanel a jury, but I don't think he needs your assistance."

"That's just the point, your honor. My client is not insane. If I may introduce the results of some psychiatric tests I've had done on Officer Grady while he's been in prison. May I approach the bench?"

"You may."

Emanuel walked up to the bench and placed a copy of the reports in front of Judge Wallace, who gave him an irritated glance. Emanuel then returned to his lectern stopping on the way to hand Sophie Mitchell a copy.

"Your honor," Emanuel began, "if you'll note, the cover letter to the report is on the letterhead of Dr. Sam Kazinski, an esteemed professor of psychiatry at Georgetown University Medical center. Dr. Kazinski's curriculum vitae is attached and it speaks for itself. Your honor, you'll see Dr. Kazinski's cover letter clearly states that after an extensive review he determined that Officer Grady is of sound mind. You can also go through the actual tests if you like."

"I will definitely do so at my leisure Mr. Adams, but for the sake of brevity today I'll assume they support your argument."

"Thank you, Judge. Now, if I could approach one more time, I'd like to submit copies of Officer Grady's annual physicals required by the New York City Police Department." Emanuel again approached the bench, dropped off the files and then gave a copy to Mitchell.

"Judge, you'll note that while these physicals did not include extensive psychiatric evaluations, they did cover cursory mental health issues. They would contain more extensive studies if an officer's behavior on or off duty deemed it necessary. You'll note in reading the doctors' findings, that first, Officer Grady's conduct never warranted a more in-depth psychological examination, and second, his responses to the cursory reviews checked out normal."

Judge Wallace gave a heavy sigh. "Okay, Mr. Adams. So, what you're saying is your client is sane and you still want to proceed with the Texas defense: 'the son of a bitch had it coming and your client was the perfect man for the job.'"

"Your honor, I can't speak for Texas, but in this case my client had an encounter with God that inspired him, if you will, to kill Reverend Winston, and my client feels the jury will believe him, and acquit him."

Judge Wallace thumbed through the yearly physical reports sighing heavily at each turn of the page. Finally, he addressed Emanuel. "I don't suppose you've considered temporary insanity Mr. Adams."

"No, your honor."

"Well Mr. Adams, I can't impose an insanity defense on your client. We both know that. But, I want you to know very clearly that this is a death penalty case with the evidence stacked against you. You should also know that I've been on the bench a long time and I know my juries. Unless you can present God Almighty as a witness to corroborate whatever story your client may tell, I can assure you the jury will find your client guilty. So, I'll let you proceed if you want to, but I will be extremely disappointed if you take that road at trial."

"Thank you, Judge," Emanuel responded quietly. Coming into the hearing he was worried about losing his argument to use the God defense, but now that he had secured it, he felt worse. He knew that Judge Wallace was right. The chances of winning on Satya's claim were very slim.

After the hearing Emanuel left D.C. Superior through the basement to try and avoid the barricade of journalists at the front entrance. There were still a few meticulous reporters covering all exits, but they were easy to break through. Emanuel knew that the press would find out about his planned defense even though the hearing had been closed to the public. Journalists were not above slipping the court reporter or bailiff a hundred to find out what was said in the courtroom. Even so, he didn't feel like talking about the case due to the pit in his stomach.

Despite Emanuel's reluctance to talk to the media, the inevitable call came that afternoon from Jude. He'd been working on his opening statement writing out thoughts by hand and furiously chain smoking. When the call came through, however, he was staring out his office window with so many images running through his head they were blurred into nothingness. He didn't hear Paula's voice through the telephone so she had to walk into his office to tell him.

"Emanuel, Ms. Michaels is on the phone."

"Sorry, Paula," he mumbled as he walked to his desk.

"Hello Jude, I've been expecting your call."

"That's right, Emanuel, we have a deal and I need something from you on this one. God told him to do it?"

"It's slightly more complicated, but I suppose, that's it in a nutshell."

"I want the complicated version."

"Listen Jude, I'd rather not discuss this on the phone. Why don't you come by my apartment tonight and we'll talk? Come late and incognito so the paparazzi don't spot you."

"I'll be there."

"Oh, and no camera."

"Got it."

Emanuel was sitting on his couch sipping a Jack Daniel's and smoking a cigarette when the doorbell rang. For the last two hours he'd been staring at the images of religious protest on his television screen while thinking about the case and planning the logic behind his defense. The thousands of people protesting every aspect of the case made his planning extremely complicated. He broke out of his thought process and begrudgingly got up to answer the door.

"Nice chest," Jude said when the door opened. Emanuel looked down and was slightly embarrassed that he had forgotten to button his black oxford.

"Sorry about that."

"Don't be," Jude said walking into the apartment, "I meant it." She was wearing faded jeans, a white tee shirt and a black leather jacket. Her blond pony tail was sticking out the back of a baseball cap. Jude dropped her bag on the floor by Emanuel's couch and took a long look around.

"It could use some work, but not bad. How about putting some paintings on the wall, for starters?"

"I guess I never got around to that. Ordinarily, I don't spend enough time here for it to matter. Now that I'm being hounded by you people though, I might redecorate."

"Don't cry, big boy, you'll be a legal icon after this one . . . if you win, of course."

"Thanks. Can I get you a drink? I have Jack or water."

"Jack's great. Rocks and a splash of water please." Jude sat down, grabbed one of Emanuel's cigarettes, and lit it. She casually scanned his coffee table, which was serving as Emanuel's home office. His laptop was open with the screen saver of psychedelic "MS's" twirling into cyber space, adding movement to the room. The rest of the table had court papers strewn about and yellow legal pads with incomprehensible notes scribbled all over them.

Emanuel returned from the kitchen with Jude's drink and sat down next to her on his couch. They clinked glasses and took long sips before they started talking.

"So, Emanuel, my source told me about your God defense, but it wasn't clear if you were pleading Grady insane or what. The source said that insanity was discussed and you'd done tests but he wasn't sure of what the outcome was. Most of us have assumed you're going insanity."

"That's the complicated part. I'm defending Grady on the basis that he's not insane and that God told him to kill Reverend Winston."

Jude took another long sip and a drag off her cigarette without taking her eyes off Emanuel. A smile slowly crept onto her face.

"You're kidding, right? I'm no lawyer, but I can't believe that defense would hold up."

"Probably not, but Satya was vehement about defending himself on that basis. He told me he had a vision where he talked to God and there was some demonstrative evidence to back it up."

"Demonstrative evidence?" Jude replied, slightly more intrigued and less amused. "What kind?"

"I'd rather not say right now, but I'll tell you, his story left enough questions in my mind that I investigated further. I found that Satya Grady is probably the brightest spot on the New York City police force and had no history of any type of mental illness. He was a pillar of his community, a family man, a leader, the whole deal."

"Maybe he just snapped one day and went postal?" Jude retorted.

"I thought of that, but psychological tests supported the fact that he is sane, and the doctors said there's no reason to believe he went temporarily insane and killed Winston."

"So, you believe him?"

"Look, do I think Satya talked to God? No. I didn't even *believe* in God before I met Satya. But, do I believe Satya became inspired somehow to do this with the belief that he was doing God's bidding and therefore, serving mankind? Yes, I do. I mean, where does inspiration come from anyway? Some will argue it comes from God. More to the point, based on the stories you've been filing about Winston, maybe Satya did everyone a great service."

"It is an incredible story. Who would have thought a televangelist could build an international financial empire, complete with his own mercenaries? He must've had one hell of a collection plate. And, the more I investigate it the more layers of suspect activity come up.

Winston was a maniac and he certainly loved power. Your problem, however, is that Satya still had no authority to kill him."

"He says he had God's authority."

"I understand that, Emanuel, but how to you prove that and convince a jury beyond a reasonable doubt?"

"A hell of a lot of Americans believed in Winston and his connection with God. Watch old tapes of Winston preaching. He was constantly saying he talked directly to God, and people believed him."

"Maybe, but at the time Winston was talking about love and living a moral life— ideas people believe come from God. If he had said God told him to create a private army and take over the world, I don't think people would have believed him or followed him. People don't expect God to promote violence."

"That's a philosophical argument, Jude. Throughout history, there were plenty of violent operations conducted in the name of God. The leaders of those movements claimed they were doing God's bidding— just like Satya."

"Emanuel, that was hundreds of years ago. Don't you think our society has evolved somewhat?"

"Has it? Look at the Israeli-Palestinian problem or the conflicts in Northern Ireland. Those are ostensibly religious battles. Tell me more about Winston's private dealings? I mean, what's the inside scoop on the paramilitary groups and the money laundering?"

"Based on the information I've uncovered, he was running a global syndicate, like a drug cartel. He'd set up all kinds of shell companies engaged in proverbial import and export. These companies funneled money to Winston's cells around the world that were training for the new Crusade. He dabbled in the drug trade as well to make more money . . . The thing is, sometimes I think I'm being played on this one."

"What do you mean?"

"There are definitely documents to support Winston's illicit activities, but I've received all of them from government sources and there are no real witnesses to back them up."

"What about Johannsen?"

"He was given to me by someone inside the White House. I didn't find him. All the rest of the church's leaders basically surrendered their rights and went quietly off to jail."

"Presumably, if they were innocent of the charges they would have fought them. You don't always have to plea bargain."

"Emanuel, not everyone is willing to walk into court and risk their lives with a thin defense."

"That hurts, Jude."

"I'm sorry. What I meant was, if the government told these guys that they had an airtight case against them and threatened them, they probably buckled."

"Threatened them?"

"I've just heard stories that sometimes the government goes further than just promising a maximum sentence. They can scare you with threats against your family and financial ruin -- a lifetime of IRS audits and no Social Security. That kind of thing."

"Don't these guys have lawyers?"

"Sure, but what's one lawyer going to do against the most powerful government in the world? You need to be realistic."

"I don't believe you, Jude. Our government doesn't need to do that kind of thing."

"Maybe in this case it felt it did."

"So, you think Winston wasn't guilty of these charges against him?"

"All I'm saying is, he may or may not be. It seems like he is, but that's still no excuse for your client to blow him away. Officer Grady didn't know what Winston was up to, and he wasn't acting on behalf of the government. So, I don't think people will buy your defense. I know I wouldn't."

Emanuel sat back and lit another cigarette. He scratched his head contemplating Jude's views. A part of him knew she was right, at least on legal grounds, but another part of him believed God had motivated Satya. Emanuel's vision of Satya in New York was so real and vivid that he was convinced that Satya possessed some kind of spiritual power. He wouldn't let himself believe he was an angel but a prophet, yes. Emanuel believed in God now and part of that belief was founded in Satya and the fact that humans can communicate with the Creator. More importantly, Emanuel had faith that he could articulate this fact to a jury so they would believe him. He felt it in his heart. It was like love, a feeling hard to describe that has no real physical signs yet he knew it when he felt it.

Emanuel wanted to tell Jude about the bombing in New York and the image of Satya although he didn't want to scare her. Plus, he didn't trust her completely and didn't want a story to appear about the crazy cop and his crazier attorney. At this point, he needed to keep it to himself and just prove to the world that Satya was a righteous man.

Jude's face had become flush with the Jack Daniel's. She felt sympathetic towards Emanuel. While covering the case and talking to him, she had become really fond of him. Although, she didn't believe Satya's story she found it romantic that Emanuel would defend someone based on a belief in God. There was also something different about Emanuel from all the other men she had met in Washington. He was so serious and pensive at times that she just wanted to leap into his head and see what was going on in there. The majority of men she met all appeared so cocksure of what they did for a living and who they were, even when they had no right to be. It was the Washington persona that everyone affected as soon as they got a taste of government power.

Emanuel on the other hand seemed sure of nothing. Certainly, Jude saw he had confidence in his abilities as a lawyer, but he didn't act like he had all the answers. While Jude devoted a lot of energy to her career she wanted an equally rewarding personal life and began to think of Emanuel in a deeper way than just a professional contact. Jude took a long look at him. He had some growth on his face that made him look rugged and his hair was messy from lots of head rubbing. It made him look like a little boy. Emanuel who had been looking straight ahead sensed her eyes on him.

"What, Jude?"

"You look tense, Emanuel. Would you like a back rub?"

Emanuel wasn't exactly shocked by Jude's offer, but something in the tone of her voice suggested to him that maybe their working relationship was about to take a more personal turn.

"Actually, that sounds pretty good. Are you sure you don't mind?" Emanuel asked besides his better judgment telling him not to.

"Of course not. Why don't you unbutton a few of those buttons again and turn around?"

Emanuel did what he was told and turned askew on the couch while Jude tucked her legs under herself. She pulled Emanuel's shirt down a bit and began rubbing his shoulders. His skin was extremely warm and soft to her touch. Emanuel was naturally muscular although his lack of exercise made his muscles slightly more elastic than they were when he was younger. Jude enjoyed the way they felt. She never much liked muscle-bound men, and anyway, Emanuel felt strong to her.

They didn't talk while she rubbed his neck, shoulders and back. They inched closer however, with Emanuel leaning into Jude's lap. She leaned forward until she could smell him. First, she smelled his hair. She could tell he used mint scented shampoo and it made her mouth water. Instinctively, her hand moved up his neck into his hair and she began massaging his scalp. Emanuel loved this feeling and closed his eyes, tilted his head back and leaned further into her. He could feel Jude's breasts and their softness comforted him.

With Emanuel so close, Jude could now smell his skin. It had an earthy smell to it with just a hint of the soap and deodorant he had used earlier in the day. Emanuel also had the smell of cigarette smoke to him and it mixed perfectly with his natural odor. It made Jude think of him as a large animal lying by a fire and it made her face even warmer.

Meanwhile, Emanuel was completely lost in the pleasurable feeling of the massage. He was indeed tense, and the sensation of Jude's strong hands kneading his back allowed him to shut his mind down for the moment. He stopped thinking about the trial, and Satya, and God. Rather, he just lay back against Jude and thought of how wonderful life could be sometimes. There were times when things were just simple, easy, and joyous. They might be brief windows in life's otherwise painful journey, but they were there and this was one of them.

Emanuel's reverie was interrupted by Jude's lips on his neck. They were hot and sent a shiver throughout his whole body. Jude wrapped her arms around him and pulled him close. She leaned further forward and kept kissing his neck and face until she reached his lips. Emanuel twisted around and they kissed. It was a long kiss with closed mouths like actors in an old movie. Then for a few seconds, their mouths opened and their tongues met.

When Emanuel's tongue hit Jude's, it sent a message to his brain and he pulled away. He looked at Jude and she looked so young and beautiful with her freckled face reddened with warmth. Her mouth and breath were delicious to him and he wanted to feast on her again, but he didn't. He brushed his fingers up her face from her chin to her cheek, to her temple, and then through her hair.

"Jude, I think you're wonderful, but now's not the time for this," Emanuel said.

"Why not?" she asked with hurt in her voice.

"Because, I think we're both involved in something heavy right now and it's brought us together. And, I'm happy about that, but I don't want us to be confused about our feelings for each other. I don't want to hurt you or jeopardize the jobs we both have to do. I'd rather we just waited and got to know each other better after this whole thing is over. I know I really like you, and I want it to be real."

Emanuel's words fit in perfectly with how Jude already felt about him. Jude usually was the one slowing the man down especially when things became physical, and despite her desire, it was refreshing to find a man who wanted to take things slow.

"I understand, I think. Now, I want the case to be over." Jude leaned over again and gave Emanuel a lingering kiss that almost set them going again before she pulled away. "I'm gonna go, okay?"

The two got off the couch and straightened up. Jude picked up her baseball cap which she had discarded and grabbed her bag. Emanuel draped his arm around her and walked her to the door.

"Jude, what are you going to say about the case?"

"I'll just report the facts without any spin. I'll say you're not pleading him insane and that he claims God inspired him to kill Winston for the good of us all. I'll get some legal commentary on justifiable homicide and leave it at that."

"Fine." Emanuel paused. "Thanks for the back rub, I really appreciated it."

"It was my pleasure. If you want to get together just to talk, off the record of course, I'd love to."

"Thanks Jude, I'd like that."

Jude walked out the door and Emanuel went back to his thoughts about the case.

19

The jury selection process took three days and hundreds of jurors. It was difficult to find twelve jurors and two alternates who knew nothing or very little of the assassination and subsequent news about Winston, especially due to the amount of public outcry occurring all over the country and in Washington. Judge Wallace quickly halted talks of moving the trial to another venue since every jurisdiction in the country was inundated with the story.

The initial group of people who had rallied on the belief that Winston was a martyr had now splintered off into many factions. There were those who still believed in the idea of Winston and the ideals he espoused, despite the reports of his evil side. Then there was still a subset of his supporters who believed a government conspiracy was persecuting him much like the Romans persecuted Jesus. Next, there were those who now fell in strongly behind President Taylor, believing he was the only force of goodness in America and that his reelection was a national priority. This group also wanted to stand up against the conspiracy theorists.

With the news that Satya Grady claimed he was acting on God's behalf yet more new groups sprang up. On the one hand, there were those who believed Satya's story based on Winston's dark side. They considered Satya a modern-day prophet doing God's will. For them, Satya was a spiritual leader incarcerated by a Godless regime. They wanted Satya freed as a prisoner of conscience. Many of this group formerly supported Winston as God's loudspeaker.

On the other side of this group were those who thought Satya was an instrument of the devil. They didn't believe his story because God didn't order assassinations, only the devil would. They wanted Satya executed to win the battle against evil.

Finally, there were the liberals who believed the whole lot of religious extremists, Satya included, needed to take a back seat in American society. They blamed President Taylor for the whole imbroglio and argued Fowler was the man to put America back on track. This group argued that the insurgence of religion into American politics created the current situation and they wanted an end to it. For them, they wanted Satya locked up for life (because they were anti-death penalty), Taylor thrown out of office, and Fowler to become the next President.

One thing was certain: nearly every American had a strong view on the subject. All the other factions now joined the Freedom activists on the Mall. There was barely any room on the Mall for all the various marches and rallies that were occurring. A carnival atmosphere descended on the Washington akin to movements of the 1960's. People were camping out and setting up vigils for their point of view. Everywhere, people were praying, making impromptu speeches, having sing-a-longs, and reading poetry. Tee shirts, hats, and food were being hawked along with booze and drugs for those just there for the party.

People also set up ad hoc monuments for lost and slain leaders who held mystical significance: Martin Luther King, Gandhi, John F. Kennedy, John Lennon, Jerry Garcia, Ronald Reagan and countless others that were not represented on the Mall. America's spirituality was exposed to the world like never before.

Even though this new group of activists was more peaceful than the Freedom party supporters during the summer, the Capitol police force and the National Guard were not considering the event a party.

They still had orders to stand watch around the clock and in full riot gear, for fear of an uprising. Washington was now truly a city under siege.

Luckily, even in the information age, there were always people who were either outside the loop of privilege or completely indifferent to the events around them, and they ended up on Satya Grady's jury.

Due to the difficulty in finding such people, Judge Wallace cautioned the lawyers not to challenge any potential juror unless they had a "damn good reason." While Emanuel wanted religious people in the box, he knew that he would not be able to remove one for being Godless under these circumstances. He just hoped that people so far removed from one of the biggest news stories in the young twenty-first century still had religion in their lives.

The demographic of the jury was fairly diverse. There were seven African Americans, five men and two women. Two of the men were senior citizens. One of the other men and one of the women were very young and had an air of defiance to them, as if they were familiar with the judicial system and distrusted it. Then there was one middle-aged Vietnamese man, and four Caucasians, two men and two women. None of the jurors worked as a professional and all of them were middle class or below. Emanuel was pleased with that fact and, all things considered, with the make-up of the jury.

The trial started as all trials do, despite the significance of the matter. It is a testament to the judicial system that procedure takes precedence over everything else. The whole country and the world might be watching, but when Judge Wallace entered the courtroom, everyone stood up in proper deference to greet him.

The procedure was also a great comfort to Emanuel. He needed something to rely on because his nerves were completely frayed. He had not slept in days due to worry and apprehension. Despite the fact that Satya wanted to defend himself on the God grounds, Emanuel still felt a responsibility for Satya and constantly doubted whether he was doing the right thing. There are times when a lawyer needs to override the wishes of his client and sometimes Emanuel thought this was one of them.

Ultimately, while tossing and turning in his bed and staring at the ceiling of his room for countless hours, Emanuel could not convince himself to defend Satya any other way. There was an insurmountable force pulling him forward in the direction Satya had pointed him. Judicial procedure, therefore, was a framework around which Emanuel could erect his defense even if the defense itself was controversial. No matter what your arguments, a trial is always conducted the same way.

Sophie Mitchell stood up to deliver her opening arguments while Emanuel and Satya, sitting shoulder to shoulder, looked on stone-faced.

"May it please the court," Mitchell began, "I am here today to prove to you beyond a reasonable doubt that Satya Grady is guilty of first degree murder for shooting the Reverend Jackson Emerson Winston."

"The law defines first degree murder as the unlawful killing of another human being with malice aforethought, perpetrated by poison, lying in wait, or any other kind of willful, deliberate, malicious, premeditated killing. It is fact that Reverend Winston is deceased and that he was killed by the bullets of a nine-millimeter handgun. It is my job to prove to you that the defendant was in fact the person that pulled the trigger of that handgun and that his conduct met that definition of first degree murder."

"If I could direct your attention for a moment to the monitor we have set up." Mitchell walked over to a wide screen monitor and turned it on. After a few seconds of static, the video of the assassination began to play. There was complete silence in the courtroom as everyone strained to see the images on the screen. The sounds of the crowd that surrounded Winston as he exited the Hay-Adams hotel the night of his death filled the courtroom. They were the sounds of excitement and fanfare and flashbulbs flashing instantly shattered by the deafening sounds of rapid gunshots. The gallery was startled by the sound of the gun bursts. Then there was a collective murmur as the video showed, from several angles, Satya taking aim and firing his weapon with policeman-like precision. Just as Emanuel had seen the video the first time, it left little doubt as to what happened.

"Ladies and gentleman," Mitchell continued, "the government contends that this video image leaves no doubt that Satya Grady planned this murder and carried it out with malice aforethought. In addition to dissecting this video for you, the government will also present testimony from witnesses to the murder, the law enforcement officers who investigated the murder, and forensics experts who will testify that the bullets found in Reverend Winston's body were the same bullets fired from Satya Grady's gun."

"I want to warn you that the defense will try to distract you from the truth in this case with stories of supreme beings ordering the death of Reverend Winston. And, while the government would never question the existence of God, we do question the half-hearted attempt of the defense to try and justify cold-blooded murder with the alleged word of God. This, ladies and gentleman, is a story that questions our intelligence and strains our imagination."

"When all the stories are finished, ladies and gentleman, you will conclude beyond a reasonable doubt that Satya Grady is guilty of first degree murder for the death of Reverend Winston and that he had absolutely no justification for killing him. Thank you for fulfilling your civic duty by serving on this jury, and I am confident that you will reach the right decision in this case."

Sophie Mitchell sat down and gave Emanuel a long look. It was a look of conviction mixed with pity, because she knew what Emanuel was about to do. Emanuel looked back with bloodshot eyes that showed his concern but did not ask for help.

"Mr. Adams," Judge Wallace commanded, "Are you ready for your opening?"

"Yes, your honor," Emanuel said rising to his feet. He looked down at his notes for the last time, glanced over at Satya and then took a deep breath.

"Ladies and gentleman of the jury, what you have just seen is a powerful and gruesome sight. It was the sight of one man taking the life of another man— nothing anybody wants to see. I wish I could tell you that the man with the gun in the video was not my client, but I can't. I also wish I could tell you that this case was a simple murder for love, money, or vengeance, but I can't. I also wish I could tell you my client is legally insane and not responsible for his actions, but I can't do that either."

"I think you know very well that this case is really about the 'why' of what happened. It doesn't make sense does it, that a police officer of high regard would kill a man for no reason? My client protects people from lawbreakers, stops crimes in progress, and prevents bad deeds with his mere presence in the community. So why did this happen?"

Emanuel paused and took a little stroll around the well in front of the jury. He looked them over and suddenly felt exhausted. They were definitely concentrating on him, but several of them had puzzled looks on their faces. Several of them he assumed were familiar with murders. After all, they lived in the District of Columbia, often referred to as the murder capital of the country. They stopped asking why a long time ago and just accepted it as a fact of daily life. They would need a lot of convincing to differentiate this case from the others they saw around them between gangs and drug lords.

"We all know that there are certain cases where we as a society allow the taking of another life," Emanuel began again. "We don't throw soldiers in jail for killing, executioners for exacting a sentence, or police officers, for that matter, who kill in the line of duty. We also allow people who are in danger of deadly harm to use deadly force in response— justifiable homicide. So, what was my client doing in that video? Was he acting in the line of duty or killing justifiably? I'll answer those questions for you."

"Part of the answer lies in who these men are, because those are not two ordinary men in that video. And who they are and what they've done in their lives is critical to this case and whether my client should be held criminally responsible for what he did."

"Jack Winston was running for President as the head of the recently formed Freedom Party. He was also a reverend and the head of a large church with thousands of members, TV shows, restaurants, and theme parks. He was a multimillionaire on the verge of becoming the President of the United States. Jack Winston preached morality and righteousness. He believed in black and white, not skin color, mind you, but right and wrong in the way people live their lives. He was running for President on the idea that if America followed the word of God, it would be a better place!" Emanuel raised his voice to emphasize this point. It was the set up.

"However, ladies and gentleman, Jack Winston also had a dark side. That dark side led him to fund a private army to spread his notions around the world and to craft a plan to use the U.S. military to do the same!"

"Objection!" Mitchell screamed, jumping to her feet. "That's argumentative and prejudicial, your honor. Not to mention that Jack Winston is not on trial here, Satya Grady is!"

"First of all, this is opening *arguments*, your honor," Emanuel said, trying to remain calm in light of Mitchell's outburst. "And, second of all, Winston's character is very much at issue at this trial," Emanuel responded.

"Unless counsel intends to show his client knew of Winston's alleged activities and then had some right to kill him, those statements are irrelevant and outside the scope of this trial," Mitchell shot back, exasperated.

"Enough," Wallace yelled, banging his gavel. "I'll make an evidentiary ruling when we get there. For the moment, the jury will disregard that last statement about Winston. Proceed, Mr. Adams."

Emanuel was pleased with this initial ruling. Winston's character was on the table, and if by some unexplainable force one of the jurors had missed the news about Winston, they knew now. Emanuel composed himself and continued.

"Who is my client, ladies and gentleman? He is a public servant in New York City, one of the toughest cities in the world. Satya Grady has worked as a police officer for 25 years turning down opportunities to sit behind a desk so he could protect his community. He is also a family man with a wife and three children. He lives a humble, middle class existence, and always has. My client believed that if Reverend Winston became President of the United States, this country and the world would not be a better place but a much more dangerous place. And why did he believe this?" Again, Emanuel paused to let the question sink in to the minds of the jurors. "He believed this because, just like Winston, he was inspired by the all-knowing and all-seeing being we all call God."

At this last point some of the jurors gasped while others smirked. Emanuel didn't know what the gasps meant but he certainly knew that the smirks belied the familiar disdain that comes when someone claims their successes, failures, or transgressions were somehow due to divine intervention. These were the cynics and would be the hardest people to convince.

"Ladies and gentleman, my client believed God wanted to stop Reverend Winston and that he chose him as His agent. It is a biblical tale much like God making a covenant with Abraham and Jesus asking Paul to spread the Gospel. Does that make Satya Grady crazy? I tell you he's not and I'll prove it to you with medical evidence. Does that just make him a killer looking for an excuse? I'll tell you Satya Grady is far from a violent man and show you there was no other motive to kill Reverend Winston. Finally, ladies and gentleman I'll put Satya Grady on the stand and let him tell you his story and ask you to decide for yourself."

"Ultimately, this case is not just about a shooting. Unfortunately, this case is about America and what kind of country we want to be. I know you didn't sign up for that kind of duty, but that is what this case is really about. No matter what happens to Satya Grady, a dramatic event happened in the history of this county. That event has given us pause to look at ourselves and ask whether we want to be governed by religious ideologies and images of right and wrong that may not cross every culture or ethnic group or belief system. We now have the chance to ask whether the vision of Reverend Winston is the right one for America or the actions of my client were the right one— to stop that type of philosophy from spreading. Good versus evil, ladies and gentleman. My client versus Jack Winston, and you'll have to decide."

Emanuel took one long hard look into the face of every juror and then sat down and tried to steady himself. Satya reached over and patted him on the arm. He was pleased with Emanuel's opening statement and already felt partly vindicated now that his explanation was out in the open.

Meanwhile, in the gallery people were stirring and murmuring as Emanuel finished his opening. Some smirked, just as the jurors had, at the pleas as a fanciful story that was a thin defense, while others nodded their heads in approval choosing at least for the moment to leave themselves open the hear Satya's story. The noise caused Judge Wallace to bang his gavel several times to restore order in the courtroom. He was already annoyed that the trial was taking this turn and he knew what was in store for him. The trial of the new millennium was underway.

20

As promised, the prosecution's case moved forward with military precision. Over the next several weeks, Mitchell used the video as a foundation for every witness's testimony. It was a clever ploy because it allowed her to show the footage repeatedly in an effort to solidify the images in the minds of the jurors. Her first witnesses were the cameramen and sound technicians who shot the video. They testified that their equipment was working properly when the footage was taken and that the video clips were accurate.

Next came the eyewitnesses who were pictured in the video. Mitchell would ask each witness to identify him or herself in the video and then confirm that the man they saw shoot Winston was the defendant, Satya Grady, sitting before them. Each one of them did. After the third eyewitness, Emanuel stood up and asked to stipulate that all of the government's proposed eyewitnesses would testify as the last three did. He did not want the testimony to become gratuitous and Judge Wallace agreed. The jury had gotten the point.

After the eyewitnesses Mitchell presented the investigating officers, led by Detective Horahan. He was a veteran cop and was well prepared for his direct examination. Horahan just read from his notes and recounted receiving the call about the homicide and investigating the scene. It was obvious there was a gunshot fatality, and all his eyewitness interviews confirmed that Satya Grady, the man in the video and at the defense table, was the perpetrator. Then Horahan described talking to Satya at the police station the night he was arrested, and testified that while Satya did not make an admission, at no point did he deny the shooting as most criminals do. Emanuel did not ask Horahan any questions, seeing that there was no point.

The forensics expert then identified Satya's weapon from an enlarged video image as a standard police-issue Smith & Wesson 9-millimeter semi-automatic handgun. Then he explained how ballistic tests performed on the bullets removed from Winston's body and from the crime scene were evaluated to show conclusively that they were bullets from Satya's gun. Each gun leaves a trace on its bullets as unique as fingerprints, he explained, so there was no question in this case that there was a match. Mitchell then led him through the chain of custody of the evidence to show that at no point did the evidence become contaminated so as to cast doubt on the credibility of the findings. Again, Emanuel asked no questions.

Next, Mitchell put on the coroner who established the cause and time of Winston's death. The conclusion was internal bleeding and trauma caused by gunshots, and his estimated time of death was within minutes of the time noted in the upper right-hand corner of the video.

Finally, Mitchell put on Hugh Quintas, Winston's campaign manager. Quintas was tall and thin and had an unhealthy, sallow look about him. His eyes were sunken into his bony head, and the bags underneath them were thick and heavy. Quintas had dyed black hair, neatly slicked back and a thin, dyed black mustache. He was conservatively dressed in a blue suit, with a yellow polka dotted tie, and a white silk pocket square peeking out of the breast pocket of his suit.

Quintas first explained that Winston was a candidate for the presidency and that he was speaking the night of his death at a political fundraiser. This testimony was simply to show how Winston arrived at the time and place of his death.

Then Mitchell asked Quintas a few questions about Winston as a person and the tears started to flow. Quintas described what an intelligent and caring man Winston was and how his death was a loss for the entire nation. He confessed to loving the man, in a spiritual manner of course, and described his personal struggles to cope with Winston's death. Emanuel allowed the testimony and tears to continue for five minutes before standing up and objecting that the testimony was not relevant and extremely prejudicial to his client. Judge Wallace appreciated Emanuel's tack of allowing some of Quintas's testimony before objecting, and agreed that the jury had heard enough crying from Quintas. Mitchell then concluded her direct examination and sat down.

Judge Wallace looked over at Emanuel expecting him to say he had no questions, but this time Emanuel told the judge that he did have some questions for the prosecution's witness. He had asked no questions up to that point because there was little to be gained from cross-examining solid witnesses just for the sake of cross-examination. Too many lawyers made that mistake, believing they have to make an effort to impress the jury. Emanuel knew however, that unless the cross-examination was seeking a specific point, prosecution witnesses should be left alone. He had reviewed all the records and proposed testimony beforehand, and there were no holes. Quintas, however, was different.

"Mr. Quintas," Emanuel began, "how long did you know Reverend Winston?"

"I met the Reverend in 1992, when I first joined the Divine Light Church."

"Can you describe your business, or rather, political relationship, with the Reverend for the jury please?" Emanuel asked.

"At first, we had the normal relationship between a clergyman and a churchgoer, but over time it became friendlier. We kept in close contact, even after I moved to Washington to work in politics. When Reverend Winston first started thinking about running for President, he contacted me to seek my advice. I, of course, thought it was a fabulous idea and instantly offered my services as his campaign manager. When he decided to run he gave me the job." Quintas made this statement with an indignant air, as if Emanuel could never understand the bond between the two men.

"In all your years of knowing Reverend Winston as your pastor, friend, and employer," Emanuel asked, "did you ever hear him talk about God?"

Quintas laughed at this question that he found extremely foolish and smoothed his mustache before answering. "Of course I did. Reverend Winston was a man of God, he probably talked about the Lord every day and in every conversation."

"I see," Emanuel said, taking a dramatic pause. "And, did the Reverend ever say he had conversations with God?" Quintas quickly realized he had walked into a clever trap.

"What do you mean?" Quintas stammered.

"I mean, Mr. Quintas," Emanuel said, raising his voice significantly, "did you ever hear Reverend Winston say something like 'I talked to God last night and he told me to run for the Presidency of the United States,' or 'God told me to open a religious theme park?'"

"I don't know?" Quintas replied quietly.

"Mr. Quintas, I will let you answer that question again, before I introduce about 100 newspaper articles in which Winston is quoted as saying he talked to God, and a three-hour video clip of Winston stating publicly that he talked to God. Would you like to rephrase your answer?" Emanuel was red in the face, and the vein bisecting his forehead was throbbing prominently.

"I suppose so."

"You suppose what, Mr. Quintas?"

"I suppose I did hear the Reverend say he talked to God."

"And did you believe him when he said it, Mr. Quintas?"

"Yes, I most certainly did," Quintas snapped, changing his meek tone to one of defiance.

"Thank you, Mr. Quintas. Your honor," Emanuel said, looking at Judge Wallace, "I'd like to introduce this collection of newspaper articles and video clips, corroborating Mr. Quintas's testimony that Reverend Winston repeatedly stated he talked to God."

"I object, your honor," Mitchell said rising to her feet. "Such evidence has no relevance to these proceedings, not to mention, the government has not reviewed the material."

"Your honor," Emanuel broke in, "these materials are very relevant to my client's defense. If the man he allegedly killed could claim he talked to God, and his followers believed him, I think my client can make the same claim and ask the jury to believe him."

"Very well, Mr. Adams. I'll allow you to introduce the evidence, but only after the government has reviewed the material for accuracy. Let's break for today, and allow the government to review overnight."

"Thank you, your honor," Emanuel and Mitchell said in unison.

"Mr. Adams, I will dismiss Mr. Quintas unless you have further questions."

"Just one more your honor. Mr. Quintas were you aware that Reverend Winston was embezzling Church funds and funding mercenary units around the world?"

"Objection," Mitchell stated instantly. "Irrelevant."

"Overruled, Ms. Mitchell. The witness may answer the question." Judge Wallace said.

"I believe all those allegations are completely false. Jack Winston was the most peaceful man I've ever met. He didn't need to use violence to spread his message," Quintas answered spitefully.

"No further questions, your honor," Emanuel said. His face was burning because he knew he went too far in asking the last question.

The trial resumed at 10 a.m. the next morning. Emanuel was there early in order to review his notes. Due to his lack of sleep he was happy to be back in the courtroom. He always found the apprehension of going to trial was far worse than the actual experience. He would be nervous and slightly scared when preparing for trial, but once Emanuel stepped into the courtroom all that angst slipped away.

Emanuel asked the bailiff if he would bring Satya out a few minutes early so they could confer and the bailiff obliged. Satya came in from the side door of the courtroom, still wearing his blue suit and looking fairly cheerful.

"Good morning, Emanuel," Satya said extending his hand.

"Good morning, Satya. You're looking well," Emanuel replied as he shook Satya's hand.

"I really enjoyed your cross-examination of Hugh Quintas yesterday. It lifted my spirits and I finally had a decent night's sleep."

"Thanks Satya, but don't get too excited. We still have a long way to go."

"I know, but where would I be without hope? You just gave me a little more hope yesterday. That's all."

Emanuel went back to reviewing his notes and before he knew it, Judge Wallace walked in and the trial began again.

"Ms. Mitchell," Judge Wallace started. "Did you sufficiently review the tapes and newspaper articles last night?"

"I did, your honor."

"Did you find any problems? Any objections?"

"No, your honor. The government would just like to stipulate to showing one video clip to corroborate Mr. Quintas' testimony, so as to not waste the court's time."

"That's very considerate of you, Ms. Mitchell. Mr. Adams, is that alright with you?"

"Well, your honor, considering the prosecution has showed the video of the assassination countless times, I'm surprised they'd object to some video of Winston talking about his numerous conversations with God."

"Your honor, these sound bites of Winston talking about his relationship with God are simply not very relevant to these proceedings, and whether the defendant shot Winston," Mitchell rebutted.

"I agree," Judge Wallace said. "Mr. Adams, I think I'm going out of my way to allow any of this evidence at all."

"Thank you, your honor. I suppose one clip should prove the point. The defense will stipulate."

"Very well, Mr. Adams you may proceed."

Emanuel got up and walked over to the large monitor that, up to that point, had only replayed the videotape of the assassination to the point of overkill. Emanuel casually slipped in his own tape and then turned to address the jury.

"Ladies and gentleman, as you may recall, yesterday Hugh Quintas, Reverend Winston's campaign manager, testified that on numerous occasions the Reverend claimed he spoke directly to God. Today I'd like to corroborate that testimony by playing you a video clip of an interview Reverend Winston gave on the syndicated talk show, Larry King Live, in January of this year." Emanuel pushed the play button on the monitor and stepped back.

There, in his usual hunched over stance was Larry King with his gray hair brushed back, and his suspenders pushed up almost to his neck. "Good evening America, this is Larry King. Tonight I'm with the Reverend Jack Winston who is currently running a very successful campaign to become the first third-party President of the United States. Reverend, how are you?"

"I'm great Larry. Thanks for having me on the show." Winston, as usual, looked handsome and polished. His blond hair was wavy and luxurious and the bright blue luster of his eyes glowed through the monitor. He had the self-assured look of a man in complete control of every factor in his life. He gave Larry a smile indicating that he could proceed.

"Reverend, the first question is why? Why would a man of the cloth like yourself want to be the political leader of this country?"

"That's a good question, Larry. As you know, I've devoted my entire life to the service of the Lord. Early in my life, I began a relationship with God."

"What do you mean a relationship?" Larry interrupted.

"I mean, Larry, that on my sixteenth birthday, I was lying in bed in a dreamlike state. You know, when you're not sure if you're awake or asleep and you're having thoughts that are deeper than normal. God came to me that night and he asked me to be his servant. He said that it was His will that I devote my life to spreading His Word. He didn't tell me how I should do it, but rather He just enlisted me in His service. It was my first encounter with God."

"How did He come to you Reverend, was it a voice or a vision?"

"It's hard to explain exactly, because it's something you just feel deep inside you, not really your brain or heart, but in your soul. I suppose though, if I had to characterize it, I would say it was God's voice coming to me, but more as an energy field than an actual human voice as we know it. I'll tell you, it certainly was not a vision because no mortal man can see the face of God."

"So that's why you went into the ministry, because God told you to?"

"Like I said, God enlisted me in His service, but He didn't say how I should go about it. That's why I went to a religious college to study as much as I could about His Word. When I got out, I decided that becoming a preacher and spreading the Word was the best way for me to fulfill God's mandate."

"So, back to my original, question, why now the presidency?"

"In all the years between the night God first came to me and last year, God never came and talked to me although I talked to Him everyday. I just did the best I could to satisfy His desires for me. But, last year, I had another conversation with God. Again, it was a similar experience to my first one. I was at home and it was late at night. I couldn't sleep so I took a stroll around my garden. It was a beautiful summer's night and the moon was full, providing just enough light for me to see the flowers and trees. As I was walking, I suddenly became very tired, to the point I thought I would fall over. I sat down in a chaise lounge in the garden, and once again, I entered that dreamlike state and God came to me once more."

"And what did He say, Reverend?"

"He told me I was doing a good job working as His servant, but that I could do more. He asked me to open my eyes wider and look at the world around me. He ordered me to find a way to reach more people and do more good works."

"He didn't specifically tell you to run for the presidency, then?" Larry asked.

"No, but when I woke up the next morning— I was still resting in the chaise lounge— I knew exactly what He wanted me to do. I saw the moral decay in this country and the corruption in Washington. I saw how Muslim terrorists where trying to bring down our economy and spirit. I saw it, but I never thought I could do anything concrete to change it. But, when I woke up that morning as the sun was coming up, I knew what God wanted me to do. He wanted me to become the next President of the United States."

At that point, Emanuel stopped the recording and paused before addressing the jury.

"Ladies and gentleman, there you have it. Reverend Winston went on national television and told the world that he was running for President because God told him to do it. Millions of people watched that and listened to him and did not bat an eyelid. That statement was perfectly plausible to them and they came out in droves to support him. My client, ladies and gentleman, is saying the same thing. God also came to him and gave him a mandate. God said that Reverend Winston was an evil man and he must be stopped!"

"Objection, your honor." Mitchell sprang to her feet. "Counsel is making an argument here."

"Objection sustained. Mr. Adams, these aren't closing arguments. Do you have anything else of relevance?"

"No, your honor. I'm finished."

Emanuel's point was made and he was satisfied. Coming into the trial he was concerned about how he might show this tape of Reverend Winston because he found it crucial to his case. He wasn't sure if the

Quintas cross-examination was going to go as planned and even if it did whether Wallace would allow him to show the tape to the jury. He was successful on both fronts.

"Ms. Mitchell, does the government have another witness?"

"No, your honor. The government rests."

Emanuel quickly rose to his feet. "Your honor, at this point the defense moves to dismiss the charges as we believe the government has not proved a prima facie case of first degree murder." Emanuel knew this ploy was futile, but it was necessary procedurally. If he didn't move to dismiss for the record, he would not be able to appeal certain parts of the government's case.

"Motion denied, Mr. Adams. The court finds the government has proven a prima facie case. We'll adjourn here and resume after lunch. Are your witnesses ready, Mr. Adams?"

"Yes, Your honor."

"Good. The court's adjourned."

"Thank you, your honor," Emanuel said quietly as Judge Wallace's gavel loudly slammed the bench.

During lunch, Emanuel didn't eat. He was happy with how the first part of the trial went, but he knew the real struggle was just about to begin. He sat by himself in the lawyer's room down in the basement of the courthouse, nervously tapping his foot on the worn orange carpet. He wanted to pray for the life of Satya Grady that he now held in his hands. He also wanted to pray for himself. He knew this case meant much more to him than just ensuring another law breaker's Constitutional rights were upheld. This case was personal. He wanted to pray, so he closed his eyes and asked God to help him. He made an impassioned plea that God guide him and protect him. And more than anything, he asked God to protect His servant, Satya Grady.

"Mr. Adams," Judge Wallace growled, "Are you ready to call your first witness?"

"Yes, your honor. The defense calls, Rabbi Samuel Goldberg." Over the next several days Emanuel intended to present religious scholars in an attempt to prove that prophets exist in all major religions and, therefore, it was possible that Satya was a prophet.

Rabbi Goldberg got up from his seat in the gallery and proceeded to the witness stand. He was a man in his late fifties with a thick salt and pepper beard. He had close-cropped gray hair with a bald spot nicely covered by his yalmulka. He wore a black suit, a creased white shirt, and a dark blue tie that looked as if had met numerous bowls of soup and seen many jacket pockets. Goldberg shuffled to the witness stand with his clunky black shoes barely leaving the ground.

"Rabbi Goldberg," Emanuel began, "could you tell the jury a little about your background and what you do for a living?"

"I have a Bachelor of Arts from Columbia University and a Ph.D. in Judaic studies from Yeshiva University. I'm currently the Rabbi for congregation Beth Israel, in Westchester, New York, and I teach Torah studies at Yeshiva University."

"Your honor, I'd like to qualify Rabbi Goldberg as an expert in Jewish studies."

"Any objections, Ms. Mitchell?" Wallace asked.

"No, your honor."

"Very well. The witness is an expert. Proceed."

"Rabbi, could you please explain to the jury as briefly as possible about the belief system of the Jewish faith."

"Certainly. Judaism is best explained through the thirteen foundations developed by the Rabbi Moshe ben Maimon, also known as Maimonides, and generally referred to by the acronym RaMBa'm. I'll try and quickly run through the thirteen."

"First, you must believe in the existence of God as the Creator of the Universe. This God is complete in all ways and He is the cause of all else that exists. He sustains life and if He ceased to exist then all else would cease to exist, therefore, His existence is beyond question. Further, if all else ceased to exist, he would still continue to exist because He needs nothing else and is sufficient unto Himself. This foundation stems from the statement 'I am Hashem your God . . .'"

"The second foundation is the unity of God. That means there is only one God. This does not mean one as in one of a pair nor one like a species that encompasses many individuals, nor one as in one object that is made up of many elements nor as a single simple object that is infinitely divisible. Rather, He is a unity unlike any other possible unity. This comes from the Torah 'Hear Israel! Hashem is our God. Hashem is one.'"

"Third, God is not physical. This means He is not a body and His powers are not physical. Our concept of physical movement and actions do not apply to Him. Any references in the scriptures to Him moving as a human would, are purely metaphorical. This idea comes from the statement in the Torah 'For you did not see any form.'"

"Fourth, God was absolute first and everything else in existence is not first relative to Him. 'That is the abode of God the first.'"

"The fifth foundation is that it is proper to serve Him— to ascribe to His greatness, to make known His greatness, and to fulfill His commandments. We may not serve any lesser beings such as the angels, the stars, the celestial spheres, the elements, or anything else formed by Him. This foundation is based in the prohibition against idolatry."

"Sixth is prophecy. And let me clarify here. By prophecy, I don't mean the ability to foretell the future, but rather, I mean an enlightened sense of perception. In other words, a person must know that there exists amongst mankind individuals who have very lofty qualities and great perfection, whose souls are prepared until their minds receive perfect intellect. After this, their human intellect can then become attached to the Active Intellect— the mind, so to speak, of God— and have bestowed upon them an exalted state. These are the prophets and this is the prophecy."

At this point, Emanuel interrupted. "Rabbi, just to clarify here for the jury. You're saying that one of the foundations of Judaism is that there are certain human beings called prophets who have direct contact with the mind of God?"

"That is correct. Would you like me to elaborate on the prophets?"

"I would rabbi, but not just yet. Please finish explaining the thirteen foundations and we'll revisit the prophets later."

"Very well. The seventh foundation is the prophecy of Moses. This means Moses was the father of all the prophets, both those that preceded him and those who arose after him. He was the chosen one from all of mankind because he attained a greater knowledge of God than any man ever attained or ever will. It is said that he could speak to God without the intermediary of angels."

"Moses is different from all other prophets in several regards. First, as I said, he did not need an intermediary to talk to God. 'Mouth to mouth I speak to him', Numbers 12:8. Second, all other prophets only receive their prophecy either when they are sleeping, as we find in numerous places 'in a dream at night', Genesis 20:3, and 'in a vision at night', Job 33:15, and many other examples. Or by day when a trance has fallen over them which removes all their senses and leaves their mind open as in a dream. Such a state of prophecy is called a vision or seeing and is referred to as 'Divine visions', Ezekiel 8:3. Moses received his prophecy during the day: 'If prophets are among you then I, Hashem, make myself known to them through a vision, in a dream I speak to him. It is not so with my servant Moshe, he is trusted in all my houses. I speak to him mouth to mouth, in a vision without puzzlement. He gazes at the image of God', Numbers 12:6-8. Third, when a prophet receives a prophecy, even though it was only a vision and by means of an angel, he would be weakened by it and his body would shudder. He would be stricken with a very great fear almost to the point that his spirit would leave his body, as when the angel Gabriel spoke to Daniel. Moses did not experience this weakness and shuddering. Fourth, all other prophets were unable to receive prophecy when they will it but only when God wished it. The prophet could wait days or years before the prophecy would come. Moses could prophesize at any time he wished."

"The eighth foundation is that the Torah, in its entirety, comes directly from the mouth of God through Moses the prophet. Moses was like a scribe for God's word. 'And Moshe said, through this you shall know that God has sent me to do all these things, for they are not from my heart', Numbers 16:28."

"The ninth foundation is the transcription, meaning that the Torah came from God and we can't add or subtract from it, Deuteronomy 13:1."

"Tenth, God knows the actions of mankind and does not turn His eyes from them."

"The eleventh foundation is that God gives reward to one who obeys the commandments of the Torah and punishes one who violates its prohibitions. The greatest reward is the World to Come, and the greatest punishment is kareis, or spiritual excision, 'cutting off.'"

"Twelfth, is belief in the time of the Moshiach or Messiah. This is a belief that He is sure to come and not to think He is late in coming. You should not set a time for Him, and you should not make calculations in Scripture to determine the time of His coming."

"Finally, the thirteenth foundation is the resurrection of the dead. Resurrection is only for the righteous, however. As it is said, 'How could the wicked be brought back to life when they are dead even during their lifetime.' The sages teach us 'The wicked, even during their lifetimes they are called dead, the righteous, even during their deaths they are called living.'"

"Thank you, Rabbi. Now if we could return for a moment to the idea of prophets. You mentioned certain things, like other than Moses, all prophets receive prophecies at night in a dreamlike state or in a trance. Are there any other qualifying characteristics?" Emanuel asked.

"In order for a person to receive prophecy, he must be great in righteousness and wisdom and completely self-disciplined. A prophet has no control over whether and when he will receive prophecy. He can only ready himself by meditating and focusing his mind in a joyous state. Prophecy can only come when a person is happy."

"How can we identify a prophet, Rabbi?"

"When God sends a prophet, He gives the prophet a sign to show that he is a true prophet. The sign that a prophet must give to prove he is genuine need not be a miracle."

"Can a prophet ever go against the Torah or violate a commandment?"

"A prophet may never add or detract from the Torah in any way. However, an established prophet may declare a temporary suspension of a Torah law, and we are required to obey him. The only exception to this is idolatry, which can never be permitted under any circumstances."

"So, for example, a prophet may kill in the name of God?"

"It's possible, yes."

"Do prophets exist today, Rabbi?"

"Prophecy has become more difficult to obtain because a higher state of holiness is necessary. In our general society it is almost impossible to obtain this state. However, I suppose a prophet could rise amongst us."

"Thank you, Rabbi. No further questions at this time your honor."

"Ms. Mitchell."

"Thank you, your honor. Rabbi are you familiar with the facts of this case?"

"I know that Officer Grady is being charged with the murder of Reverend Winston, yes."

"Have you ever talked to Mr. Grady, Rabbi?"

"Yes, I did have the occasion to talk to Officer Grady."

"Did he tell you that God told him to kill Reverend Winston?"

"He did."

"Are you prepared to say that Mr. Grady is a prophet by the definition you gave to the jury a few minutes ago?"

"While Officer Grady certainly meets certain criteria of a prophet, I cannot say definitively that he is one, no."

"Thank you, Rabbi. No further questions."

"Your next witness, Mr. Adams."

"Your Honor, the defense calls, Mohammed bin Ahmed."

An old and frail man creaked through the door at the back of the courtroom and began the slow process of walking to the witness stand. He had the quintessential long white beard without the mustache and a completely bald head covered with a white knitted skull cap. His blue suit had long ago lost its shape and the pants were pulled up high and synched with a black leather belt around his non-existent waist.

Mohammed introduced himself to the jury as a man devoted to Allah. He explained he was the director of the Washington Islamic center, and a professor of Islamic studies at American University. Emanuel asked that he be accepted as an expert in Islam by the court and Mitchell and Judge Wallace consented.

"Mr. Mohammed," Emanuel began, "you know that at issue in this trial is whether man can talk to God?"

"Yes," he answered with a strong, firm voice that seemed mismatched with his small body.

"Could you explain to the jury, whether this is a possibility in Islam."

"Certainly. Prophethood in Islam holds a special and significant status. You see, Allah created man for a noble purpose— to worship Him and lead a virtuous life based on His teachings and guidance. But, how would man know his role and purpose of his existence unless he received clear and practical instructions of what Allah wants him to do? This created the need for prophets, and Allah has chosen from every nation a prophet or more to convey His Message to people."

"Who can be a prophet?"

"Of course, this status is at the will of Allah, but in studying history, three traits of a prophet may be recognized."

"And they are?"

"First, the prophet is the best in his community morally and intellectually. This is necessary because a prophet's life serves as a model for his followers. His personality should attract people to accept his message rather than drive them away by his imperfect character. After receiving the message, he is infallible. That is, he would not commit any sin. He might make some minor mistakes, which are usually corrected by revelation."

"Second, the prophet is supported by miracles to prove that he is not an imposter. Those miracles are granted by the power and permission of God and are usually in the field in which his people excel and are recognized as superiors. If I might, I should illustrate this by quoting the major miracles of the three prophets of the major world religions: Judaism, Christianity and Islam. Moses' contemporaries were excellent in magic so he defeated the best magicians in Egypt to lead his people out of bondage. Jesus' contemporaries were recognized as skilled physicians, so his miracles were to raise the dead and heal the sick. The Arabs, the contemporaries of the Prophet Mohammed were known for their eloquence and magnificent poetry. So, Prophet Mohammed's major miracle was the Koran, the equivalent of which the entire Arab world could not produce despite repeated challenges from the Koran itself. The miracle of the Koran transcends time and space, it is everlasting."

"And third?" Emanuel asked.

"Third, every prophet states clearly that what he receives is not of his own but from God for the well-being of Mankind. He also confirms what was revealed before him and what may he be revealed after him. A prophet does this to show that he is simply conveying the message which is entrusted to him by the One True God of all people in all ages."

"You see, prophets are necessary for conveying God's instructions and guidance to Mankind. We have no way of knowing why we were created, what will happen to us after death or if there is an afterlife. Do we know if we are accountable for our actions? In other words, will we be punished or rewarded for our actions? Therefore, we need prophets that we trust and respect to help us answer these questions."

"How many prophets have been sent by God, Professor?"

"We do not know for sure. Some Muslim scholars have suggested 240,000 prophets. But, we are only sure of what is clearly mentioned in the Koran, that is, God has sent one messenger or more to every nation. That is because it is one of God's principles that He will never call a people to account unless He has made clear to them what to do and what not to do. The Koran mentions the names of 25 prophets and indicates that there have been others who were not mentioned to the Prophet Mohammed. These 25 include Noah, Abraham, Moses, Jesus, and Mohammed. These five are the greatest among God's messengers. Therefore, they are called the resolute prophets."

"Would Allah ever tell a man to kill another man?"

"Yes. Allah is just. Hence, evildoers and sinners must have their share of punishment. The righteous and the evil will not receive the same treatment in the hereafter. And, sometimes it is necessary to carry out God's work on earth. In fighting a holy war, or jihad, for example, it may be necessary to kill and of course die in the name of Allah."

"Thank you, Professor. No further questions at this time your honor." Emanuel sat down.

Mitchell got to her feet quickly. "Professor, do you think Satya Grady is a prophet?"

"Officer Grady is not a Muslim so there is no way a non-Muslim could follow the Prophet Mohammed. However, I do believe that Officer Grady is a man of great spiritual purity and faith."

"How do you know that?"

"In my discussions with Officer Grady, I detected an honesty and inner strength I've never seen in another man. He is a man at peace. So, while I wouldn't call him a prophet, I will tell you I believe his story. I only agreed to testify because I believed Officer Grady."

"No more questions, Your Honor." Mitchell should not have asked the last question and she knew it.

At this point, Judge Wallace called a halt to the day's proceedings. It was Friday and he adjourned until Monday morning. Emanuel was somewhat relieved since he was exhausted from the long week. He was looking forward to the weekend and trying to clear his mind although he was so deep in he was not sure it was possible.

21

The next day was a beautiful fall day with a bright sunshine and a warm breeze that still remembered summer. Emanuel was so tired the night before he had skipped dinner and gone to sleep at nine. He now felt energized and wanted some exercise. He decided to take a walk over to the Mall and see what was happening with the protestors. He wanted to see what effect, if any, the trial was having on the people.

The walk from his Dupont Circle apartment to the Mall was only about thirty minutes. He walked up to Connecticut Avenue and took it all the way up past Farragut Square. At that point, it turned into 17th Street, which led down past the White House and to the Mall between the Washington Monument and the reflecting pool.

As Emanuel passed the Old Executive Office Building, a gray and intricate structure, he saw the mass of people unfold beneath him. He couldn't believe how many people were now camping out on the Mall. Even from half a mile away he could hear them. It was like the hum of a large insect. As he got closer the noise grew louder and he could hear music blaring from several sources.

When Emanuel approached Constitution Avenue he had to cross the police line that was encircling the Mall. There were mounted police in a long equine line, and the foot soldiers in riot gear. They were fairly relaxed since the crowd had been peaceful in recent weeks, but they had a nervousness about them as if they weren't certain they could really control the mob if it came down to it. Emanuel also wondered where the police and soldiers came out on all these issues. One of their own was now on trial for murder and they had to have feelings about that.

After crossing the line, he headed up to the Washington Monument. The hillside surrounding the Monument was full of people lounging on the grass, playing frisbee, and strumming on guitars. They were mostly young, in their late teens and early twenties, and the scene more closely resembled the usual Fourth of July concert and fireworks display than a protest. But they were still making a stand.

Emanuel just walked among the people glad for the anonymity of the throng. Every once and a while he would hear snippets of debates typical of college students.

"Taylor is a fucking asshole man. He manufactured this whole thing just to win a fucking election."

"Satya Grady, is like, a Savior. He killed Winston to teach us a lesson."

"Grady's just a freak, like Charlie Manson, or something."

"At least he's not a fucking fundamentalist trying to impose his views on the world. That's worse."

The words came at Emanuel in bits and pieces as he strolled the Mall in the direction of the Capitol. He was actually amazed that so many young people were willing to devote their time to this cause. In his mind it showed a real caring for the future of the country. This case affected everybody in a more concrete way than perhaps any other movement. It brought God into American politics in a tangible way, and it seemed the people could not sit idle.

As Emanuel was walking past the Smithsonian, he was finally recognized. A young man in his early twenties who was lying on a blanket watching a portable monitor spotted him and came running over with a few of his friends.

"Hey, man, you're Emanuel Adams. Dude, what are you doing here? Shouldn't you be preparing for trial?"

"I'm just taking a break that's all. What are you doing here?" Emanuel asked.

"What do you mean? There's no other place to be," the young man responded.

"Shouldn't you be in school somewhere?"

"No way. I dropped out this semester just to be here. This case is everything. I have to see what happens."

"Why? Why is it so important?"

"I guess I want to see who's right."

"Yeah," a young woman chimed in. "We've been debating this case for weeks, and we can't decide what we want to happen. If Winston was so evil, maybe Satya should go free. But then again, he's definitely a murderer, unless he really did talk to God. And, what if Winston wasn't a bad guy? Who are we supposed to vote for now? It's just crazy." The young woman was exasperated.

"I know," Emanuel said smiling. "It's a tough case. But do you think the verdict will definitely bring justice?"

"Sure," the young man answered. "I mean the people on the jury are just like us, right? They'll probably just follow their gut instinct and make a decision. They're usually on target, aren't they?"

"Usually, I guess. There's typically some justice in what they decide, I've found. I just hope they make the right decision here," Emanuel said.

"What do you think the right decision is?" the young man asked.

"I think Satya Grady is a righteous man. I think he deserves to be free."

"All right," they all said in unison. "Good luck, man."

"Thanks," Emanuel said, and kept walking amongst the people.

Monday morning, the trial resumed with Judge Wallace storming into the courtroom. It looked like the weekend did not bring him much rest.

"Your next witness, Mr. Adams," Judge Wallace demanded.

"The defense calls the Reverend Timothy Watson."

Reverend Watson was, like Reverend Winston, a nationally prominent religious leader. He had a Sunday morning prayer television show and affiliated churches across the country. He was not as popular as Winston was, nor did he seek out an empire of theme parks and religious franchises. He did not profit as blatantly from his ministry as Winston did and lived a more humble existence.

Watson came to the stand and several members of the jury gawked as if he was a celebrity. He was a handsome man with thick gray hair that was long enough to fall over his shirt collar. He wore small round glasses that served as frames for his blue-green eyes. His suit was also gray and simple, but still fit his slender, athletic body perfectly. His black, capped-toe shoes were polished to a gleam, and his black tie was silk and expensive. Watson walked slowly and serenely to the witness stand as if he was walking down the aisle to a wedding ceremony.

"Reverend Watson, did you know Jack Winston?"

"I did. He was a friend and, like me, a man of God."

"It must be hard for you to be here today."

"It is. His death was a tragedy for all of us."

"So why did you agree to testify today?"

"When you called me and explained that Officer Grady claimed he was acting on God's request, I felt I should investigate the matter."

"Why is that?"

"I thought that either Officer Grady was insane, trying to beat these charges, or perhaps, I don't know, I supposed there might be something here. Plus, I just wanted to be involved to see if I could offer spiritual guidance."

"When you say, you 'supposed there might be something here,' what do you mean?"

"The Lord works in mysterious ways, Mr. Adams, and while asking a man to kill another man defies what I believe God is about, I thought there might be some other forces at work here. Officer

Grady is, after all, a police officer of high standing. I just couldn't understand why he would do such a thing."

"Did you think it was far-fetched that he claimed to talk to God, leaving for a moment the fact that God told him to kill?"

"Not at all, Mr. Adams. Christ is all around us. He is constantly there for us to talk to Him and seek peace. When you are born again in Christ, you devote your entire life to His word. Part of that devotion is constantly talking to Jesus. He hears everything, and sometimes He will talk back. Remember, Christ died for our sins."

"Reverend did you have the opportunity to meet with Officer Grady?"

"I did, on several occasions."

"Could you tell us about these meetings please."

"At first, I wanted Officer Grady to confess his sin and ask God's forgiveness. Christ is about forgiveness as, ultimately, we are all sinners."

"I didn't know what to expect. But, I quickly realized that Officer Grady was an extremely intelligent man who knew exactly what he had done and the repercussions of his actions. He is also a man of convictions and he quietly told me his story without asking for my approval or acceptance. It simply was so."

"I asked him if he was sorry for what he had done and he told me that he was sorry for causing pain to Reverend Winston's family, friends, and followers. He explained however, that God was calling Winston back to be judged and he was simply the conduit for that. He said we don't have a choice in doing God's work and that I understood."

"What else did you talk about?"

"We talked about everything. Officer Grady told me about his life and working for the New York Police Department. He told me he always tried to do his job to the best of his ability keeping in mind he was there to help people. He told me he missed his wife and children and hoped to see them again soon. Ultimately, he said, that justice would be done in this case, one way or another."

"What was your opinion of Officer Grady, as a member of the clergy, after you met with him?"

"It was strange, but I felt that Officer Grady was a person who did not need redemption. Most people I deal with are somewhat lost in their lives, and turn to Christ to find some direction, stability. Officer Grady is the most peaceful, content person I've ever met. He's certainly not insane."

"Reverend Watson, do you think God told Satya Grady to kill Reverend Winston?"

"I object, your honor," Mitchell interjected. Reverend Watson may be a member of the clergy, but there is no way he can state whether God told the defendant to kill Winston. It's so beyond hearsay it's in another category." Mitchell was exasperated.

"I disagree, your honor. Reverend Watson deals with these matters every day and is the perfect person to judge whether the defendant's claims are legitimate," Emanuel retorted.

Judge Wallace paused for a minute to mull over the objection. He was unhappy with this line of questioning and was scowling, knowing that this could be a matter for appeal. He hated to have his decisions overturned.

"The objection is sustained. Assuming that the defendant's claims are true, the witness did not personally hear or participate in this conversation with the Almighty. Further, the answer may serve to inflame the jury. You may proceed, counselor."

Emanuel looked down at his notes. He was not sure how to proceed and whether Watson could add anything further. Although Emanuel was disappointed that the objection had been sustained, he felt that the mere possibility that Watson would have supported Satya's claim would create a doubt in the minds of the jurors. Perhaps, that was all that was necessary, although he wanted to try one more angle.

"Reverend, you said that the idea that God would tell a man to kill another man defies what you believe in. Why is that?"

"First of all, why would God need a mortal hand to do his work? If God wanted to take Reverend Winston's life he would have done it himself."

"If you believe that, then my client's claim can't be true. Do you still believe that?"

"No, I don't."

"Why not?"

"Because, I thought long and hard about it, and I looked to scripture. Why did God ask Moses to go unto Pharaoh and ask him to free the Israelites? Why did Moses have to be a messenger especially when he warned Pharaoh of the coming plagues? The answer I came up with is that sometimes God needs to work through human beings in order to accomplish his goals. Why did God send his son Jesus Christ to walk among us and then die for our sins? The answer: He needed to show mankind His goodness and teach the lesson of love and forgiveness. So, I concluded in this case, that maybe, if God really wanted to call Reverend Winston home, He wanted to do it this way. For some reason, God wanted Winston killed, not taken in his sleep, and maybe, He wanted someone as righteous as Officer Grady to do it."

"Thank you, Reverend. No further questions, your honor." Emanuel sat down, extremely pleased with this answer.

"Ms. Mitchell?"

"Your honor, the government has no questions for this witness." Mitchell had learned her lesson.

"Your next witness, Mr. Adams," Judge Wallace said.

Emanuel spent the next few days putting on Satya's commanding officer on the force, Doolan and a few of his partners to vouch for his service record and a psychiatrist to vouch for his sanity. Satya's colleagues supported him fully and corroborated his fitness reports. Indeed, Satya was the model policeman on the force.

The psychiatrist testified that he conducted a full mental health examination of Satya and found no traces of dementia, schizophrenia, depression, or other types of mental illness. He also said Satya's story of talking to God and his subsequent actions were not per se evidence of mental illness. Mitchell did not cross-examine the psychiatrist because she did not want to try and prove that Satya was insane or temporarily insane.

"Your next witness, Mr. Adams," Judge Wallace said.

Emanuel paused for a moment, looked at his notes, then said loudly, "The defense calls Jesus Cruz to the stand."

The door to the courtroom opened, and Jesus walked into the room with his head held high and his arms rigidly by his side. He was smartly dressed in a new charcoal gray suit and red tie. His new black wing tips creaked as he walked down the aisle with everyone's eyes on him. As he walked through past the defense table he stopped and gave Satya a long look and a slight smile. It was a look that said Jesus would do everything in his power to extricate Satya from his horrible predicament. Jesus then sat down on the witness stand and took his oath.

"Mr. Cruz," Emanuel began, "how do you know Satya Grady?"

"Ten years ago, Officer Grady arrested me for possession of cocaine with the intent to distribute it."

"Were you prosecuted for the offense?"

"No, the district attorney dropped the case." Emanuel paused awkwardly after Jesus' response. He half expected someone to jump up in the courtroom and say, "I know it was you!" No one did and he proceeded with his examination.

"Did your relationship with Officer Grady continue after your arrest?"

"Yes sir. After I was released, I was on my own again with my serious addiction to crack cocaine. Since I wasn't prosecuted, I technically wasn't in the system. That meant no jail time to get cleaned up, no drug counseling, and no probation officer watching over me."

"What did you do?"

"Like any addict, the first thing I did was look to get high again. I came back home where my wife Marie was waiting for me. I really needed a fix so I rummaged through the apartment looking for money that I knew Marie had hidden somewhere like she always did. She tried to stop me, but I just slapped her. I knocked her down. I didn't give a damn about her or my kid, man. Just getting high." Jesus took a sip of water as he relived this painful memory.

"Finally, I found the money. She'd put it in Jr.'s crib, under his mattress. I was sick enough to even look there, man, knocking him out of the way. I remember him shrieking and Marie crying on the floor holding onto her face where I hit her. I just grabbed the money and headed out the door."

"What happened next, Mr. Cruz?" Emanuel asked.

"When I opened the door, Officer Grady was standing there waiting for me, holding onto his Billy club." A gasp went up in the courtroom.

"He had followed me home because he knew exactly what I was going to do. He said, 'Jesus, I know you're going out to buy crack, but I'm not going to let you do it. I'll give you a choice,' he said. 'Either I arrest you again and make sure you get put away this time, or you let me help you.'"

"There was a look in his eye that was so serious, and the way he was holding that club, made me realize he meant business. I was so hungry for the drugs, but his presence at my front door just stopped me in my tracks. I started crying, telling him how badly I needed the drugs. He told me he understood and marched me back into the apartment. He picked Marie up off the floor and got a bag of ice for her face. He asked me for all my money, which I gave him and he gave it back to Marie. Then he sat me down for a chat."

"We talked all night. I don't remember the details. I just know his words were so soothing. He assured me that I could get through this and it would be worth it. He told me that I wouldn't be alone and people would help me if I wanted it. He told me my family loved me and needed me so much."

"When the sun came up, we had some coffee and then he said he was taking me to a rehab clinic he knew, and I went willingly. I stayed in the clinic for six weeks, and he came to see me every day. He never stayed very long, but just enough time to soothe me."

"Once I got out, he came to see me again and said that if I ever felt the need to buy drugs, I would open my front door and he would be standing there just like he was the first time. Man, I totally believed him. I had cravings too, but I always knew he'd be there. I just knew it. He still came to see me from time to time to make sure I was on the right track. He gave me advice on careers, and even lent me money if I needed it."

"Officer Grady saved my life, and to this day I don't know why he did it. I mean, he must have come across thousands of junkies like me over the years, and why he spent that kind of time for me, I'll never know."

"How is your life today, Mr. Cruz?"

"My life is great. I have a good job with a software company, I own a house, and Marie and I now have three kids."

Emanuel paused to let the story sink in with the jury. He looked them over and they all had serious, concerned expressions on their faces. Emanuel was uncertain what the expressions meant, but at least he was certain the story touched them.

"When was the last time you saw Officer Grady?" Emanuel asked.

"Several months ago. He came by to see me. We had a coffee and after an hour he left."

"Did he seem the same to you?"

"Sure, he did. He was that same calming influence he always was. I needed it too, because at the time I was having some trouble with my boss at work. It was always like that, when I needed him most, he would show up."

"Why do you think Officer Grady killed Reverend Winston?" Emanuel asked.

"Objection," Mitchell said, standing up. "The witness's speculation about the defendant's actions have no basis in fact, and could inflame the jury."

"Your honor, Mr. Cruz is a character witness and I'm simply asking him to describe to the jury why a man of Office Grady's character would do what he is on trial for doing."

Wallace had a pained look on his face once again. He rubbed his head deeply for a minute before answering. "I'm going to allow this testimony. I agree with defense counsel that it will go as to character. Proceed."

"I don't know for sure, Mr. Adams. But what I do know is that he must have had a very good reason for doing so. The man is not violent and he is the most compassionate person I've ever met. He understands how hard life can be— he just has a sense for it. I think a man like Officer Grady would only kill if his life or that of someone he loved depended on it. Otherwise, he'd find another way."

"Thanks Mr. Cruz. No further questions, your honor." Emanuel said sitting down.

"Any questions, Ms. Mitchell?"

"Yes, your honor." Mitchell stood up and reviewed some notes she had made before speaking.

"Mr. Cruz, you stated you were a crack cocaine addict, is that true?"

"Yes, Ma'am, at one point in my life I was."

"Did you have any prior arrests before the time you were arrested by Officer Grady?"

"Yes, I'd been convicted twice before of possessing cocaine."

"Any other arrests?"

"I'd been arrested two other times where I got off. One time for petty larceny and another time for possession of marijuana."

"Ladies and gentleman, for the record, let me make clear that this character witness is a twice convicted felon with two additional arrests. Not much of a character."

"Objection, your honor," Emanuel stated. "Argumentative."

"Sustained. We don't need commentary, counselor."

Mitchell paced the well briefly and then continued. "Mr. Cruz, when you opened your front door on the night you described, what did you think Officer Grady was doing at your apartment?"

"I guess I thought he was taking me back to jail. I wasn't sure why I was let out in the first place." Again, Emanuel shifted uneasily in his seat.

"He didn't take you back to jail, though, did he?"

"No, he helped me out like I said."

"So instead of arresting you again for the same possession with intent to distribute charges, which were never brought, or arresting you for beating your wife and child, or waiting for you to go buy more crack and arrest you for that, he helped you. Is that correct?"

"Yes," Jesus responded meekly. His actions so starkly described by Mitchell brought tears to his eyes.

"Would you consider that high quality police work, Mr. Cruz?"

"Objection," Emanuel stated, jumping to his feet. "Mr. Cruz is not an expert on police work and is not in a position to testify on Officer Grady's actions in that capacity.

"Overruled," Wallace responded immediately, without waiting for Mitchell to respond. "You can't have it both ways Mr. Adams. I think the question is relevant to the defendant's character. Please proceed Ms. Mitchell."

Emanuel sat down.

"Mr. Cruz, do you think that Officer Grady's ignoring your crimes constituted solid police work?"

Jesus wiped away his tears and contemplated his answer. "Yes, I would. Busting people and throwing them in jail is not always the best solution. I was an addict. I couldn't control what I was doing. If I'd gone back to jail my life would have been over. I would have lost my family, everything. I think Officer Grady did the right thing."

"Of course you did, because he gave you your freedom. I would submit, however, Mr. Cruz, that it was very shoddy police work and not at all what we as a society, and the New York police department, expects from its officers. No further questions."

"You may step down, Mr. Cruz," Judge Wallace said.

Emanuel just looked down at his notes and tried to remain unaffected by the cross-examination. Mitchell had done an excellent job. His righteous client no longer looked so righteous.

"We'll stop here for today. Court will resume tomorrow at 10 am," Judge Wallace announced. It was not a good point to stop since the jurors would have all night to contemplate Satya's "shoddy police work," but there was nothing Emanuel could do.

Afterwards, Emanuel and Satya met in a private room behind the courtroom. Judge Wallace had agreed to the meeting at D.C. Superior instead of at the jail since Emanuel was putting Satya on the stand the next day and Wallace felt sympathetic. There was no doubt in his mind, at least, that the defense had no chance.

Emanuel was exhausted, physically and mentally. The strain of playing for the jury and leading the religious experts through their testimony had taken its toll. Weeks of sleepless nights were also catching up with him. He was in an awful pattern of falling asleep early, waking up two hours later, staying up half the night reading, and worrying, and then catching a few hours of sleep early in the morning.

Satya, on the other hand, seemed to be holding up remarkably well. Despite the fact that he was a resident of the D.C. jail, living away from his family, and that his fate was in the hands of twelve strangers, Satya had a light to him. His smile was still bright, and his brown eyes were steady and strong. Even his skin was withstanding institutional living avoiding the pale, sallow appearance that usually comes from life in a cell. Emanuel was amazed and found strength in Satya.

"I'm sorry how the Cruz testimony went, Satya, but there was nothing I could do. I couldn't avoid the fact that Cruz was a convicted felon and Mitchell was smart in questioning how you handled it."

"Don't worry about it, Emanuel. Perception is everything in life. I have no regrets about how I dealt with Jesus. Ms. Mitchell was right. I could have arrested him again, and I contemplated that. If I thought Jesus couldn't turn his life around I would have. For some people, prison time is the only thing capable of stopping them from hurting themselves and others. I knew Jesus wasn't one of those people. He did turn his life around and I'm proud I helped him. If Ms. Mitchell wants to characterize that help as poor police work so be it. I think the jury will understand that Jesus, his family, and society were better served by what I did. I'm confident of that."

"How can you maintain your optimism Satya? The odds are really against us, you know that."

"I know they are, Emanuel. But life is all about dealing with adversity. Why do you think people turn to God and religion? They want the answers to the unanswerable questions. Why do people die and where do they go after they die? Why do young children get sick? Why does life seem so difficult sometimes? Why are people lonely and scared? That is the human condition Emanuel and how people deal with that is how people cobble together a happy and rewarding life."

"I understand that, now. I never used to ask those questions but now I do, especially after it almost ended for me in New York. How I survived that is my unanswerable question."

"I needed you, Emanuel. You couldn't have died in the bombing. More importantly, America needs you to argue this case. It's your destiny."

"America needs me? You're starting to make me think you're insane again, Satya."

"I'm dead serious. The empire is showing cracks, Emanuel. We don't know what kind of country we want to be anymore. The world is rejecting the American way of life and ideology. It's happened to every empire since time immemorial. The dominant society thinks it has an obligation to spread its society around the world and the world eventually says 'no thank you.' But to accept that answer means the superpower has to accept a loss of power, and that has never happened before. America is faced with that right now. The world became increasingly hostile, attacking America violently and emotionally on September 11. How we deal with that will determine the fate of this empire."

"So, you killed Winston to stop America from making the wrong decision?"

"I told you why I killed Winston."

"You mean you didn't even think about why. You just did what God told you?"

"I'm not blind. I see what's happening in the world and I have strong opinions. Would Winston have destroyed America or worse, caused Armageddon? I don't know, but that's not the issue. The real question is what will the American people do? This empire does allow the people to make decisions. The problem is recently the people were so complacent they stopped listening to their leaders and getting involved. They were giving up their rights willingly. I knew my actions would change all that."

"They certainly did. The whole country has an opinion on this case. I wish you could walk down the Mall with me and talk to people."

"I do too. But, Emanuel, that will be your job after all of this is over. I did mine. You go talk to the people and make sure they know the truth. Give them faith that they can make the right choices and answer some of the unanswerable questions."

"What about you, Satya? I'm worried about you. I've never felt this way about a client before. If we lose I'm not sure I'll be able to handle it.

"We've already won, Emanuel. Don't you see? Just do your job to the best of your ability and everything will work out as it should. That's why I feel so optimistic. I know the end result will be the right one."

"Alright, Satya, I will."

That night, Emanuel slept deeply and peacefully.

22

When Judge Wallace knocked on the courtroom door the next morning, everyone stood up in unison. There was excitement in the gallery as everyone knew that they'd hear from the defendant today. The room was packed with people, including Jude who was sitting in the first row behind the defendant's table. Emanuel was happy to see her and it gave him an extra burst of adrenaline like a high school athlete trying to impress his new girlfriend.

Satya looked well rested and pressed in his blue suit. He gave Kim a hug and a kiss prior to sitting down at the table. Once again, he squeezed Emanuel's arm and told him everything would be fine. "We'll get through this together," he said.

After Judge Wallace settled in he gave Emanuel the nod to proceed.

"The defense calls Satya Grady to the stand," Emanuel said with conviction.

Satya got up from his chair and walked to the stand with his head held high. His hair was parted on the left without one strand out of place. He had shaved twice that morning to ensure a clean appearance. He glanced at the jury and then sat down on the witness stand.

The bailiff asked Satya to raise his right hand and then said, "Do you promise to tell the truth, the whole truth, and nothing but the truth, so help you God?" There was a pause in the courtroom as everyone realized these words carried more weight than usual, and then Satya answered firmly: "Yes."

"Officer Grady," Emanuel began, "could you please tell the jury your occupation?"

"I'm a senior officer of the New York City Police Department."

"How long have you been on the force, Officer?"

"This year was my twenty-fifth."

"Your honor, I'd like to introduce Officer Grady's fitness and service records into evidence."

"Very well," Judge Wallace said.

Emanuel handed a copy to Mitchell, one to the clerk, and a copy to Satya on the stand.

"For the sake of brevity, your honor, I'd just like to discuss Officer Grady's last report. Officer Grady, do you see the first page in the file with the date December 7, 2003?"

"I do."

"Could you read the report for the court please?"

"Certainly. 'Officer Satya Grady once again showed himself to be an exemplary officer in the New York City Police Department. Officer Grady made thirty-six arrests this past year without firing his weapon or injuring anyone in the line of duty. He worked tirelessly in the community to try and prevent crime. Once again, this year, Officer Grady volunteered his time to train young officers in crisis management and grassroots police work. Officer Grady passed all his physical and mental examinations with high marks and seems in excellent health.'"

"Thank you. Your Honor I'd like to introduce all of Officer Grady's annual reports and stipulate that they all read similarly."

"Ms. Mitchell, any objections?"

"No, your Honor, the government will stipulate."

"Very well."

"Officer Grady, have you ever received any awards for your service as a police officer?"

"Yes. I've received eight commendations, five Officer of the Year awards, I was recognized by the Mayor of New York for outstanding service, and received a Good Samaritan award for service I performed while off duty."

"Officer Grady, that report you read mentioned that you didn't fire your weapon for a whole year. Is that normal for you?"

"Yes. I've tried throughout my career to avoid the use of firearms. I've always found negotiating to work better and it's obviously safer."

"Officer, it is your defense, is it not, that you killed Reverend Winston because you were following the Word of God?"

"That's correct."

"Could you please tell the jury how you came to receive this Word?" At this question the courtroom became completely silent.

"I was patrolling my beat one night in March of this year. I was in my cruiser in the Hell's Kitchen section of Manhattan. It was late, about three in the morning and Ninth Avenue was deserted. I crossed over 57th and all of a sudden, I noticed that the wind had picked up dramatically. Large objects, like trashcans and cardboard boxes, were being blown across the street. There was a lot of dust, too, so my visibility was low."

"I slowed down and just as I did, my right front tire blew out. This was odd since we have those heavy-duty, puncture-resistant radials, but it does happen from time to time. I pulled over. I was between 53rd and 52nd, right in heart of Hell's Kitchen."

"What happened next, Officer?"

"I got out of the car and was immediately struck by how cold it was. It was only March, but it felt like the middle of winter. I looked around and noticed that there was not one person on the street. Nobody was walking around or standing on the corner— very unusual for New York. The emptiness made me a little nervous."

"I walked to the front of the car and looked at the tire. There was a gash in it like you wouldn't believe. It looked like someone took an industrial saw and just had at it. As I was checking it out I heard glass shattering. I became even more nervous because I thought that a major crime might be in progress. I was patrolling alone that night since my partner was sick."

"Right away, I radioed in and told the dispatch my location and that I was investigating a possible break-in. I drew my weapon and crossed over Ninth on foot towards the sound of the glass."

"Right as I got to the other side, I heard more glass breaking. The sound was coming from an alleyway in the middle of the block, so I headed right for it. As I was running, I was thinking how odd it was that there was an alley in the middle of the block. I know that neighborhood pretty well and I just don't recall ever seeing that before."

"I turned into the alley and ran down it. A few paces in, the alley had a turn in it, which was also really strange. I made the turn and right there, I surprised a man climbing through a huge window that he'd obviously broken. I had no idea where the window led, but the man was climbing through it."

"I yelled, 'Stop! Police!' The man turned to me and his face was covered in a black mask— not a ski mask but something really tight fitting. It almost looked like he didn't have a face, just a black space on his neck with two eyes. The next thing I knew, he pulled a gun and shot off a round, just one shot. It was a clean shot, though, right to my chest. It knocked me over and I blacked out."

The jury was mesmerized by the story. Satya's description was so detailed and his face so expressive as the words poured out of his mouth.

"Please continue Officer Grady."

"While I was unconscious I could see myself lying in a trash heap in that alley. The dream was pleasant though, as if I knew everything would be fine, but at the same time, I was positive I was dying. I could see that the wind had died down and the temperature had returned to where it should've been. I looked at my shirt and it was completely soaked in blood. I could also see the bullet hole in my chest and it was a big one."

"Then, in my dream, I started praying. I wasn't praying to stay alive, but just to prepare myself for death because I was sure the end was coming. I wasn't scared or sad. It almost felt good, as if all my hard work was over and it was time to go home."

"At that moment, I raised my head up a little bit, and I saw this figure appearing from around that bend in the alley. As the figure approached it became less and less discernible until it seemed to disappear inside of me."

"Then I heard His voice in my head: 'How do you feel, my son?' He asked. Right away, I knew it was God."

"I answered, 'I've been shot. I'm dying.' I remember thinking that I sounded scared, like a lost child. 'It is very bad,' He said. Then from inside of me He reached out to my wound and His touch sent an electric shock through my otherwise numb body."

"Then God said: 'You're dying Satya.' He said it matter-of-factly like it was inconsequential. 'Are you afraid of death, Satya?' I immediately answered, 'No, I'm not afraid. I just never thought I'd die alone in an alley. I wish my family were here.' As I said this I got the sense He knew exactly what I was going to say before I said it. 'You are a man of faith, Satya.' He said to me. It was a statement without any hint of doubt. Then I answered Him: 'Yes Lord, I am a man of faith.' As I said it, it was the most energizing feeling I've ever had— to know I was talking to God and He was talking to me.

'Satya, if I command you to undertake a task for me will you do it?'

'Yes,' I answered.

'Will you question my motives for giving you this task?'

'No, Lord,' I said.

'There is a man, Satya, who is so evil, that he has the capacity to destroy all of human kind. This man hides behind the veil of My power and My words to carry his evil plans into action. This man frightens people with My wrath as if it were his own, in order to make people do his bidding. This man is smart and cunning, and he has the power to manipulate people with his energy. He shines on the outside as if bathed in my light but on the inside, he is dark and depraved. He is now a leader of a great army but he is looking to increase his hold over people and nations. Satya, I need you to be my servant and remove this man from human society in the name of the Lord.'

'Thy will be done Lord,' I answered. 'Just tell me who this man is and it is done.'

'This man is Jackson Emerson Winston.'

'Yes Lord,' I answered.

'Goodbye Satya,' He said and touched His hand to my heart in parting. I could once again see the dark figure moving down the alley. He turned the corner and was gone.

"The next thing I knew, I regained consciousness. I reached down to my chest and felt for the bullet wound. It was gone but great pain had overtaken my body. The pain came from my shoulder and I reached for it. There was a gash there as if the bullet had simply grazed my shoulder instead of hitting me in the chest."

"I felt strong enough to get up, so I struggled to my feet and headed out of the alley, back to the street. When I got out to 9th Avenue, I looked back down the alley looking for some sign of what had happened, but it was empty. Just then, two cruisers pulled up in front of me and the officers rushed to my aid. I told them I'd been shot in the alley and then collapsed in their arms. The next thing I knew, I woke up in the hospital."

During Satya's testimony Emanuel had looked around the courtroom, which was still completely silent. The jury, Judge Wallace, and the gallery sat spellbound by Satya's story. There was something in Satya's voice that was completely believable. He didn't sound like a raving lunatic, or a religious zealot. Rather, he just sounded sure of himself and confident. It was this characteristic that made Emanuel believe in him from the start.

"Your Honor," Emanuel said, "I would like to introduce these photographs taken of Officer Grady at the hospital after the incident he described." Emanuel showed the jury the photos of Satya with a bright red wound above his right shoulder blade, and then another picture of the stitched wound. Some of the jurors were disturbed at the gruesome sight, all of them were wondering if Satya's story could be true.

"Officer Grady, what did you do next?"

"Basically, I just did some research into Reverend Winston's travel plans. I knew he was coming to Washington the next week, so I went too. Then, as we all saw on the video, I shot him with my service revolver."

"Officer Grady, do you feel remorse for shooting Reverend Winston?"

"Of course I do. I know he has a family and people who love him, just like I have. I know from being a police officer how serious death is because I've seen it too many times to count. I'd like to apologize to the Reverend's family. However, I felt I had no choice in the matter. God came to me and told me to do His work, and as a man of faith, I had to do His bidding. I'm also willing to suffer the consequences of my actions."

"Thank you, Officer Grady," Emanuel said. He didn't even look at the jury as he sat down.

"Ms. Mitchell, your witness," Judge Wallace said quietly.

Mitchell began her cross-examination from her seat. "Mr. Grady, do you admit that you planned the death of Reverend Winston?"

"Yes."

"Do you admit that you waited for him outside the Hay-Adams hotel?"

"Yes."

"Do you admit that when Reverend Winston exited the Hay-Adams hotel the night in question, you shot him causing his death?"

"Yes."

Mitchell went to her feet and approached the witness stand. "Now, Mr. Grady, you've just told the jury that the reason you carried out this act was because God told you to do it. Most of the world's religions and certainly the teachings of Jesus Christ hold that killing another human being is a sin. Do you expect the jury to believe that God told you to commit a sin, to break His Commandment, 'Thou shall not kill'?"

"Ms. Mitchell, I wish life could be so easy as to have predetermined answers. The fact is, killing is only a sin in certain circumstances. If you defend your home and family, then it isn't. God would understand. When we fight wars and kill other human beings because they threaten our way of life that isn't a sin, is it? If the jury finds me guilty I'll be put to death by the government of the United States. Is that a sin or not? Are you committing murder by asking the jury to find me guilty?"

"Of course not, Mr. Grady," Mitchell said, flustered. "I'm doing my job. The government pays me to prosecute people who break the law."

"Exactly. And, I was just doing my job, entrusted to me by a higher power than our government, God."

"But, our government is a real tangible thing, and our laws were created by the people of this country. If we go to war, or decide to execute someone, it's a group decision."

"Just because you can't see God, doesn't mean He's not all around us. That is what faith is. If you have faith, you believe that God created life and God takes it away. In this case He simply used me to take the life of Reverend Winston. That was my purpose, Ms. Mitchell, just like I'm sure you have yours."

Once again there was silence in the courtroom.

"I have no further questions, your Honor," Mitchell said, sitting down.

"You're excused, Officer Grady," Judge Wallace said with a respectful tone.

Although Emanuel normally would have closed his case with Satya's testimony, there was one more witness he had to call, the doctor from the emergency room the night Satya was shot and talked to God. He had run out of time for the day, however, and Judge Wallace called a recess.

That night Emanuel headed right for the Old Ebbitt. The hardest part of the case was over. He would have a strong closing argument but the case simply hinged on whether the jury believed Satya and nothing he could say in closing could convince them of that. Emanuel felt a combination of euphoria that the case was winding down and apprehension about its ultimate resolution. He was confident he'd done the best job he could've under the circumstances, but often in the criminal justice system that simply wasn't good enough. And, the facts of this case were worse than most others.

Emanuel thought back to his trial practice class in law school. His professor was a diehard liberal who had devoted his career to criminal defense because he viewed it as a social service. Jerry Horowitz didn't feel anyone was guilty because at some level society drove them to crime, so our government or corporations or the class system was really to blame. Horowitz always put one of these institutions on trial instead of his client, and won his fair share of hard luck cases.

While Horowitz talked like a socialist and dressed like a philosophy professor, complete with the tweed jacket with the patches on the elbows, worn corduroys, and beat up shoes, he knew criminal law better than most polished looking corporate litigators. Horowitz always said each case, no matter how complicated, came down to one fact. After you weed through all the intricacies and the testimony, one fact would make the difference in the mind of the jurors. At the moment, Emanuel's biggest problem was his one "fact" was God, and He didn't show up to testify. Emanuel knew that God meant something very different to different people, and that fact would probably kill his case. Emanuel tried to prove God's existence through piecing together smaller facts about traditional religious doctrines and more importantly, through the direct testimony of his client. But, he needed to corroborate Satya's story to convince the jurors, but at that point it looked too late. Emanuel needed a new fact.

Emanuel walked into the Old Ebbitt and was embraced by the usual noise and warmth of the early evening crowd. He hadn't been there in weeks and was happy to be back. He nodded at Tony the maître d' and hopped up the three steps to the bar. As he strode down to his usual seat in front of Doc, Emanuel could feel people's eyes upon him. People turned the heads to look at him and whispered quietly to one another. He'd become a Washington celebrity and wasn't that happy about it. All he wanted was a quiet drink, not fleeting stardom.

"Counselor, so good to see you," Doc said, placing Emanuel's martini in front of him. "This place isn't the same without you." Doc wiped his hand on his apron and shook Emanuel's.

"Doc, believe me, I'm not the same without this place." Emanuel took a long sip of his martini with his eyes closed. "Ah, the nectar of the Gods."

"Haven't you had enough of God, Emanuel?" Doc joked.

"I probably have, but these martinis have a divine quality to them."

"Cheers, Emanuel. Listen, in all seriousness, how are you? It must be tough."

"It's been a stressful few weeks, but it's winding down now. The case has gone as well as I could've expected." Emanuel took another sip of his drink. "What've people been saying around here?"

"It's a mixed bag. With the election coming up most of the political hacks are cynical. They figure one way or another Taylor's gonna win thanks to your client. They're not so concerned about whether Officer Grady is guilty or innocent, I'm sorry to tell you. It won't make a bit of difference in the election or their careers."

"I suppose not."

"Others do talk about whether Officer Grady was justified in killing Winston. It's not like many Washingtonians were looking forward to a religious extremist in the White House. Everyone in town might have lost their jobs and worse, he might have shut down this bar."

"Don't even make jokes like that. That's what the case will really come down to. If the jury thinks my client was justified they'll acquit, if not he's done for."

"Just hope for the best. You'll always have me, Emanuel."

"Thanks, Doc. That's comforting."

Doc walked away leaving Emanuel alone with his martini. He lit a cigarette, took a long drag, and then chased it with a mouthful of warming vodka. Emanuel stared blankly at the monitor behind the bar. CNN was recapping the day in court and analyzing his every move. Moreover, they were discussing Satya's testimony, which had caused an enormous stir and the talking heads were beside themselves trying to make points about God, morality, criminal conduct, the supernatural, politics, the history of assassinations, and any other angle they could find.

The court of public opinion found Satya's testimony compelling. He wasn't a raving lunatic talking about God, but a rational man talking about a strange, near-death experience. Of course, the legal pundits claimed even if Satya's story was true it still wasn't an adequate defense. The law of justifiable homicide didn't include the God defense. The pundits did talk about jury nullification as a possibility, but that was just a crapshoot. Who knew what was going on in the minds of the jurors or how spiritual they were? There had never been a case like this to test the religious convictions of a jury because there had never been a time like this in American history before.

Emanuel was happy that Satya had at least made an impact. Nobody was laughing at him or questioning his sanity anymore. Satya's method was questioned by many of the talking heads admitted that Winston's presidential bid had major problems to it, and while no one wanted to say they were glad he was dead, the message was clear.

Doc interrupted Emanuel's thoughts with another martini.

"You old dog. It was bad enough before you were a star. This one's from the lovely brunette at the end of the bar."

Emanuel looked to his right and saw a six-foot tall woman walking in his direction. She had long, dark wavy hair that fell over broad shoulders. Her green eyes stood out prominently on her gaunt and angular face as did her perfectly white teeth. She was wearing a tight gray, cashmere turtleneck sweater and a black skirt that showed the contours of her hips and fell off just before her knee- high boots started. Emanuel noticed she strutted like a runway model, placing one foot in front of the other— an odd site in Washington.

"Pardon the interruption, Emanuel, but I wondered if you'd like some company," she said.

"Do I know you?" Emanuel asked nervously.

"No. We've never met, except I watch you on television everyday."

"Really. I'm sorry you don't have better things to do with your time."

"Come on. Everyone's watching. It's engrossing," the woman said, with her hands on her hips.

"Would you like to sit down?" Emanuel asked.

"I would love to. My name's Sarah."

"Nice to meet you, Sarah. Thanks for the drink."

"You're welcome. Thank you for doing such a wonderful thing for our country."

"What am I doing for our country?" Emanuel asked.

"I think America is on trial in this case. And, you're doing a fantastic job of making that clear. We need to look in the mirror and see if we like what we see."

"That's exactly what I think. I'm glad you do to."

"I'll tell you something else Emanuel . . . I knew Jack Winston." All of a sudden, Emanuel felt extremely self-conscious, like everyone in the bar had stopped talking and were listening to their conversation. "I knew him, and I have information that might help your case."

Emanuel rubbed his hand across his forehead, summing up the situation. He took a cigarette out from his jacket pocket, lit it, and looked Sarah over very carefully. She could be some crackpot trying to throw him off the case at the last minute. After all he'd been through, anything was possible, but he decided to hear her out.

"Alright, let me have it," Emanuel said.

23

The next morning, Emanuel appeared in court exhausted. All of a sudden, this last day of testimony was turning into the pivotal point of the trial. Ultimately, he believed what Sarah told him and then stayed up half the night trying to corroborate her story and then preparing his direct examination. The first witness of the day was still the doctor who saw to Satya the night he was shot.

"The defense calls Dr. Jacob Heller," Emanuel stated.

A young man in his early thirties walked up to the witness stand in a green plaid jacked and gabardine pants. Heller had thick black hair, held neatly in place with gel that glistened in the fluorescent lights of the courtroom. He was the chief emergency medicine resident at Mt. Sinai hospital and the only thing that took away from his immaculate appearance were the dark circles under his hazel eyes that told of many sleepless nights in the emergency room.

"Dr. Heller," Emanuel asked, "Can you please tell us what happened the night of March 8, when Officer Grady appeared in your emergency room?"

"Officer Grady presented with a gunshot wound to his left shoulder. The bullet seemed to have grazed his shoulder. I just cleaned the wound and stitched it up. It was a fairly routine procedure."

"How many stitches were required, Doctor?"

"I believe it was fifteen."

"And how was Office Grady's demeanor?"

"Officer Grady seemed to be in a state of shock. He was calm, quiet, and had a dreamlike quality. Not that unusual for somebody who was just shot."

"Thank you, Doctor. No further questions, your honor."

"Ms. Mitchell."

"Doctor," Mitchell began, "in his testimony, Officer Grady claimed that he was shot in the chest and was actually on the verge of death when God came to him and saved his life by moving the wound to his shoulder. Did you see anything that might corroborate this story?"

Heller thought for a minute while Emanuel smiled to himself.

"I don't know if I can corroborate that story, but there were a few unusual things about Officer Grady's case."

"Like what, doctor?"

"First, his vital signs were way low, seventy-five over palp."

"Seventy-five over palp?"

"I'm sorry. The average rate is about 120 over 70. When the second rate is so low you can't hear it, we say 'over palp.' It's a rather serious situation."

"What else doctor?" Mitchell was uncomfortable now, but she had opened this line of questioning and couldn't back down.

"Officer Grady had also lost a lot of blood, which obviously contributed to his low vitals. I had to give him a transfusion of about five pints. I don't mean to downplay this type of injury, but in the range of bullet wounds, this was relatively minor. There was not reason for Officer Grady to have been in that condition."

"Anything else, Doctor?"

"I guess there's only one other thing that does come to mind. When I was examining Officer Grady, I did find a strange reddish rash on his chest. It almost resembled frostbite, which would have been impossible. It was small and localized and not causing him any discomfort so I thought nothing of it."

Mitchell was stunned by this testimony. She had never questioned Heller prior to the trial because she was sure he would have nothing to add to the medical reports she read. She paused not knowing how to proceed. The entire courtroom was silent as the jury and gallery contemplated the significance of the doctor's words. Finally, Mitchell stammered, "None of these observations indicate a bullet wound to the heart or chest though. Isn't that correct, Doctor?"

"That's correct. And he had no internal damage."

"Thank you. No further questions." Mitchell sat down quickly.

"Mr. Adams, do you wish a redirect?"

"Yes, your Honor."

"Doctor Heller, let me see if I understand your testimony. Officer Grady had dangerously low vital signs, needed a five-pint transfusion, and had burn marks on his chest?"

"Yes. Unusual for a gunshot wound to the shoulder."

"You are aware that Officer Grady claims he was shot in the chest and then after having an encounter with God, the bullet wound moved to his shoulder, are you not?"

"I am."

"Do you think that is a possibility considering your observations upon examining Officer Grady?"

"Objection, your honor. Is counsel really asking this witness to validate the defendant's so-called meeting with God?"

"Your Honor, I'm simply asking the witness's expert opinion as to whether Officer Grady's symptoms on the night in question were more in line with a chest wound than a shoulder wound?"

"I'll allow the question."

"Doctor Heller, where the symptoms more in line with a chest wound?"

"Mr. Adams, I can't tell you what happened to Officer Grady that night, but I will say this. I've seen hundreds of bullet wounds in my career, and a shoulder wound that requires fifteen stitches is not at all consistent with Officer Grady's other traits— the loss of blood and his vital signs. And, I still can't figure out what the rash on his chest was. On the other hand, a chest wound with internal damage will most certainly result in those characteristics. So, something strange happened out on the street that night."

"Thank you, doctor. No more questions."

"You may step down," Judge Wallace said. "Any more witnesses, Mr. Adams?"

"Yes, your Honor. The defense has one more witness that was not on the list. Her name is Sarah Miller. She's a character witness with testimony about Reverend Winston."

Mitchell immediately stood up. "Your Honor, first of all the government has not had the opportunity to depose this witness, and second, as I said during counsel's opening, Reverend Winston is not on trial here nor is his character."

"Your Honor, this case is about whether my client was justified in killing Winston. He claims he was following God's will in doing so because Winston was an evil man. Therefore, testimony about Winston's character is certainly relevant. And, as for the government's opportunity to depose the witness, I also have evidence that the government can quickly review to glean the nature of the testimony. I would like to proffer the evidence."

"Very well. The jury will retire to the anteroom until further instructions while I review this new evidence."

"Counselors, please approach the bench."

Emanuel and Mitchell walked up to the bench. Emanuel handed a stack of photographs to the judge.

"Jesus Christ," Wallace said after looking at them. He passed them over to Mitchell who just shook her head.

"Your Honor," Mitchell said after reviewing the photographs, "these photos will only inflame the jury and are prejudicial to the government's case."

"What!" Emanuel said trying to keep his composure. "The government has shown a video of my client shooting Winston countless times. What could be more prejudicial than that? You can't have it both ways, Mitchell. I admit these are tough photos, but I have a right to show my client's actions were justified."

"Your Honor, let me repeat that Reverend Winston is not on trial here. Why do we need to sully the man's memory when it has nothing to do with whether Officer Grady had a legal right to kill him?"

Wallace pondered his current predicament. He was in a no-win situation and he knew it. Either way he decided would be questioned especially if he didn't allow the evidence.

"I've thought about the character issue a long time, since it came up during the openings. While Ms. Mitchell, I agree with your arguments in principle, I do have to weigh whether the probative value of this evidence outweighs the potential prejudice. In this case, I do think I have to let the jury decide whether Reverend Winston's morality, or lack of it, was a factor in this case. Your job will be to convince them that it isn't. I'll allow the witness and the photographs."

Once the jury was back in place, Emanuel called Sarah to the stand. She entered the courtroom in a conservative black pantsuit and walked to the witness stand as she had walked over to Emanuel at the Old Ebbitt the night before.

"Ms. Miller, what is your occupation and residence?" Emanuel asked once Sarah had taken her oath.

"I live in New York City and I work in fashion."

"Please tell the jury how you came to know, Reverend Winston."

"Eight years ago, I moved to New York. I was fourteen years old and just starting out my modeling career. I was living away from home and part of the Glamour agency's development program."

"I was living the party life like most young models, going out to New York's best places, never paying for a thing. One night I was in the VIP room at an exclusive club when I was brought over to a table where a couple of men were sitting. One of them was Jack Winston."

"What did you think of him?"

"I thought he was so beautiful. He had this incredible aura around him. I was young and impressionable and I was in awe of him. He talked to me so quietly and stared at me with those blue eyes of his. I'll never forget the moment I first met him."

"What happened next?"

"We spent a few hours drinking and doing cocaine at the club and then we went back to his friend's apartment." Sarah said cocaine so matter-of-factly that Emanuel was worried the point would be missed by the jury.

"Who had the cocaine?" Ms. Miller.

"Jack did."

"How much cocaine?"

"I can't say exactly, but enough to keep doing it all night at the table. It seemed like one of us was doing a key at all times."

"So, what happened when you went to his friend's apartment?"

"He took me into a private room and all of a sudden his quiet demeanor completely changed. He became agitated and violent. He turned into an animal and started doing horrible things to me." Sarah paused there and became choked up with emotion.

"I know it's difficult, Ms. Miller, but can you tell the jury what kind of things Reverend Winston did to you?"

"He started by cursing at me. He called me a dirty little slut and said Satan was inside me. He said he needed to get the Devil out of me. Then, he handcuffed me face down on this large bed. I remember having my face buried in the comforter not knowing what would happen next. I was terrified. Then I smelled incense and the sweet smell made me sick. My head was spinning from the alcohol, drugs, and incense. But, the next sensation I felt was incredible pain. Jack had taken a riding crop and started beating me across the back, yelling all the time that I was a whore possessed by the Devil. I was crying out in pain and I could feel the blood beginning to flow on my back."

Sarah had to pause as the memory was bringing tears to her eyes. Emanuel became acutely aware of the silence in the room. Judge

Wallace had a deep frown on his face that made his forehead seem mountainous. The jurors where also riveted on Sarah. Some were covering their mouths while others looked on the verge of tears as they watched Sarah cry. Emanuel felt terrible that Sarah had to reveal this information, but he knew it was critical to his case. After a minute he prodded Sarah to continue her story.

"When he stopped beating me, he rolled me over with my hands still handcuffed behind my back. The handcuffs were cutting into my hands and my hair was in my face so I could hardly see. Then Jack moved away my hair and showed me a razor. It was one of those old fashioned flat razors and it was sharp. He took it and started shaving me, you know, down there." Sarah nodded her head forward and everyone in the room got the picture.

"He was saying that I needed to be completely exposed for his exorcism. Again, that the Devil was inside me and he needed to get him out. When he was finished shaving me he rolled me over again." Sarah stopped again.

"Sarah," Emanuel began in a quiet voice, "what happened then?"

"He, he . . . sodomized me."

The jury and the gallery cringed at this new detail. Even Emanuel was finding it hard to take.

"Anything else, Ms. Miller?"

"After he was finished, he started to cry. He was weeping like a baby. He said he was sorry he had to do that to me but it was the only way to make me pure again. He kept saying he was sorry and then he finally, he uncuffed me. He insisted that I take the riding crop and whip him. He said he needed to feel my pain. At first, I didn't want to, but then I did it. I beat him with all my might. He shrieked in pain, but I know he enjoyed it. When I was finished he told me to get out. I grabbed my clothes and left. His friend had a limo drive me home."

"Your Honor, at this time I'd like to introduce photographic evidence to corroborate Ms. Miller's testimony," Emanuel said.

"Very well," Judge Wallace said with a very dry mouth.

Emanuel showed the photographs to the jury who passed them around barely able to stomach them.

"Ms. Miller, where did you get these photographs?"

"It turns out that Jack's friend whose apartment we were at, had a hidden camera in the room. After Jack's death, he gave me copies. I guess to remember Jack by."

"What is your opinion of Jack Winston, Ms. Miller?"

"I think he was a sick man. He obviously had some incredible strengths, but deep inside he was an evil man. He loved power, but it was almost too much for him. I think that's why he liked being beaten by young girls."

"Thank you. No more questions."

"Ms. Mitchell," Judge Wallace said quietly.

Sophie Mitchell got up to begin her cross examination. She knew she'd have to shift the blame for this twisted sexual relationship from Winston to Sarah and she was dreading it. She hated when female victims were made to seem like the instigator of sex crimes and much preferred the prosecutorial role of attacking a sexual predator. In this case, however, she had to make Winston seem a little less deviant than Sarah Miller's testimony just did.

"Ms. Miller, when Jack Winston asked you to go home with him on the night you described and you said yes, was that a decision you made of your own free will?"

"Sure. I was extremely attracted to Jack."

"So, you knew that 'going home' with him meant engaging in sexual activity?"

"I suppose I did, but not . . ."

"Just answer the question, Ms. Miller. You described Jack Winston putting you in handcuffs. Did he force you to wear them or did you let him put them on?"

"I don't remember. Things were happening so fast."

"Did he beat you first?"

"No."

"So, you let Jack Winston handcuff you?"

"I don't remember."

"Fine. Ms. Miller, did you enjoy the sexual experience you had that night?"

"No. I was terrified."

"Did you see Reverend Winston again?"

"I did." The jury gasped at this testimony.

"You mean, after that experience, you claim was so horrible, you saw him again?"

"Jack was so enticing and I was so young. I thought maybe that behavior was normal. I didn't know anything about what people did in bed. Plus, Jack was also a father figure to me. I was alone in New York and when we weren't having sex he had the same calm demeanor and soothing presence as when I first met him. It was only late at night when he turned into that monster."

"The fact is though, you continued to date Jack Winston for, how long, several months a year, out of your own free will?"

"It was only a few months."

"It was out of your own free will, Ms. Miller," Mitchell yelled.

"I suppose I did," Sarah responded with her head hung down in shame.

"No more questions."

"Mr. Adams, any redirect?"

"Yes, Judge. Ms. Miller, tell the jury one more time how old you were when you met Jack Winston."

"Fourteen."

"Fourteen," Emanuel yelled. "A minor and too young to make rational decisions."

"Objection," Mitchell belted out, standing up. "Counsel is making an argument."

"Your Honor, it's a fact that fourteen is below the age of consent."

"That's true counselor, but save that for your closing. Objection sustained."

"No more questions, your Honor."

"You may be excused Ms. Miller. Any more witnesses, Mr. Adams?"

"Your Honor, at this time the defense rests."

Mitchell's closing argument was an antiseptic procedure. She once again showed the video of the assassination and then referred to Satya's testimony that clearly encompassed an admission of all the necessary elements of first degree murder. She then implored the jury not to be swayed by supernatural tales and the fact that Winston had some skeletons in his closet. "Committing adultery does not give someone else the right to kill you," Mitchell admonished the jury. "While those facts might be disturbing, they had nothing to do with this case. At the end of the day, Officer Grady had no authority to kill Winston, nor any personal justification to warrant justifiable homicide."

Emanuel, on the other hand, felt he needed a big finish. He needed the jury to put Satya and Winston next to each other and conclude that Satya was the better man. So much so that he did the world a service by killing Winston and should be set free. Emanuel stood up and gave the jury a long hard look and then glanced at Satya before beginning.

"Ladies and gentleman, one of the backbones of this country is a belief in God. The first settlers to this land, the Pilgrims, came here to seek religious freedom. They were followed by the Quakers, the Catholics, the Eastern European Jews, and countless other groups seeking religious freedom. These people lived under regimes that oppressed their faith, and they wanted to be free to pray to God in the way they saw fit."

"That freedom is one of the foundations of our democracy. While we have this freedom, there is also no doubt that God, and primarily Christianity, play a huge role in our society and our government. We constantly tussle with the First Amendment to the Constitution, which says both that there must be a separation of church and state and that the government must pass no laws that interfere with the free exercise of religion. This causes debate about whether schools should post the Ten Commandments on their classroom walls and whether public prayers before football games and high school graduations are constitutional."

"Now, we all have different viewpoints on these questions, and we're not here to decide those issues. However, one thing is clear no matter what side you're on, and that is God, religion, and faith are as American as apple pie."

"With faith, religion, and God, come responsibilities. It is not a free ride. At some level, you have to devote some of your life to God, sometimes on a small scale like going to church or synagogue a few more times a year, and sometimes, on a much grander scale. That is what Satya Grady did ladies and gentleman, and I'm not talking about the killing of Reverend Winston. I'm talking about a lifetime of service to his community. My client chose a hard job, and he did it well. He chose this job because he is a man, like many Americans, who believes that God wants us to be positive members of society. You saw my client's fitness reports and you heard his fellow officers talk about him, so you know he did his job as well as anybody could."

"Because Satya Grady did his job well and because he is a man of faith, God came to him and asked him to perform a service. That service involved the taking of a life but," Emanuel paused, "it was nonetheless, God's work."

"You can't have it both ways, ladies and gentleman. You can't be a person of faith and then deny that God often requires us to do things we may not want to do. Just like our country sometimes asks us to do things we don't want to do. When our government asks us to go to war and kill others and sacrifice our own lives, we go to preserve our democracy. We don't question it, we just go."

"Satya Grady, ladies and gentleman, is not a killer. He is not a violent man. He is a family man who wants to go back to his wife and children and his job. Who was Jack Winston on the other hand? He was a man bent on using his power and that of our government to impose his will on the world. Mind you, his will was not pure in spirit. It was hypocrisy. While he was preaching morality he was funding mercenaries, defrauding the government, and engaging in horrible sex acts with minors. He was a drug user, an adulterer, a rapist, and a sodomizer. The very kinds of things he claimed the rest of society shouldn't do, he was doing. That is the worst kind of hypocrisy, the worst kind of evil, and my client had the inspiration and the faith to stop it."

"Don't find Satya Grady guilty of being a man of faith. Don't find him guilty of following God's call to arms just as you would follow your country's. Don't find him guilty of saving us all. Allow Satya Grady to go home."

"I want to thank you for doing your civic duty in what, I know is a difficult case. I know when you look into your conscience and your soul, you will find Satya Grady innocent."

Emanuel sat down exhausted. He had worked up a lather during his closing and he wiped his forehead with his handkerchief. He poured himself a glass of water and looked at Satya as he took a sip. Satya had a serene look on his face that said everything would be all right, and Emanuel knew he had said the right things. He had done all that Satya asked, and it was no longer in his hands. Emanuel had put on a logical defense where there was no logic, only faith.

Judge Wallace explained to the jury that if they found, based on the facts presented at trial, that Satya's actions met the elements of first degree murder they must find him guilty. And, under new sentencing guidelines, if they found Satya guilty of first degree murder, the judge had no choice but to impose the death penalty. Judge Wallace did not give the jury the option of finding that Satya's actions were justified because the law does not allow for the "God told me to do it," defense. However, he said that if the jury had any doubt that Satya's actions constituted first degree murder they should find him innocent.

24

After the jury left the courtroom to begin their deliberations, Emanuel decided to return to his office. He didn't want to wait around the courthouse because he didn't want to give the impression that he thought the deliberations would be quick. It was still early and even though Emanuel was certainly not going to do any work he couldn't go home.

This time Emanuel did not try and sneak out the back of D.C. Superior. He decided to face the gauntlet of reporters and protestors with his head held high. Everyone had an opinion about the case, but he had the client. He was proud of Satya and honored that Satya chose him to defend him. Nobody would ever know what went into this trial except the two men, but Emanuel wanted the world to know that Satya Grady was a righteous man.

The reporters were the first to attack, thrusting microphones in his face and screaming questions. Emanuel couldn't discern the questions and didn't bother saying "no comment." He felt like he was walking along in an invisible cocoon protecting him from the outside world.

When he walked outside the courthouse he faced the mobs of people and their vigil to one or another actor in the drama. The faces in the crowd represented the full spectrum of culture and ethnicity that formed American society, fully enjoying their cherished

American right to espouse their unique views. Emanuel saw President Taylor hanging in effigy, Reverend Winston nailed to a cross, and Satya Grady as both an Angel of Death and an Angel of Mercy.

Emanuel stood in the plaza outside the courthouse and took in the scene. He realized for the first time, that there was no way to take the moral high ground in this case. The people who supported Winston were supporting a sexual deviant who wanted to take over the world with his own twisted version of religion, while people who supported Satya were backing a killer. As for backing President Taylor, whether people supported his efforts to "uncover" Reverend Winston's activities or not, it was clear that he was going to profit politically from the death of a rival. There were no moral victors.

Back at his office, Emanuel took off his jacket and tie, and his black wingtips, and lay down on his couch. He kept his portable monitor on in case the clerk called to notify him of the verdict, although he didn't expect it that afternoon. There was not really a rule of thumb about the correlation between the length of deliberations and the verdict. However, in a murder case, longer was usually better for the defense, and certainly in this case a short deliberation would mean the jury completely disregarded Satya's story.

Emanuel fell asleep and did not dream. When he woke up it was already evening. He got up off the couch and went over to the window that overlooked 15th Street and the White House. He figured that at that moment President Taylor, if he was home, was preparing for the last days of the election. In two weeks, Taylor would most likely win the election. With all the distractions caused by the death of Winston and the murder trial, Taylor's opponent had barely been noticed. The polls indicated that Taylor would win by a comfortable margin. Now, with Sarah's testimony about Winston, any of his former supporters would surely support Taylor.

Emanuel was numb. He felt the heaviness of the situation, but he really didn't want to think it through because it was too disturbing. He went over to his desk and opened the bottom drawer where he kept his bottle of 18 year-old Chivas. He always joked that he kept it there for medicinal purposes, and this situation definitely required it. He poured himself a hefty drink and lit a cigarette. Then he turned on his stereo and popped in a Mahler disk. The mournful music was just what he needed.

As he sipped the scotch and puffed on his cigarette, Emanuel began rehashing the events that brought him to this moment in time. He mused how funny life could be, and how cruel. Before the case, he had been living in a superficial world. He never thought about morality or spirituality, and now he had just spent two months trying to convince twelve people that God exists. More importantly, Emanuel knew that he wasn't just trying to convince the jury on Satya's behalf, but rather, he had come to believe in a higher spiritual power himself. Satya had made him believe and for that he would be forever grateful.

After another scotch, Emanuel went to sleep again on his couch. This time he began to dream. It was his dream about the airplane once again. There he was fighting his way through an airport chasing a figure ahead of him. The figure appeared to be a woman, but it was blurry in his mind. The airport was so crowded with people moving so slowly around him, oblivious that he was pursuing the most meaningful thing imaginable. Once again, he saw the figure walk through a boarding gate and Emanuel followed. He made it onto the plane just in time and the flight attendant ushered him quickly to his seat. On his way he strained to see the object of his desire but as he looked down at what seemed like an infinite line of seats, he failed to see her. The flight attendant strapped him in and the plane began to taxi. As it soared into the air, Emanuel looked out the window but all he saw was darkness. He fidgeted anxiously in his seat, waiting for the seat belt sign to turn off so he could go find the vision that he'd been chasing. The plane flew higher and higher and never leveled off. The seat belt sign stayed on, trapping Emanuel in his seat. Finally, he tried to unbuckle the belt so he could get up, but it was locked shut. The plane kept going up and up, and Emanuel began to panic. He looked around for a flight attendant and could see none. Then he realized he was the only person on the plane— all the other people were gone. The plane kept climbing and he was totally alone. At that intense moment of panic, he woke up abruptly.

For the next two days, Emanuel stayed in his office like a recluse. He ordered food from the Old Ebbitt and showered in his office bathroom. He didn't have a change of clothing, however. To pass the time he would peruse his law books reading the cases, and going through the mental exercise of finding a way to reach a different, yet plausible, decision in each case. Emanuel always thought that there was never a correct outcome to a case. Facts could always be viewed in different ways, and different arguments could be made. The law was a gray area.

Meanwhile the press was having a field day with the trial. The news of Winston's sex life exploded onto the headlines and the talk shows. It was the last fact of a perfect story. Now the case had everything, God, life, death, politics, and sex. The country was awash in debate over Winston and Satya and what their lives meant for everyone else. Emanuel just ignored it all.

On the afternoon of the second day, Jude called him on his monitor. She wanted to come and see him, and to talk about the case. She said he owed her, and, for lack of anything better to do and a desire just to see her, Emanuel invited her to his office.

She arrived, looking fresh and beautiful with her skin glowing. She was also carrying a small camera, and Emanuel knew right away what Jude had in mind.

"Jesus, you look terrible, Emanuel. I think you need a vacation," Jude said.

"Thanks, sweetheart. I knew you'd cheer me up."

"Do you need cheering up?"

"Let's just say I'm a little worried. I really care about Satya."

"Do you think you're going to win?"

"It's impossible to say. I didn't get a good feel for the jury. They all kind of looked at me with blank stares, even during my closing— or, maybe not. I don't know. I was in a funk during the whole thing."

"Listen, Emanuel, do you want to talk about it on camera? I'd love to get your feelings recorded before the verdict."

"What do you mean, my feelings? This isn't about feelings."

"Sure, it is. This whole case is about what people feel. That's what God is after all. God is passion and emotion and love, and that was what you were trying to prove. It must have affected you."

"Alright, I'll let you record me on one condition."

"What's that?"

"I want you to sign a release, that says you can only air the interview when I say so or if I die, of course."

"Deal." The two shook hands. As Jude set up the camera on a tripod, Emanuel drew up a little contract. They both signed it, and then sat down on Emanuel's couch to talk.

"Emanuel, in the next few days you'll know the fate of your client. What's going through your mind?"

"I'm scared, Jude."

"Why?"

"I'm scared for the life of Satya Grady. Satya is the purest man I've ever met. We all go through life uncertain of so many things, and Satya is the first person I've ever met who is completely at peace with how he's lived his life— including shooting Reverend Winston."

"Do you believe that God told him to kill Winston?"

"Absolutely. I never even believed in God before getting involved with this case and meeting Satya. Now, not only do I believe that God exists, but I know God came to Satya just as he described, and told him to perform this task. If you sit down close to Satya and look him in the eyes, you'll know it's true."

"Do you think the jury will believe him?"

"I don't know. When it comes to God, people want to believe the stories they like. I mean we've been reading the Old Testament for over five thousand years, and people have no trouble believing that

God wiped out the earth with a flood and turned people into pillars of salt or asked an old man to sacrifice his son. The New Testament is over two thousand years old and people have no trouble believing that Jesus walked on water, turned water into wine, and then chose to die for our sins. Maybe one day, people will believe that Satya Grady killed Reverend Winston at God's request, and in so doing, saved us all. I just hope the jury believes that now."

"Emanuel, how has this experience changed you?" Jude asked.

The camera panned in close on Emanuel's face. He paused a minute before answering.

"Jude, I've had a long and interesting life." Emanuel chuckled, realizing how that statement might sound coming from a man not yet forty.

"I've lived a long and interesting life, but something was always missing. Before, I met Satya and took this case, I never thought of things being greater than myself. If I didn't live it or experience it, then it wasn't important. I didn't care. It was my life and I wanted to live it the way I pleased. Maybe it was defending the accused; maybe it was living a solitary life completely self-absorbed. I don't know. But, after all I've gone through with this case and with Satya my view has changed."

"How so?" Jude asked.

"I've laid awake so many nights thinking about this case and about Satya's story. I was so worried about what would happen and if I was doing a decent job. And after countless nights, it became clear to me that I had only one place to turn . . . and that was to God. I realized this case had implications far beyond my control and could only ask God to watch over me and not to forsake me. I prayed, Jude, and the act itself eased my pain. But ultimately, this case was so much bigger than me, bigger than all of us. One day I'm sure there will be an answer, and it'll make sense. In the mean time, my prayers calmed me and told me that I would survive. God now is within me. I feel it."

Jude put down her microphone and gave Emanuel a long embracing look. After a minute she offered another back rub and Emanuel accepted. He took off his shirt and she began to knead his back.

"Emanuel, I want you to know something," she said. "After Jesus Cruz's testimony I looked into his case. I know you were the prosecutor who let him go."

Emanuel sat up and turned to Jude. "How come you didn't report it?"

"Because I love you. I've loved you since the first time I saw you sitting at the Old Ebbitt. Even though I was after the story, there was something about you. I think it was your loneliness. Following this story and getting to know you, I've seen there's so much inside of you— so much good. I don't want anything to hurt you. Your compassion for Cruz and your defense of Satya showed me what kind of person you are and what kind of heart you have. Some other reporter might find out one day, but I wasn't going to break the story."

Emanuel grabbed Jude and they kissed. And this time they didn't stop.

The next morning at eleven, Emanuel's portable monitor beeped. It was the clerk at D.C. Superior, telling him the jury had reached a verdict. Instantly, Emanuel's stomach did a flip and he ran to the bathroom to vomit. After voiding his stomach, he splashed water on his face to cool down. Then he combed his hair and tied his tie. He couldn't believe how bad he looked. It was as if his hair had turned gray overnight, and his eyes showed the strain.

He tried to smooth the wrinkles in his suit and then he went outside to hail a cab. It was another beautiful fall day with bright sunshine that was just a shade duller than the summer sun. There was a fresh smell in the air that always came when the cooler breezes of autumn came to wash away the sweat of summer. It was invigorating to Emanuel, especially after three days cloistered in his office.

The taxi arrived at D.C. Superior and marshals were waiting to escort Emanuel inside. The crowd had swelled so that there were people all the way down D Street and up 5th Street. Television trucks were lined up, as every news agency in the world was anxious to report the outcome of the trial of the century.

Emanuel was comforted to enter the small courtroom away from the mass of humanity. The bailiff brought in Satya and the two men embraced.

"Satya, I hope God is with you today."

"Did you pray for me, Emanuel?"

"I did, Satya. I prayed and prayed and prayed. I hope God was listening."

"He always does, Emanuel," Satya said giving Emanuel a gentle pat on his cheek. "I'm going to talk to my wife."

Satya walked back to his wife and they hugged and kissed as their tears flowed in unison down their cheeks. Emanuel sat down and waited. Finally, everyone was in place and that jarring knock came from the judge's chambers. Judge Wallace came in, looking a bit weary himself. He called for the jury, and the bailiff brought them in.

"Mr. Foreman," Judge Wallace said, "has the jury reached a decision?"

"We have your honor."

"How do you find?"

The Foreman paused and looked down at his hands, which were clasped in front of him. Then he raised his head and tears slowly trickled down his face.

"Your Honor, the jury finds the defendant, Satya Grady, guilty of first degree murder."

At that moment, time stood still for Emanuel. He could feel his heart beating and his brain seemed to stop working. His eyes were closed and he saw nothing in his mind. He had no thoughts and could not hear any of the noise that was coming from the gallery behind him. Emanuel thought, somehow, that he must have died. Slowly he opened his eyes and turned to look at Satya. His client was standing there with a slight smile on his face.

"Satya, why are you smiling?" Emanuel asked.

"Because it's perfect."

The next voice Emanuel heard was that of Judge Wallace.

"Satya Grady, you have been found guilty of first degree murder. Under the sentencing guidelines of the District of Columbia, I have no choice but to sentence you to death. You will be sent to the Federal Death Row facility in Terre Haute, Indiana, where you shall be put to death by lethal injection. May the Lord have mercy on your soul."

25

That night, President Taylor appeared before the American people yet again to discuss the case for the final time. At this point he had the election locked up. Most of Winston's supporters had come back to the Republican Party for one reason or another. Some believed everything they read about Winston, others believed Satya Grady's story and felt God wanted them to vote Republican. Still others just got scared of the unknown, an unknown party and an unknown candidate. President Taylor was a known quantity to the American people. If nothing else, they knew what they were getting and flocked back to his camp.

"My fellow Americans." Taylor began, trying to keep a somber air. "Today marked the end of a sad chapter in our history. None of us like to see our leaders, whether we agree with them or not, gunned down in the street. And this case was no different. I would have rather fought Reverend Winston in the arena of public opinion and let you the people decide what you wanted, but other forces intervened."

"My one consolation and, I hope you feel it too, is that the criminal justice performed its role in this case and justice was served. The verdict today resolves this situation and let's us move forward as a nation. Justice was done and now, let the healing begin. Thank you and God bless the United States of America. Good night."

Taylor dismissed the television crew brusquely and headed back to his private study for a nightcap with Tobias. Taylor poured himself and his Chief of Staff a hefty Johnnie Walker Black on the rocks.

"Paul, I have to hand it to you. I can't imagine things could have gone any better for us short of hiring Satya Grady to take Winston down."

"I know, Mr. President. I know," Tobias said taking a long drink.

PART IV

Epilogue

*"BUT RISE, AND STAND UPON THY FEET; FOR
I HAVE APPEARED UNTO THEE FOR THIS
PURPOSE TO MAKE THEE A MINISTER AND
A WITNESS BOTH OF THESE THINGS WHICH
THOU HAST SEEN, AND OF THOSE THINGS
IN WHICH I WILL APPEAR UNTO THEE."*

THE ACTS 26:16

26

It took Emanuel several weeks to recover from the trial. The voice of Judge Wallace reading the death sentence ran repeatedly in Emanuel's head like a skipping record. Each day Emanuel would plod through every detail of the trial trying to think of one examination, one question, or one witness he could have handled differently that might have changed the outcome. He was obsessed with this exercise and couldn't work on anything else. Emanuel bought the transcript and read through it, making notes, then rereading, until it became the script of a play in which he acted every part. One thing was certain, and that was Emanuel would leave no stone unturned on the appeal.

Meanwhile, the public reaction to the verdict was just as strong as it had been before and during the trial. The revelations about Winston's personal peccadilloes effectively ended the Freedom party and the Church of the Divine Light as no one wanted to be affiliated with that kind of behavior. While Church and party loyalists were willing to believe that a government conspiracy was trying to frame Winston for his paramilitary activities, they would not and could not accept a leader who engaged in adultery, sodomy, and statutory rape. In fact, America had never reacted well to even tame sex scandals despite the best efforts of Washington spin-doctors.

The majority of Freedom party voters stayed home from the polls in November, too disheartened to vote, while a certain percentage returned to the Republican party and helped reelect Taylor in a closer than expected vote. Fowler moved up several points just by virtue of having no involvement in the Winston case and almost caught Taylor at the end. Despite those who wondered whether Taylor and his government played a role in the events after Winston's death, Taylor's core message of removing government from the personal lives of both Americans and those around the world resonated with voters. When people awoke from the trance of religious extremism, they yearned not to have a leader that drew absolute moral lines. Taylor smartly reminded Americans of this in the weeks leading up to the election and people responded. Taylor's message was that morality and religion was best left to the individual, behind his or her bedroom door, and with his or her God, and it worked.

Emanuel eventually awoke from his trance as well and began to work again. His reading of the record ultimately gave him solace. He had some grounds for appeal, but mostly he was convinced that he had fought a smart and aggressive case. He had brought logic into the courtroom when none should have existed and while he thought he could have won, he didn't feel discouraged by the loss. The crutch of God as an excuse for antisocial behavior doesn't always work, and in fact, he mused that it works too much of the time. The jury in this case could have legitimately gone either way but ultimately it refused to justify Satya's actions in the name of God. The cost was great but the fact that Emanuel and the world learned that lesson made it worthwhile.

Emanuel now had the bully pulpit of celebrity. The media hailed his performance as one of the greatest courtroom defenses in American jurisprudence, despite the final decision. His opinions, thoughts, and words were in full demand and he took advantage of it to spread his message. He was on television constantly, wrote a book about the experience and traveled the country on a speaking tour. Emanuel felt an obligation to Satya to tell people what he knew – that Satya was a righteous man, that he was a servant of God, and that even under those circumstances what he did was not acceptable.

Larry King was one of the first interviewers who called Emanuel and when he was ready to speak out he sat across the table from the grizzled journalist. Emanuel was wearing a plain blue blazer and a white, buttoned down shirt open at the collar. King was typically hunched over like a vulture waiting for the death of his guest.

"Ladies and gentleman, we're thrilled to have with us tonight, Emanuel Adams, who fought the case of the century. His client, Officer Satya Grady of the New York City police department was accused of assassinating presidential candidate Jack Winston, and ultimately found guilty and sentenced to death. Emanuel, how are you feeling?"

"Good Larry. It took me time to recover, but I feel good. I've almost completed a book on the case and I'm working on the appeal."

"Despite the decision, do you feel justice was served?"

"I have faith in the jury system and I accept this verdict. While there are grounds for appeal, I think both the prosecutor and the Judge did fine jobs at trial. More importantly than justice being served, I think this case taught a great lesson."

"And what is that?"

"Satya Grady is a righteous man, pure of spirit. Let me assure you and all of America of that. I experienced that first hand. He taught me about God and spirituality in the most poignant way possible. He touched me and made me believe in God whereas before, I didn't. I believe that God sent Satya to us to teach us that killing in the name of God is unacceptable."

"Killing in the name of God is unacceptable?"

"That's right. The majority of wars in history were fought on religious grounds and we are currently fighting a religious war today, the war on terrorism. I think God said, 'Enough,' and sacrificed Satya to remind us that there are no 'holy wars.' God is no longer willing to serve as the excuse for violence. The message is clear."

"So, how do we fight the war on terrorism?"

"Larry, we live in the richest most diverse society ever created. Think of all the resources we have at our disposal. Let's try economic aid, food, medicine, movies, television, and acceptance of foreign cultures as equal to our own. Recall the story of Satya and Jesus Cruz from the trial. Satya could have brought Jesus back downtown to jail, but instead worked empathetically with him to recover from addiction. Likewise, we could work with the countries that breed terrorists to change attitudes and improve quality of life. People who live well don't become suicide bombers."

"But what if we're attacked again, like on September 11 or on even grander scale? How should we respond?"

"First, let me say that I've been a victim of a terrorist attack. When I was in New York investigating Satya's case I was having drinks with a friend of mine in Hell's Kitchen when a bomber ran in and blew himself up. My friend didn't make it, Larry, but I left relatively unscathed. That experience opened me up to Satya's message. Being the subject of violence is not easy and causes suffering. But, is the appropriate response violence? Is that what America should stand for – the country that can brutally retaliate against any threat or action? Should America be the empire to fear? If we continue to react that way, eventually *we* will become the greatest threat to peace. If every time a terrorist kills one of us we kill thousands of a foreign culture in response, we have become the problem and not the solution. The world will see us as the aggressor and band together against us. "

"Jack Winston was ready to take us to full scale war against Islam: Judeo-Christianity versus Islam in a battle to the death. We have superior weapons and they have superior numbers. Both sides believe they have God with them and both sides are ready to die. Who would win Larry?"

King paused and rubbed his chin. "I don't know."

"Take Satya again. He did have God on his side. I can assure you that God sent Satya to kill Winston. And what is the result: barring some miracle that I don't expect, Satya will also lose his life. No winners, Larry, just two dead men. Let's not take that to a grander scale. That is the message."

27

Emanuel spent the next four years working on Satya's appeal. First, he made a direct appeal to the D.C. Court of Appeals and then to the Supreme Court. After those losing efforts, he filed a federal petition of habeas corpus, which was denied. When he appealed that decision, he was denied again. Then the Supreme Court refused his petition for a stay of execution. Finally, on Christmas Eve, in the last year of President Taylor's second term, he asked him to pardon Satya. President Taylor had Satya Grady to thank for his second term and he now he had the ability to spare his life. He chose not to and, as Emanuel expected, there was nothing left to stop Satya's death.

The execution was scheduled for New Year's Eve, and Emanuel made the trip to the facility to say goodbye for the last time. The Terre Haute death row was a modern and clean place. Unlike other prisons, it had a calm sterile feel to it, as if it was whitewashed every day to kill any germs that might linger in an institution. This antiseptic atmosphere of the building was a stark contrast to the spectacle that was taking place outside its walls.

Over one hundred thousand people had gathered for a candle light vigil for Satya. They were orderly but passionate, singing songs of peace, waving banners proclaiming love, and praying for a last second reprieve. The scene was occurring all over the country and the world, in major cities and small towns. Emanuel's message and Satya's lesson had gained support in America and around the world. The public relations battle was being won and terrorism and violence in the name of God was being rejected. Groups who had hoped for political gain through violent activity were being rejected by most governments and ignored. Regimes that suppressed their people or violated human rights were dealt with as you would a terminally ill patient. Like palliative medicine, the nations of the world came forward with money for infrastructure, corporate investment, media outlets, doctors and teachers. Thus, dictatorships began dying painless deaths and freer nations began being born. While violence still occurred in places the movement was growing.

Emanuel and Satya sat together in a lounge area unable to talk for the first few minutes. Finally, Emanuel spoke.

"I'm sorry I couldn't have done more to save your life, Satya."

"We both know that was not the way things would turn out," Satya replied.

"I know, but now that the day is here, I'm still so sad to lose you." Satya smiled and put his hand on Emanuel's shoulder.

"You also know you're not losing me. My story and my lesson will live on. Those people outside are a testament to that, as are you."

"Thank you, Satya." Emanuel paused. "I'm not staying to watch. I can't take it."

"Good, I'd rather you didn't watch either. Let's just say we'll meet again on the other side."

The two men embraced grasping each other for several minutes. Emanuel's head was buried in Satya's shoulder and he did not want to let go. Finally, he had to, and he left. Guards ushered him out a back entrance away from the throng and a car whisked him away to the Indianapolis airport.

Emanuel sat in the bar waiting for his flight. The monitor above the bar was showing a special report on Satya and the murder of Reverend Winston hosted by Jude Michaels, Emanuel's wife.

Emanuel watched while sipping a glass of red wine. He never got tired of looking at her or hearing the sound of her voice. The broadcast rehashed the events leading up to the shooting and the trial. At the end, Jude cut to the interview of Emanuel the day before the verdict. He finally agreed to let her air it.

The interview ended and Emanuel wept. Seeing himself four years in the past shook that indescribable place that makes a human being cry. He lowered his head and felt the tears cascade over his clasped hands. They flowed and flowed. Despite the fact that he knew the answers now, the experience and Satya's imminent death were still painful. Loving another person and loss was painful, but it was also evidence of being alive and Emanuel had never felt more vibrant.

After a few moments, he composed himself and looked at his watch. It was eleven o'clock. Right now, the first drops of poison were entering Satya's blood stream. In about thirty seconds, Satya's head would start spinning and he would pass out never to wake up again. Emanuel wiped his wet face with his sleeve and then lifted his glass in homage to Satya and prayed to God that he would live in everlasting peace.

It was time for Emanuel to board his plane. He grabbed his bag and started walking to the gate. The airport was surprisingly crowded for the late hour, or maybe Emanuel's mind was so preoccupied he could not navigate his way through the corridor. The gate ahead seemed like a portal to the unknown. Emanuel nonetheless, walked through it and onto the plane. He sat down and buckled himself in. He looked around the plane, which was mostly empty.

The plane left the gate and taxied out to the runway. While it made the long, slow journey to the far end of the airfield, Emanuel drifted off to sleep. In his slumber, he saw Satya walking down the aisle of the plane towards him.

"Satya," Emanuel said reaching out his arm.

"Emanuel, I'm okay. I'm home and at peace."

"Good Satya, I'm so glad."

"Never stop telling the world about me. Keep telling the world the story of Satya Grady and his conversation with God. Make them believe."

"I will Satya. I will."

And the plane roared into the heavens.

ABOUT THE AUTHOR

 Neil Hare is an President of Global Vision Communications, LLC, (GVC), an agency specializing in strategic communications, business development, and small business marketing for trade associations, non-profits, coalitions, and corporations. He is a frequent speaker at business events on marketing and communications, inside and outside the Beltway.

Previously, Neil served as vice president of Corporate Communications at the U.S. Chamber of Commerce, where he managed public policy awareness campaigns aimed at the Chamber's three million members on issues such as tax and regulatory reform, market driven health care, energy, free trade, and expanded transportation and infrastructure. Hare is a licensed attorney in the District of Columbia Bar and began his career at a Washington, D.C., law firm, specializing in international law and litigation. He then became a legal editor for the Bureau of National Affairs (BNA), covering America's securities markets. He appeared regularly on CNBC, MSNBC, and FOX News as an expert on day trading and wrote columns on securities regulations for financial publications.

Hare received a J.D. from American University's Washington College of Law and a B.A. in international relations from Tufts University. He is active in the soccer community and is a supporter of the Arts, even performing in the Washington Ballet's performance of Giselle at The Kennedy Center. Hare is also the author of An Animal Cries, published in 1998. He lives in Washington, D.C., with his wife, two daughters and one son.

Made in United States
North Haven, CT
26 September 2023

41993874R00165